ᴛᴌᴇ ORIGINAL SIN

'Pulsing with romance, danger, and suspense . . . A compelling read.'
— *Publishers Weekly*

'Positively riveting . . . A sexy, hard-to-put-down read.'
— *Kirkus Reviews*

'The climax . . . is a real stunner.'
— *Chicago Tribune*

THE MASK OF TIME

'Spine-chilling adventure, mystery, and
intrigue . . . Superb reading entertainment.'
— *Rendevous*

'Keeps you reading while your dinner burns . . . Great fun.'
— *Cosmopolitan*

'Turns on the heat at the start and doesn't let up.'
— *Kirkus Reviews*

'A dizzying roller coaster of a story . . . that resonates with
authentic detail against a sprawling canvas of history.'
— *Gothic Journal*

A HOUSE OF MANY ROOMS

'A sexy, grip᷎ ᷎ ᷎at.'

'A profusion of surprising plot twists, relentless suspense and a humdinger of a climax. A spellbinding thriller that will keep readers riveted.'
— *Booklist*

'Bravo! The reader is kept guessing around every turn . . . touches nearly every human emotion conceivable.'
— *Rendezvous*

THE SEVENTH MOON

'Suspenseful . . . highly atmospheric . . . harrowing.'
— *Publishers Weekly*

'Few thrillers have as strong a sense of atmosphere and adventure as this fascinating tale.'
— *Chicago Tribune*

'[Gabriel has] a gift for suspense that can make you read 351 pages in a sitting.'
— *The Charlotte Observer*

'The action in this fast-paced romantic thriller rages across three decades worth of drama.'
— *Booklist*

TAKE ME TO YOUR HEART AGAIN

ALSO BY MARIUS GABRIEL

The Original Sin

The Mask of Time

A House of Many Rooms

The Seventh Moon

Wish Me Luck as You Wave Me Goodbye

TAKE ME TO YOUR HEART AGAIN

MARIUS GABRIEL

LAKE UNION
PUBLISHING

Text copyright © 2016 Marius Gabriel

Published by Lake Union Publishing, Seattle
www.apub.com

Amazon, the Amazon logo, and Lake Union Publishing are trademarks of Amazon. com, Inc., or its affiliates.

ISBN-13: 9781503936539
ISBN-10: 1503936538

Cover design by Lisa Horton

Printed in the United States of America

For my family

1.
LONDON, 1942

Chiara bent over the toilet bowl, shuddering. She tried to fight down the waves of nausea, but in the end her breakfast came up all the same. All she'd had was toast, but it didn't matter. The spiteful thing in her stomach hurled back all nourishment. Nor did the nausea end with throwing up. It persisted, darkly coiled inside her, and would probably be there all day.

At least it's Saturday, she thought as she washed her face, *and I don't have to go to work.* Still wrapped in her quilted dressing gown, she went to her favourite perch in the little window seat and curled up there, hoping there would be no more sickness. The magnificent view down the Mall was one of the advantages of living in a garret. The trees were in full summer foliage, and the elusive scent of their leaves, heated by the sun, rose up to her window.

It was literally a garret, a tiny attic apartment set in an octagonal turret that was perched on top of one of the fortresses belonging to the Admiralty. Sir George Harmon, her boss at the Ministry, had found it for her. Considering the short notice – she'd been bombed out of her comfortable flat in Tisbury Mansions, and there was no possibility of her finding a billet with her sister, Isobel – she'd been lucky to get the offer. The place had been used before her by an arty young cartographer, who'd done it up in pseudo-Jacobean style, with faux sconces and stencilled heraldic symbols. The rent was low, and it was twenty minutes by bus or Tube to the Censor's Office, where she worked. There were five flights of stairs to be climbed, that was true, but the lovely view more than made up for that. At least, for now.

And a garret suited her mood. She didn't want to see anybody outside work, didn't want to have to entertain or be entertained, didn't require room to expand. She'd lost everything she had in Tisbury Mansions anyway. Every stick of furniture, every rag of clothing, every plate and cup, the sum total of her life, had been blown to smithereens. All gone. And she had no intentions of starting to acquire things again. She was just fine the way she was. To another woman, the stone walls of the attic might have seemed bleak. To her, they were a fortification. She was safe up here, walled off from the world, not needing anything and not needed by anybody.

The flat, advantageous as it was, came with a hereditary post, that of fire warden for the building. It was her duty to ensure that fire regulations were strictly enforced. Hoses, buckets of sand, axes and ropes, pumps and bells, all in their proper places, gas turned off and the blackout observed. Less pleasantly, it was also her duty to fire-spot during air raids. She had spent several terrible nights up on the roof, watching for incendiaries as the bombers prowled the sky, raining destruction.

But in this summer of 1942, the Blitz seemed to be in abeyance. Other cities were being raided; Birmingham, Manchester, Bristol, Coventry and Exeter had all been bombed lately, but London had been spared for a few weeks. Perhaps it was owing to the brave fighter pilots who still roared over the rooftops in their Spitfires; or to the barrage balloons that made such an extraordinary spectacle, filling the London sky with monstrous, fat, silvery jellyfish; or to the tireless anti-aircraft batteries. Perhaps the tide of the war had ebbed, and the Germans really were being beaten. Or perhaps it would all start again tonight. Nobody could say.

The sky was a rich blue over the city. She sat, hugging her queasy stomach and staring down the tree-lined Mall, for the best part of an hour. Since Tisbury Mansions, she'd perfected the art of stillness. It had not been one of her talents hitherto. She'd been a gadabout, a partygoer, a pleasure seeker. A stop-out, a reveller, a butterfly. That had all ended the night of the bomb. The wings of the butterfly had shrivelled in an instant, leaving her flightless and crawling.

In exchange, she'd been given the gift of wisdom. It was a fair swap, she often thought. Wisdom was a prize. Wisdom usually took years to attain, and she had received it in an instant. And wisdom was stillness.

Unlike the other two Redcliffe sisters, Chiara had never been considered pretty or an object of concern to her family or even particularly interesting. The other two went to extremes. Isobel had been a Blackshirt and was now a Socialist. Felicity had been a nun and was now wallowing in the fleshpots of sinful Cairo. One could only shake one's head.

Chiara had never been one for the extremes of anything, especially not politics or religion, neither of which interested her. Chiara had just been Chiara. She was fun and not absolutely hideous (with her blonde hair and brown eyes, her pert nose and bee-stung mouth, she had an elfin look), and she had always been in demand. Young men had chased her, but only one man had ever captured her.

The nausea faded a little, and she decided to risk another cup of tea. She lit the gas and put the kettle on the single hob that served her as a kitchen and that was where she prepared the little she ate. The knock came while the tea was brewing. Visitors were very rare. Nobody in her former circle knew where she was now living, and the Admiralty block was all but deserted on the weekends. The knock, which was repeated, was unlikely to herald anything good.

And in fact, when she finally opened the door, it proved to be her older sister, Isobel.

The sisters stared at one another without speaking for a moment. Isobel, resplendent in a bravura navy and gold outfit that defied every tenet of Utility Clothing, was also tanned and healthy looking. Chiara, in her threadbare dressing gown that was a larger woman's cast-off, was pale and somehow transparent by contrast. Chiara remained expressionless. Isobel's handsome face wore a look of grim determination. She was breathing heavily through her arched nostrils. The five flights of stairs were taxing unless you were used to them.

'I saw you the other day,' Isobel said. 'You were looking in the window of Fortnum's.' She held out the gift she had brought, a blue-wrapped parcel from Fortnum & Mason, no doubt containing an illegal amount of precious, rationed tea. 'Here.'

Chiara ignored it. 'I saw you, too.'

'You walked straight past me in the street.'

'That's because I didn't want to see you. I don't want to see you now.'

'Chiara—'

'Goodbye.'

Isobel tried to stop Chiara from closing the door. 'Please hear me out,' she called through the rapidly closing gap. She pushed hard and managed to force the door back open. From the nursery on, Isobel had always won physical contests with her younger sisters. She wasn't just stronger; she was far more ruthless. 'We can't go on like this.'

'Isobel, even for you, this is stinking behaviour,' Chiara said bitterly. 'Go away.'

'I just want to talk.' Isobel had managed to gain entrance. She pushed the Fortnum's package into Chiara's hands.

'I don't want to talk.' Chiara opened the casement window. 'And I certainly don't want your bloody Red Cross parcels.' She threw the package out. 'Now get out.'

Isobel winced. 'There were macaroons in that.' She dominated the little apartment like a cuckoo in some much smaller bird's nest. Her bright, dark eyes swept the place. 'My God. I hadn't realised you were quite so *immured*. You're not following in Felicity's footsteps, are you? Turning yourself into a little nun?'

'Perhaps you could get to the point.'

'All right. It's better that you hear it from me. Oliver and I are getting married.'

Chiara's nausea had been returning sharply since that first rap on the door. Her gorge now rose irrevocably. She turned and fled. The toilet was separated from the rest of the apartment by nothing more than a velvet curtain (one of the arty cartographer's Jacobean touches), so her violent retching was perfectly audible to Isobel. She clung to the bowl, heaving up strings of bile, which were all her stomach contained anymore.

She was shaking like a leaf when she emerged from the stall. Isobel looked at her thoughtfully. 'You all right?'

'Stomach bug,' Chiara said tersely. 'I wish you both joy. Now, may I repeat my invitation to get out?'

'It's not all sweetness and light,' Isobel said. 'Oliver's going to be posted abroad in the autumn. You've been through all that. I haven't. I'm not looking forward to it.' She went to the window and looked out. 'There are compensations to this eyrie of yours, I see. What a view.'

Chiara would like to have pushed her sister out so she could enjoy the view at closer hand. 'Have you finished what you came to say?'

'Yes, and I'm going.' Isobel turned from the window. 'But I have to tell you that you're behaving very badly. Making a spectacle of your misery. Drawing attention to yourself like a sulky child.'

'Actually, I'd just like to be left in peace.'

Isobel gestured at her dishabille. 'Wearing these dreadful clothes. Making yourself ill and going around London, pressing your nose to the windowpanes like Mimi in La Bohème. Obviously starving yourself to punish us. It's disgusting.'

Chiara had had as much as she could take. She went to the door and held it open wordlessly. Beyond, the stairwell yawned.

Isobel went on regardless. 'What happened wasn't done to hurt you. It just happened. Oliver and I were attracted madly from the moment we set eyes on one another. It was pointless to pretend otherwise.'

'But you *did* pretend.' Though she'd sworn to herself never to engage in this conversation, Chiara couldn't keep the retort back. 'You pretended and you carried on behind my back. If I hadn't been bombed out that night, I wouldn't have found out.'

'We would have told you. We were planning to, of course. But Oliver never promised you anything, Chiara. He told me that. You were never under any illusions.'

'Wasn't I?' she said bitterly.

'Well, if you were, you shouldn't have been. He made it clear from the outset that there were no strings attached on either side. Didn't he?'

'Discussing this subject with you is beyond me, Isobel.'

But Isobel pressed on, evidently wanting to get things off her chest. 'He didn't even *want* an affair with you. You forced the issue. And you promised never to hold him responsible for your happiness. Oh yes, he told me all this. As for marriage, that was always out of the question. Oliver needs a wife who can take a proper place beside him—'

'Delightful as this conversation is,' Chiara cut in, barely in control of herself, 'I must ask you once again to leave.'

'I'm only repeating what he told me,' Isobel said briskly. 'You are free to deny it if you wish. But I've never found Oliver to be a liar, in my experience.'

'Perhaps your experience is shorter than mine.'

Isobel ignored that with Olympian calm. 'The point is that this shouldn't come between us, Chiara. We're sisters, after all.'

'I'm not likely to forget that.'

'Oliver and I are both very sorry about the bomb. And sorry that you should have found out at such a bad moment. We've tried to help, but you reject everything we do. We'd like to be your friends. Neither of us sees any reason why we should be estranged from you because of this.'

'I must beg to have my own opinion on that,' Chiara said, retreating into icy formality.

'Irony doesn't suit you, darling; it was never one of your weapons.' At long last, Isobel prepared to go. 'I hope you feel better soon. I'll come again.'

'Please don't,' Chiara said, on the edge of tears. She closed the door on Isobel's back and sat down to weep. So much for wisdom and stillness.

She'd known that some such approach from Isobel had been in the offing for weeks, but it had still been a horrible ordeal. Isobel possessed Oliver now in a way Chiara had never done. Chiara would never have used *we* and *us* when speaking of herself and Oliver. She would never have been so presumptuous. They'd never truly lived together. There had never been a *we* and *us*. Isobel and Oliver had set up house together on Park Lane. And now they were to be married. *'A wife who can take a proper place beside him.'* Bitch! *'No reason why we should be estranged from you because of this'?* They would be asking her to be a bridesmaid, next.

Oliver had never wanted to set up house with her. And she'd never pushed Oliver – never, until those last few weeks before the bomb.

She'd tormented herself by wondering whether the scenes she'd made, in particular during one awful visit to Courtfield Park, Oliver's family home in the Cotswolds, had driven Oliver into

Isobel's arms. After years of not pressing Oliver, she'd felt that she was getting too long in the tooth to be nothing more than his fling. She'd asked for something more permanent. He'd responded by having an affair with her sister.

She wiped her eyes with shaking hands. She'd promised herself never to engage with Isobel or Oliver, but to maintain a complete separation from them. To indulge in reproaches or recriminations would destroy what little peace and dignity she had left. This awful nausea had made her weak, and she'd let her resolve slip. She wouldn't do so again.

Isobel and Oliver were powerful personalities, used to having their own way in everything. Neither was ever likely to admit any fault. They thought they were above the rest, and to a great extent they were. It was just a pity for others who got caught up in their chariot wheels.

Chiara thought of the women from Oliver's past she had occasionally glimpsed while they'd been together. She had sworn she would not become one of those haunted wraiths. But Isobel's brutal description of her suggested that she already had.

She wouldn't allow that. She had to be strong. She would gather her forces. Just as soon as this nausea subsided.

❧

'I told you you'd be wasting your time,' Oliver Courtfield said.

'She's an obstinate little upstart,' Isobel replied, unpinning her hat. She was clearly irritated at having been outfaced by Chiara. 'I was kindness itself, Oliver. I had the olive branch in my beak.'

'It's rather soon,' he pointed out. He was sitting at his desk with a pile of red classified files containing aerial photographs taken by RAF bombers over the Baltic coastline of Germany. Oliver Courtfield was unmistakeably a member of the established order of things. Handsome in a very masculine way, he radiated confidence and authority. He watched Isobel as she mixed two vodka martinis at the drinks cabinet. Since Hitler's invasion of Russia, she'd insisted on replacing the gin with vodka. It was her idea of being a good Socialist and supporting a second front.

'Is it? Well, she can stew a little longer, then,' Isobel retorted. 'Come away from that damned desk. You're turning into a troglodyte.' He obeyed, joining her on the sofa near the window. The spacious flat that they'd taken just off Park Lane had charming views over Hyde Park, although the windows had been so heavily taped up against bomb blasts that one couldn't see much anymore; and, as a result, the rooms were always somewhat dark. They kept lamps on all day.

She gave him the martini, with a stuffed olive in it, and they toasted one another. 'Perfection,' he said after his first sip. 'And where on earth did you find olives?'

'Under the counter at Fortnum's. My little man there can work miracles. For a price.' She settled her curvaceous bottom next to his and kissed him. 'Well, I have to have olives for my Oliver, don't I?'

He smiled. 'How does she look?'

'Chiara? Absolutely ghastly. White as a sheet and hair all over the place. I'm shocked at how far she's let herself go. She was never a raving beauty, but the scarecrow look certainly doesn't do anything for her. Mind you, she wasn't well.'

'Oh?'

'Vomiting like Niagara. I suppose she's not bothering much with food hygiene, either.'

Oliver drank his vodka martini thoughtfully. 'Poor Chiara.'

'Darling, it's her own silly fault. She needn't live like that. We offered all the help we could. She wouldn't take it, would she? We have nothing to reproach ourselves with. Anyway, never mind her. I've something important to tell you. I was speaking to

Clem Attlee this morning before I saw Chiara. He told me there's going to be a by-election in Stepney East in December.'

'Indeed.'

'It hasn't been announced yet. But it's a Labour seat. The sitting MP is elderly and sick, and he's resigning.' She paused, her dark eyes sparkling. 'They're considering giving it to me, darling!'

'Stepney East?'

'Why do you look like that?'

'It's a tough area, Isobel.'

'But the toughs will be on my side,' she said, laughing.

'There'll be toughs on both sides,' he replied.

'The Conservatives and the Liberals won't contest it, Oliver. You know there's a sort of agreement on that. And it's very small – only four and a half thousand voters. I could just walk into Parliament!'

'I know you'd like to do this, but it's very soon. And our own position—'

'I'll be a newlywed! What could be more appealing? "Young Bride Stands for New Beginnings in Stepney." The newspapers will love it.'

'I still don't know when I'll be leaving England. I may not be here to support you.'

'Oh, I'll manage without you,' she said gaily. 'It'll look even better if you're away on service. The women will identify with me. A war bride always gets a lot of sympathy.'

'You think of everything,' he replied dryly.

'There is one thing you *could* do.'

'Make you a war widow?'

'No, silly. I want you alive. But you could get yourself on the Birthday Honours list. "Lady Courtfield" would impress the working classes greatly.'

'I've told you,' he said, smiling despite himself, 'in my line of work, knighthoods aren't dished out like toffees.'

'I know – discretion and confidentiality and all that. Ah well, you'll be piled with honours after the war.'

'After this war there'll be another war,' he said, eating his olive.

'Oh, don't start all that Red Menace stuff. The Russians are our allies. If we don't let them down now, they'll still be our allies after the war.'

'If you say so.' It gave Oliver some ironic amusement that Isobel, by breeding and inclination a member of the upper-middle classes, should have chosen to espouse Socialism and the Labour Party as her career. She had once been a vehement supporter of Adolf Hitler; she was quite prepared to discuss her spectacular conversion to the Left in great detail, and often did.

'You know I'm giving a little talk on the need for a second front next Saturday, darling. I hope you'll be able to attend.'

'I think I'm going to be busy.' He had already attended several of Isobel's little talks and felt he was by now quite familiar with her views. 'But I'll see what I can do. About this place Chiara's moved into: is it suitable, would you say?'

'No, I would not say. It's the sort of place from which you'd shoot at your enemies with an arquebus. Or do I mean a crossbow?'

'I'm not sure which you mean, Isobel.'

'It's a stark little cell at the very top of an Admiralty building at the back of Whitehall. It might do for storing suitcases, but I wouldn't call it fit for human habitation.'

'I see.'

'She has such a knack for making places cosy, but she hasn't done a thing there. It's her martyr complex. I told her so. She's making a spectacle out of her wretchedness. It doesn't impress me.'

'Poor little thing,' he murmured.

She shot Oliver a sharp glance. 'It's no use getting sentimental over her, Oliver. What's done is done.'

'I'm not getting sentimental. However, I don't like to hear of her living like that, being ill and so forth. She's your sister, after all. And she's something to me, too.'

'What is she to you, exactly?' Isobel enquired, her voice cooling perceptibly.

'You know very well what she is to me.'

'She's an ex,' Isobel said. 'Enquiring too closely after the welfare of an ex is not wise.'

'Quite right. One should never get one's Xs and one's Ys mixed up.'

'Very funny,' she said with a cold smile. 'I mean it, Oliver. Don't fall into the trap of feeling sorry for her. It's exactly what she would like. She does it deliberately.' She took his empty martini glass. 'Shall I make us another?'

Oliver glanced at his watch. 'I think I'm feeling rather peckish. Shall we stroll over to the Dorchester for lunch?'

'All right. I'll get my hat.' As they took the mirrored lift down, Isobel went on, 'I bought her a dozen macaroons at Fortnum's. They cost me nearly five shillings. You'll never guess what she did with them.'

'Threw them out of the window,' Oliver said, adjusting his tie in the mirror.

Isobel pinched him spitefully. 'You're so sharp, you'll cut yourself.'

෧౨

Monday morning began with a difficult interview. Chiara woke up more nauseated than ever, but there was no question of staying off work. All she could do was abstain from eating or drinking anything in the hope that it would suppress the retching. However, throughout her visit to the *Daily Mail* offices in Fleet Street, she felt faint and sick. The two sub-editors she was dealing with were seasoned journalists who viewed Ministry of Information attempts to meddle with their paper with a jaundiced eye.

'We've been going fifty years, Miss Redcliffe, through war and peace, and we know what we're doing,' the senior man, Paul Harding, said combatively. 'Does the Minister expect us to turn the *Mail* into a comic?'

'Well, some more cartoons would certainly cheer us all up, wouldn't they?' Chiara said, fully aware of how inane she sounded. 'However, that's not what the Minister wants. He's particularly concerned about your coverage of the bombing recently, in particular the photographs of dead and injured civilians.'

'Death and injury are what happens when a thousand-pound bomb falls on someone's street,' the junior man said sarcastically. 'They're not dropping marshmallows.'

'I know what happens when a thousand-pound bomb falls on someone's street,' Chiara said. 'It's happened to me. The point is not to suppress the news, but to report it in a way that doesn't damage morale.' She'd brought a manila folder with her, containing clippings she'd made from recent issues of the *Mail*. 'Take these photographs, for example. This one shows buildings burning. Very dramatic, but the firemen are just tiny figures against the blaze. They look ineffectual. You can't see any details of what they're doing. It looks like they're running away, in effect.'

'They *were* running away,' Harding said grimly. 'That whole block came down.'

'That's not the impression we want to convey. Panic, fear and despair are our enemies. Here are some photos of casualties in the street. This man is wearing a home-made bandage. This family are all badly hurt. This child clutching her teddy bear looks dead. There's no sign of the ambulances or any other rescue services in any of these pictures. It looks as though all these people have been abandoned to their fate. That's not the impression we want to convey, either.'

Harding tapped the clippings with a stubby, ink-stained forefinger. 'These are all powerful news photographs, Miss Redcliffe. If they don't summon up outrage, then nothing will.'

'Outrage isn't enough, Mr Harding. Screaming for revenge isn't enough. We need to give reassurance, too. Readers mustn't be left with the impression that there's nobody there to help them when the going gets tough.'

'Sentimental pictures of kindly firemen and beaming bobbies?' the junior man demanded. "London Can Take It"? That's not a story, that's just propaganda.'

'Given that a large majority of your readership are women, running pictures of dead and injured children is going to damage morale needlessly. Yes, kindly firemen and beaming bobbies are the kind of news we need to disseminate. And nurses and ambulance men and stretcher bearers and air raid wardens, too. The story shouldn't be the pasting we're taking or the suffering being inflicted. The story should be the way we're coping with the situation. You need to see this from a woman's point of view. What you're running isn't just bad propaganda; it's bad journalism, too.'

This produced an angry reaction from both men. Chiara tried to control her nausea as they browbeat her: How dare she try to teach them their job? How dare she presume to understand their readership better than they did? How did the Minister expect them to do their job with this kind of unwarranted interference? Somehow she held steady through it all and stopped herself from running off to throw up. The fact that the *Mail*'s readership was largely female gave it special importance in the propaganda war, but the *Mail* also had a long history of strained relations with the government. Lord Rothermere, its owner, had been a friend of Hitler and Mussolini, and had supported Mosley and the British Fascists during the 1930s. It had taken time for the paper to shake off that association. There was still an element of mutual distrust between the paper and Winston Churchill's War Cabinet.

The discussion was acrimonious, but Chiara had the Minister of Information behind her, and she stuck to her guns. By the time she left the offices at noon, she had spent the entire morning at it; but she had secured an undertaking from the sub-editors not to print any pictures of bomb damage or bomb casualties without a figure of authority featuring prominently in the scene.

She felt weak and shaky as she walked along Fleet Street. She wondered whether Sir George Harmon, her boss, would let her go home early today. She would have to hope he was in one of his fatherly moods.

When the hand took her arm, she knew immediately whose it was. Only one man had ever touched her in that way. She stopped, closing her eyes, suddenly breathless.

'Chiara,' Oliver said, 'can I talk to you for a moment?'

She was afraid to look up into his face, in case she broke down, but she forced herself to do so. He had changed little since the day they'd met, in December 1938. Chiara felt her heart turn to water. 'Oliver, no,' she said in a low voice, disengaging her arm.

'Just for a moment. Please. There's a little pub around the corner. We can be quiet in there.'

She was too much taken by surprise, and feeling too fragile, to put up much resistance. She allowed him to steer her to the pub, one of the many on Fleet Street, which was opposite the Church of St Dunstan. A noisy wedding party was spilling out of the porch into the street, the groom in uniform, the bride in a plain Utility dress.

The pub was just opening, and smelled of last night's ale and Woodbines. Chiara's stomach had begun heaving again, and the sight of the bride hadn't helped. She sat at a corner table while Oliver got drinks from the barmaid. His tall figure was achingly familiar. That he'd known exactly where to find her, and even when she'd be coming out of the *Mail* offices, was evidence of the power he had. She'd never dared ask exactly what he did in MI5 while they'd been together. No doubt Isobel had it all at her fingertips.

15

He took the seat opposite her, debonair as always in a dark suit, with the inevitable white carnation in his buttonhole. He was twenty-three years older than she, and would be fifty this year. He had been her only lover, and the only man – other than her father – whom she had ever loved. She'd believed he loved her in return. They had once meant so much to each other. They had belonged to each other for three and a half years. Could all that possibly have vanished forever? She watched him as he drank from his glass of beer. She didn't touch hers, knowing that the tiniest sip would result in catastrophe. For a while, they sat in silence.

At last, he said, 'I told her not to come. But you know what she is.'

'No, I don't,' she replied, surprised by the strength of her own voice. 'I don't know what either of you are. I thought I did, but I was wrong. It's a mystery to me what you are.'

He nodded, as though conceding a point. 'I'm sorry she did that. It can't have been pleasant for you. I'm sure this isn't pleasant, either.'

'It isn't. So let's make it brief, shall we?'

'All right. Isobel said you were sick while she was with you.'

She shrugged. 'Gastroenteritis.'

'Are you pregnant?'

She didn't flinch. 'Why would you assume that?'

'It's in your face, Chiara.' He leaned back, his eyes on her. 'I know you well enough by now. It shows. How many weeks?'

'Assuming I am pregnant, what on earth gives you the right to ask anything about it?'

'Because it's my baby.'

Chiara summoned up a bleak smile. 'You're very sure of that, Oliver.'

'Oh yes. You're right – I don't know what I am, but I know what you are. That's the one thing I *am* sure of. So please tell me: how many weeks?'

'Twelve, going on thirteen.'

She could see him calculating in his head. 'So it will be born—'

'At the end of January, next year,' she supplied.

'Thank you.' He took out his little black leather notebook – how well she remembered *that* – and wrote something in his neat way.

'You needn't concern yourself with any of it,' she said. 'It has nothing to do with you.'

'I don't think you can say that,' he replied gently.

'I'm not going to take out a paternity suit against you or anything like that. I want nothing from you.'

'That's silly, Chiara. I understand the way you feel now—'

'No, you don't,' she interrupted. 'You don't understand the first thing about me, Oliver, or you wouldn't be here. I don't want to see you, and I don't want to see Isobel. I don't wish you ill. I just want nothing more to do with you. I want to spend the rest of my life not hearing about you or seeing you or being closer than ten miles to you.'

He toyed with the black notebook. 'You know, of course, that her first child died in infancy. But I don't think you know this: Isobel can't have any more.'

'She never told me that.'

'She had a second pregnancy, and a miscarriage, in Barcelona during the Spanish Civil War. The conditions weren't sterile, and she developed an infection. The child's father was Willoughby, by the way. The American volunteer she was living with.'

'What does any of this have to do with me?' Chiara asked sharply. 'What are you getting at, Oliver?'

'She told you that we're getting married.'

'And?'

'I have a proposal for you. Isobel and I will take your child. We'll make all the arrangements before the birth in January. I know the right people. The paperwork will all be prepared. For the adoption,

I mean. The child will be legally ours from the day it's born. The records will be sealed, and a birth certificate will be issued recording that Isobel and I are the parents of the child.'

'Never,' she said quietly. 'That's an utterly obscene suggestion.'

'Think about it.'

'You think about *this*,' she said, rising to her feet. 'The only reason I didn't have an abortion was because my baby was conceived while I still believed you loved me. You didn't, and you were already sleeping with my sister.' The journalists and other Fleet Street employees who were filling the little pub were staring at Chiara, but she didn't care. She was enraged. 'But even if there was no love on your side, there was love on mine. And for the sake of *my* love, I kept the child.'

'Chiara—'

'I've lost everything, Oliver. Everything but this. And if you imagine that I will ever give him up to you and Isobel, then you're insane. I'd sooner kill him.'

His ruddy cheeks had turned pale. 'I'm nearly fifty. I haven't got an heir, Chiara.'

'Then father a brat on some other fool,' she retorted, walking out. 'You'll never have mine.'

࿄

A large man at the bar said, 'Shame!' in a loud voice, and there were growls of hostility as Oliver left the pub. He ignored them and searched among the crowds on the pavements for Chiara. He thought he saw her, walking swiftly away down Fleet Street, but there was no point in following. He needed to marshal his thoughts. He decided to walk back to Whitehall along the river.

He took it at a brisk pace, paying no attention to the cars on the Embankment or the boats on the Thames. He was going over the brief exchange in his mind. It was not like him to be gauche in his dealings with women, especially not with Chiara, about whom he felt twinges of guilt. But she had taken him by surprise. His suspicion that she might be pregnant had been so readily confirmed that he'd floundered and had said the first thing that had come into his head. As a result, he'd found himself, for the first time in many, many years, speaking from the heart. And that was not like him, either. He'd grown so used to thinking and speaking guardedly, as was expedient or pragmatic, as suited the realpolitik of the situation, that he'd hardly recognised his own voice.

And she – she had cold-cocked him. Chiara, always so gentle and sweet, had outfaced him, just as she'd outfaced Isobel. He'd never seen that fierce look on her face before. In it had been all the hurt he had inflicted on her, and it had silenced him.

Oliver clenched his teeth as he remembered his own words. He and Isobel, to adopt Chiara's child! Raise it as their own! What had he been thinking of? She would never accept such an arrangement, and only a madman would have suggested it. Yes, he had spoken like a madman; but in that moment, his heart had not been his. Learning that Chiara was with child, his child, had filled him with a rush of tenderness that had been close to madness. There had been many moments in the past four months when he'd regretted what he'd done. But no moment had been like that moment today.

He took a deep breath and paused to look at the new Waterloo Bridge, which would open to traffic in a week or so. He remembered the picturesque old bridge very well, with its nine Neoclassical arches. It had begun to subside in the late nineteenth century, and work on the new bridge – much starker, with only three long arches – had begun on the eve of the war. With so few men available, most of the work had been done by women. He'd watched them for the past three years, in their overalls and dungarees and boots and hard hats, spanning the river with a quarter mile of reinforced concrete.

The bridge, probably because of its great size, had been singled out for attacks by the German bombers more than once, and the women had simply repaired the damage and kept on working. There was no greater monument to womanpower in London, he reflected.

And every one of those women could do something no man could: conceive a child and bring it into the world. A truism that one took for granted, until the child was one's own. And the woman wasn't.

He was greeted at the War Office by a perturbed RAF analyst with a sheaf of notes. 'I think you're right, sir,' he said. 'There's something going on at Peenemünde. We've gone over the photographs with magnifying equipment, comparing them with shots taken two years ago, and there are several new underground structures. I've marked them in red pencil on the tracing paper. We think they're test beds for aircraft engines.'

'What sort of aircraft engines?'

'Very fast ones. That's our guess.'

Oliver took the folder. 'I'll go over it now.' He went to his crowded office. The Peenemünde Army Research Centre had been developed enormously since the start of the war, and something – as the analyst had said – was certainly going on.

He sat poring over the complex annotations. If the Germans were building some sort of secret weapon there, the possibilities were ominous. So many threats loomed: aircraft with jet engines, which could outfly conventional planes and defeat radar; rockets that could reach London within minutes of being launched; weapons containing poisons or deadly diseases; the nuclear weapon, which could theoretically burn down cities. In total war, nightmares abounded.

Oliver knew that much of the construction work at Peenemünde was being carried out by forced labour from Poland and other Nazi-occupied countries. The barracks could be seen in the aerial photographs, typical Nazi concentration camps built to house slaves. Such workers would have no loyalty to the German state that had enslaved them, and that opened up the possibility of getting information, if they could make the right contacts.

The seriousness of the issue drove thoughts of Chiara out of his mind, but he found himself thinking of her again as he left the office later in the day.

'I haven't got an heir.' The words he'd blurted out in that Fleet Street pub echoed in his own ears. He was not aware of ever having thought such a thing before today, but he'd said the words with complete sincerity.

He was forty-nine. Fifty was a turning point in a man's life, they said. The half-century. He'd had good innings so far. He'd had an amusing life. Though there might never be public recognition for the work he'd done, so much of which had been secret, he'd served his country well. He'd shown bravery and discipline, and had earned the high opinion of men whose high opinion he valued. There was the war to be won, and in ten or twenty years he could think of retiring to Courtfield Park to enjoy the countryside he loved so deeply.

He'd had several women in his life. Not as many as he could have had, but he'd been selective. And rather than passionate and short-lived affairs, he'd sought out stable relationships that had lasted a few years each. 'Marriages in miniature', a friend of his had called them. The trouble was, they all ran their course. With a mother like his, and an upbringing such as he had had, he was not constitutionally suited to long commitments. He got bored with the women, and he moved quietly on, trying not to leave too much wreckage in his wake.

He'd thought he was bored with Chiara Redcliffe after three years. Especially when Isobel had arrived in England. Infuriating Isobel, whose progress he'd followed for some years before he'd met her in the flesh; one of the few people to have been honoured with

MI5 files for both Nazi and Communist affiliations. Her extremism, he knew, was all pose. She loved to provoke and draw attention. She'd certainly provoked him and drawn his attention. She was a beautiful, stylish woman, and he would have found her interesting for that alone; but it had been out of sheer annoyance that he'd wanted to bed her, if the truth be known. That was a mistake he'd made once or twice in his life before – getting off with women because he couldn't get on with them. It had never ended well.

And so he had set in motion the course of events that had culminated in the dreadful night when he'd arrived at Isobel's to find Chiara there, bombed out and forlorn. Of course, she'd guessed at once what was going on. And that had been that.

Fifty, and a father. By the time the child was twenty, he'd be seventy. His own father had been fifty years older than he, and more than thirty years older than his mother, a French beauty barely out of her teens on her wedding day. It was simply history repeating itself. Cécile de Robillard had very quickly grown bored with marriage and motherhood, and had gone on her merry way while Oliver was still a little boy. His father had brought him up. He still saw his mother from time to time, but they were almost strangers to each other.

How long would he have continued his affair with Isobel? She was glamorous, and Chiara was not. She was maddening where Chiara was calming, aggressive where Chiara was gentle. He'd found the contrast fascinating at first. He'd even thought it might be amusing to be the Conservative husband of a notorious Labour MP; that would make for some interesting discussions at the clubs he belonged to.

But the gilding was rubbing rather swiftly off the gingerbread, and the gingerbread was proving rather indigestible stuff.

He still loved Chiara. There was no question of that. And if it came to choosing a turbulent life with Isobel or a serene one with

Chiara, he knew which was the better choice. And now that there was a child—

His child. The child that he and Chiara had made. He wanted it, and he wanted her back.

But could he swing it?

෨

Chiara's fury was so deep that it drove away her morning sickness for the rest of the day – and, indeed, for the rest of the week that followed. It was as though the hormones that had been making her nauseated had been replaced by new hormones, ones that made her feel strong and angry. Just recalling the calm way Oliver had suggested that he and Isobel take her baby away from her was enough to send her into a towering rage. The breathtaking effrontery of it! More than anything, that showed how Oliver had seen her: a passive, malleable plaything with whom he could do whatever he wanted.

She'd been so determined to make him happy for three and a half years that she had never thought about her own happiness. How yielding she had been! How soft! And here she was, seduced and abandoned, like the foolish heroine of a morality tale.

'Well, I'm glad to hear the morning sickness has gone, at any rate,' the midwife said. She was an ascetic-looking Anglican sister with a sour face, and her expression said just the opposite – that she was disappointed, rather than pleased, by any alleviation of Chiara's discomfort. Chiara dreaded her check-ups with Sister White, but there was no other choice. Medical services were strained as it was, and she, as a mere unmarried mother, rather than, say, the wife of a serviceman, was in bad odour.

A quite different odour, as of antiseptic sanctity, emanated from Sister White's wimple as she bent over and applied her ear trumpet to Chiara's smooth white belly, which was only just starting to swell like rising dough. 'The foetal heartbeat's strong, at any rate,' she said, again conveying an impression of displeasure. *At any rate* was a common phrase with her, a palliative for all sins. 'Heartbeat a hundred and fifty.'

'That sounds very fast,' Chiara said in concern.

'Perfectly normal,' Sister White replied briskly. 'I've made some enquiries on your behalf, Miss Redcliffe, through the Church, of course. Adoptions are not in such demand as they were before the war. There are so many young women in your position nowadays. And placement is even more difficult if the father is a Negro. Is the father a Negro?'

'No,' Chiara said, 'the father isn't a Negro.'

'An Englishman?'

'Yes, he's an Englishman.'

'Any insanity, venereal disease, things of that sort?'

'No.'

'That's something, at any rate.' She fixed Chiara with a cold blue eye. 'And no chance of marriage?'

'None, I'm afraid,' Chiara said.

'Then I think we can do something. You're a girl of good family, and if there are no racial snags or hereditary diseases, so much the better. There's an elderly couple who're looking for a baby. They're in their seventies, but—'

'It's very kind of you to think of me, Sister White. But I've no intention of putting my baby up for adoption.'

'What will you do with him, then?' the midwife asked in some surprise.

'Well, I'll keep him and bring him up myself.'

'Alone?'

'Alone, if needs be.'

Sister White raised one thin eyebrow. 'We'll do your enema now.'

'Do we have to?' Chiara asked forlornly. She'd detested enemas from earliest childhood. 'I'm perfectly regular.'

'Lie on your left side, please.' Sister White was already attaching the tubing to the red rubber bag that looked horribly like a hot water bottle, and (Chiara knew from experience) contained a similar abundance of hot water. Chiara stared at the rather grubby wall of the clinic as the midwife packed a towel under her bottom. 'It's not impossible, of course,' Sister White said as she worked, 'but it needs a sacrifice which few young women are prepared to face. You can say goodbye to your career, for a start. You can say goodbye to any prospect of finding a decent husband. Going in.'

'Ouch!' Chiara said, wincing.

'You can also say goodbye to your social standing. Whatever you may think now, your life will be one of sneers and whispers. The lowest will look down on you – and on your child. I'm telling you all this from experience, Miss Redcliffe. My own mother was not married to my father. I can't say that she had a happy life, though she did her duty by me. Nor can I say that I was better off in her house than I would have been in the home of a loving, adoptive family, perhaps with siblings to play with. She did what she felt was right. But motherhood is a long, hard road. At the end of it there may be neither happiness nor thanks.'

'Oh, Sister, isn't that enough hot water?'

'The best you can do for your child may not be to keep him yourself, but to let some loving family take him. Think about these things, Miss Redcliffe.'

'If I wanted to give him up,' Chiara panted, 'the father is willing to take him.'

'Well, that sounds an admirable solution.'

'It isn't. I'm not giving him up. I love him already.'

'That's it. You know where the lavatory is.'

Chiara went swiftly to the lavatory and endured the inevitable results of the enema. When she came back into Sister White's office, the midwife was making notes in her ledger.

'You must get ready to leave London now, Miss Redcliffe,' she said without looking up. 'The Evacuation Board will give you a travel allowance and a living allowance. Do you have somewhere to go?'

'I'm not leaving London,' Chiara said flatly.

'You must.'

'It's not compulsory, is it?'

'No. But there is a difference between courage and irresponsibility. You've more than yourself to think of, now.'

'I have a job to do here. I can't stand the idea of mouldering in the country somewhere, like a sow in farrow. I'll stick it out unless it becomes impossible.'

'It will become impossible, I assure you. Don't leave it too late. I'll give your details to the board, in any case.' The midwife seemed to have warmed slightly towards her. She folded her dry little hands. 'Perhaps you'll satisfy my curiosity. The father: I assume he's a married man?'

'Not quite yet.'

'I don't understand.'

This frosty old thing was the first human being, Chiara realised, to whom she'd been able to talk about her situation. She opened her heart. 'He's older than I am, by more than twenty years. He's a distinguished man. We became lovers before the war. He was always very kind, but he made it clear he didn't want to marry me. I thought I could cope with that, but, as the years passed, it grew more difficult. I started to put pressure on him; perhaps I was wrong. In any case, my flat was bombed one night, and when I went to my elder sister's place, I found them together.' Chiara swallowed the hard lump that had formed in her throat at the memory of that dreadful night. 'They'd been having an affair for some time. Neither of us knew that I was pregnant. They're getting married in the autumn.'

'Did you get pregnant in order to trap him?'

'Oh no! I'm not that stupid, Sister. It was an accident. I'd been taking all the right precautions for years. I'm not really sure how it happened.'

'Hmmm.' Sister White's expression said that she had a pretty good idea how it had happened. 'Is your sister a great deal older than you?'

'Three years. She's thirty next month.'

'May I ask why he's willing to marry her if he won't marry you?'

'Isobel – that's my sister – is very different from me. She's everything I'm not. She's beautiful and clever and fascinating. And she's ambitious. She wants to get into Parliament. She'll make Oliver a much better wife than I ever could.' Tears welled up in her throat. 'Only it hurts, you know. It hurts terribly.'

Sister White watched Chiara as she cried into her hanky. 'You're very down on yourself, Miss Redcliffe. Your sister may be ambitious, but she can't be a very moral person. You've been most cruelly treated. And they want to take your child?'

'That's what Oliver has offered, anyway.' Chiara dried her tears.

'What did you say?'

'I told him I wouldn't consider it.'

The midwife's bony face was speculative. 'It sounds to me very much as though he's kicking himself now. You could get him back, if you wanted.'

'That's the last thing I want.'

'Men are peculiar creatures. I don't have a great deal of experience myself; I took the veil at eighteen. But I've got eyes. And I see that they always want what they don't have. And when they have it, they want back what they had in the first place. You say your sister is everything you're not, but it's hard to imagine that she has your innocence, your freshness, your . . .' She studied Chiara, searching for the word. 'Your light. And now you are carrying his child. Your sister's position is very weak, Miss Redcliffe. Well, I will see you next week,' Sister White concluded briskly. Her stint as confidante was now over. 'Good day.'

Chiara hurried out of Sister White's office, through the waiting room, where several expectant mothers sat in various stages of enlargement. Soon, she thought, she would be swollen and waddling like one of these, complaining of shortness of breath and puffy ankles. The thought was not pleasant.

'Chiara Redcliffe?'

For a moment she considered ignoring the male voice and speeding on as though she hadn't heard. There was nobody she wanted to see in this place. Then she paused and turned reluctantly. To her horror, it was Simon Altringham. He was wearing a white coat over an officer's uniform and carrying a more elaborate version of the foetoscope that Sister White had just used on her. She felt her face flame with heat. 'Simon!' she gasped in dismay.

He shook her hand briskly. 'I'm delighted to see you,' he said. 'I've thought of you so often.'

'What are you doing here?' she asked, her tongue feeling thick in her mouth.

'I'm the local obstetrician,' he said. 'After basic training, the Army told me I was a captain and sent me here. I was hoping to go abroad, but apparently I have a talent for obstetrics. They need doctors to bring young Britons into the world. Probably safer than letting me loose on wounded servicemen. Most mothers know what they're about, anyway. What are you doing here?'

'I—' Her mouth remained open, but no further sound came out. Her face burned even hotter.

He frowned in puzzlement and then glanced at her midriff. 'You're pregnant?'

'Yes,' she said.

'Oh, my dear girl. Let me check you over.'

'Please, no,' she said in dismay. But he had taken her by the arm. He was much taller than she, and she was swept inexorably along. 'I've just seen Sister White,' she blurted out, 'and had my enema!'

'No enema, I promise,' he said, smiling. 'One is quite enough, don't you think? Sister White swears by them, but, between you and me, in most cases I think they do more harm than good.'

In a state of mortification, Chiara entered his office, where he made her lie on a couch. 'This really isn't necessary,' she said through clenched teeth.

'Good practice for me, though.' He deftly draped her thighs, raised her skirt and pressed the stethoscope to her belly. 'Lovely heartbeat,' he said with approval. He was far gentler than Sister White, but very thorough. He checked her pulse, blood pressure and temperature, peered in her eyes and mouth and asked a great number of questions. He did not, however, ask about her marital status – perhaps the absence of a wedding ring made the question superfluous – or the identity of the father. Perhaps that was self-evident, too. The last time she'd met him had been in Oliver's country house during the winter. It had been a particularly unhappy weekend for her. She and Oliver had argued bitterly. She'd told Oliver that she wanted marriage and children, and he'd told her in no uncertain terms that he wanted neither. Looking back now, that weekend had been the crisis in their relationship. It had probably been during that weekend that he and Isobel had begun their affair. And if there had been any unconscious decision on her part to get pregnant despite Oliver's wishes (as Sister White had hinted), then that weekend had been the turning point in her feelings, too.

Simon Altringham came from a distinguished family. His father, Sir James Altringham, was a Cabinet Minister, knighted for services to the government. His mother, Lady Altringham, was on various committees. Chiara remembered a younger brother, Adrian, who was now probably in the Army, and some other young people who had been at Courtfield Park that weekend. They'd been thrown together while Oliver and the older generation had argued politics with Isobel. It had been during a cold morning's ride out on the horses that Simon had kissed her on the lips. She'd been furious with him. It had been an unasked-for impertinence. *'You look so beautiful,'* he'd explained. *'I couldn't help myself.'*

And later, he'd imparted some unasked-for advice, warning her that Oliver would never commit himself to her. He'd told her that Oliver was not a faithful man, and had urged her to find someone her own age, someone she could rely on. Meaning, clearly, himself. She'd been angry and offended, and had told him to mind his own business.

And here she was, flat on her back with her skirt pulled up while Simon listened to the heartbeat of Oliver's child. If ever folly had stumbled and been brought low, she was it.

'You're very healthy,' he pronounced cheerfully. 'Everything just as it should be. Are you still working in the Censor's Office?'

She rearranged her clothing awkwardly. 'I generally just say I work for the Ministry of Information. People don't like the idea of censorship.'

'Ah, yes. *Suppressio veri* and *suggestio falsi*, as my old Latin master used to say. I've always wanted to ask: what do you do with all the naughty bits you snip out of people's letters?'

'I work mainly with the Press,' she said frostily. 'At a somewhat higher level than snipping up letters.'

'I know. Just teasing you.' He grinned. 'You still rise to the bait rather nicely. Quite formidable.'

'Sorry. My sense of humour has been lacking, lately.'

'We'll have to see what we can do about that. I'm giving you these.' Simon piled the packages on the desk. 'Horlicks malted milk tablets; those are rather yummy, actually. Cod liver oil, which isn't. Iron tablets and salt tablets. Take them every day, please, without fail.'

'Thank you.'

'You're entitled to some additional ration coupons from now on,' he added, writing a note. 'An extra small bottle of milk, too. And a small bottle of orange juice. You can take the cod liver oil with the juice.' He smiled at her. He had changed in the six months since she'd last met him. He had the same open manner and the same smiling look in his deep blue eyes, but he had lost the boyishness that had struck her at Courtfield Park. The transition from student to doctor had improved him, she thought. He was by way of becoming a handsome man with a very well-shaped mouth. The crooked nose, broken in some long-ago accident, was a defect, to be sure, but one soon forgot that. She was getting over the first acute embarrassment of meeting him again.

'I suppose you're wondering about Oliver—' she began slowly.

He held up his hand. 'No, I'm not. In here, I'm only interested in you and your baby. But I'd like to see you outside the clinic. We can talk as friends, then. Will you have tea with me?'

'I don't think so.'

'Why not?' he asked briskly.

'Because I feel I've been a fool,' she replied, laying a hand on her belly.

'Did you see all those patients waiting out there? Well, a lot of them feel they've been fools, too. And, between you and me, a lot of them might have been. But it's a wonderful thing, all the same. Shall we say Sunday afternoon tea at Brown's? Three thirty?'

'I really don't—'

'I shall be there, nevertheless. You come along if you feel up to it.' He reached into a drawer. 'This is the latest thing. Chock-full of good sense. Keep it as long as you like.'

Chiara took the book. It was called *Childbirth without Fear*, by Grantly Dick-Read. It had evidently been well thumbed. 'Thank you, Simon.'

He rose from behind his desk. 'Don't forget to take the cod liver oil with orange juice,' he advised, 'and don't let me down on Sunday.' He shook her hand warmly. 'Meeting you again has cheered me up immensely. No, I won't try to kiss you again,' he said as she backed away from him. 'I learned my lesson the last time.'

☙

Oliver slipped into the Conway Hall just as Isobel was reaching her peroration. She caught sight of him at once at the back of the hall but did not falter in her address. She was an excellent public speaker, lively and authoritative, and well up to dealing with hecklers.

'Are you a bloody expert, then?' someone in an officer's uniform jeered.

'No,' she shot back, her clear voice ringing out, 'I'm not an expert. The experts are the ones who gave us the Maginot Line and told us the Germans would never cross it. The experts are the ones who told us Singapore was impregnable and would never fall to the Japanese. The experts told us to put our faith in light tanks and not build dive bombers and forget about submarines. The experts told us that Hitler wanted peace and that Mussolini would come into the war on our side. I'll tell you what: if I were an expert, I'd be hiding my head in shame right now. Wouldn't you?'

There was laughter as the heckler subsided. Oliver looked around the hall. It was packed. Even the gallery was crowded. Isobel had attracted a substantial audience. Most of the gathering were ordinary Londoners, anxious to hear the truth about a war that they knew was being only half-revealed to them by a government that controlled the radio, laid a heavy hand on the newspapers and censored the letters of the men fighting abroad. They wanted to know what was really going on. And, by golly, Isobel was going to tell them.

'We should have stood shoulder to shoulder with the Russians when Hitler invaded the Soviet Union last year,' she was going on. 'I urged it then, and the experts wouldn't listen. I urge it again today because it's not too late! Thanks to the courage and endurance and good sense of the Russians, thanks to the blood they have shed for us, it's still not too late! Opening a second front now would give us victory by summer of next year.'

'Communist rubbish,' someone called out, but Isobel pressed on, resplendent in a dress the colour of poppies and a hat sporting a nodding pheasant's feather.

'Showing the Russians that we're taking our fair share of the fighting will rouse millions of Europeans, ready to revolt against the Nazis. We can trap the Germans in a giant pincer, the war on two fronts that they've always dreaded. We can bring down the whole hideous structure of Nazi power. And, with it, we'll bring down Mussolini and his thugs, leaving the Japanese to face an armed world alone.'

She concluded to loud applause. People surged forward to the podium to congratulate her, ask questions and sign the petition. Oliver remained at the back, watching, until the hall was almost clear. Then he went up to her. She was bright-eyed, her cheeks flushed with colour, and Oliver thought she looked lovely.

'It went well, don't you think?' she greeted him.

'Very well. You were a great success.'

She introduced him to the people around her, one of whom was the local Labour Party secretary. 'Your fiancée's a wonderful natural orator,' the man said, wringing Oliver's hand. 'We think the world of her – and we're expecting great things in the near future!'

He murmured something suitable in reply. He could see the excitement on their faces. They did think the world of Isobel, and with good reason. Politics had always been run by what Isobel had once called fusty frock coats. Compared to the drab politicians of the day, with their mealy-mouthed opinions and dreary speeches, Isobel was a sensation. Her jewel-like brilliance could only be an asset to a party struggling to shake off a reputation for sombre grimness. He could see it in the way they looked at her.

There were a couple of Russians, too, including the chargé d'affaires from the Russian Consular Department, on whom Oliver had a thick file. He greeted the man cheerfully and laughed dutifully when the Russian congratulated him on his forthcoming marriage and said slyly, 'I hope Miss Redcliffe will continue to be Red even after she becomes your wife.' It took half an hour to extricate Isobel from them. He steered her towards his Jaguar, which he'd parked on Theobalds Road.

'Thank you for coming, darling,' she said, squeezing his arm. She was in high good spirits. 'I was so happy to see your face. Did you really like the speech?'

'It was colossal.'

'It's going to be part of my platform in Stepney, you know – the second front. "If elected, I will put all possible pressure on the government to join our gallant Russian allies," et cetera. They're all Reds there; they should lap it up. What do you think?'

'I liked the bit about the light tanks and the dive bombers,' he smiled. 'Very authoritative.'

'I get all that sort of thing from *Picture Post*,' she said gaily. 'It's my bible. We got another five hundred signatures for the petition today. Not bad, eh?'

'Not bad at all.'

He took her to the Savoy Grill for lunch. Isobel had no patience with rationing in any of its forms. She would not stoop to Utility Clothing, lying cheerfully about her spectacular outfits when challenged, and claiming they were made from old curtains. She shamelessly bribed shopkeepers to obtain black market goods, had scented soap in abundance while other women eked out a bar of Lux for weeks, and certainly would not eat humble victuals. Almost all of their meals were eaten in restaurants. She did not cook and neither did he.

The Grill Room was crowded, but Oliver had taken the precaution of booking a table. The towering figure of General de Gaulle dominated a group of senior French officers at a corner table, and there was a large screen at the opposite corner, indicating that Winston Churchill was lunching with his Cabinet there. The remainder of the tables were occupied by an eclectic crowd of famous journalists, American officers and diplomatic staff from various countries.

Isobel perused the menu, ordering a Dover sole with new potatoes. Oliver wanted nothing more than grilled marrow bones on toast. She asked for a Pimm's Cup to start with. When the waiter had bowed himself away, Oliver looked her in the eye. 'Chiara's pregnant.'

Isobel went swiftly pale. 'How do you know?'

'I went to see her. When you told me she was vomiting, alarm bells went off.'

'Yes,' Isobel said slowly, 'they should have done for me, too. I missed that connection.'

'She's four months gone. It's due in January next year.'

'Yours, of course?'

'Yes.'

'Will she agree to an abortion?'

'No.'

Isobel leaned forward. 'Make her agree!'

'I don't think we can make her do anything in her present mood.'

'So she's determined to have it?'

'It would appear so.'

'I feel sick.' Her Pimm's arrived, a colourful confection with lemon, mint and slices of fruit. She drained most of it in one gulp. Oliver signalled silently to the waiter for another. 'Damn her,' Isobel said quietly. 'I'm starting to hate her.'

'It's unfortunate.'

'Unfortunate!' Isobel exploded. 'It's a bloody catastrophe. This is going to sink my election chances if the Press get hold of it. Weren't you taking precautions, for heaven's sake?'

'She was attending to all that. I trusted her.'

'And she's dug you a nice little pit, lined with sharp stakes. What are you going to do?'

'I suggested that you and I adopt the child as our own, but that didn't go over at all well.'

'I'm glad you didn't suggest that to *me*,' Isobel said grimly. 'Why should I be saddled with her brat? I'd sooner drown it.' Her second drink had arrived, so she got to work on it. 'I need a real drink, damn it.'

'Don't choke on the lemons,' he said ironically.

'Why has she kept it so quiet all this time, the little wretch? Hoping to drop a bombshell at the moment of maximum effect, I suppose.'

'I don't think so. She wants nothing to do with either of us.'

'If you believe that, you're a fool. She planned the whole thing. Got wind of you and me, and made sure you knocked her up. Honestly, men are such fools!'

'I doubt whether it was anything so calculated. Chiara's not the type.'

'You're supposed to be a brilliant man,' she said scathingly. 'You don't seem to know much about women.'

'Perhaps I don't.'

'You're taking this so damned calmly,' she hissed at him. 'I could stab you with this fork.'

'I've had a little more time than you to absorb it.' He shrugged, but he kept his eye warily on the fork she had snatched up.

'I'm going to see her myself.'

'I wouldn't,' he advised. 'It won't do any good.'

Isobel made an exasperated noise and slammed the fork back down on the tablecloth. She stared across the crowded room. Her face was tight. 'Why is it,' she asked, 'that every time I get a chance at happiness, it's taken away from me?'

He saw that her eyes were shimmering with tears. 'We'll work this out,' he said gently.

'Why should my child be taken from me and a child be given to her?'

'I don't know.'

'I've looked after those two sisters of mine since I was sixteen, and never a word of thanks. It's not fair. Why were my men a succession of absolute bastards, and she got you, first time? Can you tell me, Oliver? Can you tell me why she's having your child, and I can't?'

She was crying in earnest now. He handed her his handkerchief. 'I'm sorry. It's very hard.'

'The *one thing*,' Isobel said, her voice breaking, 'the one thing I can't do. It's too much.'

He said nothing, letting her cry. The waiter arrived with their dishes. The sole was perfectly cooked, accompanied by three little new potatoes and five stalks of green asparagus, all dripping butter. He went to work on his marrow bones, scooping the gobbets of fat out of each and spreading them on the hot toast. He sprinkled salt and white pepper on them. They were delicious, taking him straight back to his childhood and the meals he'd shared with his father during holidays at Courtfield Park. At the Savoy, they understood such things. After a while, she picked up her fish knife and fork and began dissecting her sole, sniffing between mouthfuls, her eyes red.

'Feeling better?' he asked.

'I've been worse.'

'Good.'

'She'll file a paternity suit against you, Oliver.'

'She says she won't.'

'You seem to have had a nice long talk to her about this,' Isobel said bitterly.

'It was very brief,' he replied calmly, 'but we covered the main points. In any case, it won't come to a suit. I'm willing to provide any support she asks for.'

'How very gallant of you. You're a shining knight.'

'I'm trying to do the right thing, Isobel.'

'By *her*. What about *me*?'

'Darling, what do you want me to do?' he asked, taking a bite out of his toast.

'Buy her off,' Isobel said. 'Offer her money. Offer her whatever she wants, but make her get rid of it. You're the spymaster general, for God's sake, Oliver! Can't you have some men bundle her into the back of an unmarked car and drive her away?'

He wiped his fingertips on his napkin. 'I assume that's a flight of fancy,' he said coolly, 'and not a serious proposal?'

'I don't know. This is an intolerable situation.'

'What can't be cured must be endured,' he said.

'You have to do something about this.'

'I will do something,' he assured her. 'But you may not like it.'

'What's that supposed to mean?' she demanded sharply. 'You're going to leave me and go back to her, aren't you?'

Oliver smiled. 'Of course not.'

'I'll kill you both if you try that,' she promised.

❧

Chiara's telephone was ringing. Praying that it was not a raid alert, she picked up the receiver wearily. The operator was on the line. 'Miss Redcliffe? Stand by to be connected to Cairo, please.'

Chiara's heart began to race. Cairo! The international telephone service had been suspended except for emergency calls since the beginning of the war. Had something happened to Felicity? Despite the difficult relationship they'd had during Felicity's years in the convent, they'd reconciled their differences, and when Felicity had left London for Egypt, Chiara had been bereft. She hadn't heard Felicity's voice since that sad parting on Liverpool Docks.

'Darling?' Felicity's voice was tiny and distant. 'Are you there?'

'Yes! Is everything all right?'

'Don't worry – I didn't mean to frighten you. I'm fine. I'm being very naughty and using one of the lines at the Embassy, though I've only got two minutes, so no silences, please!'

'Oh, it's so lovely to hear your voice!' Chiara exclaimed, feeling immensely cheered. 'Tell me everything. What do you do all day?'

'Run up and down the stairs with messages. I'm getting legs like a mountain goat.'

'Aren't you wallowing in sin, then?'

Felicity snorted. 'Hardly. Haven't sinned once since I got here. This is the dullest place on earth. Worse than the convent.'

'You astonish me, darling. I'm terribly disappointed. I thought you'd be in King Farouk's harem by now.'

'Fat chance. What about you? How are you? How's Oliver?'

Chiara hesitated. She'd had no contact with Felicity in the past several weeks, apart from an exchange of birthday telegrams, and Felicity knew nothing of her recent history. 'Oliver's left me for Isobel. And I'm four months pregnant. You're going to be an aunt.'

There was a silence. 'You're raving.'

'I'm afraid not. Oh, and Tisbury Mansions took a direct hit. I was at work, luckily, but everything's gone. I'm living down the Mall from Buckingham Palace, in a garret.'

Odd little sounds were coming down the line, and Chiara realised that Felicity was crying. 'Bloody, *bloody* Isobel! She can't bear to see any of us happy! She destroys everything. She did the same to me.'

'Please don't cry, darling. It's all over now.'

'When's the baby due?' Felicity asked, weeping.

'January next year.'

'I'll be there to share your birth pangs, I promise.' Chiara heard Felicity blow her nose. 'What are you going to do about it? Keep it or sell it to the gypsies?'

'Keep it.'

'I'm so glad. Brave girl. It'll be a beautiful child, just like you. We'll raise it together. I'm so sorry about Isobel and Oliver, darling. And so sorry about Tisbury Mansions. Did you lose everything?'

'All my clothes. All my paintings. Every stick of furniture. Everything.'

'Oh, how ghastly. Are you very wretched?'

'I'm all right. *"This life's a dream, an empty show,"'* Chiara said, quoting from the sampler that had hung in their childhood playroom. Felicity joined in, and they chanted together, ' *"But the bright world to which I go, Hath joys substantial and sincere; When shall I wake and find me there?"'*

'If I were a man, I'd never choose anybody over you,' Felicity said. 'Oliver must have lost his mind.'

'He says he and Isobel want to adopt the baby.'

'He *has* lost his mind. As if you'd ever stand for that!'

'It's not going to be easy,' Chiara said.

'Who's helping you with all this?'

'Well, nobody. I just go to see the midwife every two weeks.'

'I never thought to hear you talking about midwives. You'll be knitting tiny jumpers next.'

But before Chiara could reply, the operator's voice cut in. 'Your two minutes is up. Disconnecting you.'

'Goodbye, darling,' Chiara called.

'Goodbye,' she heard Felicity answer. 'Goodbye, darling Chiara—'

And the line was dead. Chiara replaced the receiver.

Strange, maddening Felicity! She was the youngest of the sisters, and the most unpredictable. As a teenager, she'd looked like a Renaissance angel, tall and willowy, with a cascade of blonde curls framing a seraphic face. She'd been so determined to enter that damned convent, despite all her sisters' opposition. She'd stuck it out for almost five years, fading away into illness, all her beauty and promise withering, until Chiara and Isobel had been afraid she would die.

But she'd emerged from the convent at last and entered the world again – a world very much changed from the one she had left. At first she'd seemed to be too helpless to cope with wartime life. But she'd made her obstinate way through the first hurdles, training as a cipher clerk and eventually getting a posting to Cairo.

Cairo, of all places! Notorious for its decadent lifestyle, where spies from every nation revelled in sex, booze and sin; notorious for its playboy, King Farouk; notorious as a place where no virtuous young maiden could possibly be safe.

God knew what Felicity had really been getting up to. And now, the threat to her morals was overcome by a far greater danger – that of a German invasion.

The war news from North Africa was more serious than the radio or the newspapers were allowed to report. From her privileged position in the Censor's Office, Chiara could see just how close the Germans were to seizing Egypt. Led by their brilliant general, Rommel, their tanks had scored victory after victory in Libya. Cairo was in their sights.

Evacuation from Cairo, Chiara knew, was going to be almost impossible for the British forces there. And that might mean capture and internment in a Nazi concentration camp.

Despite all that, Chiara felt buoyed up by Felicity's call. Their lives were all in turmoil, but at least they had lives. The years that Felicity had spent as a postulant had been so very awful. She'd felt that Felicity was lost to her forever. She remembered the ghastly visit she'd paid to the priory when Felicity had been so ill. She'd felt then that Felicity was dying.

Had her own years with Oliver been something similar? She'd spent almost the same length of time as Oliver's mistress that Felicity had spent as a nun. And she, too, had withdrawn from life in that time. So much of it had been spent waiting for Oliver to come home from overseas postings, never knowing whether he was alive or dead. And of course she'd never so much as looked at another man in all that time.

Before Oliver, she'd had so many suitors that Isobel and Felicity had joked about her 'First Fifteen'. She'd never loved any of them. Only Oliver had conquered her heart. She had been faithful to him, sitting at home like Patience on a monument, refusing all offers of a social life. She'd lost touch completely with the old crowd. And here she was now, in her late twenties, dispensed with. And going to be a mother. She'd always thought Felicity a fool, but perhaps she herself had been the foolish one. At least Felicity had been able to begin again. She would never be able to do so.

When the telephone started ringing again, she thought Felicity might have wangled another two minutes. But this time it really was Air Defence.

'Raiders on the way,' said the clipped voice in Chiara's ear. 'Take your posts, please.'

A moment later, as she started scrambling into her blue serge overalls, the sirens began to wail, that unearthly warble that always sounded to her like all the dead of London calling from their graves. Her heart was thudding heavily. It was all very well to lecture newspaper editors about keeping morale high and not spreading panic; the only emotion one felt during a raid was blind terror.

She was loaded with equipment as she clambered onto the roof, most of it absurdly ineffectual, in her opinion – a shovel, a stirrup pump, a bucket of water, her cumbersome gas mask, a handbell and a pair of binoculars that were supposed to see in the dark but that she'd always found useless. She resented the bucket of water the most. She was always kicking the thing over in the dark confines of her post, and, in any case, what was *that* supposed to do against a real fire?

Her post on the roof was a little wooden hut that had been surrounded with sandbags. There was a telephone inside it that connected to the fire service. And if you found an incendiary bomb, you were supposed to slash the sandbags open with your knife and scoop sand onto it with your shovel. She'd never heard a worse idea in her life.

The searchlights were already reaching up into the sky from all around the city. There were three batteries in the Mall below her, all mounted on heavy trucks whose engines were revving to keep their charges up. The bright, reedy beams wavered up into emptiness; she recalled that it had been another cloudless day and that the moon would soon be rising, illuminating the city for the greedy eyes of the pilots from Germany.

And within half an hour, the swelling drone of the bombers came, growing loud enough to drown out the engines of the searchlight trucks. Chiara huddled in her outpost, hugging herself. The helmet was heavy but gave her little sense of protection. It was like a soup bowl mockingly strapped on her head, leaving her slender neck exposed. The Germans wore a much more efficient-looking coal-scuttle arrangement. She was horribly afraid. During the first raids she'd sat through, she'd been in a state of indifference as to whether she lived or died. Sometimes her misery had been so profound that she hadn't known how she would get through the next five minutes, let alone the next five days or five months. A direct hit would have been a mercy.

And she hadn't known she was pregnant at first. Or, if she had, she hadn't thought about it. She hadn't thought of herself as carrying an extra life. Tonight was different. Tonight, as the first bombs began to fall somewhere in the East End, she was acutely aware of that tiny, trusting heart beating a hundred and fifty times a minute inside her. Her body felt like a very frail shelter for that precious heart to which she had promised a life.

An explosion a mile or so away made her jump in fright. She tried to peer through the darkness. Like a giant stamping towards her, the explosions grew louder and louder until the very air lit up orange and beat against her like something solid. She was next. The long whoosh of the falling high-explosive bombs could be heard before each blast. Screaming, she covered her ears and crouched down, her eyes squeezed shut.

A massive blast knocked her brutally against the wall. She sprawled in the debris, hunching her body around her womb. She felt the Admiralty building swaying; what had seemed an impregnable fortress now felt like a child's tower of blocks, unstable and disjointed. The anti-aircraft batteries close by were firing rapidly now, adding their staccato voices to the thunderous cacophony. Chiara picked herself up, her ears ringing. She was shaking so much that she could hardly gather her scattered equipment. What madness it was to stay up here, exposed to hellfire. She was an expectant mother. She had a duty to something more important than herself or anything else in the world. The idea of wallowing in the countryside, like a sow in farrow, was suddenly very attractive. She had to force herself not to run back down the spiral staircase to shelter.

She was bruised all over. She dared not think of what the blast might have done to the little creature clinging in her womb. The roof of her little shelter had been blown to pieces – it had only been made of wood and canvas – but when she wound the telephone handle, it was still working. That seemed to be an omen of some kind. She decided to stay on the roof. She felt that if she gave up any hope of getting down from there alive, she wouldn't be so frightened.

There was an orange glare in the sky now, from the other side of her building. She couldn't see properly. She climbed the rungs of the iron ladder that led to the highest part of the roof. Now there was nothing between her and the hideous sky, clawed by the searchlights and riven by the bombers. She walked along the ledge until she could see the next block.

The glare was hot enough to make her shrink back. A stick of incendiaries had fallen onto the row of buildings that fronted Waterloo Place. The roofs were pouring sheets of flame into the sky. She noted which parts of the block were burning most fiercely, then scrambled back down to her telephone and called the fire in, describing its location and intensity.

The noise of the explosions and gun batteries was so loud that she could hardly hear the calm voice on the line. 'Can you remain in observation to direct the engines?'

'I can try,' she shouted back.

'Stand by, please.'

She waited, staring across the rooftops. This was the heaviest raid she'd ever been through. London had become a landscape designed by Dante. High above, where the invisible enemies droned, the bursts of flak flickered and danced, seemingly ineffectually; the restlessly sliding, intersecting searchlights had yet to find a single one of the bombers that were shedding this devastation. Below, the city burned from east to west. Despite the blackout, the familiar skyline was perfectly visible against the countless conflagrations. At the end of the Mall, she could see Buckingham Palace lit by the flames. The King and Queen had remained in London throughout the Blitz, lending their support to the citizens of the beleaguered city. No doubt they would be in their shelter now, just like all other sensible people.

The rumble of the bombers had faded a little, but they would be back. They retreated after the first run, waiting for the fires they'd started to take hold and spread to adjacent buildings. Then they returned, guided by the flames, and used them as targets for more bombs, intending to kill the firemen and other rescue workers, and spread the fires wider. All this she knew, and she knew that the blaze in the next block might bring more bombs soon. But, somehow, her terror was fading, or perhaps she was numbed by the noise and devastation around her. The child inside her was having a baptism of fire. If he was to have a fiery death, then she would be with him.

The telephone shrilled and she picked it up. 'The engines are in Waterloo Place,' she was informed. 'I'm going to patch you through to the local commander. Can you liaise with him, please?'

The next hours became an exhausting marathon of climbing over the roof to observe the fires and climbing back to the telephone to guide the firemen. By now the bombers had returned, and the continuous thunder of the bombardment sometimes made it impossible to talk on the phone.

Every anti-aircraft battery in Whitehall was firing, pumping shells into the night. Chiara's head was splitting with the noise, which was like the barking of monstrous guard dogs. The flashing of the guns was somehow even worse, stabbing into her eyes. The darkness fled and rushed back so swiftly that it was hypnotic. Everything became unreal after a while, a blur of noise and light and darkness that she moved through, as though in a film or on a stage. Even the bomb blasts seemed somehow contrived, 'effects off' that weren't really happening. She stopped thinking of the danger to herself as the hot winds buffeted her on her rooftop like fiery wings. She sucked the air, hot and poisonous with smoke and fumes, into her labouring lungs, and crawled to and fro on burning hands and feet, like a beetle waiting to be flicked off someone's lap.

Orange dandelion seeds scattered across the sky above her. The shrapnel from the airbursts fell around her like hot steel rain, tinkling merrily when the pieces were small, rattling with menace when they were large. From her vantage point, she directed the firemen below, telling them which sections of the building were burning, which were safe to go into.

Numbed exhaustion overwhelmed her. But floor by floor, window by window, the fires started to subside in Waterloo Place. Blackened holes, like missing teeth, replaced the orange glare. Guided by her, the firemen had been able to locate all the incendiaries and put them out. But the fire had done its work, destroying floors and ceilings so that apartments had collapsed into one another, and a gracious Georgian block had been damaged, perhaps beyond all repair. *What sense is there in that?* she wondered tiredly. *How does it help Hitler to ruin the great work of time?*

She retreated to what remained of her shelter.

At first she thought the glow in the sky was from another, vaster blaze; then she realised that dawn was breaking. On cue, the rumble of the bombers began to fade. Like vampires, they fled before the light. She looked at her watch. Seven hours had passed since the first warning. As far as she had been able to tell, not a single German plane had been shot down. She sagged in exhaustion against the parapet. The all-clear began to wail.

The scrabbling of boots made her look up. An ARP warden had come onto the roof to join her. His torch stabbed at her, making her wince. He was an elderly man, his face blackened with soot and grime, his tin hat askew.

'You all right, lovey?' he called.

'Yes, thank you.'

'How was that for a Saturday night?' He surveyed her wrecked observation post. 'Gawd blimey. You all alone up here? Nobody with you?'

'Just me,' she said, trying to smile.

'They shouldn't have left you all on your own. Look at the state of you.'

'I'm all right.' Behind him, two firemen had followed. Their blackened faces were split with grins.

'I told you she'd be a cracker,' the first man said to his friend. He shook Chiara's hand. 'We came to have a dekko at you. We've been fighting the fire down in Waterloo Place. The radioman was calling you "the angel on the rooftop". We knew you had to be a looker because your voice was that sweet. *You* ought to be on the radio.'

'Never mind him, he's married,' his friend said, also shaking her hand. 'I ain't. It was worth the climb to see your face. You're a brave kid.' They clambered back down to join the rest of their crew.

'They've made tea down in the street,' the ARP man said. 'Come down and have a cuppa. Jerry's shot his bolt and buggered off.'

Nobody refused a free cup of tea these days. She sat on a rickety box in the street in the pale light of dawn, drinking hot, sweet tea with a motley collection of people from the surrounding streets, many still in their pyjamas. Fire engines were clanging to and fro. The street was littered with the night's debris: broken glass, rubble, shrapnel and leaves. A double-decker bus that had been abandoned when the sirens had sounded now sat forlornly in a heap, all its windows shattered and half its side blown off. The Mall had been barricaded while the remaining fires were dealt with. Smoke was rising into the sky all around, but the morning air blowing into the city was cool and clean, smelling of new-mown grass.

She sat, half-listening to the conversations around her. She was practically deaf from the explosions, but she wasn't interested in their tales of near misses and German planes shot down, anyway. She was thinking of her baby. She'd had a terribly narrow escape.

She'd sworn to have nothing to do with Oliver, accept no help from him and cut him out of her life. But perhaps giving her child to Oliver and Isobel was the best thing she could do. Oliver had money, lots of it. Since the loss of Tisbury Mansions, she was no longer comfortably off. Raising a child on her own was not going to be easy. He could give the child a name, a background. The boy or girl – she was prepared to consider the possibility of it being a girl – would go to the best schools and follow Oliver to Cambridge. He'd said he wanted an heir. That meant the child would inherit on Oliver's death. And would join the established order of things as a gentleperson, knowing all the right people and having all the right connections. Not as the slighted offspring of a fallen woman.

Could she do it, though – give him up? And could she stand by, as they'd want her to, and watch them make him their own? Could she bear to see Isobel in her place, Isobel whom she knew to be utterly ruthless and selfish? She saw herself peering through a window for the rest of her life, forever on the outside. That would be unbearable. Yet would it be any more bearable to think she'd deprived her child of his birthright?

2.
CAIRO

'*aites vos jeux, mesdames et messieurs.* Ladies and gentlemen, please make your bets.'

The Egyptian croupier dropped the little white ball onto the wheel. It scurried across the spinning slots. Felicity watched it. In one hand she held her last chip. In the other, she held her drink, a glass of flat champagne – or what passed for champagne on a Saturday night in Cairo.

The decor of the club was a hybrid of Louis XIV and Ramses the Great. Under a gazebo of fake roses, the orchestra struck up a fresh tune. A group of wealthy Egyptians had arrived and was flocking gleefully around the baccarat table. This casino did not bar 'natives', provided they were rich and fashionable. With the Nazis at the gate, promising to liberate Egypt from colonial rule, many 'natives' were openly jubilant. They laughed in British faces and made sly jokes in Arabic and generally behaved as though the proximity of Rommel were a jolly good thing.

Beyond this gilded cage, the world was engulfed in war. War from palm to pine, war from pole to pole. Men and women were dying by the hundreds of thousands. The London she had left behind her – and where her sisters still lived – was burning, pounded nightly by Goering's Luftwaffe. Paris was lost, so were Oslo, Copenhagen, Warsaw, Budapest, Amsterdam, Athens. And now it was Cairo's turn.

She made her last bet of the evening, and, to her surprise, won the grand sum of three pounds. She picked up her winnings. As she left the table, there was a scramble to get her seat, two women both trying to claim her place. The younger and prettier of the two succeeded. She was a New Zealander with the War Service Auxiliary, faced with the unenviable task of feeding hungry Kiwis all day. Like Felicity, she was out for some Saturday night distraction.

'Maybe I'll get some of your luck,' she said to Felicity with a bright smile, settling her pert backside on the red leather.

At the cashier's desk she exchanged her chips for three crisp pound notes. Her gait was slightly unsteady as she walked down the stairs to the lobby. That last glass of champagne was starting to hit her. She was still not used to alcohol.

She was greeted by the popping of camera flashbulbs, clapping and cheers. But the applause was not for Felicity. The young King of Egypt had arrived with his entourage and his mistress. Farouk was wearing a black bow tie and white evening jacket, a cigar cocked between the fingers of one hand. The mistress, a handsome, blonde Alexandrian Jewess, was poised on the other arm, her magnificent bosom well displayed in a low-cut Parisian gown.

Felicity curtseyed dutifully and was rewarded with a wave of the royal cigar.

'Ah, Miss Redcliffe.'

'Your Majesty.'

Farouk inspected her from his commanding height. Under his heavy lids, which gave him a sleepy look, the pale eyes were assessing. 'We hear a certain young English lady has been storming the roulette table tonight.'

She blinked. He had just entered the casino. How had he heard these things? He had spies everywhere. He prided himself on knowing everything – and doing nothing about anything. 'I was lucky.'

'Unlucky at love, then, hmmm?'

'I wouldn't know about that, Your Majesty.'

'And how is the esteemed Ambassador?'

'Working hard, I'm sure,' she replied.

'Ah. Keeping us butterflies safe while we sip nectar.' He was looking down her cleavage with interest. 'We don't see enough of you,' he went on. 'You must come to Helwan. I'm having a palace party this weekend. You play tennis, don't you?'

'I play a little.'

'You shall play a lot. And I shall admire you bouncing around while I eat iced watermelon in the shade of an umbrella.' The Jewess, who was holding a small, woolly, white dog under one arm, was regarding Felicity with sharp eyes. Felicity got the impression of a keen but not very happy intelligence. A divorcée who had reportedly cleaned out her very rich husband, she was supposed to be keeping Farouk anti-German for the time being, a task in which Sir Miles Lampson, the formidable British Ambassador, was failing signally. The fate of the free world might depend on that splendid bosom. 'And we'll have mixed swimming in my pool,' the King went on. 'And then an early supper. Champagne and lobsters. And then dancing girls!'

'So terribly sorry, Majesty,' Felicity began, 'but I can't—'

He cut in. 'I'll drive you myself. Bring your prettiest négligée. We're all sleeping on the roof. And, of course, a bathing suit.' He moved in close, his voluptuous lips caressing her ear. Flashbulbs cracked, capturing the moment, his wink, her expression of cross-eyed outrage. Damn it! She would be in the society pages tomorrow, looking like a fool. Farouk chuckled as he moved on, puffing at his cigar. 'I'll make all the arrangements! Pip-pip toodle-oo!' Having been educated at the Royal Military Academy at Woolwich, the young King of Egypt was fluent in the argot of the British upper classes, and spoke with only the faintest of Levantine accents.

Felicity marched out of the lobby. Farouk had tried it on with her on more than one occasion, the first time when she had just arrived in Cairo. He tried it on with every pretty woman he saw, though (as people remarked) he didn't always get it off. Despite his youth, he was becoming corpulent, his boyish good looks fading. Irritatingly, he'd got hold of the information that she'd spent several years in a convent before joining the Army as a code officer. It seemed to make him friskier than ever, as it did with some men. The street outside was quiet, the air cool on her flushed face.

'Taxi, *hanim effendi*!'

The *suffragi* was holding open the door of a cab for her. But the thought of returning to her dreary little room and trying to sleep was repugnant. She had been billeted in a tiny cubbyhole, no bigger than a closet, in a shabby hotel off Ismailia Square, which she shared with a quantity of mice. The other cipher girls called it 'Cockroach Palace'. After six weeks in Cairo, there was no sign that she would be found better accommodation, and she was getting cabin fever. 'No, thanks. I'll take a walk.'

The *suffragi* called after her, but she did not turn around.

The embankment was lined with tall palm trees, overlooking the Nile. This part of Cairo was a square mile of luxury and pleasure, where the clubs and casinos, the smart restaurants, grand hotels and fashionable coffee shops offered the wealthy places to party, gossip and intrigue. Behind the façade, however, the scene changed.

She took a shortcut through a narrow street, haunted by hollow-ribbed dogs and feral cats, but otherwise deserted. On a corner, though, there was a sign of life, an old man sitting with his donkey and his tray of flat loaves. The idea of hot, fresh *baladi* bread was appealing.

As she started to cross the road towards him, a man jumped in front of her. One hand held a knife with a wickedly curved blade.

The other hand made rapid beckoning movements, indicating that he wanted her bag.

As she backed away, she registered the bad teeth, the drug-polished black eyes. He followed her, the knife slashing at her face. 'Give me,' he shouted in broken English.

She turned for help to the old street vendor, but he was already trotting swiftly away on his donkey, leaving his wares scattered in the road. He did not look back. She retreated, her heart racing. The contact of cold stone against her shoulder blades woke her paralysed instincts. Without thinking, she thrust her hand into her bag and pulled out the little revolver. Her elder sister, Chiara, had given it to her before she'd left London. She pointed it at the thief's legs and pulled the trigger.

She felt the kick of the pistol, saw the shower of sparks, was deafened by the report. The knife clattered to the ground. Her attacker hopped away, clutching one foot. Her bullet had taken a chunk out of his left shoe, which was dribbling gore. He looked at the blood on his hand, then hobbled off up the street, howling in Arabic.

Felicity turned to run the other way. She did not get far. The gleaming black flank of a limousine pulled up next to her.

The door of the car opened. The driver was a foreign-looking woman with long black hair, wearing a glittering white evening dress. 'Are you all right?' she called in English.

'He just tried to rob me,' Felicity replied shakily.

'I saw the whole thing. You were *formidable*.' The other woman pulled her hair back behind one ear, revealing a dangling earring with spectacular diamonds. 'I think the best thing would be a graceful departure. Don't you?'

'Shouldn't we call the police?' Felicity's legs were starting to shake in reaction. 'I shot him!'

'You British are not so popular right now. Do you want to be here when an angry mob collects?'

'No, I don't want that.'

'Then let's go!'

'All right,' she said. She got into the car. The interior was luxurious, lavender leather and burr walnut, the doors thumping shut to insulate them from the brutal alternatives of life outside. They passed the knife-man, stumbling along as fast as he could with his wounded foot.

'Maybe I should drive over him?' the woman said speculatively, slowing the big car to a crawl. 'Teach him a lesson?'

'Please don't,' Felicity said. 'I think he's had his lesson.'

'Maybe you're right.' But she drove up on the pavement and swerved so close to the boy that he had to flatten himself against the wall. She speeded up and turned the corner. 'My name is Rabiah Bakhtiar.'

She took the small, firm hand. 'Felicity Redcliffe. I have to go straight to the Embassy.'

'Why?'

'I work there. I have to tell them what happened.' The prospect of explaining this to the Ambassador was not a pleasant one. 'They're going to be furious.'

'Will it do you any good to tell them?'

Felicity hesitated. 'I doubt it.'

'Then don't tell them.' She dug in the crocodile skin bag at her feet and produced a little gold-plated flask. She tipped her head back and swigged from it, then passed it to Felicity. 'You like cognac?'

Felicity drank from the little golden flask. The spirit flooded her chest with heat, making her choke. 'Oh, God. What a night.'

'Thank God for a little adventure in this dull town. Let's have breakfast at my place.'

⁓

The Honourable Malcolm Tennant was in bed, but the bed was not his own. Nor was the woman beside him his wife. He pushed her away, propped himself up on one elbow and looked at his watch. 'I have to go.'

'Not yet, *habibi*.' Leila Suleiman stretched her arms up to him. Her long, crimped hair, bleached in imitation of a Hollywood blonde, was spread over the pillow. 'Stay.'

'I can't.'

'You can tell them you have been attending to a crisis.'

He snorted. 'My dear idiot, there *is* a crisis. That's why I have to get back to the Embassy.'

He rolled out of bed and began dressing. He was a tall man with a bony, prominent nose, rather dark-skinned for an Englishman, not handsome by conventional standards, but with the kind of face that inspired confidence in the British. He looked and sounded like what he was, the product of a famous public school. He dressed hastily. Leila was smoking an oval Cleopatra cigarette as she watched him. The scent of the Turkish tobacco was sweetly narcotic.

'What is this crisis, *habibi*?' she asked, hugging her knees. Her catlike face was intent, her dark-rimmed eyes fixed on him.

'Nothing for you to worry about.'

'But I do worry. The Germans?'

'Yes.'

She exhaled smoke at the ceiling. 'I thought you said they were being contained?'

'Not anymore.' He popped the gold links that had belonged to his father through his starched white cuffs. 'The First Armoured Division has been destroyed by Rommel. Seventy tanks gone. The rest scattered. He's broken through the Eighth Army, and he's racing for the Egyptian border.'

'My God.' She stubbed out the cigarette, looking anxiously at him. 'Are they going to invade?'

'That's the general idea.'

'Don't we have any forces there to stop him?'

He shrugged. 'Nothing substantial.'

'But there must be a plan!'

'Our leaders have a touching idea that Rommel is exhausted and will pull back at the last minute to rest. In my opinion, that's like hoping a man will pull back to rest when the girl's got her knickers off and her legs open.'

'So what will the Army do if he crosses the border?'

'A strategic withdrawal, darling.' He stooped, tying his laces.

She lit another cigarette and smoked reflectively. 'You're going to abandon me to be raped by the Italians. And then the Germans.'

He smiled sourly. 'You'd enjoy that, wouldn't you?'

'No, I wouldn't enjoy that.'

'Rubbish. You lot can't wait for them to get here and boot the *inglizi* out.'

'That's not true.'

'Don't lie to me.' He slapped her buttock hard enough to make her cry out. He had to hurry. The apartment that he had rented for his trysts with Leila was conveniently close to the Residence, but he had stayed far too long – as usual.

Leila listened to his shoes clattering down the stairs, the slam of the street door, the sound of his car driving away. When silence settled, she swung her legs out of the bed and went to the cupboard. She opened the latticed door and reached behind the pile of her underclothes. The little eight-millimetre camera was still turning. German-made, it was compact and all but silent. It had been taking eighteen frames per minute for the past hour through its precision Zeiss lens, recording the obscene things Tennant liked to do to her. She stopped the camera. With this, she could threaten to crush Tennant. He would pay a fortune for this film, one day. And keep paying.

She filled the douche with salt water. Another abortion right now would be more than she could bear – and would put her out of action for weeks. And Tennant himself was too indifferent to care about protection. He wouldn't even consider a strategic withdrawal. Preventing conception was her business. He didn't care how she did it so long as she did it and it didn't interfere with his pleasure.

When she was quite sure she had removed every trace of Tennant, she dried herself and put on her old, patched dressing gown, huddling into it, for the night was cool. Then she picked up the telephone to make her report.

'He was here for an hour,' she said. 'He's just gone.'

'Did he talk?' the voice on the other end asked.

'A little. They're frightened. He said that the British have insufficient forces at the border to stop the invasion. Their tanks are scattered. They're relying on Rommel pausing to regroup. If he chooses to advance, the British will retreat.'

'He said this directly?'

'Yes.'

The man grunted. 'Good. Write a full report.'

'All right.' When this was over, she would cut her hair short again, let the curls and the peroxide grow out, and resume her life. There was a war. Men died, lost limbs, had their minds broken. This was her part.

∾

Barbara Tennant was not asleep, either. She lay on her side of the bed, staring at the ceiling. Her husband's side of the bed was smooth as a prayer book. He would return in broad daylight, smelling of another woman, telling her there was a war on. Another all-night crisis at the Residency. Saving the Empire.

Of course there was a war on. A cast-iron excuse for what he had been doing since the first year of their marriage. He was making love to a woman half his age. She had seen the girl, had her pointed out by a kind friend, in fact: a little, sallow, haughty trollop with arched nostrils and red lipstick. Up to all sorts, you could tell just by one look. The Honourable Malcolm Tennant. What a joke. He was the least honourable man she had ever known.

She went to her dressing table, thinking of Orlando Hescott, the war artist who'd arrived in Cairo. He was quiet-spoken and wore khakis, like a common soldier. In the garden of the Residency, she'd seen him with his shirt off for the heat, sketching Jacqueline Lampson. His body had been smooth and suntanned. Beautiful. He'd asked if she would sit for him.

I'm not daft, she thought. She knew exactly what he meant. Lie down for him, more like. He was a calmly handsome man with steady eyes, a way of looking at you that women said was more exciting than being caressed. Women could be such fools. Moira Hamilton – the same kind friend who'd pointed Leila Suleiman out to her – had said that when an artist painted your portrait, he saw you more clearly than your husband ever would.

He'd made official portraits of Farouk, Queen Farida, Lampson and Nahas. And they said he'd done more than paint Farida. They said he'd got her into bed and that 'she was panting for more' (Moira again). He'd painted Queen Mary and Winston Churchill and the Duchess of Windsor, and was currently billeted with the daughter of that old Lebanese scoundrel, who was the most scandalous woman in Cairo.

'Why on earth would you want to paint me?' she'd retorted, with her most awkward laugh. It had happened during the afternoon tea that Miles Lampson had given him at Groppi's. Moira Hamilton had picked up the murmured exchange over the chocolate-covered dates and pastries smothered in crème Chantilly. 'He's trying to get off with *you*, of all people,' she'd giggled. The giggle had been set with barbs.

Am I, then, so undesirable? Barbara wondered.

She began to brush her hair with hard, sweeping strokes.

Farouk's favourite *salle privée* was painted from floor to ceiling with swags of roses twining on an extravagantly gilded lattice. Dotted here and there were naked marble nymphs, not very successfully concealing their charms under their hands. 'Pretty girl, that little Felicity Whatsername.' He used his thumbnail to slice open the cellophane wrapper, opened the new deck and began stripping it. He only liked to play with high cards. 'Nice figure.'

'I thought you didn't admire "girls who look like boys",' Zipporah Mizrawi remarked. The Redcliffe girl was of the modern type, slim and light on her feet. She'd always heard Farouk extol bodies like her own, curvaceous and soft, with deep bosoms and wide hips. That, at least, was what he demanded from the flocks of Italian, Balkan and Egyptian starlets who formed his constant entourage.

'I like that combination of eyes and hair. That sort of English-woman never shaves between her legs. Do you think it's blonde there, too?'

'I'm sure she makes sure both places match.'

He ignored the waspish note in her voice. 'We must find out. What does she like? Silk? Chocolates?'

'You're not serious?'

'Not serious about what?'

'About getting her to Helwan.'

'Why not?' He smirked at her. 'Don't be jealous, Zippy.'

'I'm not jealous. But she works at the Embassy. Or had you forgotten?'

'And I'm the King of Egypt.'

Zippy fed her poodle a biscuit. The trembling little animal snapped it up, intelligent eyes rolling in its snowy wool. 'Lampson would shoot you.'

'Half the men in this room want to shoot me,' Farouk said, squinting over his cigar smoke at her. 'Look at dear Colonel Naguib over there. Did you ever see such a death's head?' He waved languidly to the grim-faced Egyptian Army officer, who responded with a stiff bow. 'That chap wants to shoot me because I'm supposed to be pro-British. The charming red hats at the table behind him want to shoot me because I'm supposed to be pro-German. I can't win.'

'I hope you're not really pro-German, dear boy.'

'But there's a lot to be said for the Germans. They have a sense of fun. Know what Hitler gave me for my birthday?'

She watched his epicene, perfectly manicured hands shuffling the cards. Soft hands that had never done a useful thing since birth. 'Yes, I know. A red Mercedes convertible. And the British gave you a set of golf clubs.'

'I rest my case.'

'The Germans' sense of fun isn't always very amusing. They would send me to the gas chambers.'

'And what a waste that would be,' he said with calm indifference. 'Dr Goebbels was *très amusant* while he was here. A most cultured man.'

'He's hideous.'

'Well, dear Edward likes the Nazis well enough. And he has the most perfect taste I know.'

'They made *dear Edward* abdicate.'

'They didn't make him abdicate because he was pro-Nazi. They made him abdicate because he was pro-Wallis.'

'My point is that you should watch out the same thing doesn't happen to you.'

'They wouldn't dare.' He looked up at her with his sudden smile. 'I don't want you to be sent to the gas chambers. You really are a handsome creature.'

'At least my hair is natural.'

'You think she dyes hers?'

She shrugged. 'I don't care. I don't like the subject.'

He leaned forward and lowered his voice. 'Tonight you shall undress for me. Slowly. And get me excited. Until I can hardly contain myself. And then you will get on your hands and knees and—' He broke off as his poker partners arrived, two Balkan millionaires and a director of the Suez Canal Company. He leaned back. 'You fellows are late, damn you.'

'We've been waiting for an hour and a half, Your Majesty,' the Frenchman said, masking his irritation.

The King scoffed. 'Nonsense. Sit down. I hope you chaps have brought plenty of money. I'm feeling lucky tonight.'

Zippy watched Farouk direct the three men around the poker table, making them get up and change places until he was satisfied. Almost three times his age, wealthy and powerful as they were, they obeyed the young King with weary patience. From childhood, he had been denied nothing, indulged in everything. None of them was going to disappoint his expectations. Tonight would cost them money, sleep and pride. Farouk never got up from the poker table until his pockets were bulging with chips. But the patronage he dispensed was essential to conducting business in Egypt.

Farouk was invariably 'dazzlingly handsome', 'golden-haired' or 'godlike' in the gossip columns. In fact, Zippy thought, watching him now, he was just a pudding-faced boy with dirty blond hair and sleepy eyes. His best feature, in her estimation, was his mouth, which was childishly sensitive. And he could produce a sudden, enchanting smile when he was really amused. He ordered drinks all round, chattering facetiously, telling the silly jokes they had all heard a hundred times before, but at which they all dutifully laughed, concluding each joke with 'Don't you think that's rather good?'

'Have you heard the war news?' the Frenchman asked. 'The Eighth Army—'

'*Khalas, khalas*,' Farouk said, waving the subject away. 'No damned war news tonight. I've had enough of the British and their war.'

'Very good.' One of the Balkan millionaires chuckled unctuously. He lit a cigar with a diamond-encrusted cigarette lighter and puffed like a dragon at Zippy. She resisted the temptation to wave the acrid smoke away from her eyes. They detested her – she knew that well enough. The Balkan, who was rumoured to be the personal financier of King Zog of Albania, had brought a flat parcel with him. He slid it across the baize to Farouk. 'This may be more to your taste, Majesty.'

'We were just talking about presents, weren't we, Zippy? I hope this has nothing to do with golf.' He tore the wrapping open greedily to reveal a photograph album bound in gold and green. He opened it and burst out laughing. 'Oh, I say, Mukhtar, that's rather good.' The others craned their necks to get a look. Over Farouk's shoulder, Zippy saw that the photographs were startlingly pornographic. Farouk flipped through the images, each one more obscene than the last. The financier grinned at her.

'Homework for you, Mam'selle.'

'Yes, homework for you, Zippy,' Farouk said with his merry laugh. She kept her smile in place, refusing to show them that the insult had stung her pride. They treated her like his whore. But these worldly men knew little about Farouk. He was a sexual *ingénu* in many ways. His teenage wife had already embarked on affairs so notorious that the Allied troops sang about them. At times she wondered how he had managed to father two children. There was only one thing he liked to do with her, which was over in a few minutes and could hardly lead to conception. The album would go into his vast collection of pornography, to be catalogued and forgotten.

The drinks arrived: vintage champagne and cognac for the men; an iced bottle of the violently coloured orangeade that he loved for Farouk, the dutiful Moslem. He gulped down a glass of the fizzy, sweet stuff and belched, settling back into his chair with the cards. *'Yalla, bina.* Let's play.'

MARIUS GABRIEL

The British Embassy in Garden City was thrumming like a beehive at four in the morning. Every room was lit. A continual stream of clerks jostled up and down the grand central staircase from the Cipher Room on the ground floor to the Ambassador's suite on the top floor, carrying freshly decoded messages up and hastily scrawled replies down.

Malcolm Tennant slipped past the guards outside the Ambassador's door with a nod and tried to mingle with the crowd inside, unnoticed by Sir Miles Lampson's eagle eye, which was not easy, since the huge British Ambassador towered over all others by at least six inches.

'Any more news?' Tennant muttered to an aide.

'Rommel's tanks have reached the frontier, sir,' the man replied out of the side of his mouth. 'The Eighth Army's in total confusion. Units scattered, losses unknown. It's a rout.'

Tennant nodded. 'And Auchinleck?'

'Furious. Wants a counteroffensive, but our forces are too widely dispersed to do anything effective. Word is, Rommel's going to capture Benghazi imminently. Oh, and Hitler's restyled the Afrika Korps. Henceforth it's going to be "Panzer Army Africa".'

'That certainly has a ring to it.'

'Malcolm!' The Ambassador's booming voice rose above the murmur of voices. A large finger beckoned.

Tennant pushed through the throng towards the Ambassador, who led him into the little back room. Lampson closed the baize-lined door and turned on Tennant. 'Where the hell have you been?'

'Went out for a breath of fresh air,' Tennant replied.

'Breath of fresh air, my foot.' Lampson was an enormous, intimidating man with a face that Tennant had heard the cipher girls describe as 'like a bag of spanners'. He glared down at Tennant from his full height of six foot five. 'You went out to that bint of yours.'

'I needed a break. I've been here since yesterday morning,' he said defensively.

'So have I. So have all of us.' Lampson got the bottle of Laphroaig out of the cupboard and poured them both a generous slug. 'I wish you could remember who you're married to, Malcolm. Barbara's a decent woman.'

'Barbara and I don't get along. You know that.'

'A strong marriage keeps a man sane in a place like this. And I need hardly tell you that keeping a mistress is not quite the thing for an undersecretary.'

Tennant shrugged wearily. Undersecretary! He should have been an ambassador by now. It was all very well for Lampson to preach. A few years ago, at fifty-four, Lampson had married a raving beauty of seventeen. The bewitching Lady Jacqueline Lampson, exotic and flirtatious, was the undisputed queen of Cairo society. Lampson was in clover; while Tennant had been tied for twenty years to a dull, spiritless woman he neither loved nor liked, stuck in a career rut that never led anywhere. 'I'll take that under advisement, Sir Miles.'

Lampson gulped his Scotch. 'Things are getting a damned sight too sticky. You heard about Rommel reaching the frontier?'

'Yes.'

'He has Alexandria in his sights, now. If he takes Alex, he takes Cairo. If he takes Cairo, he takes Suez. And if he takes Suez, he takes the war.' Lampson put the Laphroaig back in the cupboard. 'Suitably refreshed as we are, shall we get on with the defence of the realm?'

❦

The house was near the pyramids at Giza, in an area where the rich escaped from the overcrowded city. The palatial villas concealed their ostentation with high walls. Only glimpses of tiled roofs were visible among lush palm groves.

'So nouveau riche, I know,' Rabiah said to Felicity, 'but living in the old town is really impossible these days.'

She had pulled up outside ornate wrought-iron gates. A *bowab* hurried out of his sentry box to open for them. A distant cock was crowing. The sky was light.

Gravel spurted under the wheels of the Hispano Suiza as Rabiah drove to the house along a driveway lined with palms. By the light of the rising sun, it was revealed to be a curvaceous Mediterranean palazzo. Rabiah parked the limousine in a cavernous garage, beside a mustard-coloured Army staff car. Felicity was still in shock after the incident. A feeling of unreality had settled over her, a feeling that this was all a dream, horrible in parts, over which she had no control.

The vaulted kitchen that they entered was silent. 'The servants aren't up,' Rabiah said. 'Lazy dogs. However, we can manage to make coffee, I think. It can't be difficult.'

But she obviously had little experience with the cafetière. Felicity had to put it together and make the coffee while Rabiah pulled out drawers, hunting for spoons. She was about Felicity's age, with olive skin and cloudy green eyes, her black hair tinted with henna. 'You don't do much in the kitchen, do you?' Felicity said.

'Not if I can help it. I wonder if Orlando is awake. He wakes early. Just when I am going to bed.'

'Your husband?'

Rabiah laughed as she clattered with the tray. 'Orlando is my house guest, darling. An artist. A beautiful creature.' Rabiah cocked her head, listening. 'He is awake. Come and meet him.' She put the coffee pot on a tray with three tiny gold cups and led Felicity through the house. High-arched rooms opened into one another, revealing vistas of Persian carpets and oversized furniture. They emerged onto a veranda. In the garden beyond was a tiled swimming pool, which rippled and glittered as a swimmer exercised in it.

'That's Orlando,' Rabiah said. 'Quick, before he gets out. Look!' An easel and a tray of oil paints stood in the centre of the veranda. The large canvas on the easel was covered with a cloth, which Rabiah whisked off. 'He hates people to see his work before it's finished. But isn't that lovely?'

The painting was of a naked woman sprawled on a sofa with striped cushions. Though the work was half-finished, it was clear that the nude was Rabiah herself, and indeed, the vacant sofa was there to be seen on the veranda, standing in front of the easel. Felicity was not an art expert – that was more the province of her sister Chiara – but even she could see that the painting was the work of a fine modern artist. The lines were dynamic, and the colours had a vivid brilliance that reflected Rabiah's own vitality.

'It's very good,' she said sincerely.

'I'm sure he'll want to paint you,' Rabiah said.

'Not like that, I hope.'

'Are you a prude?' She laughed and threw the cloth over the canvas again. 'To be painted by Orlando Hescott is no small thing, my dear. You may hang in a museum one day. And that's immortality.'

'Is he an old friend?'

'He's painted me before. In Paris, just before the war. He was in the Welsh Guards. He fought at Benghazi and Mersa Matruh. Quite a hero. But he's far too valuable to risk on the battlefield anymore. You might as well put Renoir in a tank. So they've made him an official war artist. He's here to paint portraits of the most important people. He's already done Farouk and the Queen. And me. Again.'

The pride in her voice was unmistakable. Felicity wondered how it must feel to lie naked like that while a man painted you, and whether Rabiah and the artist were lovers. They took the tray to the poolside and sat to watch the man swimming. He swam with the precision of an athlete. All she could make out was sleek, dark hair and muscled arms. The morning air was deliciously cool on her flushed cheeks. 'Do you live here all alone?' Felicity asked.

'I look after my father. Gaga,' Rabiah added succinctly. 'Doesn't know who he is or who I am. When he dies, I'll be the last of the line.'

'You're not Egyptian?'

'We're Lebanese. My father came here from Beirut with one suitcase, and made a fortune.' She gestured at the magnificent surroundings. 'As you see. It will be my job to squander it all once he's gone.' She laughed gaily.

Orlando Hescott finally hauled himself out of the water. He straightened, dripping. He was wearing trunks, his torso smooth and tanned. Rabiah threw him a towel. 'Look what I have brought you, Orlando,' she said. 'Miss Felicity Redcliffe, an ice-cold British beauty who is lucky at cards and unlucky in love. And she has killed a man this morning.'

He wrapped the towel around his waist and shook Felicity's hand. A thick lock of his hair hung over his forehead in the manner of a ladykiller. His eyes were a deep blue and very steady. 'Have you really killed a man?' he asked quietly.

'Of course not,' Felicity replied.

Rabiah told the tale. She made it sound like a schoolgirl prank. Seated in a chair, Orlando Hescott listened gravely to Rabiah, with water droplets glistening on his skin. Felicity tried not to stare at him. He was a thrillingly handsome man who made few unnecessary movements. Every man and woman in the whole world was jumping into other beds, Felicity reflected, and as always, she was the only one clinging to her maidenhead – even though the Army doctors had diligently supplied her with cervical caps and shown her how to use them.

'Given the current mood in Cairo,' he said when Rabiah had finished, 'tonight's events may produce something of a situation. You work at the Embassy, Miss Redcliffe? In the Cipher Room?'

'Yes.'

'You're in a delicate position. You're supposed to report any sort of trouble with the locals. Especially something like this. Are you all right?' he asked Felicity, who had started to cry.

'I wish I'd never gone to that wretched casino,' she replied, blotting her eyes with her handkerchief. 'I keep seeing that boy, blood squirting out of his shoe.'

'Do you think he saw you get into Rabiah's car?'

'Yes.'

'Rabiah's car isn't hard to identify. It'll be all over the bazaar by lunchtime.'

'Oh dear!'

Rabiah shrugged. 'Don't worry about me. I can take care of myself.'

'You'll have to tell the Ambassador, Miss Redcliffe, if only to protect yourself.'

'I suppose so.'

He stood up. 'I'll get dressed and drive you to the Embassy.'

Rabiah sighed after he'd left. 'Trust a man to make things complicated,' she said. 'We shouldn't have said anything.'

'I'm afraid I've got you into dreadful trouble!'

'I like trouble.' A nurse wheeled an old man out into the garden. He sat in a wicker bath chair, wrapped in a splendid gold-embroidered dressing gown, but his face was vacant and unresponsive as Rabiah greeted him and fussed with his hair.

Orlando Hescott returned. He had dressed in a khaki shirt and trousers, and his hair had dried, revealing itself to be a dark gold in colour.

'Ready to go?'

Felicity nodded. 'Yes.'

The Honourable Mrs Malcolm Tennant, called 'Barbie' behind her back by the cipher girls, was a matronly woman whose English tea-rose complexion was not suited to the Egyptian climate. Her cheeks were now flushed pink, and there were beads of sweat around her mouth as she glared at Felicity.

'The last thing we need at this point is any trouble with the natives,' she said, dabbing her upper lip with one of the Pond's tissues she took with her everywhere. 'Do you have any idea how foolish you've been, Miss Redcliffe?'

'To be fair to Miss Redcliffe,' Orlando said in his quiet way, 'she was caught up in events beyond her control.'

'That's what they all say, Mr Hescott. There's going to be trouble, but perhaps we can contain it.' She reached for the telephone. 'I'm going to call my husband.'

Felicity was starting to feel very tired, her eyes gritty and burning. She was grateful for the steadying presence of Orlando Hescott beside her. He was being kind through this ordeal. The Military Police sergeant who was with them sat stolidly, tugging his ginger moustache.

Malcolm Tennant, the undersecretary, entered the hot little room. His face was sallower and more aquiline than ever. He looked as though he hadn't slept either, and he was impatient. 'What is it, Barbara?'

Felicity's adventures were explained in some detail to Tennant, who leaned against the door with his hands in his pockets.

'Damned stupid girl,' he said in his clipped way when the story was told. 'Why did you shoot the wretched man?'

'I was all alone in the street! And he had a knife,' Felicity said, gulping down the tears that threatened to reappear at his harsh tone.

'You can't go around Cairo shooting people. This isn't the Wild bloody West. Where's this popgun of yours?'

Meekly, Felicity reached into her handbag and produced the little pistol Chiara had given her. Tennant took it, sniffed and put it in his pocket like a teacher confiscating a yo-yo. 'You never had this, understand? It doesn't exist.'

Felicity nodded. 'Yes, Mr Tennant.'

'This is probably going to require disciplinary action of some kind,' he said. 'In the meantime, say nothing to anyone. You weren't there, it never happened, and it was two other people.'

'But Malcolm—' Barbara began.

'Too late for anything else,' Tennant cut in. 'Can you keep your mouth shut?'

'Yes, Mr Tennant,' Felicity said.

'Then do so.'

'You'd better go home directly,' Barbara told Felicity brusquely after her husband had left. 'I'll get one of the other girls to stand in for you today.'

'That wasn't quite the reaction I was expecting from Tennant,' Orlando said as he walked Felicity out of the Embassy. He had taken her arm in the most natural manner. 'Not entirely wise, in my opinion, but there it is. I'll get you another pistol, if you like.'

'No, thank you,' Felicity said with a shudder. 'No more guns for me. You've been very kind, Mr Hescott. I don't know how to thank you enough.'

'Please call me Orlando. And there is a way you could thank me, Felicity. I wonder whether you would let me paint you. You have a very arresting face.'

Felicity thought of the nude study of Rabiah on the striped cushions. 'I don't think—'

'Just a preliminary sketch,' he cut in smoothly. 'Head and shoulders. If we both approve, we could move on to a fully developed portrait.' They walked out of the shady portico into the garden, which was brilliant with flowers, and then into the rumble of the street. 'I've been wanting to sketch some of the cipher girls for my portfolio, and you—'

He was interrupted by a ragged chorus of shouts. Across the street, a small mob of Egyptians had gathered, most wearing the *galabeya* and loose turban of poor men. There was usually a rather sullen crowd hanging around outside the Embassy these days, but today they were far more agitated. Felicity saw fists being shaken, angry faces yelling. It seemed that this animosity was being directed at *her*. One young man, in particular, was screaming at the top of his voice. He was propped up on two makeshift crutches. One of his feet was bandaged. With a sickening shock, she realised that he was the boy she had shot in the alley. He had recognised her and was jabbing his finger at her furiously.

'That's the boy from last night!' she gasped.

The crowd began to stream across the street towards them. The sentries at the gate emerged from their sentry boxes, lifting their rifles to their shoulders uncertainly. At once, the Egyptians stooped, reaching for missiles. A hail of stones flew across the street. Felicity saw the Military Police sergeant who'd been with them in the Embassy stagger, clutching his bleeding face. A passer-by in a suit crumpled to the ground, struck by a half-brick that had laid his forehead open. The morning heat buzzed with stones and bottles.

Orlando Hescott jerked Felicity out of her dazed trance. 'Run,' he commanded sharply. His Vauxhall was parked fifty yards down the street. They pounded along the pavement towards it. Felicity heard the mob howling behind them in hot pursuit. Stones clattered around them. A car windshield shattered into fragments nearby. There was a shot, then another, followed by screams. Something struck her heavily between the shoulder blades and she stumbled, gasping with the pain, but Orlando yanked her forward.

'Come on!'

She threw a panicky look over her shoulder. To her horror, a gang of about twenty men was chasing them. Sticks had now appeared in their hands; others held rocks or knives. Their faces were savage, and they were howling for blood. Her heart almost failed her. Her vision blurred, as though she were going to faint, but Orlando wouldn't let her stop. He grasped her wrist and pulled her with him.

They reached the car. Orlando threw the passenger door open and bundled her inside, slamming the door. She shrank under the dashboard as the mob surged round the Vauxhall, fists pounding on the bonnet and roof, faces snarling at the windows. The car began to rock, as though they were trying to turn it over.

She glimpsed Orlando, fighting his way through the crowd. Limbs flailed at him, hands clawed at his face. He disappeared into the mass of drab *galabeyas*, and she felt he was going to be killed. But he emerged from the mêlée somehow, wrenching his door open and scrambling behind the wheel. His clothes were torn, and his previously immaculate hair was hanging over his eyes, but he seemed remarkably calm.

'This car isn't a very good starter,' he informed her, as though commenting on the weather. He twisted the key, and the engine churned asthmatically. Fists continued to pound on the car's roof and sides. With a sharp crack, the window beside her starred. A man was swinging a brick against the glass. 'Cover your face,' Orlando said. She obeyed.

The engine took with a wheezy roar. Leaning on the horn, Orlando edged forward slowly. The crowd was reluctant to part. A youth flung himself on the bonnet, his face a few feet from Felicity's, distorted with fury as he cursed her. She could only stare back at him numbly. Another window cracked under a blow. Inching forward, blasting the horn, Orlando cleared a passage at last, and the Vauxhall trundled down Ahmed Ragheb Road. A few of the crowd ran alongside for a while, shouting, drumming on the car, and then fell back one by one as it picked up speed. Orlando turned down the road that ran alongside the Nile. The street was busy but orderly here, the river glinting grey-brown under the morning sun. He ran his fingers through his hair, raking it back from his forehead. His blue eyes were calm.

'That was an interesting few moments. I think the Honourable Malcolm Tennant's scheme of keeping this quiet is a dead duck. Are you all right?'

'No. I'm not.' Felicity had started to shiver with shock. She looked back through the rear windshield, noticing for the first time that it had been broken in. 'They wanted to kill me!'

'Don't worry, they're not following us. So that was the boy you shot?'

'Yes, I recognised him and he recognised me. They know who I am. Oh, God.'

'The nationalists are certainly stirring the pot rather effectively.' He glanced at her white face and trembling hands. 'I think you need a drink.'

❧

'I've got more than that to worry about, damn it,' Miles Lampson said. He waved the memo at Tennant. 'This is from the War Cabinet. We've been ordered to burn all the classified GHQ files immediately.'

'How?' Tennant asked laconically. 'There are rooms full of them.'

'Don't I know it.' The Ambassador grunted.

'The incinerator can't possibly cope with all that. We'll have to make a bonfire in the garden.'

'I'd like to put bloody Farouk on it. With the fat on him, he'd burn until Rommel gets here. You'd better get started.'

'Me?'

'Yes, you.'

'Can't someone else do it?' Tennant asked resentfully.

'You're responsible for handling and disposal of classified files,' the Ambassador pointed out. 'Best get going, Sunny Jim.'

Tennant went downstairs to get the process started. He'd hoped to be in bed by now. He tried to mask his fury with his usual stoical face. As he had pointed out, there were three rooms full of strictly classified files. Most of them couldn't be of any possible interest to the Germans, but orders were orders. The road outside the Embassy was quiet again. The mob had vanished as efficiently as it had formed. This morning's skirmish had resulted in relatively light damage: an MP sergeant with concussion and some damage to the Embassy railings, which Lampson had had freshly painted (his notion of boosting morale in the face of imminent defeat).

He commandeered the huge braziers the gardeners used for burning dead palm leaves and chose a spot in the courtyard. Under his orders, secretaries and soldiers began lugging boxes of manila-brown files out of GHQ. He doused the first few in kerosene and set them alight, but the files were slow to burn. They curled languidly and writhed coyly. Probably treated with some kind of flame retardant, Tennant thought wearily. Damned things made to last forever, instead of for a swift annihilation. Somebody should have thought of that. Like everything else in this bloody war: bad planning, bad timing and insufficient manpower. Was he supposed to stand here all day, tending this bonfire, like the stoker at the furnace of Hell?

More files were dumped on the blaze. He watched their edges grudgingly blacken. The heat was frightful. He stripped to his shirt-sleeves, sweating profusely already. His eyes burned. His heart was pounding dully. This was going to give him heatstroke.

He groaned aloud as he saw the figure of his wife approaching across the courtyard, wearing one of her ghastly flowered dresses and a straw hat. Why had she never learned to dress elegantly? As her figure grew more matronly, he found her more irritating than ever, her bosom obtrusive, the swish of her plump thighs infuriating. The hat cast a speckled shade over her face, which wore its customary slab-like impassivity. 'You look hot,' she said.

'Did you come out here to tell me that?' he growled.

'No, I came to tell you that the young man Miss Redcliffe shot has made a formal complaint to the police. They're saying he was a boy from a good family, on his way to the mosque for early prayers. No mention of any knife or any robbery, of course.' Barbara studied his crimson face unsympathetically. 'This isn't just going to go away, as you said it would. Miss Redcliffe will have to be got out of the way as soon as she can be found. Put under lock and key somewhere safe.'

'Yes, well, there's nothing I can do about it now, is there, Barbara? The girl has run off with the oversexed genius.' One of the staff emptied another carton of folders onto the bonfire, which was starting to spew a column of black smoke into the cloudless sky. 'And cipher girls are your responsibility, not mine.'

Barbara dabbed her face with a Pond's tissue. 'I wonder exactly what you think *is* your responsibility, Malcolm.'

'You're supposed to see to their morals,' he retorted.

'I'm supposed to see to their well-being. I can't follow every twenty-year-old girl on her night out.'

'Well right now, as you can probably see, I'm rather occupied with this.'

She turned her slow gaze onto the bonfire. 'This is an absurdity,' she commented.

'Most of my life is an absurdity,' he said savagely.

'I'll try to find Miss Redcliffe.'

She walked back to the Embassy. Tennant was longing for a beer. More trouble. Perfect. The Germans bombing Alexandria. And Ramadan just around the corner.

Bloody girl. Silly little fool with her huge, frightened eyes and quivering lips. There was no end to the folly of the cipher girls. Anyway, as Lampson had said, they had more than her to worry about now.

He watched his wife's substantial figure plod up the garden path. A vision of Leila Suleiman rose in his mind, sprawled naked on the bed that smelled of their lust, wiry and lithe. God, he wanted her again. He would go back to the apartment on his way home, when this was over, he decided. Might be the last time, who could say?

∽

'I don't want any more alcohol,' Felicity said. Orlando ignored her – she had learned that men generally did ignore what one wanted – and pushed the gin and tonic in front of her. They were sitting in a dark corner of the bar at Shepheard's. Everybody in the room was drinking resolutely and untiringly. The war effort – she had long since learned this, too – sailed on a river of alcohol. One could only hope that the enemy were drinking the same amount.

'Drink up,' Orlando commanded. 'I'm going to make some phone calls.' He went to the telephone at the end of the bar. Felicity was feeling extremely shaky. She lifted the glass to her lips, nauseated by the smell, and tried to get the stuff down. The furious faces of the mob haunted her.

After making several brief calls, Orlando replaced the receiver and came back to the table. 'Barbara Tennant wants you out of Cairo. You're not to show your face anywhere, on pain of death. Felicity *non grata*. The Embassy's in ferment, burning all their secret files. Sounds like they expect Rommel any moment.'

'Where am I supposed to go?'

'Rabiah's going down to Aswan until everything blows over. She has a houseboat on the lake. A lovely old thing. We're invited.'

'We?'

'You and I.' His calm, blue eyes met hers. 'We could do worse. It's very pleasant down there. The lake is majestic. The boat is very comfortable. We could start work on that painting, and' – he smiled economically – 'get to know each other better.'

Felicity looked down. His hands, handsome and smooth like the rest of him, were spread out on the scarred table, his fingertips touching hers. She drew her hand back. 'Just out of interest, aren't you and Rabiah having an affair?'

'Anything like that has been amicably settled.'

'And she won't object to watching us have a little fling?'

'I should think it would charm her greatly to observe it. She might even decide to join us in our revels.'

'It's a kind offer,' Felicity said wearily, 'but all a little too modern for me, thank you.'

'You don't have to decide right away. However, I will probably go down with her. She's closing up the villa here. So that leaves me without a billet.'

'And me on my own.'

He shrugged, as though at her innocence. 'Egyptians are chafing to throw off the British yoke and seething over the Jewish Palestine project. A paleface villain is just what they want. You'd be quite safe down in Aswan. It's peaceful and still pro-British. Here in Cairo, you're in danger. Where are you going to go?'

Felicity put her head in her hands. Did she really have to choose between a lynch mob and seduction by Orlando Hescott? Her former life, the years in the silence of the convent, her ups and downs with her sisters, were like a dream to her now, sweet and remote, compared to this vivid and horrible present. She missed Isobel and Chiara so much, maddening as they were. She would give anything to be with them now.

Was this what she had wanted when she'd pushed her way out of the priory gate? She didn't even have any nice clothes to wear on a houseboat. That, on its own, was enough to make her recoil from the idea. Orlando Hescott tapped a cigarette out of his packet of Woodbines and offered it to her.

'I don't smoke,' she said.

'Try it. It'll soothe your nerves.'

Hesitantly, she accepted the cigarette. He lit it for her with a steel lighter. She tried to inhale, the way she'd seen women do in the movies. The smoke caught in her lungs, making her choke. A wave of giddiness produced an alarmingly light-headed sensation. 'That's awful,' she choked.

'You'll get used to it. Keep going. And I think you need another gin,' he said.

❧

Malcolm Tennant was still sweating profusely and blackened with smoke when he arrived at Leila's. Her eyes widened with alarm as she opened the door. '*Habibi*! What's happened?'

He pushed past her. 'Get me a beer.'

'You smell of smoke. And you look awful. What have you been doing?'

'Tending the bonfire of the vanities,' he growled.

'I thought you must have been caught in the rioting. It's all over Cairo.'

'I've noticed. I'm not blind. Get me that bloody beer, would you?'

She went to the little fridge and got him one of the bottles of Australian lager she bought for him on the black market. He took it from her and poured it into his gullet, belching loudly between draughts. 'What is the bonfire of the vanities?' she asked.

'Instructions from London to burn all classified documents,' he said. 'The old bastard gave me the job, of course. He hates my guts.'

'You had to burn all the documents? Why?'

He tugged his tie loose. 'To stop them falling into Rommel's hands.'

'Are things that bad?' she demanded.

'Christ knows,' he replied. 'There are tons of papers. Ridiculous bloody performance. I'd have been there all day. I cleared out and left the *bowabs* in charge. Let *them* sweat.'

'Does this mean the Germans are close?'

'You're always so damned full of questions,' he said sourly. 'Worse than Barbara. Are you selling information to the enemy?'

Leila didn't flinch. 'Would you like another beer?' she asked, seeing that he had drained the bottle.

'No. Tell you what I do need, though.'

She smiled at him. 'Come on, then. But shower first. You stink.'

This seemed to annoy him intensely. 'Oh, I stink, do I? And who the hell are you to complain? Cleopatra?' He was black-browed. His expression disquieted her.

'You're not getting into bed with me like that,' she said.

'I'll get into bed with you any damn way I please.' He took her wrist in a hot hand. 'I pay for the bloody bed and I pay for you.'

Leila tried to laugh at him. 'Don't be silly. You're filthy. You'll spoil the sheets.'

'I'll do more than that, I promise you.'

He pulled her, half-protesting, half-laughing, to the bedroom. 'You're hurting me, *habibi*. Wait!'

He slapped her face hard. She felt her teeth rattle. Numbness spread through her cheek. He was in a savage mood, she realised, and not joking. His fingers bit into her flesh, bruising her as he man-handled her onto the bed. The more she fought, the more brutal he became. She was soon breathless and stopped trying to reason with him, concentrating on protecting her breasts and face from his hard elbows. He had never been a gentle lover, but now he was not like a lover at all, but like something else, a thug taking what he wanted and enjoying the pain he inflicted in the process.

He dug a knee into her belly, winding her, and tore her blouse open, grasping her breasts cruelly. 'It's time you bloody people learned who your masters are,' he said through clenched teeth. 'I've paid for you!'

'*Habibi*, no!' she gasped. Dazedly, she thought of the camera in the closet. She hadn't had time to turn it on. This, whatever it was, should be recorded. Sex had never been anything but an ordeal with Tennant, but she'd had no idea it could become so violent and terrifying. She clutched at the bedposts to try to get away from him. It was no use.

Afterwards, Leila curled into a ball, too shattered to even cry. He got up. She heard him get himself another beer from her fridge and gulp it down. Distantly, the noise of the rioting could be heard; the mob had reached the Embassy. There was the sound of a shot. The hubbub died down for a moment, then rose up again, redoubled.

'Here.' He threw something into her face. She opened her eyes dully. It was a handful of dirty money. Her stupor drained away, to be replaced by rage. After every sacrifice she had made for him, every piece of herself she had given up, he had taken the last thing that was her own.

'Yes,' she said in a shaking voice, 'I'm selling information to the enemy.'

He turned. 'What?'

'Not even selling it. I give it away joyfully.'

'What the hell are you talking about?'

'Everything you tell me. Every word. I pass it straight on to the Moslem Brotherhood.'

He loomed over her. 'You're lying.'

She laughed at him bitterly. 'It's true. You've made me a whore, but I've made you a traitor.'

He grasped her arm and jerked her upright, glaring into her face. 'I've never told you any classified information.'

'You don't know what you've told me!' She returned his gaze fearlessly. 'I've hated every moment we've had to spend together.

Do you think I submitted to you because I was in love with you? You're an arrogant fool, Malcolm. You disgust me. And I'll tell you something else: I've killed your babies. Two of them.'

'That's your business,' he rasped.

'Your fat English wife can't have children, can she? No one to continue your noble family line. And now there never will be. You'll die alone.'

Her venom seemed to take him aback for a moment. 'Shut up, Leila—'

'I've filmed you. Look in that cupboard!'

Tennant stared at her for a moment, then strode to the cupboard and opened it. He took out the German camera and stared at it blankly. Then his face suffused with blood. He tore the back of the camera open and ripped out the ribbons of celluloid film. 'Bitch!'

She threw back her head and laughed again. 'I've got others. I'll send them to your wife. To the high and mighty British Ambassador. To everybody in Cairo. You're finished. All you British are finished!'

~9

The taxi that took them to Felicity's hotel had to thread its way through a maze of back streets. The rioting was spreading across the city and the bigger roads were all choked with people. Orlando made her crouch down on the back seat, not so much because anyone might recognise her as because the sight of any British female might attract a stone or worse. He himself sat with a small sketchpad on his lap, scribbling quick impressions of the scenes he saw. Out of the corner of her eye, Felicity watched his pencil race across the rough paper. The graphite scribbles resolved somehow into running figures, angry faces, domed buildings. He was really a very good artist, able to capture images with magical speed. Even watching sideways, with her head practically on his knee, she could see that. It was just rather crushing to know that all this violence was somehow her fault. She felt bewildered and lost.

Ismailia Square was crowded, but there seemed to be no violence there yet, just large crowds of men in *galabeyas* milling around aimlessly, like extras in some Biblical epic, waiting for instructions from Cecil B. DeMille. The taxi pulled up outside the hotel, and Felicity hurried in, Orlando close behind her. She scuttled into the lobby, to be confronted by the duty manager, Mr Riada, who came gliding out from behind his desk to greet her, rubbing his hands together unctuously.

'Oh, Miss Redcliffe! We thought you'd never get here!' He inclined his brilliantined head close to hers and muttered, 'He's up in your room. With his people!'

'Who is?' Felicity asked in alarm.

Mr Riada, who claimed an Irish grandfather, pressed his finger to his glossy moustache, rolling his yellow eyes. 'Shhh. Go up at once. Hurry!' He glanced suspiciously at Orlando. 'Your friend can wait in the bar.'

'I'd rather go with her, if you don't mind,' Orlando said. 'Especially if there's going to be any trouble.'

Mr Riada flashed him a scornful glance. 'No trouble in my hotel, Mister, thank you.' He signalled to the burly bouncer who prowled in the lobby, on the lookout for undesirables visiting the cipher girls who made up the majority of the lodgers. The man laid a large hand on Orlando's shoulder. 'Bar's open, old son,' he said. 'Run along and buy yourself a beer.'

Separated from her protector, if that was what he was, Felicity went up alone in the lift. The gins she'd drunk at Shepheard's had dulled the edge of her weariness (and eased the throbbing bruise between her shoulder blades) but they had also made her feel somewhat plastered. She was having difficulty walking in a straight line or keeping her thoughts in order. Whoever was in her room – probably some furious official from the Embassy – the coming interview was likely to be very unpleasant. She took a deep breath and tried to walk down the unlit corridor without bumping into the buckets of sand that stood in melancholy rows. It felt as though she were walking at the bottom of the sea, in one of those iron suits that divers used, at once ponderous and weightless.

The door of her room was ajar, and there was a tremendous bustle inside. She peered in cautiously. Her room was full of Egyptians. Her suitcase was on the narrow little bed, apparently being packed – or, rather, clothes were being stuffed into it and pulled out again with much argument. The cupboards and drawers were all gaping open, the contents in disarray.

'I say, these will never do.' King Farouk, resplendent in a cream linen suit, turned to greet her, holding up a handful of her shabby old brassieres. 'These are shocking. You need some new lingerie immediately. And haven't you any nylons? I can't find any at all. Where do you keep them?' He resumed pawing through her underwear drawer.

'What on earth are you doing?' Felicity demanded in astonishment.

'Getting you packed for Helwan,' he replied. 'I told you I'd make all the arrangements. We're setting off in an hour.' He picked up a pair of her sandals and sniffed them. 'Do you have sweaty feet?'

Indignantly, Felicity snatched the shoes away from him. 'Tell them to stop mauling my clothes at once! This is outrageous!'

'Somebody had to pack for you. I've been waiting for you for ages. I thought you'd never get here. Don't worry – talcum's just the thing for sweaty feet. But I insist on varnished toenails. Deep red. I've got some bottles at Helwan.'

Felicity pushed one of the entourage away from her suitcase fiercely. 'Make them stop. I'll call the police!'

'But I'm the King,' he said calmly. 'The police grovel to me. Frankly, Miss Redcliffe, none of your clothes are remotely suitable. The only thing for it is to equip you once we get there. Even if it's a yashmak that covers everything but your sparkling eyes.' He burst out laughing. 'Or nothing at all! I say, that's rather good, isn't it? *Mieux d'aller nu que n'être pas à la mode,* what?'

'I can't possibly go to Helwan with you,' Felicity said.

'You can't possibly stay in Cairo,' he retorted with unexpected sharpness. 'The whole city's baying for your blood – or hadn't you noticed?' Felicity was silenced. 'You need to disappear. The longer you hang around, the worse things will become. You'll be safe with me.'

Felicity closed her eyes, swaying. This was like a dream. She didn't know whether she would be any better off in Farouk's palace at Helwan than in a cosy *ménage à trois* on a houseboat with Orlando and Rabiah at Aswan. But there was something about Orlando's smoothly predatory manner and Rabiah's fierce lunacy that frightened her more than Farouk's vulgarity. A burst of angry shouting from the square down below jogged her into wakefulness. 'What would the Ambassador say?' she asked in a faint voice.

'Old Lampson will do exactly what I tell him,' Farouk said loftily. 'I'll speak to him now, if *that's* what you're worrying about. Where's the nearest telephone?'

There was one fixed to the wall in the corridor. Farouk shooed away the cipher girl who was attached to it, tearfully trying to get through to her boyfriend in Alexandria, and dialled the Embassy. Felicity watched him as he talked to the operator. He stood straddle-legged, one hand in his jacket pocket, his voice loud, high and confident. Young as he was, he was already pudgy, his belly straining the buttons of his pink silk shirt. He offered protection, but at what price? Could she really think of losing her maidenhood to this ostentatious Levantine princeling? Did she really have to lose it at all? She recalled something one of the girls had said to her in the East End, while she'd been working in the canteen: *'You got to give it to someone, haven't you? May as well be him.'*

The other cipher girls, in curlers or hairnets, poked their heads curiously out of their doors all along the corridor as his voice penetrated the thin walls of the hotel.

'I don't care about that, Sir Miles,' Farouk was saying, apparently having been connected with the Ambassador, 'this is a question which affects me personally as head of state. I'm taking Miss Redcliffe under my protection. Yes, that's right. Under my wing. I see it as my duty. Absolutely my duty. We'll spend the weekend in Helwan. By the time we get back, the whole thing will have blown over.'

He held the receiver away from his ear, smirking at Felicity as a prolonged response ensued. Felicity recognised Sir Miles Lampson's ferocious tones, reduced by the instrument to an impotent clicking, like that made by some large but harmless beetle.

'Biting the carpet in rage,' he whispered to her in glee. 'No,' he said aloud into the receiver, 'I'm afraid you can't talk to her; she's most indisposed. This whole business has taken a terrible toll on her nervous system. I shall see to it that she gets the best restorative treatment at Helwan.' He rolled his muddy green eyes drolly at Felicity.

'Are you really going off for a weekend with the King?' one of the girls whispered to Felicity in awe. 'They say he's a terror with women!'

'I don't know *what* I'm doing,' Felicity muttered back, reflecting that she'd never spoken truer words.

'No, Sir Miles,' Farouk trumpeted, 'there's absolutely nothing I can do to calm the situation in Cairo. This is a state of affairs entirely created by the heavy-handed behaviour of your police.' More furious clicking. 'No, I'm sorry, I refuse to intervene or make any kind of statement. It's Thursday night, the start of the Moslem weekend, and I shall be going to Helwan to relax and pray. We can discuss this when I get back.' He hung the receiver up in mid-crackle. 'That settles *that*,' he said triumphantly to Felicity.

Felicity, who had never heard anyone talk to the Ambassador like that, was shocked. 'He'll have apoplexy.'

'I jolly well hope so. Ghastly man. Now. Let's get you packed, shall we?'

Felicity had reached her decision. 'All right. I'll come. But I have to tell Orlando Hescott. He's waiting downstairs.'

'Oh, Mr Hescott is one of your pals, is he?'

'I barely know the man. But he invited me to Aswan.'

'You've had a lucky escape, I should say,' Farouk replied.

She went down to the bar, where she found Orlando nursing a beer and staring into the mirror behind the bottles. 'It's King Farouk. He's asked me to spend the weekend with him in Helwan. I'm so sorry, Orlando. I think I'd better go with him.'

He observed her calmly. 'Good for you. I can't compete with a king.'

'It's not a competition,' she snapped irritably. 'I'm not a bloody trophy!'

'Of course you're not,' he replied. 'Enjoy Helwan.'

She relented. He was really the handsomest man she had ever met, and so far he had been an absolute gentleman. 'Thank you for everything you've done for me. You've been terribly kind.'

'Not at all. Some other time, then. I'll be in touch. I still want to paint you.'

'Even granted that the bar is not set very high in Cairo, what could possibly be interesting about me?'

'Oh, you're very interesting, I assure you.' He kissed her lightly on the cheek and left.

༄

'Look here,' the Ambassador said to Sir Walter Monckton, 'we've got rather an unpalatable radio broadcast to make.'

'Yes?'

'We have to tell the friendlies to get out of Cairo. Dutchies, Belgians, Frogs, anti-Fascist Eyeties – the lot of them. Advise them gently to clear out.'

'Are things really that bad?'

'We don't want a lot of wretched civilians clogging up the roads and railways when Rommel gets here. We'll need them for our own people.'

Monckton looked startled. 'All right.'

Lampson grunted as he rose. He walked out onto his balcony and glared around. The street outside the Embassy was empty, but only because the Military Police had cleared it and there was a platoon of soldiers guarding each end. The distant clamour of the crowd could be heard clearly a few streets away, still chanting anti-British slogans. He made out the shouts: *Rommel! Rommel! Rommel!* He clenched his massive jaw. He would have liked to have shot every man jack of them. Out of the cloudless evening sky, a scorched sheet of paper drifted down, then another, and another. He snatched one out of the air and marched to Barbara Tennant's office with it. 'Where the devil's your husband?' he demanded savagely.

Barbara flinched as though she'd been struck, her double chin wobbling. 'I can't find him anywhere.' She was pale and looked drained. 'He's not at home and he's not—'

'We both know *exactly* where he is,' Lampson snapped. 'Shall you look for him there, or must I?'

Barbara, weak and blurred a personality as she was, had reached a barrier she would not go through. 'I think you must, Sir Miles,' she said quietly. 'I cannot.'

'Then I shall.' He tossed the scorched sheet onto her desk. 'In the meantime, it's still raining Top Secret documents. They're everywhere. Know what the street vendors are doing with 'em? Using them to wrap monkey nuts. Monkey nuts, I ask you! Appropriate, isn't it? I left him with a simple job to do. A child of ten could have done it. And he couldn't even finish that before slinking off to his little—' He stopped himself. Barbara was weeping into a handkerchief, her plump shoulders heaving. 'Oh, damn it all,' he said wearily, and left her to her tears.

He thrust his head into the office next door, where a group of secretaries was huddled around a radio, listening glumly to the BBC bulletins on what it was calling 'The Battle for Egypt' at El Alamein, only sixty miles from Alexandria. Lampson listened for a few moments. There had been a run on the banks in Alexandria. The gold reserves had already been sent to Khartoum. The British fleet had fled the harbour for Haifa and Beirut. The Italian population of Alexandria, some fifty thousand strong, was forming a welcoming committee. The arrival of the Afrika Korps was expected at any moment. Mussolini had landed in Libya to back up Rommel, complete with a white stallion and crates full of medals for the coming triumph.

Studying the secretaries, the Ambassador chose the plainest and most capable-looking, a starched spinster in her fifties. He beckoned to her, then returned to Monckton, who was still sitting in his office, staring into space. 'Better get weaving on that broadcast, old chap,' he said. 'No time to waste.'

෧෨

'Now,' chortled Farouk, as they hurtled through the busy evening traffic in his flame-red Mercedes, 'you simply have to tell me all about the nuns.'

'What about the nuns?' Felicity asked cautiously. She was sitting in the front with him, the rear seat occupied by three Italian aides-de-camp whom Farouk retained on purpose – as he gleefully told Felicity – to annoy Sir Miles Lampson.

'Tell me all the naughty things you used to get up to in the convent,' he urged. 'I'm dying to hear all about it. Every sordid detail!'

'We didn't get up to any naughty things,' Felicity protested, repelled by the suggestion.

'Oh, rot! I can just imagine! Didn't you indulge in flagellation? Whips and canes?'

They were driving past the central railway station. Felicity twisted in her seat to stare out of the window. The station was jammed with civilians carrying suitcases and bundles, most of them British, to guess by their appearance. Huge queues had formed in the street where the donkey boys and their asses waited, hoping for work. Fleets of taxis were bringing more, forcing Farouk to slow down. 'What on earth's going on?' Felicity demanded.

'The Europeans are all getting out,' Farouk said offhandedly. 'Heading for Suez, Ismailia and Port Said. Every train going east is crammed. Didn't you creep into each other's beds after lights out? With bananas and things? Tell me about the bananas. Or was it cucumbers?' he added with relish. 'I bet they were randy old things!' He honked his horn imperiously at the cars ahead of him, which tried to move out of his way.

Felicity was too shocked at the sight of this mass evacuation to be bothered by Farouk's scurrilous suggestions. It appeared as though every civilian in Cairo had descended on the railway station in panic. Men, women and children, some dragging dogs on leads, were jostling for places in the queues for trains. In the dim street lights, it looked to her like a scene from Dante's *Inferno*.

By dint of hooting furiously and rushing at the other cars with his Mercedes, which was impossible to mistake for anyone else's car, Farouk forged a passage through the dense traffic. Behind the station, Felicity glimpsed more disheartening sights: shops with photographs of Rommel in the windows, swastika flags draped where once the Union Jack had hung. There was even a portrait of Churchill ostentatiously tossed out with the rubbish. The night streets were full of Egyptians celebrating, buying falafel and kebabs from stalls, waving photographs of Hitler. She found this so upsetting that she began to cry. Her world was coming to an end, and a new and horrible one was being born.

A small group of street children, recognising the King's car, ran behind it, shrill voices clamouring for *baksheesh*. No adults joined them. Nor did anyone in the car notice Felicity's sobs, and the crimson Mercedes picked up speed, hurtling onward towards Helwan. Farouk fiddled with the car radio until he found a German station. It was playing 'Lili Marlène', the marching song of Rommel's Afrika Korps. The female singer's plaintive voice was joined in the chorus by the crash of soldiers' boots and the triumphant roar of their voices.

One of the Italians leaned forward, grinning. 'England finish,' he said to Felicity. 'Italia, Germania! Now is our time!'

ॐ

The Ambassador clumped up the narrow and malodorous stairwell, followed closely by the starched secretary he'd pulled away from the radio, Miss Herrick. He checked his watch. It was coming up for nine in the evening.

'Think this is the place,' he grunted, reaching a shadowy doorway. He was out of breath. He got too little exercise these days, his daily golf game having been curtailed by the crisis. He pounded on the door and looked around at the flaking walls and cracked tiles of the landing. 'Not very romantic. Can't imagine what would drive a feller to leave his nice, clean wife at home and come to a hole like this for a woman like this. Eh?'

Miss Herrick maintained a stony silence but managed to convey the impression of a decent woman twitching her skirts away from contamination. There was no reply from within. Impatient, Lampson put his shoulder to the door and heaved. With a sound of splintering wood, the flimsy lock gave away. The door sagged open. They went inside.

The little apartment had been done up in rather pathetic Arabian Nights style, with gaudy scarves covering the cracked plaster walls and chichi Egyptian furniture. It was lit by coloured glass lamps from the souk, some of which lay broken on the floor among a litter of beer bottles. This décor had no doubt been chosen by the woman who lay on the bloodstained bed, rather than by the Hon. Malcolm Tennant, who sat with his face in his hands in an armchair at the opposite end of the room.

To her credit, Miss Herrick did not scream or have hysterics, but went quickly to examine the woman. For his part, Lampson closed the door, congratulating himself on having followed his instinct to come and investigate in person.

'Is she dead?' he asked.

Miss Herrick, who had some first aid training, was trying to find a pulse. 'I don't know.'

Ignoring the silent hunched figure of his undersecretary, Miles Lampson prowled around the apartment, surveying the tawdry knick-knacks, sniffing bottles of scent. He picked up the smashed camera and examined it, noting the open cupboard facing the bed. There were also some notebooks that he picked up, glanced at and pocketed. At last he stopped next to Tennant. 'Well?'

Tennant raised his head like a man awakening slowly from a horrible dream. 'She filmed us,' he said in a hoarse voice. 'She was going to send copies to Barbara. To everybody. She said she was working for the Germans. I would have been ruined, Lampson. My career—'

'I don't give a damn about your career,' the Ambassador said contemptuously. 'Did you tell her anything?'

'I can't remember.' He lowered his face into his hands again and began to sob dryly.

'What the hell has gone wrong with you, Tennant?' Lampson asked.

'I don't know,' Tennant said between his fingers. Lampson saw that his knuckles were cut and raw.

Miss Herrick had gently rolled the battered head to the light so she could examine the face. 'She's got a pulse,' she said, 'but it's very weak. She's badly hurt. Nose broken, some teeth knocked out. There's a telephone. Shall I call the hospital?'

'In a minute.' Lampson went to examine the woman on the bed, who was whimpering as Miss Herrick tried to sponge the crusted blood from her mouth. She was in a bad way, her face pulped, and a broken collarbone by the look of it. Probably some ribs gone, too. Tennant had used her like a punch bag. The situation simply got better and better.

'Right,' he said brusquely, 'only one thing for it. I'm calling the Military Police to arrest this woman. Stop fussing with her, Miss Herrick.'

The secretary gasped. 'Arrest her? But, sir! She needs a hospital!'

'She's a spy, isn't she?' the Ambassador retorted. 'Use your head. We can't afford another bloody Egyptian limping round in bandages, telling everyone what bastards we are. We've got to get the lid on this, fast. She'll be charged with espionage and thrown into a cell and kept out of sight. Hopefully, she'll die. If not, she got the injuries resisting arrest.'

Miss Herrick, tight-lipped, began cleaning the woman's blood off her hands.

Tennant lifted his head again, shuddering. His eyes were glazed. 'I don't know what got into me,' he whispered. 'I hate this bloody country.'

'If this gets out,' the Ambassador replied, 'it will kill your father, and probably your wife, too. So keep your damned mouth shut until I tell you what to say. Understand?'

Tennant nodded. 'Yes.'

Lampson picked up the telephone. 'Operator? Get me the Military Police.'

∽

In the brilliant morning light, the nail varnish gleamed like metallic blood. Farouk, his head bent over Felicity's bare feet, was doing a remarkably neat job, coating each toenail in turn with the little brush. She was still in her nightgown. He'd woken her very early, bursting into her bedroom in a red fez and white canvas ducks, dragging her out onto the terrace to join him in a breakfast of freshly cut watermelon, figs, mangoes and Muscat grapes. His boyish exuberance was exhausting; they'd arrived late last night, and she'd had no more than a few hours' sleep after a shattering day.

'That's rather good, isn't it?' he said, leaning back to admire his handiwork. 'I could hardly close my eyes, worrying about your toenails. You have very pretty feet.'

'Well, this is the first time I've ever had my toenails painted,' she said, wiggling her toes, which he had thoughtfully separated with cotton wool.

'No, really?'

'My mother disapproved. And, of course, in the convent nothing like that was allowed. It's certainly the first time I've ever had them painted by a king,' she said, smiling at him. 'Thank you, Your Majesty.'

'You don't need to call me Majesty unless other people are around,' he said, capping the varnish bottle. 'You shall call me Farouk, and I shall call you Felicity. People whose names begin with

"F" are lucky for me – did you know that? That's why I chose you. I made my wife change her name to Farida, and my daughters are called Farial and Fadia.'

He was cultivating a downy moustache, she noticed, which set off his plump, almost girlish features rather dashingly. He had good teeth, white and even, which he showed in a frequent, appealing smile. This was quite a small palace, as she'd discovered, set on the banks of the Nile, with a beautiful garden. There was a swimming pool and a tennis court, but so far – apart from the staff – they were the only two guests to have appeared. In this intimate setting, Farouk appeared more youthful than she had thought he was. 'May I ask how old you are, Your Majesty?' she asked.

'I'm twenty-two.'

Felicity was taken aback. 'I thought you were much older! I'm almost twenty-four.'

'I shan't hold that against you,' he said tranquilly. 'I was King at sixteen, married at eighteen, a father at nineteen. I shall probably be dead by your age. My wife's awfully jealous, but don't worry, she never comes here.' He chortled.

'What does your wife say about Miss Mizrawi?' she asked boldly.

'Zippy? Zippy's ancient. My wife only gets annoyed about younger women. Anyway, Zippy's getting ready to cut and run. Packing her bags. She's a Jewess, you know. She thinks Rommel will send her to a concentration camp. Might do her some good. Goebbels told me they're practically health farms. She's getting awfully fat.'

'You're not very gallant about Miss Mizrawi. And your wife might be happier if you were more faithful to her.'

He glanced at her with soft hazel eyes that were rather like a gazelle's. 'Shall I tell you something? My wife's been having affairs since the day we got married.' Felicity said nothing, but studied her gleaming toenails. She'd heard the rumours – everyone had. 'She's currently having an affair with Prince Wahid Yussri,' he went on.

'You can read about it in the gossip rags. She prefers older men. Athletic and debonair men of the world. She says I'm just a boy. That's why I've only fathered two girls. A *real* man would father sons, you see? Girls are a dire disappointment to the nation.'

'I'm sorry,' Felicity murmured.

'And she went to bed with your Mr Hescott while he was painting her portrait.'

'Oh.'

'That was rather insulting. He's not even a prince. My mother's having a passionate affair, too. With my old tutor, Prince Hassanein. I rather looked up to him.' Farouk sighed. 'They don't get along. My two queens, I mean. They hate each other like poison. Too alike, you see? They have terrible screaming matches that the whole palace can hear. I rushed in with my revolver once and threatened to blow both of their brains out. *That* shut them up. But not for long. I don't have much authority over either of them. Farida can be very nasty. And my dear mother has lost her head completely over Hassanein. As for my sisters . . .'

'I'm very sorry,' she said sincerely.

'So now you see why I like film stars, parties and fast cars,' Farouk concluded. 'They take my mind off things.'

'I can understand that.'

'And why I like gentle, quiet, English girls like you.' He smiled at her. 'As soon as your polish dries, we'll attend to your toffee.'

'Absolutely not,' she said, knowing what he was talking about from the chatter she'd heard at the Embassy.

'Oh, have you already had it done?'

'No!'

He looked disapproving. 'It's essential.'

'Not to me.'

'You can't have all that hair down there. It's not decent.'

'It's perfectly decent,' she retorted, 'and I'm attached to it.'

'You shall be unattached.' He called to a young Egyptian woman who was standing at the table of sliced fruit. She hurried over. She was veiled to the eyes, but, at a word from Farouk, she hoisted her robe and revealed a naked and completely depilated pubic mound. 'You see?' he said, stroking the hairless cleft of her sex. 'Much more attractive.'

'Please stop doing that,' Felicity said, feeling hot all over, 'and ask her to go away.'

'You're much too prudish,' he said, dismissing the girl, who seemed quite unembarrassed by the episode. 'It's because you never have sex. Now, I have sex every day. I have no inhibitions, I assure you. I'm very healthy. They say I have a dirty mind, but I don't. I'm just completely open about such things.'

'You're shocking,' she said, trying not to squirm with the embarrassment he'd just caused her.

He appeared offended. 'I'm not shocking!'

Felicity took a deep breath. He was barely an adult, she thought, a boy who had been raised in the midst of fabulous wealth, whose every whim had been granted and whose imagination could never exceed what he could attain. Marriage and the crown of Egypt had plunged him into nightmarish personal difficulties. It was hardly surprising that he was an *enfant terrible*. What was surprising was that he was not an absolute monster. In fact, there was something almost endearing about his innocence. He had the natural charm of a pretty child who has never been rebuked. 'All right, I'm sorry. But I'm not a doll, either. Painting my toenails is quite enough. Nothing more!'

'But I want you absolutely perfect for when you give me your virginity,' he said plaintively.

'You've got completely the wrong idea about me,' she said firmly. 'I'm not about to hop into bed with you just for the asking!'

The garden was starting to fill with people, servants in dark red livery, some guests in sunglasses and hats (it was already very hot) and a little string orchestra, which had begun tuning up under a pergola. A very elegant-looking middle-aged couple were approaching, calling Farouk's name. He pressed Felicity's hand, kissing her knuckles. 'I think you underestimate,' he said, his gooseberry eyes moist, 'how very fond I've grown of you, Felicity.' He jumped up to greet the middle-aged couple. 'The Count and Countess Pefanis,' he said. 'May I present Miss Felicity Redcliffe? She can't get up. I've just done her toenails, and they have to dry. Don't you love the colour? Exactly the same as my Mercedes.'

'*Enchanté, Mam'selle,*' the man said, clicking his heels and dipping his aquiline nose over Felicity's hand. The woman, in a beret with a little veil, offered languid, slender fingers.

'Albanian Blackshirts,' Farouk whispered loudly to Felicity. 'Terribly pro-Mussolini. Spying like mad against the British, so don't talk about the war!'

⤳

Barbara Tennant was having breakfast when her husband finally came home. She watched him blunder through the hall, knocking a sheaf of newspapers off the console. They scattered on the tiled floor, a litany of bad news in heavy black type. He did not look at her as he wandered into the kitchen, but she saw that his hands were bandaged, and his face was the dead, rubbery white of a toad's belly.

'Is there any coffee?' he asked hoarsely.

'It's on the stove,' she replied, spreading marmalade on her toast.

He fumbled with the percolator and gulped the coffee down, not noticing he was swallowing the grounds. 'I'm going to bed,' he announced.

They were, she thought, like two guests in someone else's home. 'I want a divorce.'

He turned to her slowly. His eyes appeared lifeless. 'I won't give you one. It would ruin my career.'

'Yes, you will. You've been having an affair with another woman. Not for the first time, of course.' She heard her own voice, quiet, calm and somehow proceeding from some source outside herself. 'But this time, I'm not letting it go. I won't be humiliated like this. I won't spend another day like yesterday. Everybody knows about her. I can provide witnesses in court, including the Ambassador. I'll subpoena him and everyone else, if necessary. It will be a scandal. You won't be able to fight it.'

'She's dead.'

Barbara put the toast down. 'What do you mean?'

'I killed her.'

'What are you talking about?' she asked in alarm.

Tennant looked at his hands. 'She was a spy. She played me for a fool. I was angry with her, and—' He swallowed. 'She died two hours ago.'

Barbara felt sick. For many years, he had been like a stranger to her. Now she felt how little about him she really knew. She wanted to recoil in horror, but her body felt lumpish, as though made of wet clay. She felt half-afraid of him, of the rage she'd always known was inside him and that might one day have been turned on her. 'Are you going to be charged?'

'They'll cover it up. They cover everything up. You know that.'

They heard the distant sound of shots, which had become dreadfully common in Cairo over the past days. 'Did you love her?' she asked him at last.

'What does that matter, now?'

'It doesn't, I suppose. I'm sorry for you, Malcolm. But you can't drag me through this any longer. I'm going back to England.'

❦

99

The orchestra had been playing foxtrots valiantly all morning, though the performers, three of whom were young European girls, were shiny with sweat and almost fainting in the heat under their pergola of bougainvillea. Having been pumped by the Albanian Blackshirts, who vainly tried to find out all about her work at the Embassy, Felicity had fallen in with more congenial companions, a pair of Free French officers in dashing uniforms, complete with képis. She hadn't caught their names, but one had the number 29 on the drum of his képi, and the other 32, so she had mentally christened them Vingt-Neuf and Trente-Deux. They took turns bringing her plates of sliced mango and chunks of crimson watermelon with big black seeds.

'You like Farouk?' Vingt-Neuf asked her as the King's high-pitched laugh rang out across the garden.

'I suppose I feel sorry for him,' Felicity said.

'Why should you feel sorry for him?' Trente-Deux enquired, smiling. 'He is a very rich *bouffon* who possesses everything he could desire.'

'I don't think he's a buffoon,' she replied. 'Nor do I think he has everything he could desire. He has the things that others desire.'

'That would be enough for me,' Trente-Deux said. 'Does he possess you?' He was the bolder and more handsome of the two and was trying hard to get off with her.

'No, he doesn't.'

'But he expects to possess you.'

'We saw him painting your toenails,' Vingt-Neuf added. He was a plain boy, his face scarred by adolescent acne, but she liked him better. 'A woman does not usually permit such intimacies unless . . .'

'Nevertheless,' Felicity said, 'he doesn't possess me.'

'Surprising. *Bouffon* as he is, he has only to snap his fingers and the women come running. He has them two and three at a time. Then he gives them a pretty little trinket and sends them away and snaps his fingers for more.'

'The sort of girls who can be had for a pretty little trinket may not be worth having,' she said. 'I don't think that's happiness.'

Trente-Deux shrugged. 'I am not so complicated. For me, that would be happiness.'

'We wait for the crumbs that fall from his table,' Vingt-Neuf added with a wry smile. 'You have heard the news from Alexandria?'

'I don't want to think about the war,' Felicity said.

'You British may soon end up like we French,' Vingt-Neuf replied, 'an army in exile. I wonder how you will like that?'

'I was very depressed on the way here,' Felicity confessed, 'seeing all the traffic headed east. But then, outside Cairo, we came across hundreds of tanks heading west, so I cheered up again.'

'I say, you fellows are talking about me, aren't you!' Farouk was approaching. His expanding girth, though well disguised by his tailoring, made his gait an unathletic waddle. Under his red fez, his forehead was beaded with sweat. 'I can always tell! Anyway, I'm the only subject worth talking about in Egypt – because I'm the only one who isn't a subject. That's rather good, isn't it?'

The French officers laughed politely along with Farouk. 'Very good, *Majesté*.'

Farouk clapped his hands imperiously. 'It's getting time for a swim. Put on your bathing costumes.'

The Frenchmen went off obediently to change. 'I don't have a bathing suit,' Felicity said.

'I've thought of that,' Farouk said, taking her arm. 'Come along!'

They went to her bedroom. The swimsuits were laid out on her bed enticingly, all in bold patterns or vivid colours. He'd even given her a basket containing sunglasses, sun cream and some sun hats.

'Oh, my goodness,' she said.

'Don't you like them?' Farouk demanded impatiently.

'They're lovely. But I can't accept them.'

'Nonsense. They were bought for you. They're the latest style, you know.' He held up a buttercup-yellow two-piece. 'Go on, try this one.'

'I've never worn such a thing in my life. I don't think I have the figure for it.'

'Of course you have.'

'I'm not one of your starlets.' But she was touched by the gesture and tempted by the swimsuits. 'I'll try them, but I can't promise to appear in public.'

He beamed. 'Excellent. I'll just sit here and give advice.'

'Oh no, you won't,' she said firmly. 'You'll go out of my room while I change.'

'I can't keep popping in and out like a jack-in-the-box,' he said plaintively. 'It's not dignified. I'm royalty, you know. And the two guards are outside the door. We're perfectly private.' He locked the door with a rattle and settled into a plush armchair and covered his face with his fez. 'I promise I won't look while you're bare. You just tell me when I can open my eyes.'

'I don't trust you an inch.'

'Think of that sparkling blue water awaiting you. It's ninety in the shade out there.'

'Don't you dare look.' For extra security, she pulled open the closet door and changed behind that.

'What were those two Frenchmen saying about me?' he asked hollowly from inside his fez.

'They were envying you your success with women.'

'That sort of poor devil always does. They think I get girls because I'm rich.'

'And why *do* you get girls?' Felicity asked, lacing up the bottom of the two-piece, which was rather daringly open at the side.

'Because I'm irresistible, of course. I say, that pubic hair of yours isn't so bad, after all.'

'You didn't see anything,' she said indignantly, retreating behind the closet door.

He had removed the fez from his face and was craning his neck to see her. 'Yes, I did. I'm astonished. I thought it would be blonde, like your head.'

'I'll never trust you again!'

'Well, I'm very curious. I haven't seen a lot of pubic hair, you know. Egyptian women are all shaved. And the starlets, too.'

'I don't want to know about that.'

'I'm shaved, too, of course. The Egyptians say it's cleaner. The heat, you know. And the starlets want you to see everything they've got.' He came up to her and began caressing her naked arms with surprisingly gentle fingers. 'Your private parts are a rather strange arrangement, you women, don't you think?'

'Our arrangements are perfectly normal to us,' she retorted. 'It's yours that are peculiar.'

'I suppose it's what you're used to looking at in the mirror. Can I have another look?'

'You've seen far too much already.' There was no sense of threat from him as there might have been from a different kind of man. And, silly boy as he could be, he was tall and handsome, and undeniably a king. 'Your guests are waiting for you.' Laughter and splashing could be heard distantly from the pool.

'They can wait. They're all just parasites, anyway. They hate me, and I hate them.' He kissed her forehead with his moist, pink mouth. His expression was meltingly tender. 'I've grown terribly fond of you, Felicity. I just want to stay here with you.'

'And do what?'

'You promised me your virginity.'

'I never did,' she said. 'That's just your wild imagination.'

'You look magnificent in that two-piece,' he said. 'What a figure you've got, by Jove!'

103

She backed away cautiously. 'Oh, Farouk. You're very sweet, but I can't just hop into bed with you.'

'Why not?'

'I don't love you, for a start.'

'Do you know how many times I hear that?' he exclaimed. 'Everybody says it. *"I don't love you."* It's terribly hurtful. Why shouldn't I be loved? It's all I want. I shall tell you something I've never told anybody. I've never had a virgin. Somebody's always been before me.'

'What about your wife?'

'I have my doubts about *her*,' he said darkly. 'She was only sixteen on our wedding night, but she knew a lot more than she should have done. I think if I ever find a real virgin, I'll marry her right away. I'm a Moslem – I can have four wives, you know. I'm so generous to everybody, but nobody's generous to me, or even kind.'

Felicity felt sorry for him. It was also undeniably exciting to be desired by a king. *That* was something neither Isobel nor Chiara could say, far more experienced though they were! She wondered what they would say if she told them she had given her virginity to a king. But she didn't love Farouk. He aroused almost adolescent feelings in her, of naughtiness and innocence, of arousal and curiosity. 'I'll be kind to you,' she promised.

'When?'

'I don't know.'

'Why not now? I'll be very gentle, I promise.'

'I'm sure you would be,' she said regretfully. 'You're a very gentle man. But I really don't want to. I'm not ready, honestly I'm not.'

Farouk groaned lustfully. 'You've got such wonderful breasts. Much better than anybody else's. Angels have breasts like that, soft and white, floating as though they had invisible wings. I get awfully randy, you know. It's a great burden.'

'I expect it is.'

'Don't you get randy?'

Felicity smiled. 'Sometimes.'

'Awfully randy?'

'I suppose so.'

'And what do you do about it?' he asked.

She felt herself blush slightly. 'What everybody does, I suppose.'

He was interested. 'Show me.'

'No,' she said firmly. 'I want that swim. Let's go down to the pool.'

He was panting with excitement. He kissed her on the cheek before unlocking the door. 'You *are* an angel,' he said. 'I think I shall fall in love with you. Come! I want to show you something. It's rather good.'

◌◌◌

The council of war was being held in Sir Miles Lampson's office, with the door locked. Among the senior staff present were Walter Monckton and Bernard Burrows. Malcolm Tennant sat behind them with his head in his hands, lost in his own grief and seemingly oblivious to the gravity of the situation. He was ignored by the others.

'Auchinleck thinks he can stop Rommel at El Alamein,' Lampson said. 'There's another tank battle shaping up as we speak. As soon as the sand storm dies down, the planes will take off and the fighting will resume. We'll be kept posted, of course. But in case Auchinleck can't hold Rommel, he wants us to prepare for further retreat while keeping up morale and making sure the Egyptians don't defect en masse. The Army's expanding the defensive positions between Alamein and Alexandria. For our part, we've got to secure all the approaches to Cairo. That means getting ready to mine roads and blow bridges when the time comes. They've also asked us to flood large areas of the Nile Delta to make them impassable to tanks.'

He unrolled the large-scale map on the wall, and they crowded around it to follow Lampson's directions. Tennant raised his head and quietly reached for the whisky bottle while nobody was looking and poured himself a tumbler full. He drained it in one gulp, barely aware of the burning in his gullet. He had loved Leila, in his own crooked way, and he had killed her. Barbara was going to divorce him. It would be in all the papers, a public humiliation that would destroy his career.

The war had ceased to have any meaning for him. It simply didn't matter. Nor did his career, his marriage, his existence or anyone else's. He was only aware of the rising darkness in his own soul. It was extinguishing what little was left of him. When the last little area of light was darkened, there would be nothing remaining.

He glanced at the men in suits, crowded around the map. *Each man kills the thing he loves,* he thought. *Yet each man does not die.* He refilled his glass, seeking oblivion.

∞

One of the grinning Italians unlocked the door, which they had reached along an underground passage. 'Be very quiet,' Farouk whispered to Felicity.

The room was dark. Felicity could hear the muffled chatter of women's voices. The door was closed behind them, and Farouk drew back a heavy curtain. She paused in shock as she was confronted by a naked woman smiling and tucking her hair into a bathing cap. Then she realised that the woman was standing behind a pane of glass. She and Farouk were looking into the ladies' changing rooms. There was a lot of naked female flesh on show; several women in various stages of nudity were getting ready to go into the pool or dressing after having got out.

'It's one-way glass,' Farouk whispered into Felicity's ear. 'I had it put in specially. They think they're looking into a mirror. They have no idea we're here.'

'This isn't very fair!' Felicity hissed.

'Rather good, though, isn't it? You're the only other person I've ever brought in here.'

'I rather wish you hadn't,' she retorted, feeling hot at the imminent prospect of meeting these women in their clothes over drinks or food.

He ignored her indignation. 'Don't you find it exciting?' he asked. 'I spend hours down here sometimes.'

'I'm sure you do.'

'Well, I can choose who I want to be with later on, you know. It can be very stimulating. Don't you think? Look at them!'

Despite herself, Felicity was fascinated. She hadn't seen many naked women in her life. Only glimpses of her sisters, and they didn't count. The remainder of her knowledge came from art galleries. The variety and lushness of the female form was a revelation. Art galleries didn't show you how breasts could vary from tiny to enormous, or how they swayed with their owners; or how thrilling a naked woman in movement could be, just towelling her hair or pulling on a swimsuit. She could well understand Farouk's excitement, even share it. Watching these pretty women from this secret window was an erotic experience. She wondered what she herself would look like among them. Taller, probably, paler and slimmer than most.

'Look,' he said, 'I told you they're all shaved. See? Except for that one – she's left a little tuft. That looks silly, don't you think?'

'Ummm . . .'

'You're shocked.'

'A bit.'

'But excited, too. I can see it in your face.' He chuckled.

Her journey towards sexual maturity, from the nunnery to the emancipated 1940s, was slow, but it was thorough. Eventually, she thought, she would lose whatever it was all these men seemed to want from her, and presumably join some kind of grown-ups club in exchange; but in the meantime, she was learning a great deal about the foibles of the male sex, who seemed to like looking as much as, if not more than, touching. She recalled Frank Carrillo's fascination with blue movies in London. And now Farouk and his voyeur's booth. Even Orlando Hescott, with his paintings, loved to undress women.

She wondered what would have happened if she'd decided to join Orlando instead of Farouk. She thought of Rabiah's smooth, brown body, of the tacit invitation to get into bed with both of them.

'I think I'd like to go,' she said, her skin tingling all over.

'Spoilsport. Let's stay here and do things.'

'No!' She was getting agitated and breathless.

'Don't be silly.' He kissed her neck with warm lips, his hand cupping her breast. She squirmed away, her heart racing.

'Let me out of here!'

Laughing at her discomfort, Farouk finally let her out. The smirking Italian outside offered Felicity a cigarette. She accepted it – this was another vice she was picking up, in addition to the overconsumption of alcohol – and puffed inexpertly, hoping to soothe her nerves.

'Farouk *numero uno*, eh?' the Italian said.

'He certainly is.'

Missing her irony, he gave her a thumbs-up, showing gold-capped teeth.

'I didn't know you smoked,' Farouk said.

'Nor did I. But I need something, after *that*.'

'We'll soon get rid of your inhibitions,' he said, beaming.

'I hope so,' Felicity said, coughing on the smoke. 'I can't wait.'
'Come on,' he said. 'Let's go and swim.'

After her bath, Barbara Tennant stood in front of the mirror and studied her body. Malcolm had never desired her. He had once told her she was as sexless as a blancmange. That had been in the early days, when she was wounded enough to make scenes. She no longer made scenes. His systematic cruelty had been matched step by step by her weakness. Tango dancers advancing and retreating. She was weak, weak, weak.

Her face, a blancmange. Her breasts, two blancmanges. Her belly, blancmange; her thighs, blancmange. Pale, sweet blancmange. Some men loved blancmange. Why hadn't her husband? She was not yet forty-two. What had become of the dreams? The desires, the castles in Spain?

What had become of her anger? She tried to feel it now, summoning up the outrage of those early years. But it was dead inside her. And even if it wasn't, this damned war had condemned them to stay in their traces. The war was a prison that confined them all. At least, her generation. There was another generation, the cipher girls she was supposed to be mother to – and what a joke that was – who fornicated and got drunk and danced to American music. And the boys who died. And then there was her lot, weighed down by the leaden chains of patriotism, convention and inertia, who did not see the war as an entertainment laid on for them. And could not even die, unless one was lucky enough to catch one of Air Marshal Goering's thousand-kilogram bombs.

Well, she'd be going back to all that shortly. The bombing and the weather and the rationing and bloody Britain. She cupped her breasts and lifted them, feeling their weight. God, they were heavy.

Her mother had died of cancer of the breast. Perhaps the same fate was waiting for her. Perhaps they would do Goering's work for him, see her off. If they had to be amputated, they were heavy enough to be dropped on Berlin. They would do a fair bit of damage, one would think. She let them sink again and touched her hair. That, at least, was rich and youthful. Her crowning glory, Mummy had called it.

She had been aware for some time of an intermittent drumming sound coming from downstairs. She wondered whether Malcolm had come home. They had agreed to sleep in different bedrooms until her departure for England, which was booked for mid-August. However, he rarely appeared in the house at all, and when he did, he was blind drunk. Perhaps he had lost his key and was on the porch.

She fastened her peignoir and went downstairs, dreading the thought of facing her husband. If they could only avoid meeting for the next three weeks, life might be bearable.

There was nobody at the door, and the house was silent and empty. She looked around her at the furnishings of a life, the knick-knacks they'd collected in Singapore and India; the piano she had once pretended she played, now shatteringly out of tune; the silver-framed photographs of the dead and the forgotten. The furniture that had been chosen for its glossy wood and expensive fabrics, not because anyone would ever be comfortable on it. The dining set they had so seldom used. All as futile as the wreckage floating on an empty sea after a shipwreck.

She was about to go upstairs again, when she caught a few more faint thumps. They seemed to have come from the kitchen, although they stopped almost as soon as they'd begun. Perhaps a stray cat or dog had got into the house. That had happened before. She picked up one of the silver-plated candlesticks from the table (more useless flotsam) and went into the kitchen cautiously, armed.

It was empty. Just to be sure, she pushed the pantry door open. The door thudded against something. Alarmed, she peered in, her candlestick at the ready. She found herself facing her husband's dangling legs.

She looked up. He had hanged himself from the beam in the ceiling. He was staring down at her, his head awry, his face a terrible leaden colour, his tongue blue and protruding from his mouth, his eyes bursting out of their sockets.

The shock washed through her like high voltage. 'Malcolm!' she screamed. 'Oh, God, Malcolm, what have you done?'

◈

It had been an evening during which the war had been utterly forgotten, with a banquet of crimson lobsters and glossy caviar, gallons of champagne and dancing to a real orchestra in white evening suits and fezzes at the pool. The pool was an extravagant, Hollywood production, with Roman mosaics and white marble columns supporting a trellis over it, from which hung the crimson blossoms of a trumpet vine. As midnight approached, Farouk had lured some unworldly – or perhaps all too worldly – young starlets into jumping into the darkened pool wearing only their underwear. He had then turned on the underwater lights, with predictable resultant hilarity. A number of gallant gentlemen had then plunged in fully clothed to provide moral support, followed by a similar number of clothed ladies to whom it had suddenly seemed a good idea.

After this episode, a cabaret had been laid on, with belly dancers, all of whom stripped to complete – and of course hairless – nudity, to appreciative applause. A female crooner began to sing Egyptian love songs in a deep and sultry voice. Couples melted into the shadows, clinching various carnal deals.

Felicity found herself next to Vingt-Neuf in the garden in the early hours of the morning. He had changed out of his dashing uniform and now looked quite ordinary in an evening jacket that was a size too large for him.

'Where's your friend?' she asked him.

'With a little Albanian film star,' he replied. '*Au moins*, she said she was a film star. Perhaps she is only a *soubrette* who does the ironing for a film star. They're in the house somewhere.'

'Leaving you alone?'

'He is more handsomer than I am. They always go for him first. Sometimes I am lucky and they go for me second.'

'You seem philosophical about that arrangement.' Felicity had drunk a lot of champagne and had been feeling very blue. She wanted to be amused. The only amusing person here was Farouk, and he had hardly looked at her all night, being too busy with more glamorous companions. He was at the centre of a group of young women now, teaching them a new dance step. One of the girls was wearing only her brassiere. 'Do you know any jokes?'

'I can't think of any,' Vingt-Neuf said. 'I've been listening to the radio. A lot of young Australians and South Africans are dying for us at El Alamein. That is not very funny, I think.'

A lump rose in Felicity's throat, and she started to cry. 'It's all such a bloody, *bloody* waste,' she said. 'I don't want anybody to die for me.'

He took out a cigarette and lit it. 'This will help.' He offered it to her. The smoke smelled very peculiar, but also familiar. She'd caught pungent whiffs of it in the souk sometimes.

'Is it hashish?' she asked.

'*C'est ce qu'ils disent.*'

'I don't want to be sick.'

'It won't make you sick. Try.'

The smoke was pleasant in her lungs, not as harsh as the Woodbines that all the soldiers smoked. She looked up, trying not to cry anymore. The sky above the palms was velvety, sprinkled with stars. 'You can hardly see the stars in Cairo.'

'One never can in the city. I miss the dim and wavering stars of Paris.'

For some reason, this image cheered her up. They shared the cigarette companionably. Felicity's head was spinning and expanding at the same time, as though some mischievous person were blowing it up like a balloon and tossing it around. The Egyptian crooner implored her *habibi* to fulfil her innermost desires, and the orchestra throbbed and wailed sinuously in empathy. Her head felt very light, as though it were going to float away among the stars. 'Goodness, I feel strange.'

'But pleasant, I hope?'

'Very pleasant. Lighter than air.'

Vingt-Neuf bent down to inspect the chair she sat on. '*Effectivement*, you are floating three centimetres from the grass.'

Felicity burst out laughing. 'It's so funny the way you French say centimetres. What's wrong with inches?'

'Nothing, indeed.' He watched her inhale the last of the hashish. 'Would you like to go inside and make love?'

She considered, wondering if any of this were real or just a dream. 'I'd like that very much. You wouldn't have to be second,' she said generously. 'In fact, you'd be the very first.'

'I'm glad to hear it,' he replied gravely.

'And Farouk will find only an empty glass,' she added.

'*Quoi?*'

'"*And when Thyself with shining Foot shall pass,*"' she recited, '"*Among the Guests Star-scattered on the Grass, And in thy joyous Errand reach the Spot Where I made one – turn down an empty Glass!*"'

'Let's find an empty bed,' he recommended.

'Let's.' The hashish had made her feel very randy, as Farouk would have said, far randier than any man had managed to make her feel so far. Irresistible and delicious desires were swelling in her, hardening her nipples and the peak between her thighs and making them protrude so that they rubbed insistently against her garments. She was also conscious of the mysterious hollow place within her, which she had so seldom explored in her twenty-three years.

'Come.' He seemed to be in a great hurry, pulling her along by the hand towards the palace. The lights whirled round and around, and music thumped her like a wave as they passed the bandstand. She felt herself floating higher, almost washed off her feet. She pulled her hand out of the Frenchman's.

'Let's dance!'

'*Mais non, Félicité, allons.*'

'I want to dance,' she insisted.

'We can dance after.'

'I want to dance *before*. Stop pulling me!' The orchestra unleashed a great wailing blare of affirmation. Felicity lifted her arms and wiggled her hips, as she'd seen the belly dancers do. She tossed her hair and shook her breasts, with their shameless exclamation points. Making love couldn't be better than dancing.

'I say, that's jolly good!' Farouk had appeared, very dapper in an evening jacket with a crimson cummerbund round his waist and his fez at a rakish angle. 'Have you been taking lessons?'

'So you've finally noticed me,' she panted. 'Do I have to take all my clothes off to get your attention?'

'Forgive me. There were a lot of boring people who had to be amused.'

'You didn't look very bored when that girl was tying her underwear round your head!'

'One has to pretend to be entertained. *Noblesse oblige*, you know. I'm the host.'

' *"A host of yellow daffodils."* It should be crimson poppies.'

'Let's go inside,' Farouk said, offering his arm.

She took it. 'All right. I don't really like Egyptian music.'

The French officer spread his hands in dismay, his ugly face crumpling. 'You were with me!'

'So sorry,' Felicity said over her shoulder as she left him, 'but Farouk is Numero Uno and you are only Vingt-Neuf.'

❧

For some reason there was no *bowab* in the garden hut, no soldiers outside, nobody to help at all. There was a stepladder at the back of the hut, Barbara remembered. They used it for clipping the hedge. She found it, a rickety thing with broken rungs. She dragged it into the house, its feeble limbs clattering behind her. Terror was clenching her lungs. She couldn't breathe. Her heart was hammering.

Malcolm was swinging slowly to and fro in the pantry but his legs were no longer twitching in any way. His eyes were open but lifeless, starting from his face like a fish's upon a fishmonger's slab. She didn't know whether the ghastly look on his face was because he was dead or because of the strangulation.

'I'm coming,' she gasped, hauling the stepladder into the little room. 'I'm coming, Malcolm, hold on.'

She scrambled up the ladder and put her arms around his chest. For all her soft bulk, she was not a strong woman. Lifting him was a huge effort. She groped for the knot around his neck, whimpers squeezed out of her by the exertion of supporting his weight. He'd hanged himself with the clothesline. The narrow cord had bitten deep into the flesh of his throat. The knot was buried beyond the reach of her fingernails. His dead-haddock eyes bulged at her as she struggled to get her hand under the cold skin of his jaw.

'No use,' she wheezed in despair, 'no use. Can't.'

Her strength was failing. He was sagging in her arms. Sinking Lethe-wards.

A knife. She had to get a knife and cut the clothesline.

'Wait,' she said.

She slid down the ladder, leaving him dangling, and lumbered into the kitchen. There were sharp, bone-handled knives in the drawer, wedding gifts, more useless jetsam. She snatched one up and ran back to the pantry. Up the ladder she scrambled, putting one arm under his armpit, hauling his dead weight as best she could. She sawed at the clothesline over his head with the knife in her free hand. She could smell that his bladder and bowels had voided. *Does that mean he is dead?*

The clothesline parted with a twang. At once, they both crashed down heavily onto the floor, dislodging several of the pantry shelves, which tumbled bottles of pickles, bags of flour and tins of bully beef onto their tangled bodies.

∽

'It's just as well you came along when you did,' Felicity said.

'You weren't really going to go off with that little French fellow, were you?'

'I'm afraid I was.'

'Honestly, I can't take my eyes off you for a minute.'

'Well, I've been smoking hashish,' she said, 'and it's made me feel awfully sexy.'

He brightened. 'Excellent! Now you can show me what you do!' They were back in her bedroom, where the day had started. 'Go on. I can't wait.'

'I thought we were going to make love?' she said.

'You start. I'll join in later, when you get going.'

'You're terribly lazy,' Felicity said reprovingly. She felt wise and bright and lighter than air. She floated around the room as she talked. The future was so clear to her, as clear as the past and this radiant present. 'And you eat far too much. I was watching you with those lobsters tonight. You're going to get very fat. You'll lose your good looks.'

'Never mind all that. I'm waiting for the show.'

'There's not much to see. I don't have anything that sticks out or squirts stuff, you know. It all happens inside.'

'Do you need a cucumber? Or a banana?'

'I mean inside my head, silly. I don't stick anything in me.'

'Go on, then.'

'I don't think I can, with you watching. I'm not an exhibitionist like your starlet friends.' Nevertheless, she touched herself lightly, her eyes closing.

'Don't stop!' he begged, his voice slightly breathless with excitement.

'I'm surprised you're so interested,' Felicity said dreamily. 'You can go down to your little cubbyhole any time you want to and ogle every woman in the palace. And those so-called film stars of yours will do absolutely anything you ask.'

'But it's all pretend,' he said. 'You're real. That's the big difference. That's why you're so special. They just want me to give them diamonds or introductions to movie directors. They're like dogs that sit up and beg for a biscuit. You don't want anything.'

Felicity could hear sharp women's voices calling Farouk's name from the garden. 'They're looking for you.'

'Let them look. What are you thinking about?' he asked.

'I'm thinking about what I'm doing.'

'Don't you think about anyone else?'

'Sort of,' she murmured. 'I'm thinking about myself thinking about what I'm doing to myself.'

'Think about those women,' he said slyly. 'Those naked women we watched, walking around in front of us.'

She curled her toes. 'You're so naughty.'

'Can I do it for you?'

'If you're gentle.' His touch was pleasurable at first, but he was clumsy, and when he tried to put his fingers inside her, she moved her hips away. 'Not there. You don't know what to do.'

She was amused by his naïveté. A king with so many eager courtesans searching the palace for him, and here he was, fascinated by her virginal meditations. He was panting with excitement. He pulled down his pants and began to rub himself. 'You're beautiful,' he gasped. 'More beautiful than any of them.'

It was perhaps the hashish, or perhaps the sexual barriers she had crossed, that made her so aroused. They watched each other without speaking. As she approached her climax, Felicity raised her hips higher, needing him to see. Separately, simultaneously, they reached their conclusions.

Farouk was delighted. 'That was wonderful. The best of my life!'

'Mine, too,' she said. She felt very happy and very sleepy, even though she hadn't yet managed to enter the grown-ups club.

He went off to join his guests, looking like the cat that had got the cream. Felicity lay on her bed, drifting in and out of sleep with perfect ease. She was having the most wonderful, kaleidoscopic dreams. Although they were military in nature – she was seeing huge parade grounds full of soldiers marching and manoeuvring in perfect formation – the colours of the uniforms were so pretty that it was soothing rather than the reverse. Outside in the garden, under a velvet sky, the Egyptian crooner wailed to the dim and wavering stars.

ᏟᎲᎧ

Malcolm Tennant opened his sticky eyes. He was in terrible pain. Everything was red and misty, and there was a roaring in his ears. A vast, doughy face swung into his view. It was, with its bristling moustache, huge chin and pale eyes, unmistakably the face of Sir Miles Lampson.

'Is this hell?' Tennant asked. Or, rather, that was what he wanted to ask. In fact, he was unable to move his jaw, stir his tongue or make his vocal chords respond. Nor could he make head or tail of whatever it was Lampson was saying to him. It was nothing more than a distant burble, muffled by the roaring of his ears.

The pain was crushing. It radiated from his neck down his back, around his throat, into his chest. God, he hurt. If he could have screamed, he would have done. He averted his gaze from Lampson's face and stared at the high, white ceiling above his bed. He was starting to remember things now. Coming home very drunk. Not wanting to face the next day. Not wanting to face Barbara. The determination to end it all. The hope, as he mounted the shelves with the washing line in his hands, that it would be quick. The realisation, as he swung free, the noose jerking appallingly tight around his throat, that, cretinous as he had been, nothing in his life had been as cretinous as what he had just done.

Had he broken his neck? Was he paralysed? He stirred his fingers and toes experimentally and found that he was not. That was a mercy, at any rate. But he was all wrenched out of joint. As consciousness returned, the pain grew worse. A tear of self-pity slid down his cheek.

He was remembering other things now. How very unpleasant it was to die by hanging, not to be able to breathe, to feel one's brain exploding in one's skull. Trying desperately to hook his feet back onto the shelves. And failing. His shoes dropping off, one after another. His stockinged feet too slippery to grip on anything.

The dim recollection of Barbara's face appearing below him, just as life was leaving him forever. Of surging hope just as the blackness closed in for good. Presumably she had cut him down after that. Under the circumstances, it had been very decent of her to do so. She could just as easily have left him to swing.

He swivelled his eyes sideways, still unable to move his neck. Yes, there she was, a large and flowery bulk at the other side of his bed. He tried to give her a smile of gratitude.

The failed hanging had not only hurt his throat dreadfully – he was now aware that his neck was in some kind of large, stiff bandage – it had also affected his hearing. The roaring in his ears was obtrusive. It was to be hoped that particular phenomenon would fade away soon.

In fact, the roaring was clearing away intermittently. He could make out Lampson's burbling more clearly now. Lampson was calling him 'old chap', and talking about 'a tragic accident'. Hoping to see him 'back in harness very soon'. Assuring him that 'everything was going to be all right'.

Wonderingly, he saw the Ambassador melt back into the red mist. Lampson's place was taken by Barbara. She loomed over him. One of her arms, he noticed, appeared to be in a sling. Tennant forced his throat to work. 'Barbara,' he whispered.

'I can't tell you how glad I am to see you open your eyes, Malcolm,' he heard her say. 'I want you to know that I understand why you did it. I drove you to it.'

He blinked at her. 'Drove me?'

'No more lies between us, Malcolm. I should never have said what I did. I was very hurt and very angry. But I've been talking it over with Sir Miles, and my mind is clear, now. I don't want a divorce. Can you imagine me as a divorced woman? The publicity? The effect on morale?' She shook her head briskly. 'It wouldn't do. And your career would be over. But you've shown remorse, and I'm prepared to accept that. This will bring us together again. Allow us to make a new start together. Wouldn't that be better, after all the wretched, unhappy years?'

He nodded wearily. 'Yes.'

'When I saw you hanging there, it all came home to me. How stupid we've been. Both of us. It's not too late for us. We'll patch things up. Life's hard enough. What's the point of being unhappy?'

He squeezed her hand. 'No point.'

'No point at all. We have to make it work. Together. And that means you must change. You can't treat me like that anymore. You have to treat me with respect. Do you understand? Can we make a new start?'

'Let's give it a go,' he mouthed.

At this, Barbara's stiff expression softened. 'I'll learn to trust you again. And so will Sir Miles. If you earn it.'

A ward sister now appeared and gently coaxed Barbara away from his bedside. 'Mr Tennant has to rest now. I'm sure he'll feel more like talking tomorrow.'

'I hope you've learned from this,' Barbara said. 'I'm going to give you one more chance. Goodbye, Malcolm.'

Tennant, who had no more intention of making a new start with Barbara than he had of flying to the moon, managed to force his mouth into a grimace that approximated a smile.

He felt her kiss his brow. Then he was alone.

You've got a charmed life, old boy, he thought. *Who'd have thought it? Barbara squared, Lampson squared. Everything's going to be all right after all.*

❧

It took Felicity a long time to attain consciousness. Her brain felt distinctly slow. Thoughts were languid in taking shape. She found herself staring vacantly at things like her toothbrush or her soap, rather than picking them up and using them. The memory of last night's erotic encounter, which had been so enjoyable at the time, was now rather embarrassing. She looked out of the window. The rolling green lawns – evidence, more than anything in Egypt, of Farouk's wealth – were peopled with frolicking guests. She could make out Farouk himself, wearing only white bathing trunks and a panama hat, surrounded by *baigneuses* at the edge of the pool.

There was a note next to her bed: *Look under your pillow.* She did so and found a pair of emerald earrings in a velvet box. The stones were small but bright and appeared to be quite valuable. Her closet, upon opening the door, also proved to contain gifts: some pretty summer frocks and, as he'd promised, some really lovely underwear and nylon stockings. She was doing rather well in the trinket line.

She went downstairs in one of the bathing costumes he'd given her. It was mid-morning and already very hot. There were at least a hundred guests in the palace gardens, a good number of them young women. No doubt Farouk would have vetted them all through the one-way mirror he had installed in the changing rooms.

There was such a crush around him that only his laughter could be heard. The press of plump, swimsuited young female bodies reminded her of feeding time in the seals' enclosure at London Zoo. She gave up trying to speak to him and sat in the freckled shade of the palm trees, which were now heavy with huge racemes of immature dates. There was no sign of Vingt-Neuf and Trente-Deux. Perhaps they had been called back to arms. She felt rather sorry for Vingt-Neuf. There was no doubt she had led him on, rather. She determined to smoke no more hashish. The results were not predictable.

'*Hanim?*' An obsequious *suffragi* in a red monkey jacket with gold buttons had approached her. 'Madame Mizrawi asks you to join her.'

Felicity's heart sank. With something of the feeling of a poacher with a rabbit in his pocket going to face the gamekeeper, she followed the *suffragi* to the tennis court. Waiting for her there was Zippy Mizrawi, Farouk's Alexandrian mistress. She was wearing a white sharkskin swimsuit, which set off her splendid bosom and tanned limbs. As usual, she was carrying her little white poodle under one arm. In the other hand, she was swinging a tennis racket.

The dog watched Felicity with sad, friendly eyes. Zippy greeted Felicity coolly. 'I hear you play tennis?'

'Very badly.'

'Find a partner. Farouk and I will play you.'

To Felicity's great relief, Vingt-Neuf appeared. Wearing shorts and a vest, he looked wiry enough. Farouk bounded onto the court, wearing only his bathing trunks, grinning broadly. It was the first time Felicity had seen him naked from the waist up. His chest was covered in dark curls, though she knew he was shaved below. He must look very odd completely naked, she thought.

He and Zippy made an unexpectedly strong opposing team. For all his bulk, Farouk was able to hit the ball with formidable force and accuracy, and Zippy more than made up for his lack of nimbleness around the court. In addition, Zippy cheated with unblushing aplomb.

'That was in,' Felicity protested after finessing a particularly good cross-court forehand.

'Out by a mile,' Zippy said serenely. 'Our service, I think.'

'They're shameless,' she complained to Vingt-Neuf.

'We will need all our skill to defeat the forces of the pharaohs,' he smiled. 'Remember Napoleon.'

It was Felicity's turn to receive Farouk's service. He bounced the ball a few times, grinning. She could see by the look in his eyes that he was expecting an easy kill, perhaps a love game on his service. He had the advantage of her in brute strength and weight, but he was already sweaty. She spun the racket between her hands as she waited, trying to anticipate his serve.

It came onto her backhand, a cannonball with no attempt at spin or any other subtlety. He was relying on sheer power to get past her. But she was not intimidated. She'd learned her tennis in a hard school – playing against her elder sister, Isobel, who thought it screamingly funny to cover Felicity with bruises. She swung her racket double-handed and slammed the ball back, giving it as much topspin as she could get into the stroke. The ball swooped over the net and bounced by Farouk before he could even get a racket to it.

'Love–fifteen,' Vingt-Neuf said. He was smiling slightly as they changed sides.

Unfazed by his lack of initial success, Farouk bounced the ball, smirking, then tossed it into the air and slammed it across the court. This time the ball was on her forehand and travelling, if anything, faster than before. She could only keep one hand on the racket, and she felt the impact jolt up her arm. But she had hit the ball with the meat of the racket, and it slipped past Farouk as before, leaving him flat-footed.

'Love–thirty,' Vingt-Neuf called. 'You are good,' he murmured as they crossed sides. The excited audience was applauding wildly.

Farouk was looking baffled and somewhat thunderous as he prepared for his third serve. He still had not learned that crude power would get him nowhere. This time, Felicity swatted the ball straight at Zippy. She skipped out of the way with a yelp and turned to watch the missile's trajectory. There was enough topspin on the ball to make it plunge to earth just inside the tramline.

'Rule, Britannia!' someone shouted from the crowd.

'Love–forty,' Vingt-Neuf said. Zippy was too surprised to even challenge the call.

Farouk was glaring at Felicity. She guessed that it was rare for him to have his mighty service answered, especially by a woman. There was a flush on his broad face as he prepared his serve. He took his time about bouncing the fluffy white ball and estimating the distance between himself and Felicity, as though he were at Wimbledon.

His service was a fraction long, and just over the line, but Felicity did not want to face a challenged call from Zippy. She stepped forward and slammed the ball back, two-handed. She sent it exactly down the centre line, and it rocketed between Zippy and Farouk without either of them even getting close to it.

'Game to us,' Vingt-Neuf said. There were cheers from the Allied contingent among the spectators.

Farouk was in a belligerent mood. 'Where did you learn to hit the ball so damned hard?' he shouted across the net.

'Playing against Mother Superior,' she replied sweetly.

Farouk's eyes widened. Then he let out a squeal of laughter. 'Treat the Germans the way you treated my serve, and you British will have no problems,' he said.

Felicity caught Zippy's eyes. For a moment, the other woman held her gaze, her green eyes brilliant. She shook her head slightly, a movement that was imperceptible to everyone except Felicity. But Felicity understood. It was time to fade into the background.

The rest of the match was played out amicably. Felicity kept her natural competitiveness and skill in abeyance. Vingt-Neuf had been doing exactly that right from the start. And she also noted that Zippy worked extremely hard to save her partner from any further humiliations. Her lithe brown legs were in constant motion and must have been wearied by the time the match ended in a defeat – though an honourable one – for Felicity and Vingt-Neuf.

They plunged into the pool to cool off. The crowd of young women once more engulfed Farouk. He splashed happily among them like a sea lion with his harem. 'Thank you for losing,' Zippy said quietly to Felicity in the water. 'Farouk isn't used to defeat.'

After their swim, Zippy and Felicity sat at the poolside while the men frolicked with the starlets. Vingt-Neuf's showing on the court had brought him some admirers, Felicity was glad to see.

'Where *did* you learn your tennis?' Zippy asked.

'Playing against my sister. She takes no prisoners.' Iced sherbet was brought to them in a gilt service by the *suffragi*. 'Farouk said you were leaving Cairo,' Felicity said, aware of the apologetic note in her voice.

'You needn't look so guilty,' Zippy replied calmly. 'I don't have any objection to your presence. It's true that I'm all packed.' She was reunited with her poodle. She stroked the dog's pinkish chest with one finger. 'Mimi and I do not intend to be here when the Germans arrive. You understand? I'm a Jew. We're waiting to hear what happens at El Alamein. It's still in the balance. It's probably the most important battle of the war.'

'What's the news?'

'It's touch and go. Rommel's supply lines are being stretched thin. He should have let his troops rest and waited for reinforcements. But he was arrogant. It's the German flaw. He thought he had the momentum and that the Allies' morale was low. Now he's up against colonial troops – South Africans, Indians, New Zealanders, Australians. They're tough. Cairo's very quiet. It's rather eerie. Even the rioting has stopped.'

'And here we are,' Felicity said, 'drinking iced sherbet from golden cups.'

'Yes. Here we are.' Despite Farouk's assertions that Zippy was 'ancient and fat', it was evident that she was neither, being an extremely handsome blonde in her late twenties. She'd done rather well in the trinket line herself, wearing a spectacular diamond bracelet with a ruby 'F' dangling from it. 'You needn't feel guilty about that, either. Neither of us started this war.'

'But it's our duty to help.'

'In our own way. With our own weapons.' Zippy sipped her fruit juice, her imperturbable green eyes surveying Felicity over the gold rim of her cup. 'So, did you bestow it upon him, this famous virginity of yours?'

Felicity flushed despite herself. 'Not exactly.'

'I didn't think you would. But he spent the night, I hear. That's quite an achievement in itself. You'll both be able to boast of your wild sexual exploits.'

'They were hardly wild exploits, Miss Mizrawi.'

'They never are with Farouk. As you've probably gathered by now, he's not equipped by nature or education for wild sexual exploits.'

'He's very kind,' Felicity said defensively.

'He can be very kind, as he can be very cruel, without caring much either way.'

'You sound as though you don't like him.'

'Do you like him?'

'Yes, I do.'

'Well.' Zippy crossed her slender ankles. Her toenails were painted the same fire-engine red as Felicity's. 'That's also an achievement, in its way. Very few people like him. He had a miserable childhood, you know. His father was never there, and his mother was too busy with her lovers. He was brought up by his father's first wife, who did her best to corrupt him from boyhood. The palace is run by squabbling women – aunts, stepmothers, cousins.'

'So I gather.'

'They keep him tied to their apron strings. They give him everything he wants and nothing he needs. He'll always be a child.'

Felicity looked around. 'A very rich child.'

'And a powerful one, in his way. He could steer Egypt to greatness if he were a different sort of child. But he isn't. He will remain eternally immature. So what *did* you do with him last night?'

'As a matter of fact, we didn't even touch each other.'

'He adores to be sucked,' Zippy said practically. She fed her poodle a biscuit and brushed the crumbs off its moustache. 'He's not very fond of intercourse. In fact, he can barely manage it. You might bear that in mind if you get another chance.'

'That doesn't sound very nice.'

'It only takes a moment. And he'll be very grateful. But you'll have to fight for your time with Farouk from now on. His attention span is very short. He gives a little to many. You may have had your moment. I mean that kindly.'

'You seem to have secured your place.'

'Don't you believe it. I stick around to remind him of what swine the Nazis are, but he's no more faithful to me than to anyone else. I put up with him because I consider it my part of the war effort. I am saving Jewish lives. We have to use whatever we have. It's a pity you're not more experienced. But perhaps that's your strength. You should hold an auction for your virginity. You'd probably get a good price for it.' Her smile took the sting out of the joke. 'It's a rare commodity.'

'It's starting to feel rather like an unexploded bomb.'

'Well, let's hope it goes off with the required bang.' Zippy nodded her blonde head at the bevy of young women around the King. 'You see these creatures who surround him? Turkish, Albanian, Greek – who knows what. Whores and would-be whores. Neither they nor the men who procure them have any love for Britain. They would like to turn the world into one huge concentration camp, with themselves as the guards.' She glanced at her watch. 'I must get back to Cairo. I only stopped by to meet you.'

'Why?'

'You're rather special, in your way. For once, Farouk has shown some good taste. I'd like to think I'm leaving him in good hands if I have to disappear. You understand?'

'I think so,' Felicity said slowly.

'The decent girls, you see, will have nothing to do with him. If you do get a chance to speak to him about the war, point out that he'd be considerably worse off under the Germans. He tends to imagine otherwise.'

'I'll try.'

'And remember the other thing.' Zippy put on her sunglasses, rose and held out her hand. The diamond bracelet clicked expensively as they shook hands. 'I hope we'll meet each other again in happier circumstances. Good luck.'

'Same to you.'

Felicity watched Zippy walk away, the white poodle under her arm. There was rather more to 'the Jewess' than was apparent. Being recruited as a replacement was an odd feeling. She was not sure she was at all suited to the job. She certainly didn't want it. It sounded very much like whoring, and that was shameful. But perhaps it was more shameful to pretend she was in an ivory tower when there was so much at stake.

As she strolled pensively among the crowd, she thought of having that pink protuberance in her mouth. It was generally understood that men enjoyed that sort of thing, but it was not an appetising prospect. In Farouk's case, one didn't know where it had been. The thought of presenting herself to the Army medics with a venereal disease was hardly attractive.

There was something symmetrical about her progress from nun to whore. If Sister Teresa Margaret could see her now! The thought made her laugh aloud. Well, she had been her own kind of nun. Perhaps she could be her own kind of whore.

There was little opportunity for whoring during the rest of the day, though there was another Lucullan banquet in the early afternoon, with whole roasted lambs on spits and mountains of summer fruit. Farouk barely glanced at her, being occupied with his coterie of starlets, who fought to nestle in his lap and caress his cheek. Felicity sat with Vingt-Neuf and Trente-Deux, who discussed the battle unfolding at El Alamein, which they seemed to understand in great detail. It was obviously a crucial point in the war. Despite El Alamein, however, several young officers remained at the palace, and, as the heat wore off, the band assembled again, and everyone changed for dinner and dancing under the stars, as though there were no war to be waged and nothing in the world but pleasure to be had.

∞

The caravanserai set off from Helwan well after midnight. The road from the palace was brilliant with the headlamps of cars making their progress back towards Cairo. In some cases, it was a very erratic progress owing to the overindulgence of the drivers on Farouk's champagne. Although Farouk himself had, as usual, drunk nothing stronger than lemonade, he was very excited and was driving recklessly, surging past other cars on the wrong side, honking imperiously at all and sundry and going much too fast for Felicity's liking.

They were the only people in the Mercedes. He had given his Italian minders the slip, as he put it. 'I'm rather good at that,' he said, chuckling. 'Perfected the technique when I was at school in England. While they thought I was swotting in my study, I was actually enjoying wine, women and song in the town with Prince Edward. Well, he enjoyed the wine and the song; I took the women!' He roared past a donkey cart trotting to early morning market, making the little animal gallop off the road with its load of cabbages. Fields of sugarcane twinkled in his headlights. 'He was a real sport. We hit it off right away. Two of a kind. I suppose they'll make me abdicate, too, someday.'

'Do you think so?' Felicity asked, clinging to her seat as the powerful car careered round a corner.

'Edward and I will probably end up in the same hotel in the Riviera somewhere, chasing the same girls. I wonder what he will say to me when we meet? Something witty, I'm sure. He has such a sense of humour. I'm jolly well going to enjoy myself before they do kick me out, I can tell you.'

'You're driving terribly fast,' she protested.

'I've been driving since I was six. Don't worry – I'm an ace. Better than Nuvolari. Still smarting from the thrashing we gave you on the tennis court?'

He had no idea, she reflected, that she'd let him win – that people let him win every game he played simply because he was Farouk. 'You're a very good player,' she said diplomatically.

'Of course I am. I'm good at everything.' He was in high good spirits. She'd done a little whoring in her room before they'd set off, just enough to produce the desired result. As Zippy had said, it didn't take long. She'd simply had to let him watch her touching herself. He'd done the rest all on his own, apparently with great satisfaction. She'd found herself aroused, but not enough to go any further. So far, she reflected, they had never even kissed one another. Like that faraway boy in that long-ago bathing hut, it had been largely 'I'll show you mine if you show me yours.' Yet Farouk seemed to imagine he was a great lover, the Sheik of Araby. 'Women can't resist me, you know,' he was boasting. 'They've been throwing themselves at me since I was a boy. It's quite amazing, this magnetism I have. Everybody comments on it.'

'Of course they do,' she murmured. He had odd moments of self-knowledge, she thought, and then was swept off by dreams, leaving reality far behind him. But the powerful headlights of his Mercedes, as they scythed across the night, revealed a landscape of poverty: wretched dwellings, humble figures bent by labour. This golden bubble in which he lived would surely be punctured irretrievably sooner or later. His predictions of being deposed might be closer than he imagined. 'Long live the King,' she added.

'That's the spirit,' he chortled.

They reached Cairo at dawn. The spectacular, swift Egyptian sunrise was about to begin, but the city was still in a dreamy, mauve spell, its minarets and domes serene against a pellucid sky. Farouk was going directly to the Abdin Palace on official business. He dropped her outside her hotel off Ismailia Square. 'I'll give you a call,' he promised. 'Pip-pip, toodle-oo!' He roared off, leaving her in the silent street. The wail of a mosque began, followed by another, then another, until the air was ringing.

There was nobody to help her with her suitcase, so she lugged it up to her room alone. She had slept very little over the weekend, and she was tired. She didn't bother to unpack, just stripped off and clambered into her little bed. However, it seemed that her eyes had no sooner closed in sleep than she was awakened again by a banging on her door.

She dragged herself out of bed to answer it. One of the cipher girls, who was still getting herself into her khaki uniform, grinned at her. 'Call for you. The men are all after you, aren't they?'

'What time is it?' Felicity asked.

'Nearly nine. I have to be at work – unlike some people!' She ran off down the corridor, the seams of her stockings awry.

She had slept for a few hours, anyway. She wrapped her gown around herself and went to the telephone. 'Hello?'

'It's Orlando Hescott. I heard you got back last night. Hope I didn't wake you.'

She stifled a yawn. 'You did, but it's fine. I should be up by now.'

'How was Helwan?'

She thought. 'Very odd.'

He laughed quietly. 'Didn't you have a good time?'

'It was instructive, at any rate. I learned a few things. Are you still in Aswan?'

'No. As a matter of fact, I'm back in Cairo. That's why I'm calling you. I'm going up to El Alamein tomorrow. I wanted to see you before I left.'

'El Alamein!'

'Yes. I'm getting a ride with the Long Range Desert Group. I'm starting a new series of paintings on a larger scale. Battle scenes. But never mind any of that. This might be our last chance to see each other for a while. Are you free?'

'As far as I know,' she said slowly, 'I'm still banned from the Embassy. So I suppose I am.'

'Good. I'm staying at Rabiah's villa. She went back to Lebanon last night. Says things are getting too hot for her. Would you like to come here? We'd have the place to ourselves. We could swim and sunbathe. And I could get started on that sketch of you . . .'

There was a silence. 'Yes,' she heard herself say, 'I'd love that.'

He sounded neither triumphant nor surprised. 'I'll pick you up in my car. Shall we say an hour from now?'

'I'll be waiting.'

He rang off. Felicity walked slowly back to her room. Her heart was beating in an odd way, hard yet steady. She felt that she'd reached a decision without considering. Or perhaps she had been considering without thinking about it.

Orlando came for her in the desert-coloured staff car. The windows that had been broken by stones had been patched with brown tape, giving it a very raffish appearance. However, among the general dilapidation of Cairo vehicles, nobody paid any attention.

As usual, he was wearing faded khakis, his shirt open at the neck to reveal that he was even more tanned than before. He took in her pale aqua dress approvingly. 'You have an eye for colour,' he said.

'It's borrowed. There aren't any nice clothes to be bought anywhere anymore. I'm in despair.'

He navigated the Cairo traffic without losing his temper or his composure. 'Did His Majesty behave like a gentleman?'

'He was his usual self,' she replied. She showed him the emerald earrings. 'He did give me these.'

'And did you have to sing for your supper?'

'I might ask you the same question,' Felicity replied tartly. 'The houseboat must have been *très intime* without me.'

'I told you,' he said tranquilly, 'Rabiah and I concluded our relationship on a happy note some time ago. There's no more to be said.'

'Do you always conclude your relationships with women on a happy note, Orlando?'

'I try to.'

'Farouk told me that you seduced his wife while painting her portrait.'

'It was hardly a seduction,' he replied equably, unsurprised by the question. 'She pursued me, not the other way around.'

'Who says the age of chivalry is dead?' Felicity murmured, looking out of the window.

'The lady in question is bored out of her skull,' he said. 'She's stuck in the palace with nothing to do all day.'

'The last I heard, she had two young children.'

'She never sees them. An army of servants takes care of everything.'

'Except her boredom.'

'They take care of that, too, usually. But, as she so charmingly put it, after looking at blue wallpaper all day, red and gold makes a change.'

'And so you added a queen to your conquests.'

'I believe that one should always sleep with royalty where possible. It's the only way to make progress.'

She couldn't help laughing at his coolness. 'I even saw you making up to Mrs Tennant. You're shameless.'

'Barbara? I like her. And she deserves some joy. She's married to a complete bastard.'

'I must say I don't like Mr Tennant very much.'

'Younger sons of earls are usually difficult customers.'

'You're the expert on the upper strata of society.'

Half an hour later, they arrived at the villa, which was deserted. It was now approaching the hottest part of the day. They went straight to the swimming pool, which sparkled enticingly in the sun. Orlando had brought a bag of yellow mangoes with him. He put these in a bowl at the side of the pool. 'There are no servants, and I can't cook. I hope you like mangoes. Want to swim?'

'Yes, please.'

He stripped off his clothes and, unembarrassedly nude, plunged in. Felicity had brought one of Farouk's swimsuits with her, but it seemed priggish to put it on while he was naked, so she undressed and followed him into the warm water.

His company was relaxing. He made few demands on her, asked no further questions and could be very amusing. He'd met and painted all sorts of important people, including Churchill, and had anecdotes about all of them.

'Churchill's a nudist,' he told her. 'So's Montgomery, for that matter. They both insisted on sitting in the buff. In Churchill's case, actually in the bath. I had to set up my easel under the hot water boiler and keep my brushes in the sink. Very steamy, it was. His secretaries kept coming in and out with despatches, completely unfazed. I painted the clothes in later. Monty in uniform, with his beret; Winston in a suit. One can't imagine Herr Hitler sitting for his portrait in the altogether.' He'd also painted Wallis Simpson in the South of France, after the abdication. 'She's a fascinating subject. Very sexy. Trying to capture her vitality is a challenge.'

'I hope you didn't sleep with the Duchess,' Felicity said.

'It was tempting, but no, I didn't. He's a charming man, but she wears the trousers.'

'Did you paint him?'

'No. He refused. He just wanted a portrait of Wallis. It came out rather well.'

'Farouk thinks he and Edward are alike.'

'They couldn't be more different,' Orlando said. 'Edward is all nerves. Farouk is a jellyfish.'

'Are they very much in love – Mrs Simpson and Edward?'

'Oh yes. But he didn't relinquish the throne for love. He never wanted to be King in the first place. Hated the idea. He could see what his life would be: an endless mummery. That was what he had to look forward to, excruciating boredom and being good in the public eye. It was like making a fox terrier sit still with rats about. He was delighted to have an excuse to bail out. He thought people would think him noble, or at least romantic. He also thought he would continue to be important. He was the man who wouldn't be King.'

Orlando hauled himself out of the pool, water streaming from his brown body. Felicity watched him drying himself. He was hard and athletic, unlike Farouk. The sexual parts of his body were also much more grown-up-looking than Farouk's, which gave her pause for thought. He reached out his hand to pull her out of the pool. After a short hesitation, she accepted. He hauled her up with easy strength and studied her nakedness without reticence. 'You're very beautiful,' he said in that calm way he had. 'We can start on that painting now, if you like.'

She wouldn't sit in front of him completely nude, though he asked, so they compromised and she put on the bottom of her two-piece swimsuit. He put on his pants, at her insistence. They worked in the shade of the veranda while the sun beat down on the lush garden. He made a few quick sketches of her in charcoal and then began with oils.

'Can I talk?' she asked.

'Except when I'm doing your mouth.'

'What made you want to go to El Alamein?'

'Ambition.'

'Won't it be dangerous?'

'I was on active service in the Western Desert before the war artist business came up. I can't say I miss the fighting. It's much more fun painting kings and generals and hopping into bed with their wives. But portraits will only get you so far. I want my work to be famous after the war, and that means some big set pieces. Landscapes, battlefields. Large canvases. There's no substitute for being there.'

'You're a bit of a bastard yourself, aren't you?' Felicity said, displeased by that reference to the wives. 'At least as far as women are concerned.'

'I know what I want,' he replied. 'This war's a bloody mess. It ruined my civilian career as an artist, so I'm bloody well going to get something back out of it. I want a knighthood and a row of medals and my work hanging in galleries all over the world by the time it's finished. And yes, I want women, too. Women want men. Why shouldn't it be me? I'm a damned sight better than other men in bed.'

'I see.' Felicity was silenced by his directness.

'What do you want out of the war?'

'I've never thought of it like that. I suppose I just drift along aimlessly. I'm not like you. I don't feel I've grown up yet. My two sisters have, but I don't know if I ever will.'

'You will,' he replied, looking at her critically with his brushes in his hand. 'According to the gossip, you've bestowed your maidenhood on Farouk.'

'I don't know why my maidenhood should be the subject of so much concern to everybody,' Felicity snapped. 'It's nobody's business but mine!'

Orlando was amused. 'Keep your hair on.'

'I'm sick and tired of being talked about.'

'Then you shouldn't be such a little sphinx,' he said, smiling. 'You keep this aura of virginal blonde mystery about yourself that piques curiosity. And you're maddeningly pretty. You must have made a lovely nun.'

'Actually, I was hideous. My hair fell out, and I nearly died of asthma.'

'Self-denial will do that,' he said, resuming his work. 'Didn't you ever want love?'

'Once, long ago,' she replied. 'In Spain. I thought I was madly in love. But he went for my sister instead. Men generally do.'

'So you entered a nunnery with a broken heart?'

'Nothing so trite.' She watched the smooth muscles of his stomach move in and out of relief as he painted. 'Or perhaps it was a little like that.'

'How long were you a nun?'

'Almost five years. I went in at nineteen.'

'When did you come out?'

'At the beginning of this year.'

He whistled. 'You really have started a new life.'

'I'm trying.'

He studied her naked breasts as he sketched them. 'And the maidenhead? Did you bestow it on Farouk?'

'No,' she said shortly.

'Why not?'

'I thought I'd wait for someone who knew what he was doing.'

Orlando met her eyes. He stopped work and put down his brushes. He held out his hand. 'Come on, then.'

∽

Still unable to do more than croak, Tennant listened impatiently as the doctor enumerated a number of things he shouldn't do. He shouldn't drink alcohol – as if he was going to take *that* seriously; have anything but soup at his meals for a week; attempt any vigorous exercise; talk; or drive his car. On that basis, he was allowed home. He nodded his acceptance of these conditions.

He was feeling weak, but in a cheerful mood. Hanging himself had wrenched all the muscles in his back. He could sense people whispering about him as he shuffled through the wards in his slippers. Despite the silly cover story that he'd had a throat infection, he knew that everybody knew. *There he goes. The attempted suicide. Silly ass. Look at his lovely wife.* (Barbara was holding his arm proprietorially.) Well, bugger them all. He was going to damn well get on with it.

'Goodbye, Mister Tennant.' The ward sister was beaming at him kindly as she adjusted the scarf around his battered throat. 'Do us all proud and make a full recovery.'

He thanked her as they shook hands. Then they were shuffling through the bustle of the entrance. A one-legged soldier, his empty trouser leg pinned up neatly, swung past them on crutches, moving at twice their pace. 'All right, mate?' he called cheerily over his shoulder. Tennant mentally consigned him to damnation and hell-fire, but put a genial smile on his face.

'Brave fellow,' he croaked, raven-like.

The heat outside was like the blast from a furnace. Tennant closed his eyes against the blinding glare. Barbara had brought his sunglasses. She put them neatly on his face. 'There you are, Malcolm.'

'Thank you, dear,' he said. *The first thing to do,* he was thinking, *is to find a replacement for Leila. But not an Egyptian, this time.* He'd been mad to take that risk. No, he would find someone from the typing pool at the Embassy. Some randy young thing, eager for fun and grateful for an older man's experience. That was the ticket. Or even one of the older ones. They were much less flighty. And you never knew what fires might lurk in a middle-aged breast. He squinted against the sun, feeling a tingle of excitement at the prospect.

As they shambled unsteadily towards the car, a young Arab came up to them. 'Mr Tennant,' he called in a loud voice. They paused uncertainly. The young man shouted a few words in Arabic. Tennant caught the name *Leila Suleiman*, and felt a chill. The young man raised the pistol he was carrying, pointing it directly at Tennant.

Oh no, Tennant thought tiredly, his shoulders slumping. *Not a charmed life, after all.*

He closed his eyes as the Arab fired two shots. He felt the bullets punch into his chest. There was a moment of agony and then a spreading numbness.

Barbara tried to catch him as he subsided, but she was weak and he was heavy. He lay on the pavement, seeing blood spurting from his own chest. The young Arab was grappling with the police now, still shouting in his own language.

Tennant looked up at Barbara, who was kneeling over him, calling his name. He wanted to curse her for having steered him into the bullets, demand why it had to be him, and not her, dying on the pavement, but his throat was choked with blood. The arterial pumping was slowing. The spreading stain on his breast was huge, dark.

Bloody poet chappie got it wrong, he thought. *Each man kills the thing he loves. And each man dies.* For a moment, his venom and spite were alive. And then his eyes closed, and the life left him.

***

Orlando knew what he was doing. There was no question of that. They'd found an empty bedroom with a pretty white four-poster bed invitingly made for them. The room was hot, but the fan in the ceiling had languidly stirred the atmosphere, making the air a caress on their naked skin.

She hadn't dreamed that her body was capable of feeling so much, so intensely, for so long. The actual moment of losing her virginity – in a technical sense – was unexpectedly joyous; but by then she'd passed through several stages of bliss that had initiated her in other ways. She had the feeling of being a rather small glove carefully squeezed onto a rather large hand; but once he was inside her, the discomfort swiftly faded, to be replaced by a feeling of excited completion.

'There,' he murmured, looking down at her with beautiful, deep blue eyes. 'Done. Does it hurt?'

'No,' she whispered, linking her arms behind his neck.

Whereas the other things had been thrilling and exquisite, this was primal. She clung to him, feeling her body heat up and losing her self-awareness, her thoughts and finally herself, until she was nothing and everything.

Afterwards, she lay in his arms, aware of parts of her body that tingled or throbbed or ached according to the treatment they'd received. She couldn't remember ever being happier. 'Thank you,' she said quietly.

'Thank *you*,' he replied courteously.

'You're right. You're wonderful in bed. No wonder all the women chase you. You're the Mozart of the boudoir.'

'And you're all his piano concertos played end to end.'

'What a nice thing to say.'

He stroked the rich blonde tresses of her hair. 'I hope it was worth the wait, anyway.'

'Of course it was. Except you're going to El Alamein tomorrow. And even if you survive that, you'll never come back to me.'

'Oh, you never know,' he replied, inhaling the scent of her scalp. 'I rather think you and I might have a future.'

Felicity raised herself on one elbow to look into his face. 'What sort of future?'

'It's too soon to tell. But this doesn't have to be goodbye forever.'

She searched his eyes. 'Do you say that to everybody?'

'No.'

'Don't smile, Orlando,' she said very seriously. 'I must know whether your idea of ending your relationships with women on a happy note is to leave them with vain hopes. Because that wouldn't be very kind.'

'I never claimed to be kind,' he pointed out gently. 'But I'm not a liar, either. I don't say things I don't mean. When I say that I think we might have a future, I mean that I'd like us to have one. It doesn't mean that we *will* have one. The war takes decisions for us sometimes. But if you're still here when I get back—'

'All right.' She kissed his well-shaped mouth to stop him from saying any more. 'You can get away with that.'

☙

Before they made love again, he finished the painting of her. She was very happy with it. He'd made her beautiful, she thought, with a quizzical look in her eyes that she recognised as belonging to her. She was delighted when he presented it to her, making her promise to sit for him again. The extraction of that promise was worth even more than the gift.

And before they made love for the last time, they ate the yellow mangoes in the twilight. She would never again smell the fruit without that evening coming back to her mind.

And then it was time to say goodbye.

3.
LONDON

One of your seedy little men is outside, Oliver,' Nigel Barrington said, 'and I'll take that, thank you.' He deftly appropriated Oliver's *Sunday Times* as Oliver rose from his armchair.

'It's all rubbish, anyway,' Oliver growled as he left the Coffee Room. His Sunday mornings at the club were sacrosanct. Boodle's was his refuge from women, seedy little men and other pests, and he did not like infringements.

He walked out of the portico onto St James's Street. He spotted the seedy little man, one of his regulars, loitering outside Justerini & Brooks, the wine merchant. He strolled over. 'Hoping for a stray bomb?' he greeted the old man dryly.

'I wouldn't mind,' the man replied. 'Been a while since I had a decent drink.'

'Every bottle in the shop would be broken, so you'd be out of luck anyway. What is it?'

'The blonde girl, the one in the Mall.'

'Yes?'

'Big fire there last night during the raid. A stick of incendiaries fell in Waterloo Place. Burned the flats down. Thought you'd want to know.'

He felt as though he'd been struck in the heart by a bullet. 'Is she hurt?'

'No, I saw her outside on the street early this morning. But she was up on the roof all night.'

'What are you talking about?' he demanded.

'She's the fire warden for her block. She was up there all through the raid, directing the fire brigade.' The old man grinned at Oliver, showing yellow teeth. 'She's a game one, Guv'nor. Everyone's talking about it. Poor little thing was black as a chimney sweep when I saw her. Asleep on her feet. She had a cup of tea with the neighbours, then went back inside.'

Oliver drew a deep breath. The adrenalin that had surged through his system was settling painfully in his stomach. He dug in his pockets and passed the man a ten-shilling note. 'Keep me informed.'

The old man pocketed the note. 'You've gone pale, Guv'nor. They'll be opening soon. Go and have a stiff one.'

He shuffled off down the street.

Chiara slept deeply for two hours but then awoke with violent nightmares and surging nausea. She was trembling with the memories of the raid. After almost a week without morning sickness, she found herself retching into the toilet again.

She was in no mood to face Oliver himself when he arrived at her garret in a cold fury a short while later.

'What the hell are you playing at?' he demanded as soon as she opened the door. 'This has to stop, Chiara.'

'What has to stop?' she asked tiredly.

He pushed past her into her flat. 'You're four months pregnant. You shouldn't even be in London, let alone spending the night on the roof in an air raid!'

'How do you know about that?' she demanded. 'Are you having me watched?'

'It's my child,' he snapped.

'What's that got to do with it?'

'I have a legal right, Chiara—'

'You have none,' she cut in sharply. 'You're not my husband.'

'But I'm the father.'

'How do you know? The father is who I say it is.'

He took her shoulders in his hands. 'Don't be a little fool!'

'And don't touch me!' Furious in her turn, she knocked his hands away. 'How dare you patronise me? After what you've done! I'm not a *little* anything, Oliver. I'm twenty-six years old!'

He made a visible effort to control his temper, though there were dangerous white patches around his mouth. 'What if you'd fallen last night?' he demanded. 'What if you'd been hit by shrapnel? Can you keep exposing yourself and your baby to that risk?' She was silent. 'Chiara,' he went on, more quietly, 'dearest Chiara, please listen to me. Pregnant women are being evacuated to the country-side for a reason. It's bad enough that you're still in London, with all the danger and all the anxiety. But to live alone here, to be on the roof yourself during raids – that's madness.' He took her hands and stared into her face. 'Please promise me you'll never do that again.'

Chiara withdrew her fingers from his. 'I was never afraid until last night,' she said in a low voice. 'I saw the midwife yesterday, and she told me she could hear the baby's heartbeat. It somehow didn't seem real until then.'

The last of his anger faded visibly at her words. 'The heartbeat?'

'Yes. She has a sort of ear-trumpet thing that she presses against my stomach. A hundred and fifty beats a minute, she said.'

'So fast,' he said, almost to himself, 'like a little bird. Are you still being sick?'

'That stopped for a week, but this morning it came back.'

'Do you think the baby was hurt in some way?'

She shook her head. 'I think he's fine. It's just me.'

He'd never been in her attic before. He prowled around now, inspecting everything with sharp grey eyes. 'You can't live like this. It's so uncomfortable. It'll be freezing in the winter. How will you manage five flights of stairs when you're heavier? You don't have any useful neighbours, and there's nobody at all on weekends. You're absolutely alone. What if something goes wrong? What if you need help?'

'I'll find somewhere better.' She sighed. 'This was all I could get at short notice.'

He sat in her window seat, his tall figure silhouetted against the light. 'Chiara, Courtfield Park is standing empty.'

She snorted. 'No, thank you.'

'Please hear me out. You'd be safe at Courtfield Park. No bombs, only peace and quiet. You'll have help, clean air and fresh, healthy produce, not like the rubbish you get in London. There's a doctor and a midwife in the village.'

'What about your mother?'

'I promise that you'd never see her there. Or Isobel. I'll keep them away. You'd be sole mistress. You'd have the whole place to yourself.'

'And you?' she couldn't help asking.

He shrugged. 'I come down on weekends. But I wouldn't bother you.'

'It sounds terribly convenient for you,' she said. 'The town wife and the country wife.'

'I don't mean anything like that.'

'Don't you?'

'There isn't going to be a town wife. We're putting off the marriage.'

'Why?'

'Under the circumstances, it doesn't seem advisable.'

Chiara considered him. 'That's the sort of language we use at the Ministry. It means absolutely nothing whatsoever.'

'I'm due to be posted abroad again shortly, for one thing. There are other details to work out. One shouldn't hurry these things.'

'Is Isobel happy about this?'

'I haven't told her yet.'

Chiara raised her eyebrows. 'You're getting cold feet, aren't you? I wonder whether Isobel will let you off the hook as easily as I did.'

'She's very different from you,' he replied obliquely.

'Very,' Chiara said. 'She'll make you the kind of wife you can be proud of. I was clearly not up to the mark.'

'I never thought that.' She couldn't see his expression clearly against the light, but his voice was quiet. 'Courtfield Park is yours for as long as you want it.'

'Even if I accepted, what would I do all day, buried in the country? At least here I'm occupied.'

'If that's the problem, I can find you war work to do. I could bring it up on the weekends.'

Chiara surveyed him sceptically. 'And once I'm established there, I'll be stuck, well and truly. No way out.'

'I suppose I can't ask you to trust me?' he said gently.

Chiara laughed briefly. 'No, you can't.'

'There are no strings attached. If you don't want to see me there, you don't have to. You'll be as free as a bird. There'll be a car at your disposal, with a driver and plenty of petrol. You need only to ask for anything you want, anything at all.'

'You must care very much about this child of yours.'

'I care very much about you, Chiara.'

Despite herself, Chiara flinched at his tone. 'That's all finished between us. I don't want anything from you. I don't want to be bound to you in any way.'

Oliver looked around. 'This is impossible, my dear. You can't stay here any longer.'

'I told you. I'll look for somewhere better.'

'There's nowhere better than Courtfield Park. Please accept my protection.'

'You sound like something out of Jane Austen,' she retorted. But she was affected by his words and the sincere way he'd said them.

'You don't have to give me your answer now.' He rose. 'But every night you stay here, you're putting yourself and our child at risk. Don't leave it too late.'

There was a silence. 'I'll think about it,' Chiara said at last. She held the door open for him.

'Thank you,' he said as he left. She didn't reply.

∽

As he walked up the Mall, Oliver was conscious of an ache in his heart. Chiara had looked tired and pale. Had she been flourishing, she might have affected him less. While he'd been with her, his emotions had been a turmoil of pity, regret and desire. He'd longed to sweep her up in his arms and cover her wan face with kisses. She'd probably have scratched his eyes out. And, as his father had liked to say, *'Softly, softly catchee monkey.'*

Nevertheless, he was anxious to get her out of the flat and up to Courtfield Park. He'd looked for, and found, the slight curve that was now appearing on her belly. His child. The child he hadn't even known he wanted. He wanted it now, by God, and he wanted Chiara with it. He was going to have to talk to Isobel. Soon.

∽

Chiara walked into the English Tea Room at Brown's Hotel at three thirty precisely. Having made up her mind to come, unpunctuality was not in her nature. The long, elegant room, with its ornamented ceiling and mahogany panelling, was as bright and gay as if the war were a figment of the imagination. Every table was occupied and lit by a pretty little lamp. An elderly waiter led her to the end of the room, where Simon was already seated. He rose to greet her, and this time he did kiss her, though chastely, on the cheek.

'You look radiant,' he said appreciatively.

She was wearing gloves and a hat, as befitted the occasion. He was wearing his captain's uniform, without the white coat this time. 'And you look very martial,' she replied, settling opposite him.

'Unfortunately, I'm only a struggling junior doctor.'

'Brown's is rather grand for a struggling junior doctor,' she said.

'Well, I thought a Lyon's didn't quite rise to the occasion. How are your vital signs?'

'Rather dull at the moment,' she confessed. 'I was fire-spotting on the roof all last night.'

He raised his eyebrows. 'Through the raid?'

'Please spare me the stern lecture. I've already had one today. But if I fall asleep halfway through tea, just stick a butterknife in me.'

'This is not a joking matter,' he said. 'You're going to have to get out of London.'

'I've been told that, too.'

'I mean it!'

'I'll go right now if you keep on at me,' she threatened, half-rising from her seat.

'All right, I won't lecture you. Sit down.'

They perused the menu and decided to share a pot of oolong tea with cakes and sandwiches. After the waiter had left, Simon crossed one leg over the other and surveyed her with his bright blue eyes. 'I might as well tell you, to save you explanations, that I've made enquiries about you.'

'Have you?'

'Yes. I know all, as they say in melodramas. Various members of my family and yours were only too eager to dish the dirt. I might add that none of us particularly liked Isobel at Courtfield Park. I'm sure you remember that.'

Chiara laughed. 'Yes. You all thought she talked too much.'

'Well, Oliver will thoroughly break her heart, as he's broken yours, and that will be her reward.'

Chiara looked away. 'I don't wish that on her.'

'I'm only interested in your situation. What plans have you made?'

'None,' she said. 'Though Oliver has made some suggestions. I saw him this morning. He's the one who gave me the lecture.'

'And what were Oliver's suggestions?'

'He wants me to go to Courtfield Park and be pampered until the baby comes.'

'To which you said . . .?'

'I said I would think about it. He also said he and Isobel would adopt the baby.'

'How does Isobel feel about these proposals?'

'I don't really know. They can't have children together, and now Oliver says he wants an heir.'

'An heir! Is that what he's calling it?'

'He's fifty this year.'

Simon Altringham had a very steady gaze. 'Do you still love him?'

Chiara was silent for a while, assessing her own feelings. 'I loved him very much,' she said at last, 'but I don't think that he loved me. Not in the way I wanted. And he wasn't the person I thought he was. And I've changed. It's as if those two people weren't us. They were actors, playing parts.'

'You haven't answered the question.'

Luckily, the waiter arrived with their tea and a silver cake stand piled with ten shillings' worth of dainty little sandwiches, scones and cream, and, on the top level, iced cakes. Chiara's nausea seemed to have vanished. In fact, her appetite had increased startlingly. She began to eat. Simon was apparently content to admire her putting the nourishment away. 'While you're busy with that sandwich,' he said, 'let me say that I think Oliver's ideas are very bad ones. For you, I mean. He clearly wants you back, and he'll ditch Isobel to get you. He'll offer to marry you. But as I said to you at Courtfield Park a few months ago, Oliver will never change. He'll never be faithful to you. He's not capable of it. Besides which, none of this can be the basis for a happy marriage. You're best out of the whole thing.'

Chiara reached for another sandwich. 'That's a pretty devastating assessment.'

'But an accurate one.'

'If you say so.'

'I do say so, and I know Oliver. If you'd listened to me last year—' Chiara gave him an old-fashioned look, and he didn't finish the sentence. 'I have a better suggestion, Chiara.'

Chiara inspected the diminishing supply of dainties. 'Go on.'

'You're going to marry me.'

She almost choked. 'Don't be funny at my expense, Simon.'

'I'm perfectly serious.' And he certainly looked it, holding her gaze steadily and without smiling.

Chiara put down the sandwich she'd selected. 'Then you're mad.'

'On the contrary, it's a very sane solution. You need a husband and I want a wife.'

'Like the farmer in the nursery rhyme? It's not that simple!'

'We have the same background. We come from the same part of the country. We have friends in common and we're the same age. Do you know why I kissed you that winter morning at Courtfield Park?

Because I said to myself, "That's exactly the sort of woman I'm going to marry." I tried to prise you away from Oliver then, if you remember.'

Chiara felt her face flushing hotly, the way it had done when she'd first met Simon at the maternity clinic. 'You may have fancied me, but please don't pretend to be in love with me.'

'I'm not pretending to be in love with you. I'm simply proposing to you. That's much more straightforward. If you want me to go down on one knee and produce a ring from my inside pocket, then I suggest a more private setting, with moonlight and nightingales. And I'll need time to buy a ring. But we don't have the luxury of time.'

Chiara's heart was beating very unsteadily. There was something compelling about Simon, something that – for all his matter-of-fact delivery – made her feel weak. 'I don't know what to make of you,' she said. 'I wouldn't have come here today if I'd known you were going to be like this.'

'Listen to me, Chiara,' he said. 'Marrying me will save you from disgrace. They say people are more broad-minded now because of the war, but nothing's really changed that much.'

'I've already had this talk from Sister White, thank you,' Chiara said.

'Sister White knows more about it than most people. If anyone bothers to count the period between the banns and the birth, they can assume what they like. You'll be a married woman, and your child will have a father. And I do mean a father. We can have a few more, but they'll be no closer to my heart, and no more completely mine, than this one. I'm fond of Oliver and quite prepared to love the child as my own. However, I will be the father, and not Oliver. There's no question of anything else.'

'I see,' she said faintly.

'Nor is there any question of your going back to Oliver. Oliver's first wife died of a broken heart, and so would you. I won't have that. Compared to Oliver, I'm a poor man. I can't offer you Courtfield Park. You'd be a struggling junior doctor's wife for a while. But I do have prospects. I'm specialising in obstetrics, which is a wonderful field, and one day I will be a Harley Street man with a thriving practice. We'll be very comfortable in a few years.'

'That's nice to know.'

'It's also true that we may not love each other at the beginning, but that will come quickly. I am ready to love you and have been since the moment we met. I'm sure that you'll grow fond of me in time, and that fondness will grow into love by and by. That's how the Victorians got married.'

'And they were bloody miserable.'

'Not all of them. Anyway, we won't be, I promise you.' He refilled their cups from the elaborate silver teapot. Chiara found herself looking at his hands and wondering whether her future lay in them. They looked safe, competent hands, what people called 'doctor's hands'. She transferred her gaze to his face with its long, kinked nose and generous mouth. It was the sort of face that might grow even more handsome with time, or at least become more distinguished. His ears were neat. His hair was very nice – thick, dark and well cut. Was she really thinking these thoughts? She looked at the tables around her, feeling that she was in a very peculiar dream and that nothing that had just been said had been real.

'Are you all right?' he asked.

'I just feel rather dizzy,' she said.

'You shouldn't have wolfed down those cakes so quickly,' Simon said. 'You're probably hyperglycaemic.' He reached across the table and took her pulse. 'Your heart's racing. And not very regular. Too much sugar. The stuff's been rationed for so long that it's like a drug now. Would you like to go out for some fresh air?'

'No, thank you, I think I'll just sit here, if you don't mind. Is there anything else you'd like to say?'

'Yes. I'm renting digs near the clinic, but I want you out of London as soon as possible. As soon as you say the word, I'll apply for a transfer to a provincial hospital away from the bombing. Any place you choose. We'll get a little house of our own. Somewhere small but comfortable. Cosy. You know what I mean.'

'I have some money,' she heard herself say.

'That would certainly help.'

'A lot was tied up in my flat, which is gone, but I have two thousand pounds in the bank.'

'And I have about the same. We've got more than enough for a house.'

'Simon—'

'Yes?'

'Is this a game to you?'

'No. I've already told you. You're the woman I want to marry.'

'Only, young doctors are high-spirited. You may be saying all this, and even believing it yourself, but you'll wake in a muck sweat tomorrow wondering how you're going to explain that it was just a whim.'

His fresh young face was serious. 'But it's not just a whim. I'm as certain of this as I can be. You would make any man alive a wonderful wife. An obstetrician needs a family. Unlike, say, an anaesthetist, who can do without one.' He smiled. 'A charming wife is an immense asset. It's hardly a gamble on my part.'

She rested her chin on her hands to study him. 'What a nice young man you are. Mothers everywhere must be hopefully grooming their daughters. Aren't there any charming young ladies interested in you?'

'At least a dozen.'

'All snowy virgins, of course?'

'I don't want any of them. None of them are a patch on you. I only want you.'

'Sir James and Lady Altringham won't share your enthusiasm,' Chiara said with a wry face. 'They weren't exactly keen on me at Courtfield Park.'

'I'm not governed by my mother and father.'

'But this would cause a rift in the family.'

'We'll take that as it comes,' Simon said calmly. 'If there is a rift, we'll heal it. We're a very loving family. When they get to know you, they'll understand why I chose you.'

'They'll say you're ruining your life to save me from ruining mine. They'll say this is a Quixotic gesture that you'll regret for the rest of your days.'

He leaned forward and took her hand. 'Whether I regret it or not is up to you, Chiara. You could see me as a fool who laid down his cape for you. Or you could put everything into it, as I'm going to. Learn to love me, as I will love you. Put the past behind you, forget Oliver and think only of our future together. You have your half of this to do. I'm not offering charity. I'm offering a partnership.'

Her head was spinning even faster. He was very eloquent. Once before he'd produced this maelstrom inside her, and if she had listened then, things would have gone better for her. 'Please stop. I've listened to you, and I'll think about everything you've said. But I can't listen to any more. I want to drink my tea and eat scones and talk about anything except the bombs or the war or my tragic predicament.'

'Got it,' he said. 'Now, you picked up that potted shrimp sandwich and then put it down again. Does that mean you don't want it? I'm rather partial to potted shrimp.'

'I do want it,' she said, cutting it in half, 'but we can share it.'

'So the morning sickness has gone, I take it?'

'I was as sick as a dog this morning. I'm fine now.'

'It's me. I have the healing touch.'

'You've certainly got the gift of the gab. If medicine doesn't work out, you could sell brushes door to door. Did you rehearse in front of the mirror?'

'I just spoke my mind. I don't have much guile. You'll find that out.'

'You may be right about the sugar,' she said. 'I haven't had such a delicious tea since the war began.' She surveyed their table with its antique silverware and delicate china. 'Look at all this: real jam! Clotted cream! Fondant icing!' She smiled at him. 'Thank you for bringing me here, Simon. I really needed this.'

He shook his head slowly. 'When you smile at me like that, you take my breath away.'

'You promised no more speeches.'

'This is a medical issue.'

After tea, they strolled through the Royal Arcade together. Simon took her arm in the most natural way. How agreeable it was, she thought, to have a man beside her after months of walking alone. Her mood was bittersweet. Like a dream that was both happy and sad, and you couldn't disentangle the two emotions. The arcade was crowded with couples and families. The fine weather had continued, and the afternoon sun shone brilliantly through the vaulted glass roof of the arcade, glowing with colour in places and shedding a crystalline allure over the shops. They stopped in front of a jeweller's window that was particularly dazzling. 'Aren't they beautiful?' Chiara said, looking at a collection of emerald and diamond rings.

'I don't think I can stretch to one of those,' Simon said.

She was chagrined. 'You know I didn't mean that!'

'I know. But one day we'll come back to this shop.'

'I've never thought of myself as a girl who deserved such things,' she said as they wandered on. 'I'm not special in any way.'

'I think you're very special. You should never have got entangled with Oliver. And he should never have chosen you.'

'It just happened.'

'Nothing just happens with Oliver. He always chose women who could defend themselves. Women older than you, I mean. Women bored with their marriages, divorcées, women of the world. They all understood what the terms were and accepted them. You were an exception. You hoped it was for keeps. You didn't know the rules; we could all see that. We all knew it was going to be hard on you. That's why I tried to warn you.'

'Don't be too severe on Oliver.'

Simon stopped and turned to face her. 'Chiara, he's having an affair with your sister! If he did that to you, there's nothing he won't do. You can't go back to him.'

'I didn't say I was going back to him. I just know that I can't match up to Isobel.'

'We all saw *that* coming, too. It was obvious to everyone except you. But Isobel will fare no better at his hands than any of the others. People like Oliver don't care who they hurt or what damage they do. They're abnormal personalities. They can only love themselves, and sometimes not even that.'

As the sun began to sink lower, they walked through Green Park. The trees were at their fullest now, their millions upon millions of leaves rustling and shimmering in the breeze. The deckchair men were having a busy day; hundreds of striped canvas deckchairs were spread out across the grass as Londoners took the sun. Above, against a cerulean sky, the blimps were a shoal of tethered, silver whales. Simon was holding her hand now; she'd taken off her gloves because it was so warm, and her palm was naked against his, their fingers interlaced.

'Thank you,' she said quietly. 'Whatever happens, I'll always be grateful to you for this day and for the things you said to me. You gave me hope. I'll never forget a moment of it.'

He kissed her gently on the lips, and this time she didn't protest.

⁓

Oliver stood naked at the drinks cabinet, studying the bottles. The vodka had run out. Brandy was the obvious choice, but the heavy decanter was a liability, as were the delicate balloon glasses. In the end, he decided on the Islay malt whisky that he had been drinking for so many years. He poured a substantial slug into two sturdy cut-glass tumblers and took them back to the bedroom.

Isobel, too, was naked. She lay sprawled on the silk sheets of the bed, her arms stretched out above her head. He studied her for a moment with a long pang of regret. She was a magnificent creature. Every detail of her was thrilling, from her dark and tumbled hair to the glossy red ovals of her perfect toenails. He let his eyes wander over her, dwelling on the luxuriant triangle between her thighs, her full breasts and rounded limbs, the arch of her ribcage, her lovely throat. In comparison, Chiara was a Dresden doll, delicate and ethereal.

Languid from their lovemaking, she turned her head and smiled lazily at him. 'Enjoying the view?'

'It's the best view in town.' He settled on the bed next to her, and they clinked glasses. She wrinkled her nose at the flavour of the whisky. 'I don't know why you like this stuff so much. It's very peculiar.'

'The distillery is on the shore in Islay in the Hebrides. You can taste the sea.' He rolled the fiery spirit round his mouth. 'My father introduced me to it years ago. It was his favourite tipple. One summer, when I was about seventeen, we sailed to Islay together, just the two of us. It was a wild place in those days, lonely and beautiful. Peat and wildflowers and whisky distilleries and not much else.' He swirled the amber liquid in the glass. 'We went to the distillery where they make this stuff. They made us sample a dozen different barrels, perhaps more. We came back gloriously drunk. It was the first time I'd ever been so drunk. I don't recall more than a few words exchanged between us in all that trip, and most of those had to do with sailing the yacht. But I was happy.'

'Aren't you happy now?'

He smiled wryly. 'Youth is a very special liquor. It produces a very special intoxication. One never thinks the bottle will run dry. But it does.'

Isobel propped herself up on one arm. 'Didn't you enjoy making love?'

'Very much.'

'So did I. As far as I'm concerned, you've got your youth still – in every way. Why are you so melancholy?'

'Because this was the last time. For a while, anyway.'

Her smile faded. 'I don't understand you.'

'I can't marry you, Isobel.'

He saw gooseflesh wash over her, her nipples tightening into hard knots. 'Why not?'

'I'm going back to Chiara.' He drained his glass before uttering the next words. 'I'm going to marry her.'

She stared at him with her large, dark eyes for a while. 'I knew this was coming,' she said at last.

'She's having my child. I can't ignore that. I didn't plan to leave any trace of myself behind in this world. I haven't been a very good man, and I haven't liked myself enough to want to produce an heir. But now that a child is on the way, my feelings have changed. I'm going to be fifty soon. I want the child. And to have the child, I must have Chiara.'

Isobel rolled out of bed and pulled on her dressing gown. She lit a cigarette and exhaled the smoke sharply at the ceiling. 'So you're dropping me just like that?'

'It doesn't have to be a permanent rupture,' he said obliquely.

'What do you mean?' she asked in a tense voice.

'I mean that there must be a marriage. It will be quick and quiet, of necessity. Chiara will be established at Courtfield Park. She'll have the child there and bring it up there. I'll keep this flat. I rather like it. After all, my work is here, five days a week. I'll see her

159

on the weekends. After a decent interval – perhaps only a month or two – there's no reason why you and I shouldn't continue to see each other.'

'My God! You're inviting me to become your mistress while you marry my sister!'

'You are already my mistress,' he said, smiling. 'My dear Isobel, you are a woman of the world. Neither of us is a dewy-eyed innocent. I think we understand each other very well.'

She studied his long, lean nakedness on the bed. 'Actually, I feel that I'm seeing you for the first time.'

'Do you like the view?'

'No.' Her tone was flat. 'I'm not standing for it, Oliver. You can forget this little scheme.'

'I'm afraid I can't. It was never my intention to hurt you, but this child of Chiara's has changed everything. We all need to adapt to the new circumstances.'

'You mean adapt to suit your vanity and selfishness?' she said, her eyes glittering. 'I'm afraid not. You told me you wanted to marry me, and I accepted. I've told all my friends. I've told everyone in the Labour Party, including Clement Attlee and Ernest Bevin. I told them I'd be standing for Parliament as a married woman. And now you expect me to sit quietly by while you marry Chiara? How am I supposed to face the world? I will not allow you to humiliate me in this way.'

Oliver was watching her rather as a ringmaster might watch a tigress, confident of having the whip hand, but wary of the claws and fangs. 'In the immortal words of Robb Wilton, what are you going to do about it?'

'I'm a public figure.' She stubbed out the half-smoked cigarette. 'I'm a journalist and a writer. I'll expose you for what you are – a man without scruples. I'll tell the world what you did to Chiara. I'll make your name stink.'

'And how will you do that without making your own name stink even more?' he enquired. 'If I behaved badly, you were worse. Are you going to tell the world that you betrayed your own sister and broke her heart? I don't see *that* doing your political career much good.'

'*You* broke Chiara's heart, you bastard!'

'As I remember,' he said dryly, 'you jumped into bed with very little prompting.'

'You seduced me!'

'Come now,' he scoffed. 'You're thirty years old. It's absurd to talk of seduction.'

'You were never serious about Chiara! How could you be? She's just a child. She knew you would never marry her. What sort of wife would she make you? You'd be tied to a nonentity. That's why you chose me, because you and I are alike. It was the logical choice for both of us. Think of the brilliant future we have together, Oliver!'

'All that may be true, but I repeat that things have changed. I'm planning a different future now. It may not be so brilliant, but it includes a child.'

'You're disgusting!' she hissed back at him. '*You*, to talk of a child! What do you know about children?'

'As much as you, I suppose,' he said calmly.

Her eyes filled with tears; of rage or grief, he couldn't tell which. 'I had a child, and he was taken away.'

'Then you should understand how I feel now. I can't give this up.' He paused. 'There is also Chiara's welfare to consider.'

'Oh, for God's sake!'

'She can't face this alone. It would destroy her chances in life.'

'Please spare me your tender feelings for Chiara, or I may be sick. You don't give *that* for her,' she said, snapping her fingers. 'You've never had one moment's regret about her until now.'

'That's not true. I would have spared her any suffering if I could have done. It wasn't possible, that's all.'

'And now you think you can gallop back to her on your white horse and make everything all right? She won't have you!'

'She will,' he replied. 'I know Chiara. And there's no other course of action, Isobel. The sooner you see that, the better. The best thing you can do is accept this calmly, make as little fuss as possible and get on with your life. I won't embarrass you with a big wedding, of course. We'll marry quietly at Chipping Norton. It can be kept out of the papers. Everything will be quickly settled, and you'll hardly be affected.'

'I'll tell Chiara exactly what you've just proposed,' she said fiercely. 'Will she still have you when she knows that you have no intention of being faithful to her? That you've told me you'll keep seeing me – or God knows who else – while she's nursing your child?'

He rose from the bed and put on his own gown. 'You won't do that.'

'Why won't I?'

'Because it's her best hope.'

'I'd be saving her from a life of wretchedness with you! You don't care a thing for her!'

'And you? Weren't you suggesting only the other day that I bundle your sister into an unmarked car and forcibly abort her child?'

'That was not said in earnest!'

'But this is,' Oliver said, belting the sash around his lean waist. 'If you play rough, then I can, too. Much rougher than you.' Despite herself, Isobel took a pace backwards as he turned to her, his face cold. 'Have you forgotten who I am? The files I have on you are enough to have you interned in Brixton jail for the duration of the war, along with your old pals, the Mosleys and the other British Fascists.'

'Oliver!' she gasped.

'You associated with Hitler and Mussolini, the leaders of countries with which we're at war. Under Defence Regulation 18b, you can be detained indefinitely, without charge or trial. The person being bundled into the back of a Special Branch car will be you, not Chiara.'

Isobel was white in the face. 'You bastard! We've just made love, and you stand there, threatening to have me imprisoned! By God, Oliver, I'll tell everyone who'll listen exactly what you are.'

'But nobody will listen.' He was growing icier as she grew more emotional. 'Under 18b, there are no committees, no panels, no tribunals. No statement you make will be printed. You will be silenced completely and utterly. You'll be branded forever a traitor and a Nazi. I don't enjoy saying these things to you, but you are forcing me to say them. Please understand that I have the power to do what I promise.'

Tears spilled down her cheeks. He was struck by how her beauty had vanished in the past few moments. 'I believed that you loved me,' she said. She put her face in her hands. 'My God. A moment ago, I was so happy!'

'I've been happy, too. You're a beautiful, brilliant woman. We would have made an excellent team. I don't want to lose you. I certainly don't want to do you any harm. Don't force my hand.'

'How cruel you are, now that I see you clearly.'

He laughed. 'Come now, darling. Don't be melodramatic. The situation is difficult enough as it is. Let's spare each other the insults and recriminations, shall we?' He took the tumblers back to the drinks cabinet and poured two more stiff tots of Lagavulin. The decanter was nearly empty, he noted. He would have to drop in at Justerini & Brooks when he next went to his club and order another case. He took the whisky back to Isobel. 'You don't know this,' he said, handing her the tumbler, 'but I've been protecting you ever since you came back to England. There were senior people in Five who wanted you interrogated, then. It was only because you were Chiara's sister that I stopped the investigation. I vouched for you. You stayed out of Latchmere House thanks to me. You wouldn't have lasted a day there.' He watched her as she raised the glass to her lips in both trembling hands and gulped down the whisky. 'I'm as disappointed as you are,' he said in a gentler voice. 'We've been close friends, and close friends we should remain. To become antagonists now is the greatest folly we could commit.' He tried to stroke her cheek, but she flinched away from him.

'For God's sake,' she said shakily, 'don't touch me.'

Her face was a ruin. It seemed to have slumped like a bombed building. It was hard to believe that ten minutes ago she had been lovely. He'd seen shock and violence do this to other faces, and he felt sorry for her. 'Buck up, old girl,' he said. 'You're going to be an aunt. That's something, at any rate. We're all going to be tied together. One happy family.'

She started to sob. Oliver glanced at his watch. He knew this was just the beginning. It was going to be a long night.

෩

'Dr Altringham tells me you're a friend of his,' Sister White said, writing her notes.

'Yes, we know one another,' Chiara said. 'Is he here today?'

'He's in the operating theatre. An emergency Caesarean section. We think a great deal of young Dr Altringham.'

'Do you?' She wondered whether Simon had asked Sister White to put in a good word.

'Oh yes. With so many new doctors going into the Army, we're terribly short of obstetricians. They've been wheeling geriatric cases out of retirement. Some of them quite senile. Still prescribing laudanum and paregoric. It's a great relief to have a promising junior like Dr Altringham on our ward. He'll be delivering your baby, of course.'

'Will he?'

'He's insisted. You should consider yourself lucky not to be in the hands of old Dr Thornton. Or Mr Somerset – he's nearly ninety. Dr Altringham's a born obstetrician. Safest pair of hands on the ward.'

'Then I'm lucky,' Chiara said.

'Yes, indeed. You're *extremely* lucky, Miss Redcliffe.'

The midwife had spoken the last sentence with enough emphasis to give Chiara the strong impression that she was talking about more than the delivery.

'The thing is,' she said, 'I don't know Dr Altringham all that well. We spent a weekend together once, and that's all, in fact.'

'I hardly think that matters,' said Sister White briskly. 'I don't believe in looking a gift horse in the mouth.'

'Has Simon – Dr Altringham, that is – said anything to you, Sister?'

'He has said something,' she said without looking up.

'He's made an extraordinarily kind offer, but I—'

'*Kind?*' Sister White looked up sharply. 'The man is an angel in human form.'

'Well, I suppose that's what I mean. It's a great sacrifice on his part, and I suspect he's doing it out of some sense of obligation because Oliver's practically family to him. His parents are Oliver's oldest friends.'

'I don't believe that either you or Dr Altringham would be making a sacrifice of any kind. It's an excellent match on both sides.'

'But I think—'

'There's far too much *thinking*,' the midwife snapped, her face frosty. 'The present generation does nothing but *think*. In my day, we didn't think about things half so much. We simply jumped to it. If something needed to be done, we did it. We didn't ask why or wherefore. Nowadays, if I ask my nurses to do something, I see them chewing the cud over it, with a gormless, cow-like expression. I can't bear it. God knows how they manage in the Army, but I can't bear it. I give them the rough edge of my tongue, I can tell you. And though my veil prevents me from using coarse language, it's surprising what can be achieved with a few well-chosen words.'

'Yes, Sister,' Chiara said meekly.

'If you were standing on a railway track, with the Paddington Express hurtling towards you, would you stand there thinking about what to do?'

'No, Sister.'

'You're not a fool, Miss Redcliffe.'

'No, I don't think I am.'

'Then don't behave like one.'

As she walked out past the row of patients with their burgeoning tummies, Chiara was thinking of the way Simon had described the place he was thinking of: *A little house of our own. Somewhere small but comfortable. Cosy.* How wonderful that sounded! She was so tired of her garret, of the loneliness and the fear. Sister White was right. She'd be a fool to look a gift horse in the mouth. She thought about Simon in the operating theatre, of those sure, safe hands delivering a child.

When she got back to her little flat, a large bouquet of red roses was waiting for her on the doormat. Among all the privations of wartime, and with every garden turned over to vegetables, fresh flowers were scarce and expensive. Roses were almost non-existent. She read the note: the roses were from Oliver. Their spicy, heavy scent made her dizzy for a moment. This was so typical of him.

She took the bouquet into her garret. To keep them might be a sign that she was weakening. But to throw them away – red roses in wartime! – would be a dreadful waste. She couldn't bring herself to do that.

She put the roses in a vase with water but tore up the note.

And the day ended on another bright spot. Just before she went to sleep, she got a call from Felicity in Cairo.

'It's all happened,' Felicity said excitedly.

'What's happened, Fee?'

'I'm in love.'

'Truly?'

'And that's not all. I've joined King Farouk's harem and become a fallen woman.'

'No!'

'Yes! Well, not exactly. But I've become his protégée, and go to his palaces for the most decadent parties. Lobsters and champagne and dancing girls who take all their clothes off.'

'Fee, I don't believe you. You're making this all up.'

'Cross my heart and hope to die. Oh, I've such a lot to tell you, darling! I've shot a robber in the foot with the pistol you gave me and started a riot and had my car stoned by a mob.'

'*What?*'

'Yes, it's true. And Mr Tennant has been shot dead by an Egyptian Nationalist. His wife has gone back to England. And the most important thing is that I've met the most wonderful man, a war artist called Orlando Hescott. He's at the front line now, and I'm dreadfully worried about him, but I know he'll come back to me, because it's meant to be.'

'Felicity, I'm so happy for you!'

'Doesn't sound like me, does it? But it is. It's the new me. Bullets and begonias. I'm calling from the palace now, and I only have a minute, but I'll tell you everything when I'm back in London. We're two fallen women, darling. Isn't that just perfect?'

'I may not be fallen, after all. I've had an offer of marriage.'

'Good heavens! Who from?'

'Simon Altringham. He's a doctor now.'

'That's a bit close to home, isn't it? Isn't his father one of Oliver's friends?'

'Yes. We met at Courtfield Park in the winter, and he kissed me on horseback.'

'Oh, well, *that* seals it. Was he wearing shining armour at the time?'

'A smelly hacking jacket, as I remember.'

'This is fate. Are you madly in love with him?'

'No.'

'Is he madly in love with you?'

'I don't think so.'

'Sounds like the perfect basis for a happy marriage.'

Chiara laughed. 'Well, we like each other very much – and he says love will come. He says we're ideally suited, and that's the most important thing. Sister White – that's the frosty old midwife – says he's an angel in human form, and I'd be a fool to refuse him.'

'Do you think Sister White is the best person to advise you?'

'Sister White might be a sour old stick, but she knows human nature well enough.'

'So you're going to accept Simon?'

'I'm running out of choices. Oh, Fee. I'm not suited to being lonely and miserable. I don't want to be an unmarried mother. I want to be happy in life. I want my baby to have a father. And Simon really is wonderful. He's handsome and kind and generous and funny and caring—'

'I'll have him, if you don't want him.'

Chiara smiled. 'I *do* want him. I just feel I'm taking advantage of his good nature to a shocking degree. I'm sure his parents will loathe me for it forever.'

'Oh, sod that.'

'Fee! You're picking up awful expressions!'

'It's because I mingle with licentious soldiery. But really. Sod that. You're the one who's been imposed on. You're a treasure, and you'll make him a wonderful wife. I'm not surprised he wants you. Never mind his parents. Let them loathe you. Think about yourself for a change. And just think – this is one in the eye for Isobel, all right! She's stuck with nasty old Oliver, and you'll have juicy young Simon! She'll be livid.'

Chiara laughed out loud. 'It's so wonderful to laugh again. And it certainly makes a change for me to be getting advice from you.'

'Well, Orlando has taught me one thing, and that's to grab life with both hands. I've spent most of my life hiding away, and there's so much I've missed, so much I'll never get back. I'm not missing any more, darling. And you shouldn't, either.'

'I know you're right.'

'So do I. Don't have any more second thoughts. Grab your Simon with both hands.'

৶৹

Oliver found his wine merchant in turmoil. Men in aprons were carrying cases of wine up from the cellar and loading them onto a lorry parked in St James's Street.

'We're moving most of our stock out of London, Mr Courtfield,' the manager told him. 'Can't risk it anymore. The vibrations from the bombing are starting to spoil some of the burgundies. As for a direct hit, the less said, the better. What can I do for you, sir?'

'I wanted a case of Lagavulin.'

The manager sucked his teeth. 'Ah, now, Lagavulin, you say?'

'Is there a difficulty?'

'Malt's very hard to get hold of nowadays, Mr Courtfield. The government's making the distilleries export all their whisky to bring in foreign revenue. The Americans are buying up all the good stuff. We need their dollars. We're bankrupt, sir, that's what it is.'

'You must be able to find a few bottles, surely.' He leaned over the counter. 'What would it cost me?' he asked in a low voice.

'Double,' the manager replied without hesitation. 'Forty pounds'll get you a case of fifteen-year-old.'

'I've never paid such a price in my life!'

'And I can't put it through the books, you understand, sir. Don't ask me to put it on your account.'

Oliver slid eight large, white five-pound notes across the counter. 'Send two bottles to my club and the rest to the flat, all right?'

Crossing the road to Boodle's, he found himself yawning. It had been a wretched night with Isobel. She had been far worse than he would have imagined. She had screamed, wept, raged. It had only been with the crudest threats that he'd managed to silence her in the end.

Women, he'd found, were physical cowards. They cracked easily under interrogation. They couldn't withstand bodily pain, and, of course, threatening their children was effective. But there was a certain steely strength to them, even though you couldn't see it. You thought they were beaten, but there were hidden reserves. Perhaps it was nature's way of allowing them to cope with the childbirth thing. You could never bank on having completely broken them. It could be unnerving.

Isobel seemed broken now, but what if she wasn't? She'd promised to attack him in public. That would not go down well at Five. Getting her to shut her mouth might be a serious problem. What if he had to carry out what he'd threatened her with? It would not be pleasant. Perhaps only a hint would do the trick: have her arrested and taken to Ham Common for a day or two of questioning. She'd soon see sense in an isolation cell. Or would she? She was the sort of woman who pushed back. And once one had got a certain distance down that road, there was no turning back. It would end in internment, and it might be very difficult to deal with Chiara while her sister was in Brixton.

He lunched alone at his club, pondering. It was possible that he'd have to deal definitively with Isobel before he was finished. At all costs, he had to prevent her from poisoning Chiara's mind against him before he could effect a reconciliation. Swift action was required; the swifter, the better. He would go to speak to her again after lunch.

The orange fool was on the menu today, and he ordered it, but before it could be brought to him, he was summoned to the telephone. The call was from the War Office.

'We've got the analysis from the latest aerial photographs,' the terse voice informed him. 'I think you'd better take a look.'

He hurried out of his club, leaving the orange fool untasted.

༄

'Is there any chance you'll be sent abroad?' Chiara asked Simon.

'Who can say? I want to serve my country,' Simon replied. 'But, according to the powers that be, England needs obstetricians more than ever. And we've got my brother Adrian overseas already. I don't mind, as long as I can do something. I'd prefer to heal people, not kill them.'

'Sister White says you're a born obstetrician. I'm sure you must have paid her to sing your praises.'

'Did she sing my praises?'

'At great length.'

'And she's a woman of excellent judgement.' He grinned at her. She'd invited him up to the garret after work. They were sitting on her tiny bed – the window seat was too small for two – with the late afternoon sun shining through the window, the anti-blast tape making striped patterns on the stone walls. 'She's rather keen on you.'

'She's rather keen on *you*,' Chiara replied. 'She told me you're an angel in human form, and I'd be a fool to pass you up.'

'But you're not going to pass me up, are you?'

'I haven't decided yet,' she said primly. 'How did your Caesarean go?'

'Mother and baby both doing well. It had a few tricky moments. It was a breech delivery that had to be rushed to theatre. The saddest part is the anaesthesia – delivering an unconscious baby from an unconscious mother. That's dangerous for them both. And not the way God intended it to be. Have you read *Childbirth without Fear* yet?'

'Only a few pages, between one thing and another. Sorry. I'll get round to it.'

'Dick-Read is a great obstetrician. He's an advocate of natural childbirth. He was ridiculed and lost his practice because of it. But people are finally starting to listen to what he's saying.'

'Isn't all childbirth natural?' Chiara asked.

'You would think so, wouldn't you? But spend a week on a maternity ward and you'll see how little really is natural. We treat the whole business of childbirth as though it were a disease – and a shameful disease, at that. We knock the mothers out with chloroform or scopolamine, even if they don't ask for pain relief. Most of them are hardly aware of what's happening, and the babies are born limp and sluggish. We don't let the mothers get into a comfortable position. In fact, we often clamp their arms and legs. We routinely perform episiotomies and then sew the mothers up like virgins afterwards, so the whole, agonising thing has to be done again for the next birth. Nearly every birth is a forceps delivery, and we pull the placenta out before it's naturally expelled. As soon as the babies are born, they're taken away from the mothers, and it may be hours before they're reunited. No,' he said, shaking his head, 'there's not a lot about it that's natural.'

'You make it sound awful,' she said, staring at him with large eyes.

'I'm not going to let any of that happen to you, I promise. Or to any of my patients. I'm going to make a lot of changes on my wards. *My* patients are going to have the fulfilling experience that childbirth should be.'

'You sound as though you've had a couple yourself.'

'Well, I've seen enough of the present system to know it's badly organised and downright wicked. Read *Childbirth without Fear*, and you'll see how it should be.'

'I will, I promise. This is a very strange situation,' she said with a sigh. 'I don't know whether to think of you as my suitor or my doctor.'

'I could be both,' he said, amused. 'Have you really never thought of me since we last met at Courtfield Park?'

'Only with irritation,' she replied. 'You were so obnoxious.'

'I've thought of you countless times. And not with irritation. Was I really so obnoxious?'

'Yes.'

'Why?'

'Well – lecturing me. And kissing me like that.'

'I suppose I was anticipating things a bit.' He studied her mouth with more than professional interest. 'But now that we're engaged, surely a spot of kissing is de rigueur?'

'We're not engaged!'

'Very nearly engaged, then. We should get into practice for when we plight our troth.'

She laughed. 'You make it sound like a medical procedure.'

'Well, it seems absurd to be considering marriage on the strength of only one kiss.' He put his arms around her. He always touched her so naturally, never clumsily or with any awkwardness. He leaned forward. She closed her eyes. His lips were warm on hers for a moment. 'There. That wasn't so bad, was it?'

'Better than the first time.'

'Better in what way?'

'Gentler. The first time was much too hard.'

'Well, I was on horseback. I suppose we're lucky we didn't knock each other's teeth out. But thank you for the hint. Let me try again.' This time the kiss was longer and even more tender. 'You have the nicest mouth,' he whispered. 'It's so soft. Exquisite.'

'Nice of you to say so,' she whispered back. 'Your technique is improving.'

'Well, I'm much more familiar with the other end of things, you know. I know my way around there.'

She couldn't stop giggling. 'If you make me laugh, we'll never get anywhere.'

'Let me kiss you again.' He put his lips to hers again, at first experimentally, as though looking for the best fit, then with increasing eagerness.

'I think you've kissed lots of girls,' Chiara murmured.

'Only in the interests of research.' He kissed her again, drawing her close. Abstinence and pregnancy, she found, had charged her libido. She didn't have to play-act; desire welled up in her, warm and real, as warm and real as the man in her arms. Simon was here for her, that was all that mattered. It had never once occurred to her to doubt his motives. He was right; there was no guile in him, and so she responded to him without guile.

She'd forgotten how delightful kissing was, kissing for the pleasure of kissing, for the intimacy and the warmth of sensitive mouths exploring one another. Oliver had never kissed her very much; he'd regarded it as a greeting, not a caress. Now she felt like a furnace, heating up steadily and steamily as the fire was stoked. She put her arms round Simon's neck and kissed him back. He was enchanted. 'I say, you're hot stuff.'

She drew back, her cheeks flushed. 'Simon, what are we going to do about – you know?'

'Sex?'

'Yes.'

'Well, as a doctor, I can tell you there's no danger to the baby if we're not too rambunctious. And choose the right positions. However, there's an aesthetic dimension, too, isn't there? Perhaps you might prefer to wait until after the birth. Make a new start, as it were.'

'That's months away. Can you wait that long?'

His eyes sparkled. 'There are other things we can do in the meantime.'

'I'm very glad to hear it.' Chiara lay back on the little bed, watching him as he took off his uniform.

The afternoon that followed was as full of delights and surprises as the best Christmas morning she could remember. And, like the best Christmas morning, what was hoped for and dreamed of became real and exceeded all hopes and dreams. Simon was able to show her just what a good understanding of female anatomy he possessed, and she was able to reciprocate in kind, to his delight.

When they were slaked, they lay together, holding one another. The sun was setting, flooding the little room with a deep, rich, red light. It was like being imprisoned in a ruby.

'Will you marry me?' he asked.

'There. I was just waiting to be asked nicely. Yes, I'll marry you.'

'Thank God. I can't live without you.' He covered her face with kisses. 'Thank you, thank you. You've made me the happiest man alive.' He raised himself on one elbow and looked down at her. 'We've got to get you out of London, darling. I've been thinking. What about Oxford?'

'Oxford?'

'It hasn't been bombed yet. They say Hitler's given specific orders that it must never be bombed. He wants it left intact to show he's a cultured fellow. It's a beautiful place, and the university's my old alma mater. And there are lots of hospitals where I can work, and there's bound to be work for you, too, until the baby is born. What do you say?'

'I don't think I want to work anymore. I've been working since I was seventeen and never had a holiday in all that time. I'm just going to be a sow in farrow for a year or two. So you take the decisions, Farmer Altringham.'

'Are you sure?'

'Quite sure.'

'Then Oxford it is.'

'Poor Sister White. She little knew that I was going to steal you away. She'll curse my name.'

'She's an excellent midwife. Perhaps we can take her with us.' He kissed her tenderly. 'This is rather wonderful. Isn't it?'

'Yes,' Chiara said, smiling up at him, 'it's rather wonderful.'

The scent of Oliver's red roses hung on the air, fading as the flowers withered.

∽

Oliver climbed the final flight of stairs with something of an effort. It had been a long and difficult day, filled with crises that had forced him to put off this interview until almost midnight. There were few cabs, and he'd walked from his office through the blacked-out streets that were full of perils. His legs and his mind were alike weary. At the top of the stairs, he stopped to catch his breath. He rubbed his face, summoning up his flagging energies. He would need all his powers of persuasion, now. Nothing could be accomplished here with threats or roughness.

He knocked at the door. After a pause, Chiara opened it. Her eyes widened. 'Oliver!'

'May I come in?'

She hesitated. 'It's very late. What do you want?'

'Just a few words. I won't keep you long.'

Reluctantly, she admitted him. She was wearing a quilted dressing gown that had obviously been made for a bigger woman. 'I was just about to go to bed.'

He reached into his pocket and took out the little velvet box. He held it out to her. She took it hesitantly. He watched her face as she saw the pearl and diamond ring inside. 'I bought that for my wife, Margaret, in 1919. She was dead three years later. It's been in a bank vault ever since. I got it out today.'

'Margaret means "the pearl", doesn't it?' she said quietly.

'I'd like you to wear it for me.'

'I can't.'

She hadn't said it angrily or defiantly, but with a calmness that made his heart sink. 'I was hoping to have more time in England. There's so much to do. But the war is always my master. I have to go abroad soon, very soon. In a matter of days.'

'I'm sorry. And I'm sorry for Isobel. It will be hard on her.'

'I've told Isobel I can't marry her,' he said. He saw her expression change and went on before she could speak. 'There's only one woman in the world I want to marry. I made a terrible mistake, Chiara. I wounded you deeply. I can never forgive myself for what I did, but I want you to believe that I'm bitterly sorry for it. I would give anything to take back the hurt I caused you. I realise that it'll take years to win your trust back. I'm begging you to give me those years. Forgive me. Come back to me. Marry me.'

She was studying his face with those gentle, brown eyes of hers. 'You look so tired,' she said almost absently. 'Do you really have to go back?'

'Yes. There's a new threat, a new weapon, and I have to find out what it is.' He was puzzled at her lack of response to his proposal. 'Can't you learn to forgive me, Chiara?'

'I think I've already forgiven you.'

His heart rose. Was it going to be as easy as that? He took heart. 'My Chiara!'

'How is Isobel managing?' she asked.

'She's angry. Very angry. She may come to you and say terrible things. You must be prepared for that, my dear. I can't control her. She's raging.'

'Oh, I know Isobel can say terrible things when she's raging. I'm quite prepared for it. She's been deeply hurt, you see. The same way you hurt me. She made the same mistake I did – of believing in you.'

He wanted to take her in his arms, but something about her stillness stopped him. 'I'm asking you to believe in me again.'

'I'm sorry, I can't.' She gave him back the ring with a gesture so sharp that he was taken by surprise. 'I'm going to marry someone else.'

Oliver was stunned, as though by an unexpected blow. 'What? Who?'

'I'm going to marry Simon Altringham.'

For a moment, he didn't know whom she was talking about. 'Young Simon? Sir James's son?'

'Yes.'

'He's just a boy!'

'He's twenty-six, the same age as me. He's a doctor now, specialising in obstetrics.'

'I don't understand,' Oliver said blankly. 'You hardly know him.'

'I feel I know him better than I know you,' she replied. She seemed very calm, and that was the most shattering part for him. 'He's a person without guile, like me. That makes getting to know each other very easy. We have a lot in common. I feel I can love him, and I believe he can love me. I don't know why he wants to marry me, but I'm terribly grateful. It's my salvation, you see – in every sense.'

Oliver wanted to sit down, but there was nowhere in the wretched little cell. He was pinned fast where he stood. 'You're carrying my child!'

'I'm sorry, Oliver.' Her voice was gentle. 'It's not going to be like that. The child will be ours – Simon's and mine. It will be loved and provided for, but you will have no rights and no obligations.'

'We'll see about that,' he said with a sudden, bitter surge of anger. He saw her eyes widen. Then her face closed. She took a step back, and he immediately regretted the outburst. 'I'm sorry,' he said hoarsely. He covered his eyes with his hands for a moment. His head was aching. 'Chiara, darling, please. I beg you, don't do anything precipitate until I get home. I'll be back before the winter. We can work everything out then. Just wait for me. Please.'

'Oliver—'

'You can't marry Simon Altringham,' he burst out. 'I don't understand how you can even contemplate it!'

'I don't think I understand it myself,' she replied slowly. 'Maybe there's nothing to understand. Maybe it's just one of those things that happen because they're right.'

'You're acting out of anger. That's always a terrible mistake.'

'I'm not angry,' she replied. 'In fact, I'm calmer and happier than I've been for months.'

'Marrying a man you hardly know! Chiara, this isn't like you. It's madness. You were always so sensible!'

'Perhaps I'm not anymore. Perhaps I've changed. Or perhaps I only seemed sensible to you because I did everything you wanted; and I only seem mad now because I won't.'

'Marry me now. If I die where I'm going, you and our child will inherit Courtfield Park.'

'No, Oliver.'

'You can't go through with this. I won't let you.'

'I can and I will. Please don't say any more – it won't do any good. I've made my mind up. Go home and rest now. You look ill.'

At Bletchley Park, Oliver had been shown the huge calculating machine that the engineers had built to crack the Nazi secret codes. You fed information into it; it whirred and clicked for a while, and out came the answer. When you changed the information, it whirred and clicked some more and gave the new answer. He felt, now, like that giant machine, whirring and clicking but unable to find the new answer. The information could not be broken. 'Please,' he heard himself say, 'please wait until I get back. I implore you.'

'Do what you can for Isobel,' she said. 'She's not as strong as she seems. It's late now, Oliver. Go home.' She held the door open for him.

He had been quite determined not to leave until he'd got what he came for, but a new wave of weariness washed over him. He could only make things worse now. He was not ready to argue with her, reason with her, win her over. He had nothing, he realised; no arguments, no reasons, no persuasions, no excuses, no justifications. Only a ring that belonged to a woman twenty years dead. Why had he brought the thing? It had been a terrible mistake. He could hardly have chosen a worse opening gambit. It had blighted everything he'd tried to do tonight.

And as he groped his way down the darkened stairs, he saw that his every step since learning that Chiara was pregnant had been a misstep, one poor move after another. Against Isobel, against Chiara. Chess games that he had played badly. One dreadful error after another. Pinning himself into a corner in a succession of faux pas.

Perhaps the missteps had begun earlier, when he'd first decided he wanted Isobel; his lust and folly then, his arrogance, his vanity, all had led him to this dark descent. He recalled the weekend it had begun, when he'd slipped into Isobel's bedroom in Courtfield Park, and they'd laughed softly in the dark. And yes, Simon Altringham had been there that weekend. He remembered now! The boy had kissed Chiara out in the woods! She'd told him about it. They'd argued, he and Chiara, because Chiara had said she wanted a child, and he—

He paused on the landing, his heart thudding. He'd told her to go to Simon if she wanted children. He'd said those words.

He fumbled his way down, clutching the cold iron rail. By God, those chickens had come home to roost. Everything he'd said and done that weekend had come back to haunt him: lust, folly, arrogance, vanity. The four horsemen of his personal apocalypse.

He emerged from the building into the inky street. In the blackout, London was frightening, an alien landscape. A man walking might fall into a bomb crater, crack his skull on a lamp post, be run down by a shadowy car, trip over invisible sandbags, be stabbed by criminals. And yet he was safer here by far than where he was going. In a day's time he would be travelling up to a secret base in Scotland and crossing the North Sea by submarine to Sweden. From there, impersonating a crewman on a fishing boat, he would attempt the most dangerous of all landings, on the German coast; and not only on German soil, but close to one of the most closely guarded of all Nazi installations, the experimental base at Peenemünde. A long, cold chill rolled down his spine. He was getting too old for these missions. He would celebrate his fiftieth birthday on a trawler, in the Baltic fog. Who could say if there would ever be another birthday? He had never lacked courage, but he knew that with each mission, the odds stacked up against him.

It had to be him. There was nobody else with his experience, his fluency with languages, his skill at surviving unperceived in enemy territory. Nobody else who'd been so close to the Nazis in the occupied countries and survived so long. Nobody else with the contacts in the German anti-Nazi Resistance. Or what was left of it.

He looked up. There was no light to be seen in Chiara's turret, of course. But she was in there – and carrying in her womb the only vestige he would leave on this earth, should he not return. He stood there for a moment, staring up at what he could not see. Perhaps that was what mattered, in the end; to leave one's blood behind. Should he never get to see that child, or sail with him to Islay, yet there would be something of him remaining.

A taxicab chuntered out of the darkness – he recognised it more by the sound of its engine than by its almost imperceptible roof light – and he darted into the road, holding up his hand.

'Taxi!'

The cab stopped. The pale face of the driver peered at him. 'Where to, Guv'nor?'

'Park Lane.' He clambered in, shut the door, and rolled away into the night.

ᕼ

Chiara clasped her belly in both hands. She felt swollen and tender there for the first time. The interview with Oliver had been painful. She'd expected him to argue fiercely, but there had suddenly come a look of defeat in his eyes that she'd never seen there before. He'd walked out without even saying goodbye, as though in a daze.

What had he been thinking of, bringing her that ring? She shuddered. Margaret was wearing it in the painting of her that hung over the mantelpiece at Courtfield Park. It was an ominous thing, and he should have known that. He was not himself.

And soon he would be out of England again. How many months she'd spent alone while he was away on these mysterious trips, wondering if she'd ever see him again! At least she didn't have to go through that any longer.

Her womb ached. Had the baby responded in some way to Oliver? *It's a wise child that knows his own father.* She'd never thought of the child as Oliver's, strangely, only as hers. And now, as Simon's. But perhaps the child knew better?

The ache sharpened, making her gasp. She held her abdomen, waiting for the pain to pass, but it didn't. She sat on the bed and tried to drink her Ovaltine, but it had gone cold, and the pain wasn't going away. A new cramp made her double over, sharp and terrifying.

There was warmth between her legs. She raised her dressing gown. Her thighs were slippery with bright scarlet blood.

Whimpering, she picked up the telephone. 'Simon,' she said through her tears, 'come quickly!'

෧ର

Oliver let himself into the Park Lane flat. The bedroom light was still on. Bracing himself for more drama, he went in. Isobel was packing a suitcase. The dress she was going to wear was spread out on the chair. For now, she was wearing only her girdle, stockings and a bra. He couldn't remember having seen the underwear, which was oyster-coloured silk, before tonight.

'Are you leaving at this hour?' he asked.

She didn't look at him, but at the blouse she was folding. 'I'm only taking this suitcase for now. I'll send for the rest of my things later.'

'Have you got somewhere to go?'

'Yes.'

When she didn't elaborate, he said, 'It's one in the morning. You won't find a cab at this hour.'

'I've ordered one from the night porter. It'll be here in twenty minutes.'

His eye was drawn to the smooth white expanse of her thigh, framed between her stockings, the girdle and the lace-trimmed suspenders. 'You could spend the night. Leave in the morning.'

Isobel glanced at him. 'Ah. I take it she turned you down.'

It was pointless to dissimulate. He was too bitter. 'Yes.'

'I told you she wouldn't have you back.' She resumed packing.

'She says she's going to marry Simon Altringham.' His voice was strained.

Isobel shrugged. 'Why not? He's a very good catch and mad about her. Good luck to her.'

'It seems I played badly.'

'Very badly, my dear.' She picked up two pairs of high-heeled shoes, debating which to pack.

'I'm sorry, Isobel. For everything.'

Finally, she turned to face him. He was astonished at how she'd collected herself since he'd last seen her. Her face was beautiful again, and if it was held together with the make-up she'd painstakingly applied, that was not noticeable in this dim light. Her chin was up and her eyes met his unflinchingly. Her gallantry took his breath away. 'What do you want, Oliver?'

'I want you to stay the night.'

'It's over between us. If nothing else is clear, that is.'

'I know. But I'm leaving tomorrow. Tonight's my last night in England.'

She studied his face. 'You never loved me, did you?'

'I desired you. I still desire you. One more night, Isobel.'

'Will you get on your knees and beg for it?'

'No.' He reached out and unfastened the little gold clip of her suspender. 'But I want it very much.' He caressed the inside of her thigh with his fingertips. 'Did you ever love me?'

She held his gaze steadily. 'Yes. Very much. But you killed it stone dead.'

'Forgive me.' His fingers slipped under the elastic of her gusset, probing her moist flesh. His eyes narrowed with desire. 'I want you.'

She put her hand on his crotch, finding him erect and hard. 'Once more, Oliver. And then never again.'

Wordlessly, he lifted her onto the bed.

❧

Chiara opened her eyes slowly to a white world. She was supine, her head resting on a hard pillow that smelled of bleach. The starched white linen of the bed was pulled up to her chin. The bed itself was like a steel cage, enamelled white, its sides raised. A bottle of clear liquid hung above her, attached to a drip that fed into her arm. She was alone in the small room.

It was morning. She could see a patch of blue sky in the gap between the curtains. Memories of the night surfaced like fish under the frozen surface of a lake, dimly remembered shadows of fear, pain, blood. She tried to interrogate her womb, but there was no feeling there. She no longer felt that she contained a new life. Everything was empty. Tears slid down her cheeks.

The youthful face of a nurse appeared at the door, then vanished. She heard her voice in the corridor: 'Tell Captain Altringham his patient's awake.' The nurse reappeared, holding a steel dish. 'And how are we feeling this morning?' she asked cheerfully, putting a thermometer under Chiara's armpit.

'Is the baby dead?' Chiara whispered.

'You'll have to ask Captain Altringham about that,' she replied, ignoring Chiara's tears. That was answer enough. Chiara's body felt numb, her mind unable to focus. Her thoughts, those fish under the surface of the ice, flitted dimly to and fro without ever coming into focus properly. 'You may as well sleep,' the nurse said, writing her notes. 'He'll be along as soon as he can. Try not to upset yourself.'

She must have slept, because she surfaced again to feel a warm hand on her forehead. She opened her eyes and saw Simon bending over her.

'Simon,' she cried out, reaching up. He took her gently in his arms. 'Did I lose the baby?' she asked.

'No.' He stroked her hair. 'He's still in there. But you've had a bleed, and you're going to have to lie quiet in bed for a couple of days.'

She grasped his hand. 'Are you lying to me?'

Simon's eyes widened in surprise. 'No, darling,' he said. 'I'll never lie to you.'

'Sorry.' She sank back onto the pillow. 'Sorry. I know you won't. Just – my mind's so blurry.'

'That's the scopolamine. Awful stuff, I know, but we need to keep you quiet. We'll taper it off after today.'

'Oliver came to see me.'

'I know. You told me last night.'

'Did I? It's all so confused. I told him about us. He looked exhausted. I felt sorry for him. He just walked out without saying a word. Then the pain started.'

'The bleeding has stopped,' he said. 'It slowed down a few hours ago, while you were out cold, and there's been nothing since. I can't tell you that you're out of danger, though. You'll be in bed for a while, so get used to it.'

'Did it happen because we made love?'

'No. If there had been penetration, perhaps. But what we did couldn't have hurt the baby. An orgasm – or several – won't cause a miscarriage.' He paused. 'I think it was caused by the bomb blast and clambering around on the roof.'

Chiara closed her eyes. 'Oh no. Oh, God.'

'You've had an abruption – a tear between the wall of the uterus and the placenta. If it's very severe, then it can be dangerous for you and the baby. But we're going to manage it as safely as we can, so it can heal. And if I think there's any continuing danger, you may have to have a Caesarean a few weeks early. Let me take a look.' He pulled the bed-clothes away and explored her belly with careful fingertips. 'Any pain?'

'No. I can't feel anything.'

'You're sedated, of course. But your uterus feels normal again. It was hard and swollen last night. I'm monitoring you for pre-eclampsia, though I don't think that's the problem.'

'I feel so guilty. What a fool I've been.'

'It may not have been your fault. It happens spontaneously sometimes. Please don't blame yourself, darling. Whatever has caused it, the answer is bed rest. If there's no more bleeding after a few days, you can be discharged. But you can't go back to your old place, I'm afraid. No more stairs for you from now on. Don't worry about it now. I'll work it all out.'

She clung to him. 'I'm frightened, Simon.'

'Don't be. You're one of the more boring of my cases.' He smiled at her and prepared a syringe. 'I don't like doing this, but it will help you rest.' He inserted the needle into her intravenous line and slowly depressed the plunger. She kept her eyes on his as long as she could while she sank back under the dark surface of the lake.

◌◌

Oliver's departures were always lonely affairs. In the interests of secrecy, he was to travel to Scotland on the night train, and nobody was to see him off at the station – not that there was anybody he wanted there. He equipped himself with a newspaper and boarded the train with a battalion of Highlanders.

Despite having paraded smartly on the platform at King's Cross, the Highlanders, once entrained, swiftly turned their compartments into squalid pits. Packed four a side, they filled the racks with their kitbags and rolls. They took off their boots and jackets, releasing long-imprisoned smells. Sealed in with the blackout shutters as they were, they lit up cigarettes, unwrapped rank packages of food, swigged surreptitiously at bottles of beer they had smuggled on board and fell asleep sprawled across one another, leaving the air thick with smoke and the floor littered with cigarette ends, bits of food, bottles and greasy paper.

They ignored Oliver in his shabby civvies, deliberately unshaven and uncombed, who stared, unseeing, at his newspaper. But the carriage became unbearable to him. He folded the paper and eased himself out, then spent most of the night standing in the darkened

187

corridor, peering out of a lowered window at the dim fields that flickered by, a dark and unseen landscape peopled with unknown and unknowing souls for whom he was fighting.

At times the train rocked swiftly, clattering through the darkness to its destination; at times it slowed so much that it was barely moving, the squeal of metal on metal dying into prolonged silences.

He tried not to think of Chiara and what he had lost and what he was leaving behind, but his thoughts kept returning again and again to her, to Chiara; for he knew now it was not just the child, but her, for whom he was grieving. Chiara, with her ineffable sweetness, whom he had spurned for a mirage.

He looked back on his years with her now as on a lost paradise. She had always been there, waiting for him to return, gentle and loving. The companion of his peaceful hours. She would not be there any longer. He had lost her to a younger, better man, someone who knew the prize he had gained. By the time he returned, she would be Simon's wife, lost to him forever.

Losing Isobel mattered little to him now. The excitement of that had swiftly worn off, and marrying her, with her tantrums and vanities, would have been hellish. At least he'd spared himself that. The final sexual act between them had been violent, almost brutal, a definitive farewell to all the illusions they'd had about each other. He'd rammed into her as though wanting to crush every last fragile thing, and she had clawed him like a lioness.

The only other person he'd seen before he left had been his mother, Cécile. She'd patted his cheek (she seldom kissed him) and said only, 'You're a fool, Oliver.'

She was right. He had been a fool. He had lost the only woman he'd really cared about, wounded her so deeply that she would never return to him.

He felt in his pocket for the little monogrammed flask of Lagavulin. He'd intended it as a last farewell to British soil, but he needed it now. He swigged, draining it in a few swallows, feeling the liquor burn down into his belly. Then he tossed the flask out of the window. It made no sound as it struck the embankment and vanished, but a blast of soot rushed in, stinging his face and eyes. He hauled the window shut and leaned, swaying, against the cold glass.

~

Chiara surfaced again in the afternoon, very drowsy, and was fed some soup and a custard pudding before dropping off again. In the evening she was dimly aware that Sister White was at her bedside, patting her reassuringly. 'Safest pair of hands on the ward,' she kept repeating. She was also aware that Simon came several times, a reassuring presence whose touch was like no other's.

She slept right through the night until the clattering of the day shift woke her at around 5:00 a.m. She was aware of feeling pregnant again. It was the most wonderful feeling in the world. She thanked God for it. Her escapades on the roof had been a hideous folly that she would never repeat. She had finally understood her responsibilities and grown up.

She was feeling better – and very hungry. She had to be content with a cup of orange juice and a bowl of very thin porridge; but she was allowed to sit up and waited eagerly for Simon's arrival. Half an hour after her breakfast, a nurse poked her head through the door. 'You've got a visitor, Miss Redcliffe.'

Chiara put on her brightest smile, but the person who walked into her room was Isobel.

Chiara was shocked at her appearance. Though she was wearing a smart green outfit with a felt hat, she looked somehow reduced, her face gaunt and ashen, her eyes red from crying, with dark shadows beneath them.

'He's gone,' she said by way of greeting.

'Oh, darling,' Chiara said, holding out her hands. 'I'm so sorry.'

'Don't you *dare* feel sorry for me,' Isobel said in a brittle voice. But she allowed Chiara to take her hand briefly. She pulled up a chair and sat beside Chiara. She reached into her bag and took out a pale blue and gold package from Fortnum's. 'I hope you won't throw these out of the window.'

Chiara smiled. 'Not unless Simon orders me to.'

'Ah, yes, I've heard about Simon. So you're going to be a doctor's wife.'

'So it seems.'

Isobel slumped. 'He left England yesterday. Oliver, I mean. Top secret and hush-hush. It's all over between us, of course. I won't bore you with the details. It didn't end easily or cleanly.'

'It's because of the baby.'

'In part.' Isobel smiled without humour. 'Who would have imagined that Oliver would turn broody? Tough old Oliver, all leather and whipcord. Drivelling on about his son and heir. I'd as soon have expected him to take up flower arranging or macramé. Still, it takes people in different ways, doesn't it?' She made a stiff little gesture at Chiara's stomach. 'I did this to you.'

'Did what?'

'The baby. I prayed for you to lose it.'

'Oh, Isobel, no.'

'I did.' Tears were suddenly streaming down Isobel's cheeks. 'I did. Say you forgive me, darling. Please, I beg you. When I heard you were in hospital, I wanted to die. I realised how mad I've been. Clean off my rocker.' She took Chiara's hand in both of hers and pressed her lips to Chiara's knuckles. 'Forgive me, forgive me.'

Feeling wretched for Isobel, Chiara stroked her sister's dark, lustrous hair with her free hand. 'You didn't hurt the baby. It wasn't you. It was me and my stupidity.'

'You don't know how terrible I've been,' Isobel wept. 'I've hated you. I've wished you dead. And all for a bloody man!'

'I've been angry, too,' Chiara said quietly. 'I'm no better than you.'

'Yes you are! Far, far better than I can ever be! I loathe myself for what I've done.' She raised a tear-streaked face to Chiara. 'I loved him so much!'

'So did I. He has the ability to make people love him.'

'He's a heartless bastard.' Isobel wiped her face. 'If I told you half the things he's said to me, you wouldn't believe me. Oh, my bloody mascara. I knew I shouldn't have worn any.' Chiara waited while Isobel got herself under control and repaired her blotched make-up. 'I've been at my worst,' Isobel said at last. 'I've been a bitch at various times of my life, but this was my absolute worst. It must be turning thirty that drove me off my rocker. And, you know, I always persuaded myself I never wanted another child, but when Oliver told me you were pregnant, it destroyed me.'

'I didn't know about what happened to you in Spain. After you lost the baby, I mean.'

'I didn't lose it. I aborted it. Of course I said it was a miscarriage, but it wasn't. I wasn't proud of it. I could have had the baby. I just didn't want to be burdened with it. I think it broke Willoughby's heart. The only decent man I've ever had. I drove him away. And, you see, I was punished for it. God took away my ability to ever have another child.' She squeezed Chiara's hands. 'I'm sorry, so sorry.'

'So am I.'

'Can you forgive me?'

'Yes, but, please, let's all be sane from now on. I've had enough madness.'

'Amen.' They embraced. Chiara felt Isobel trembling in her arms. What a mystery she was, this big sister of hers, so strong and dominant where she herself was so quiet, so ruthless where she was yielding, so passionate where she was gentle. She found herself crying, too, crying for all the lost, wasted years, all the loneliness and the pain. Why did nothing turn out as one expected? Where did the years go? 'We'll be close from now on,' Isobel whispered, echoing her thoughts exactly. 'Life's too bloody short.'

Chiara drew back to dry her eyes. 'Felicity called me the other day. She's in King Farouk's harem, living on lobsters and champagne. And she says she's in love with a war artist.'

'You're joking.'

'I'm not. He's called Orlando Hescott, and he's apparently brilliant. He's also supposed to be sex on two legs.'

'My God. She's out of the frying pan and into the fire.'

'Perhaps not. I have to say, she sounded different.'

'Not her usual gormless self?'

'Well, more grown-up. Confident, in control. Mad as ever, of course – I don't suppose that'll ever change – but very happy.'

'That's all that matters, isn't it? Good for old Fee.'

'I'm sorry about you and Oliver. I really did think you would make a perfect couple.'

Isobel grimaced. 'One day I'll tell you the whole sordid story. You'll be very angry. My vanity, as usual, got the better of me. Oliver knew how to flatter me. I was so blind. But, at the end, he was frightful. He told me he'd have me arrested and locked up for years if I didn't keep my mouth shut. I was terrified.'

'He would never have done that!' Chiara exclaimed.

'I don't know. I think he's capable of doing it. He's utterly single-minded. I don't know why I'm attracted to such bastards. He's every bit as bad as Roberto. Same type. Handsome, ruthless, selfish.' Absent-mindedly, Isobel opened the package from Fortnum & Mason and began eating the coconut macaroons it contained.

'Oliver looked awful that night. I felt rather sorry for him. Did he say where he was going?'

'No. He just gave the impression that it would be dangerous.'

'I think it always is. It's sad that it ended so horribly for you.'

'He fell between two stools. Trying to be off with the new love before he was back on with the old. It'll take me ages to get over this. Every time seems to get worse.' She shrugged tiredly. 'It's all over now. Just have to pick up the pieces. Never mind Oliver. Tell me about this wonderful Simon of yours.'

Chiara smiled. 'He *is* wonderful. He took a liking to me that ghastly weekend at Courtfield Park. He kissed me in the woods, as a matter of fact, and tried to talk me out of Oliver, though I wouldn't listen, of course. Anyway, when we met again on the maternity ward, and he found out I was pregnant, he proposed to me. Just popped the question. I thought he was making fun of me at first. The midwife says he's an angel in human form, and I think she's right.'

'He's very handsome.'

Chiara glowed. 'Do you think so? I do, too. He broke his nose in a horse-riding accident, but I don't mind that. It'll keep other women away. No offence.'

'None taken. I hear he's going to be a brilliant fanny doctor.'

'Obstetrician, darling. Yes, he's brilliant. He loves his work.'

'I couldn't do it,' Isobel said. 'All that screaming, blood and babies. No, thank you. But I'm quite prepared to accept his brilliance. Anyone who wants to marry you shows great intelligence. And I say that sincerely, even though I prayed for your death a few days ago.'

'It's a good thing you're so even-tempered,' Chiara replied.

'I know, isn't it? I didn't pay much attention to Simon at Courtfield Park, I'm afraid. The usual story, too busy blowing my own trumpet and missing the really important things going on under my nose. Anyway, I can't wait to meet him, though I'm sure he thinks I'm an absolute cow, and if he does, he's right.'

'I hope you're going to get on. And I hope his parents accept me. They were rather frosty with me at Courtfield Park.'

'They were absolutely loathsome to *me*. If they snub us, we'll snub them.'

'I'm going to try hard to make them like me.'

'Of course you will. They'll love you.'

'We're going to live in Oxford, among the dreaming spires. Simon says Hitler won't bomb it because he wants an honorary degree when he marches in. It's supposed to be safe. Simon's applying for a hospital there.'

Isobel made a face. 'Must you? How dreadfully provincial. I think I'd rather have the bombs. Oh well, you'll love it, and at least you'll only be an hour from London.' She laid her hand on Chiara's stomach. 'Is the baby really all right?'

'I think so. Simon says the placenta was torn when I was blown up on the roof. I was mad to do it. But somehow I didn't really want to believe I was pregnant. It was all just too much – losing Oliver and then finding I was pregnant. I tried to pretend none of it was happening.'

'I'm sorry I wished a miscarriage on you, darling. As soon as I heard you were in hospital, I offered God my own life in exchange for the baby's.'

'In my experience, God doesn't pay much attention to those sorts of proposal,' Chiara said with the ghost of a smile, 'which is probably just as well, really.'

'Didn't you wish any bad things on me?' Isobel asked curiously. 'No.'

'Not even a disfiguring disease – or falling down the stairs?'

'No, of course not. I love you. I would never wish any harm on you.'

'Loving people never stops me wanting to kill them when they make me angry.'

'We're different.'

'You're unnatural.'

'I suppose so.'

Isobel ate another macaroon. 'After Mummy and Daddy died, I had to be strong for all of us. You and Felicity were two little upstarts, and I had to quell you – you know, to stop you running into the traffic or walking on frozen ponds and so forth. I suppose I became a thug, but what was I to do? I learned to be decisive. I couldn't have the luxury of being kind and sweet and nice to everybody, could I? You'll find that when you're a mother. It can't all be sugarplums. It has to be the back of the hairbrush sometimes.'

'Don't, you're making the backs of my legs all tingly,' Chiara said, remembering Isobel's application of that particular implement of justice.

'Had to be done,' Isobel said through a mouthful of macaroon. 'I had to mould your characters.'

Simon came into the room, looking – Chiara thought – particularly angelic in a white coat, with his stethoscope around his neck. He glanced swiftly from Isobel to Chiara. 'Everything all right?'

'No scratching or biting,' Chiara assured him. 'We've just been having a little talk.'

'Good. *"Sweet is the voice of a sister in the season of sorrow."*'

'Who said that?' Isobel asked.

'I think it was Benjamin Disraeli.'

Chiara beamed with pride at Isobel as if to say, *You see how wonderful he is?* Isobel picked up the Fortnum's packet. 'I'd offer you a macaroon,' she said, 'but Chiara has eaten them all.'

Even this calumny couldn't dim Chiara's happiness. She felt as though the clouds were lifting from her life.

From one squalid world into another. As Oliver clambered down the rungs into the belly of the submarine, the smell hit him – twenty unwashed male bodies, stale food, diesel, cigarette smoke. It was stiflingly hot, too. He had left behind the cold, clean air of the loch.

The crew ignored him as he groped through the constricted, noisy world, ducking under bulkheads, squeezing past obstructions, clutching the oilskin pouch that contained his false papers. Submariners were used to peculiar passengers and asked no questions. They talked to one another in a slang he could not follow, their voices monotonous and low by habit. The metal surfaces were wet with condensation. It was easy to slip, easy to crack a shin or an elbow or a head. As so often before, he had to fight down a rising sense of panic. He'd always detested confined spaces.

He found his bunk, tighter than a coffin, and eased his lanky body into it. He could only fit by drawing himself in like a turtle, his chin digging into his breast, his knees pressed against the bunk above him. The journey would take three or four days, and he would spend most of that time here, in this cramped bunk, seeing nobody and speaking to nobody.

He tried to rid himself of the deep feeling of regret that had been weighing on him for days. It was no way to begin a vital mission, filled with self-reproaches and sorrows. He had to leave those behind.

He wished now he hadn't drunk the last of his whisky on the train. It would have done right at this moment to buck him up. He closed his eyes and tried to sleep, though, of course, he couldn't. Hours passed. Now and then an unintelligible announcement clanged on the Tannoy. He wondered how the crew understood it, for it was meaningless to him. At last the engines started, and he heard the crew bustling as they readied the boat. More time passed, the air growing thicker and hotter. Then, with a succession of lurches, they were in motion.

The boat was oddly quiet now, as though everyone had abandoned it. He realised that the crew were all up on the hull, taking a last look at home, a last cigarette, a last breath of fresh air. Only he was down here, having already said all his goodbyes.

Goodbyes were bad, too. He didn't want to think about them anymore. He tried to ease his cramped body and to focus his thoughts on where he was going. He heard the men's boots thudding down the companionway as they came down from the deck. There was an appreciable increase in pressure as the hatch was sealed. Again, he felt that long, cold, rolling fear, close to panic. There was no way back now. There had never been a way back. The submarine was breasting waves as it met the open sea, surging nauseously.

A voice came through the Tannoy. 'Diving stations. Diving stations.'

Men hurried to find a handhold, calling softly to one another in their own argot. Oliver grasped the edge of his bunk in both hands. The submarine blew ballast, tipped steeply and sank into the depths.

∽

Chiara's wedding was a surprisingly large one. On her side were a number of uncles and aunts, including her redoubtable Aunt Patsy – not a real aunt, but a distant cousin – who had tried to warn her off Oliver Courtfield three years ago. Fortunately, she managed to restrain any I-told-you-so's and was moved to tears, or at least a lace handkerchief, throughout the service. There were also Sir George Harmon, her boss at the Ministry of Information, and at least a dozen others from the office. To her surprise and pleasure, Fleet Street also sent envoys: no less than four editors, a number of sub-editors and several reporters and photographers formed a very jolly group, despite the fact that they'd all suffered Chiara's interference since the beginning of the war. Predictably, they became unruly later in the day.

There was also a contingent of her pre-war, pre-Oliver crowd (mainly young women, since the young men were all away) including Moira Gilligan, who had once also tried to warn her off Oliver during a Christmas dinner at the Savoy. Unlike Aunt Patsy, Moira wore a definite I-told-you-so expression for much of the time.

Sister White also came, looking very pleased with herself, as though she were the sole architect of this happy union. In her veil, she was the only other woman wearing white in the church, and made a stark, uncompromisingly Anglican figure against the multi-coloured blaze of stained glass over the altar (Corpus Christi in Maiden Lane had been chosen out of deference to Chiara's all-but-extinct Catholicism, and the charming parish priest had agreed to share the service with an Anglican vicar to avoid offending any sensibilities of men or angels).

And, of course, there was Isobel, resplendent in non-Utility suit and hat, crying passionately in the front row but looking none the less glamorous for that. Sitting beside her, somewhat surprisingly, was Cécile de Roubillard, Oliver's French mother, sphinx-like and beautiful as always. Chiara hadn't seen her since she and Oliver had separated. Nobody could remember having invited her, and it was possible that she had invited herself.

On Simon's side there was a similarly large group, beginning with his brother Adrian, who was back home on leave and who was his best man; several aunts, uncles and cousins; the Granvilles and their daughter Bryony; and a large contingent of young doctors and nurses, some of whom had hurried so precipitately from work that they still had stethoscopes trailing from their pockets.

There were two shadows. One was that Simon's parents, Sir James and Lady Altringham, did not attend, expressing their clear opposition to the match. Simon declared that he didn't mind and assured her that they would 'come around in time', but Chiara felt that the snub was an evil omen for the future.

The second and more serious absence was that of Felicity. She'd sent a long telegram, full of loving wishes, but she'd been unable to get out of Cairo. With the assistance of Farouk, she'd also sent a sumptuous wedding present through the Turkish Embassy, an ornate and clearly very expensive silver tray. Chiara suspected that Farouk had paid for the tray. Felicity was obviously a favourite. At least, now that Rommel had been decisively defeated, she was no longer in immediate danger.

Despite Felicity's absence, Chiara thought the service was very beautiful. There was even a choir. She managed the kneeling and the standing well, though Simon kept an anxious eye on her throughout. She was just starting to show against her plain white wedding gown, which one of Simon's cousins had lent her, but everyone told her she looked lovely, and a number of photographs appeared in the Press over the next few days to bear that out.

Married, they emerged into Maiden Lane with the choir singing behind them, into a chorus of cheers and a shower of torn rose petals (rice and paper alike being rationed, the wedding party had equipped themselves from the stalls at the nearby Covent Garden). There were several rival photographers on hand, so that took some time, but Chiara could have remained there for hours. She was floating on clouds of happiness. Her beautiful new husband, in his officer's uniform, was if anything even happier than she was, beaming at everyone with brilliant blue eyes while his hand was shaken and his broad back was slapped and his cheeks bedaubed with lipstick.

The reception was held at the Strand Palace, a grand art deco hotel that was now buzzing with American servicemen waiting to be sent abroad. They cheered Chiara wildly as she passed through the lobby to the Winter Garden, which they'd been lucky enough to book for the day. There, under the great domed ceiling, among towering potted palms, the wedding breakfast was served.

As usual with really good hotels, wonders had been worked in the kitchen to provide delicious dishes from the limited range of ingredients available.

'I can't remember a wedding like it since before the war,' Aunt Patsy said, examining the canapés approvingly. 'And real champagne. You've done things in style, young Chiara.'

'Simon arranged it all,' she said happily. 'I didn't do a single thing.'

'They tell me he's a very promising young man,' Patsy said. 'And Oxford's an excellent idea. Are you settled there?'

'Almost, Aunt Patsy. Simon's been accepted at a good hospital, and we've taken a little house a few streets away. It's being set up for us now.'

'Very sensible. I'm truly happy for you, darling.' She cocked a sharp eye at Chiara. 'His parents didn't attend, I notice.'

'No, they didn't. I feel awful about it.'

'They'll come around.'

'That's what Simon says.'

Chiara circulated among the crowd. Everybody wanted a moment with her, to tell her how lovely she was looking and to wish her joy. There was no chance to taste any of the delicious food or to have more than a sip of the champagne – which, in any case, Simon had told her was not good for the baby. The Fleet Street contingent were surprisingly warm, evidently forgiving her freely for having been such a thorn in their side for years. They also ate and drank more than all the other guests combined. Sir George Harmon, from his towering height of six foot six, told her she would be sorely missed at the Ministry, and Bryony Granville, her plump face streaked with tears, told her she was the bride of the season.

At a certain point, she found herself face to face with Oliver's mother, Cécile de Robillard, who was rather severely dressed in a grey and white suit that had evidently been made for her either in Paris before the war or by one of the Parisian dressmakers who had escaped to London. Chiara put out her hand. 'I'm so glad to see you, Cécile. Thank you for coming.'

'*Mes félicitations*,' Cécile said, taking Chiara's fingers in her cool ones. Her green eyes dropped to Chiara's midriff. '*T'attends un bébé?*'

There was little point in denying it. '*Oui.*'

'*Félicitations encore. De combien?*'

There was no point in trying to hide that, either. '*Quatorze semaines.*'

It was hard to tell what Cécile made of that. She asked nothing about the paternity of the baby. Perhaps she already knew that she was the child's grandmother. She released Chiara's fingers. 'I should have been glad to have you as a daughter-in-law,' she said quietly. 'But for my sake, not yours. You will be much happier with Simon Altringham. He loves you very much. You remember what I told you about my son?'

'Yes.' Cécile had told her that Oliver had been betrayed by the two most important women in his life, his mother and his wife, and would never trust another woman. 'I've never forgotten.'

Cécile nodded. 'There are no grapes on thorns, or figs from thistles. Enjoy your day. You are beautiful, and your life will be beautiful. Make a little room for me from time to time.'

The day was indeed a beautiful one, and their wedding night was spent in a suite on the fifth floor of the hotel, with a corner window overlooking the Strand. As the late summer evening closed in, tinting the sky with hues of violet and ochre, a chambermaid tapped at the door and drew the heavy blackout drapes, shutting out the world.

'You won't be disturbed again, Captain and Mrs Altringham,' she said with a demure smile, and went out.

They'd taken a bottle of the champagne up to their suite. Simon popped the cork and poured two glasses. 'You're allowed a glass now, Mrs Altringham,' he said, kissing her. 'Are you tired?'

'No, I'm not at all tired.' She clinked her glass against his. 'I want to make love.'

'My sentiments exactly.' He smiled.

'But properly,' Chiara said. 'Not just hands and mouths.'

He looked at her. 'Are you sure?'

'I've always been sure. And now that we're husband and wife, I'm more sure than ever.'

They undressed. When she lay back on the bed, Simon kissed the smooth mound of her tummy. 'How's he feeling?'

'Do you know, I think he rather liked the champagne.' Her husband laid his cheek on her belly, and she stroked his thick, dark hair. 'You really don't mind about him?'

'Of course not. If it wasn't for him, we wouldn't even be here. I'll always be grateful to him. I owe him my happiness. Can I ask you a question I asked you once before? Do you still care for Oliver?'

She thought for a short while. 'When someone hurts you so terribly, you're stunned at first. You're like someone who's been shot in the heart and doesn't know it yet. Then you start to die. There was a time when seeing Oliver was unbearable to me, and I suppose I still loved him in some way then. Some dying way, I mean.' She looked at Simon's intent face. 'That last night, when he came to me with Margaret's ring, I felt completely calm inside. I could look at him and see what he was. If I felt anything, it was pity for him. I told him I was going to marry you. He seemed so shattered. He stumbled down the stairs, and he looked grey, old, sick. But pity isn't love, Simon. I had stopped loving him. And you must know by now that I love only you. Always and forever.'

They made love gently and slowly. In the past few weeks, Simon had introduced her to a range of pleasures that she'd been completely ignorant of. He was generous and kind and skilled, and she'd never known that her body could feel such delight so naturally and so deeply.

Tonight their lovemaking was completed, not just by the delights that were given and taken out of joy but by the full union of man and woman that had a deeper and more serious purpose. For her it was touching in a way that nothing else had been, and she was in floods of tears. She knew that he was moved in the same way. They lay together, cradled in each other's arms, and dreamed of the life they would build.

∽

The song of the season was Bing Crosby's 'White Christmas', which Isobel detested. One heard the syrupy thing everywhere. It was playing somewhere in the house now, on the radio, at the slow tempo of a sentimental drunk groping down a passage. The house smelled greasy, of fried food. She had been kept waiting half an hour already, and she was a busy woman. She had the Beveridge Report firmly under her arm, annotated by herself, with dozens of markers in various pages.

At length the door opened and Mr Perk came in. He was wearing carpet slippers, balding corduroy trousers and a cardigan that bore what she and her sisters used to call in the nursery a breakfast medal – a splash of egg yolk on the breast. This presumably accounted for the greasy smells and the half-hour wait. Mr Perk was a rotund man, but not a bonhomous one. His little pebble eyes were cool as he shook Isobel's hand. He sat opposite her, leaning forward, his hands on his knees.

'Sorry you've had to wait. I wanted to save you the embarrassment, Miss Redcliffe.'

'What embarrassment?'

'I'm afraid it's bad news. The Selection Committee's going to turn you down. I've asked you round here to spare you having to appear in person.'

'Turn me down!' Isobel was shocked. 'But I was told—'

'Yes, you were. You *were* told. But *you* also told *us* you would be standing as a married woman. As we understand it, that's no longer the case, is it?'

'The wedding has had to be postponed for confidential reasons—'

'Come off it,' Mr Perk said rudely. 'You had a bust-up with him, didn't you? Over your own sister, wasn't it? Now, maybe you were wronged, and maybe you did the wrong. It's not my place to judge. But the Labour Party prides itself on family values, Miss Redcliffe. We can't afford scandals. Especially not where women are concerned.' He took out a pipe and a tobacco pouch.

'There is no scandal!' Isobel said, outraged. 'And my private life is my own affair!'

'No, it ain't,' Mr Perk said, stuffing tobacco into his pipe with a blunt forefinger. 'Not in politics, it ain't. Stepney East may look like a safe seat, but if there's any hint that our candidate isn't as clean as a whistle, you'll see a dozen Independents jump up to contest it. We've had experience of that, and, I can tell you, it doesn't always go our way at the ballot.'

'So much for the rights of women,' Isobel said furiously. 'I thought Labour was the party of emancipation and individual liberty!'

'I think you're mixing us up with the Free Love Society,' Mr Perk said dryly. 'We certainly don't support women stealing their sisters' husbands.'

'Mr Perk!'

'And there's more.' Mr Perk lit up his pipe without asking Isobel's leave. The little parlour swiftly filled with acrid clouds as he puffed vigorously. 'You're a butterfly. A dabbler. You're in this because you fancy the limelight, not because you really have any convictions. We can't use butterflies, Miss Redcliffe. We need workers.'

She tried to keep her temper. 'This is going to be my platform, Mr Perk.' She brandished her copy of the Beveridge Report. 'Have you read it?'

Mr Perk squinted at the cover. 'Anybody can read that who's got two bob to spare,' he said ironically. 'Which is more than I have.'

'A new Britain after the war. A functioning National Health Service, education for all, jobs for all—'

'The answer's no.'

'I want to put my case to the Selection Committee!'

'Who do you think asked me to talk to you?' he said between puffs. 'They don't want you to put your case. They want to save themselves – and you – the embarrassment.'

'This is Fascism!'

'Well, you would know, wouldn't you?' Mr Perk pulled his pipe out of his mouth and pointed the mouthpiece, wet with saliva, at Isobel. 'Your past's going to catch up with you. It is. You've been a British Fascist.'

'I changed my opinions! I was at the Siege of Barcelona during the Spanish Civil War! I was bombed by the Nazis before anyone in Stepney was!'

Mr Perk was unimpressed by these credentials. 'Like I said – a butterfly, flitting from flower to flower.'

'Everyone knows that I recanted—'

'No, they don't. Most voters have got very simple minds, Miss Redcliffe. The Luftwaffe's been blitzing 'em since 1939. Those people have brothers and husbands and fathers fighting abroad. They ain't going to listen to your explanations of how you saw the light and want to send them off to fight for the Communists. No, I'm sorry, but it won't do. Give it up, Miss Redcliffe. Try something else.' He rose to his feet, and Isobel had no option but to follow suit.

205

'This is outrageous,' Isobel said, on the verge of tears. She felt that the ground had been cut away under her feet.

'Well, I'm sorry you see it that way. I realise that certain people might've given you the impression that you had a future as an MP—'

'They most certainly did! Very senior people!'

'As I say, I'm sorry. But we're the poor devils who have to fight the election, and we've already chosen our candidate.'

'What! Already? Behind the scenes?'

'If you like to put it that way.'

'Might I ask who it is?' Isobel demanded, pale and tight-lipped.

'Frank Dobbs. He's a very good young man. Wounded at Dunkirk, comes from a solid Labour family.'

'I've met Mr Dobbs. He's completely undistinguished. Nobody's ever heard of him. I have addressed audiences of thousands in the United States and elsewhere, Mr Perk. My name is known. I've written articles, books. I have a *presence*.'

'You're a toff,' Mr Perk said, unkindly. 'It's in your voice and in your face and in the clothes you wear. You don't look or sound like any Labour politician I've ever met, and I've been an election agent since the end of the last war. No offence, Miss Redcliffe, but the moment you open your mouth in Stepney, you're going to put people's backs up. You go home and write another book.'

'You're making a terrible mistake,' Isobel said, her voice quivering. 'You're going to regret this.'

'I don't think so. We're going to get young Dobbs into Parliament, nice and safe, and that'll be very satisfactory all round for the Party and for the voters of Stepney East.' He surveyed Isobel's clothes with his hard little eyes, the pipe clamped in his teeth. 'I'll tell you what, Miss Redcliffe: you're ahead of your time, and I'm sorry for you, but that's the best I can say for you. Ahead of your time by a long way.'

'And I'll tell *you* what, Mr Perk. I'll stand as an Independent myself. And I'll see your Frank Dobbs off, I can promise you that!'

Mr Perk looked shocked. He took his pipe out of his mouth. 'You wouldn't do that.'

'You just watch me,' Isobel said.

৶৹

She was met in the drawing room by Violet Attlee, wearing an overcoat and an armband, obviously just about to leave the house on some war work.

'Oh, my dear, how unfortunate,' she said, putting on a scarf. 'I'm just about to go out to my mobile canteen.'

'I should have called first. So sorry. I wondered if I could have a word with Mr Attlee?'

Mrs Attlee hesitated. 'He's still in his dressing gown. They sat till very late last night. Wait here. I'll see if he's presentable.'

Isobel studied the books on the shelves while she waited. The Attlees had amassed a large collection of Victorian and twentieth-century political writings. The leather-bound tomes seemed to symbolise everything she herself aspired to – permanence, respectability, a place in history. She was still seething with anger.

Bloody, bloody Oliver. She'd known the moment he'd ditched her that getting into Parliament was going to be a great deal more difficult. If the truth were known, she'd taken him into her bed principally with an eye to what he could do for her political aspirations. There had been very little love in it. Now, four months after their separation, with Oliver still abroad and unheard-from, any heartbreak she'd felt was long over – Isobel was not a great believer in languishing – but the blow he'd dealt her ambitions was bleeding afresh.

Bloody Oliver. And bloody Mr Perk. She'd show them.

Violet Attlee returned. 'He'll see you, but please don't keep him long, dear. You know how busy he is.'

'I promise it'll only be a moment. And thank you!'

She was admitted to the inner sanctum, where the man who was both Deputy Prime Minister and Leader of the Opposition was hunched in an armchair, wearing a very shabby dressing gown and wreathed in pipe smoke. He was dictating to a male secretary who was producing documents from a large box of papers. He looked rather less benign than usual, the sparse hair at the sides of his head ruffled, his face bony and tired. 'What can I do for you, Isobel?'

'It's about Stepney East, Mr Attlee.' She launched into an account of her rebuff from Mr Perk that morning, but, before she had got very far, he waved her to silence rather irritably.

'And what is it you are asking me to do?' he demanded.

'Well, I understood that you supported me as a candidate—'

'*Encouraged*, my dear Isobel, encouraged. That is not the same as *supported*.'

'Isn't it? When you told me to stand for Stepney East—'

Attlee cut her off again. 'I encouraged you to try your hand, since you had expressed an interest in standing for Parliament. But if the Stepney East Selection Committee have already decided on a candidate, then I'm very much afraid that's that.'

'Can't you intervene?'

'Absolutely not.'

'You're the leader of the Labour Party!'

'So I am. But I do not intend to intervene.'

'But a word from you! Just a word! You began your political career in Stepney, Mr Attlee. You were Mayor there in 1919! It would take only a hint from you, and they would change their minds!'

'I am incapable of giving that hint,' he said firmly.

She felt angrier than ever. 'Why did you *encourage* me, as you put it, if you had no intention of *supporting* me?'

He puffed on his pipe, all but obscuring himself in a cloud of tobacco smoke. 'As I understand it, your personal circumstances have changed somewhat.'

'That again! Is a woman only to be valued by whom she's married to?'

'Not at all. Take my own wife as an example. She has had an outstanding career. She's been a pillar of the Red Cross for nearly thirty years. She is doing a great deal to support the community, now, with her mobile canteens, working with the YMCA. Why don't you follow her example? There is much for you to do.'

'I want something more than that!'

Attlee peered at her through the wreaths of smoke. 'More?'

'I have gifts, Mr Attlee! I have talents that go beyond charity work and mobile canteens. I thought you could see that!'

Attlee seemed to be unable to form a response. His secretary cleared his throat meaningfully. 'Deputy Prime Minister, this letter requires your urgent attention.'

'Quite so, quite so.' Clement Attlee waved his pipe at Isobel in what was unmistakably a valedictory manner. 'Must be getting on, my dear. Do drop in again at any time.'

'I told Mr Perk I would stand as an Independent,' Isobel said. 'And I will. Good day, Mr Attlee.'

She swept out of the room, but not fast enough to miss Attlee whispering to his secretary, 'This is what comes of humouring the half-baked.'

❧

She took the bus home. Now that she was a woman of the people, she was made of sterner stuff than riding in taxicabs. After Oliver, she'd taken a flat in Langham Mansions, a red-brick block in Earl's Court, near the Brompton Cemetery. It was close enough to Knightsbridge to walk to her favourite shops, and the area had escaped the worst of the bombing so far. The bus dropped her on the far side of the cemetery, and she had to walk through it to get to Langham Mansions. She didn't mind that at all, since the cemetery itself was rather majestic, with a broad path between the monuments, and the walk took her past the memorial to Emmeline Pankhurst, with whom she felt a spiritual affinity.

It was a cold, somewhat misty December day. As she strode along, her mind was working furiously.

What a ghastly morning. Perk, telling her she was a butterfly and a toff; Attlee calling her half-baked. She'd show them. She would eclipse Frank Dobbs, a nonentity whose only claim to fame was that he'd stopped a German bullet, hardly (in Isobel's eyes) an accomplishment to boast of.

Through her anger, a trickle of excitement was starting to flow. This was fate; this was destiny. She was better off without Oliver. The way he'd treated her at the end had given her a taste of how awful married life with him might be; and it was far nicer to be on good terms with Chiara, now happily settled in Oxford with Simon and in her seventh month of pregnancy. And she was better off without the Labour Party. She was independent. Independent in spirit and independent in politics. Why should she chain herself to the Labour Party? She didn't need them. Mr Perk himself had said that Independent candidates could defeat the Labour entrant if the conditions were right. She would stand on her own terms, with her own platform and her own manifesto. She would talk to the voters face to face, house to house. Would they be able to resist her? Of course they wouldn't. She was everything that Frank Dobbs was not – articulate, worldly-wise, brilliant, female. The men might look askance, but the women would love her. And in this female-weighted constituency, with most of the men away fighting, that would be her ace.

And when she'd won her seat, just let Clement Attlee come creeping back on his knees and beg her to join the Labour Party!

She had reached the central circle of the cemetery, which was a very grand area reminiscent of the Forum of Rome, serene apart from a large red crater where a stray German fifty-kilogram bomb had blown several eminent Victorians out of their graves. A group of elderly gravediggers was working to reinter them, the men's breath condensing in the cold air. She became aware that a very tall and very familiar figure had emerged from the mist ahead and was approaching her from the opposite direction. She stopped short. There was no question that it was William Willoughby.

He was bareheaded despite the cold and wearing an American soldier's leather jacket; and he looked so much as he had when she'd last seen him in Barcelona three years ago that here – in this noble old cemetery, in the fog – she had the unsettling feeling that she was look-ing at a ghost. She put her hand involuntarily on her breast. 'William!'

'Hello, Isobel.'

His familiar voice didn't sound like a visitor from the beyond. She peered at him. Tall, rangy, he appeared to be the same Willoughby from 1939. 'Is it really you?'

By way of answer, he took her in his arms and lifted her off her feet. 'God, I've missed you.'

'Put me down, William!' she demanded indignantly. The gravediggers had stopped their work to stare at them. 'You're crushing my ribs! What on earth are you doing in London?'

His eyes were bright. 'Well, I could say, "Fancy meeting you here," but when you get home you're going to find my note under your door. I was just coming back from your flat. It's taken me a little while to track you down.'

'I thought you were a ghost.'

'Well, *you* look very much alive.' He kissed her on both cheeks, 'Alive and glowing and lovely, as always.'

'I'm an old hag, really,' she said, feeling unaccountably pleased at the compliment. 'You look good, William.' And he did. His eyes, especially, were very fine, grey-blue, with the same level and intelligent gaze that she knew so well. They were almost exactly the same age, so she knew he was thirty now. Six long years, filled with wars, had passed since they'd first met in the south of Spain in 1936. They'd been so young then! It seemed a lifetime ago. He had filled out a little since their last parting in 1939. They had both been half-starved in Barcelona, with the Fascists at the gates of the city; people had eaten cats and dogs to stay alive, and Mussolini's bombers had rained incendiaries nightly. Now he was broad-shouldered and confident again. 'Did you really come to find me?' she demanded. 'What are you doing in England?'

'I've been a war correspondent for the *Herald Tribune* since 1940. I just got back from Libya. That was a hell of a show. Not sure where they'll send me next, but I wanted to see you while I was here.'

'And now you behold me.' She was unaccountably cheered by this meeting with her old lover and rather pleased with herself for having drawn him back to her. She linked her arm through his. 'Come back to the flat with me. I've got some awful stuff they call coffee, but if you put a splash of whisky in it, it's not so bad. We can catch up with each other.'

It was, indeed, cheering to see Willoughby again. Her ego had taken a knock with the Oliver Courtfield debacle, and the fact that Willoughby had sought her out was consoling. Not that they had parted on good terms in 1939. William Willoughby had inspired some of her best behaviour – and some of her worst. One of the best things she'd done was take him in when he'd come back from the Segre, wounded, battle-weary and blinded by shell shock. She had nursed him with a tenderness she hadn't known she possessed. And one of the worst things she had done had been to abort his baby when she'd found that she was pregnant, and to sever relations with him the same day, with a brutality she hadn't known was in her, either.

Willoughby had also inspired some of her most creative impulses. The novel she'd written, *A Country of the Heart*, had really been the story of their affair (with a few adaptations – the abortion had become a miscarriage, and the fictional Isobel had behaved rather better than the real-life one). Without Willoughby, she might never have tried her hand at fiction.

By the time they reached Langham Mansions, she'd told him all about Mr Perk and Clement Attlee, which had led back to a brief account of Oliver (of course, she had left out or cleaned up some of the details).

'So you're determined to stand as an Independent?' he asked as he followed her up the stairs to her flat.

'Come hell or high water,' she replied. 'Do you think I'm a lunatic?'

'No.'

'Liar.'

'I'll see what I can do. Maybe the *Tribune* will take a piece about you. Could give you some good publicity.'

'That would be wonderful.'

'Have you got a manifesto?'

'I will by tonight!'

'Get a copy to me. I'll give it all the air I can. It's a good story. I've done a couple of pieces about how women are taking over from the men. This will be an interesting variation.'

She lit the gas fire in her little sitting room and brewed him the coffee she'd promised. He stood in front of her bookshelves, studying the titles. 'I thought you'd write another novel,' he said. '*Country of the Heart* was brilliant.'

Isobel shrugged. 'It sold quite well, but the publishers aren't exactly chasing me for another. Printing books in wartime is almost impossible with paper shortages. And the critics panned it.'

'They were shocked at all the sex,' he said with a smile. 'You certainly laid our private lives bare.'

She glanced at him quickly. 'You aren't angry about that?'

'No. It was all true, anyway.'

He was the same Willoughby, but she was aware of some indefinable change in his demeanour. 'Oh, I don't know about that. That heroic, tough woman wasn't me. I'm not a heroic person. I made her up. The parts about you are true. You're a true hero, and the book was about you.'

'You have a great deal of heroism in you,' he replied. 'But heroism isn't pretty except in paintings.'

She added a stiff tot of Johnny Walker to each cup. 'I'm sorry about the way it ended,' she said, without looking at him again.

'So am I. I didn't understand you until it was too late, and you were gone by then.'

'I don't know if I ever understood myself. How did you get out of Barcelona?'

'In the back of a truck, with a dozen other *brigadistas*. By then, the French had closed the border, so they drove us up to the Pyrenees, and we crossed on foot.'

'In the middle of winter?'

'It had its moments. And you?'

'I got a boat to Marseilles.'

'I bet that had its moments, too.'

'We're here, now.' She raised her glass. 'Cheers, William.'

'God bless.'

They drank, studying each other as former lovers will do. Their time together had been very passionate in all senses: a lot of desire, a lot of love, a lot of anger. Perhaps, given the circumstances they were under – both exhausted, both under the severe pressure of the final months of the civil war – it had been doomed from the start. 'I want to tell you something,' she said. 'After the abortion,

I got an infection. I can't have any more children. So I paid for what I did.'

Willoughby's expression changed. 'Isobel, I'm so sorry.'

'Anyway, I would have made a ghastly mother,' she said with a short laugh. 'Clearly, God thinks so. He took away my first child when he was only a year old. Perhaps that's why I couldn't face having another. At least I'm going to be an aunt. Chiara is having a baby in a few weeks.'

'Congratulations.' He smiled sadly. 'I remember that you made me look out of the window in Barcelona and asked me if this was a world to bring a child into.'

'It was a dreadful time. The night I realised I was pregnant was the night the air raids began again.'

He nodded. 'I remember.'

'The next morning we found that little girl crying in the street. Remember? Her family had all been killed. I thought there was no hope for any of us. I was in despair, William.'

'I'm sorry about the infection. I guess the guilt is half mine.'

'We were both crazy. I wonder whether we're any better now?'

They glanced at one another. 'I passed through Cairo,' he told her. 'I'd heard Felicity was there, but she wasn't at the Embassy any longer, and I couldn't find her. Someone said she was with King Farouk at his palace in Helwan. But then, at El Alamein, I ran into her beau – a war artist named Orlando Hescott. We were both attached to the Press Corps.'

'Oh, what's he like?'

'Very talented. I watched him sketch.'

'I don't care about his talent! Is he going to behave decently? Did you demand to know what his intentions towards Felicity were?'

Willoughby smiled. 'Something like that. We had a chat about her, at any rate. He seems to care for her. Thinks the world of her, in fact.'

'And so he should.'

'I told him how much she meant to me. He promised he would be good. But I suspect he's a bit of a ladykiller. He's very good-looking, smooth, amusing. I don't think he has any shortage of female company.'

'God help him if he hurts her. I'll find him and kill him.'

Willoughby was amused. 'I think he knows he's under surveillance. But I wouldn't worry about Felicity too much. She's learning to take care of herself pretty well, by all accounts. Very much out of her shell. And I liked Hescott. He looks you in the eye. You learn to judge people quickly in wartime. Not that we had a lot of time to socialise. El Alamein was a bloodbath. The Germans were using eighty-eight-millimetre anti-aircraft guns against our tanks. Almost a whole brigade was lost in one attack. If Montgomery wasn't such a ruthless son of a bitch, Rommel would have steam-rollered over us. But the Afrika Korps is broken now. I've never seen so many dead and wounded men. Twenty-five thousand of the enemy, thirteen thousand of ours. And a sea of burning tanks. Hescott drew; I wrote. He gave me a couple of his sketches, as a matter of fact. They're very vivid. I've got them somewhere.'

Isobel made a face. 'Haven't you had enough of war?'

'Yes. More than enough. I tried to sign up for Uncle Sam. They offered me a desk job. I turned it down – I'd rather see action, even as a reporter. But it's good to be in London. And good to see you.'

'We're still friends, aren't we?' Isobel asked.

'Always,' Willoughby said, raising his drink to her. 'I never wanted to be anything less.'

Isobel met his eyes, feeling something stir in her belly. 'You're a good man, and I'm a bad woman. You should have learned your lesson by now.'

'I should. But I haven't.'

She knew that expression on his face so well, a mixture of desire and frustration. Perhaps, like her, he was remembering those months in Barcelona when they'd made love two or three times a day, insatiable, never tiring of each other. There had been no food, no heat, no safety; but they cared only to fit their bodies together, like pieces of a puzzle that only made sense when it was united. The physical side of their affair had generated an incandescent heat that she'd felt in no other relationship. It was the emotional side that had been the problem. It had always been in the wrong place, at the wrong time. It would be so easy to make a gesture now, the subtlest gesture, that would tell him she wanted him, too. But dared she think that the right time had come at last? Did she want to risk derailing her life all over again?

As if reading and understanding her thoughts, Willoughby rose. 'Thanks for the coffee. I'd better be going. I have a piece to deliver.'

'I want to see you again,' she heard herself say.

'I've got a room at the Adelphi.' He gave her his card. 'The telephone number's on there.'

'Thank you.' She lifted her face to be kissed. His mouth touched her cheek on both sides, but perilously close to her lips. She felt herself flinch.

'It seems we always meet in winter,' he said as he zipped up his leather jacket.

After he'd left, she stood at the window, watching him cross the foggy little square and disappear, wondering what it was about him that was different. Physically, he was little changed. He had always been handsome and well made. His manner was perhaps a little quieter, but that didn't account for the sense she had that he was altered somehow.

Later that night, while working on her manifesto, a phrase came into her mind: *The Shadow Line* – a novel of Conrad's, wasn't it? – the almost imperceptible border between youth and maturity. That was it. The end of youth.

William had crossed the shadow line. And so had she.

❦

Two days later, Isobel declared herself an Independent candidate for the Stepney East constituency by-election. This was, she found out, no straightforward undertaking, but it did bring her a small ripple of attention in the Press.

She was obliged to prove that she was over eighteen years of age, a British subject, and not a member of the aristocracy or of the police forces or the armed forces; was not a civil servant or a judge; that she was not a bankrupt and had not had her estate sequestrated in Scotland.

She also appointed herself her own election agent and was obliged to open her finances to inspection. She submitted a nomination form, together with a deposit of fifty pounds to the returning officer.

In exchange for all this, she earned the right to have her name put on the ballot paper and the right to use certain public rooms for meetings.

The immediate result of this was that three reporters called on her to enquire about her political affiliations. She gave them each a copy of her manifesto and spoke to them very graciously. Explaining her lack of party political credentials, she stated that she intended to stand as an Independent candidate without attachment to the Liberals, Conservatives or the Labour Party, though her ticket was based on social reform and a rapid implementation of the policies proposed in the Beveridge Report after the war.

She also declared that she stood for unity at this time of national emergency and that she believed that the war must be won as a nation, and not by any political party. They would find her a staunch patriot and an indomitable foe of Fascism, a political system that she abhorred, having experienced it first-hand herself.

Yes, she was a single woman, divorced for several years now from her Spanish husband. Yes, she would be her own election officer and would canvass the constituency herself, in person, starting immediately. Yes, wartime by-elections were very quick affairs, and she realised she had no more than a couple of weeks in order to impress the electorate with her policies. She welcomed this swift though democratic process and she looked forward to a fair fight with the only other candidate, F. Dobbs (Labour).

After these statements had been made and taken down, two of the reporters (elderly and dry) immediately went back to their offices, looking thoroughly bored. The third, however, who was a young woman, remained behind.

'Oh, Miss Redcliffe,' she said earnestly, 'I've been waiting for this moment!'

'Have you?' Isobel replied cautiously. She hadn't paid much attention to the reporter so far, being more intent on broadcasting her own opinions, but now she saw that she was a pale and rather dowdy person in her early twenties, whose plain features were enlivened by a pair of glowing, pale-blue eyes. 'That's very kind of you, Miss—'

'Julia Throgmorton,' the reporter said, putting out her hand. 'Somerville College, Oxford.'

'But what moment, exactly, have you been waiting for?'

'The moment when a modern woman stands up boldly to confront the male hegemony of a cynical and deadlocked party political system.'

'Oh,' said Isobel. 'What paper did you say you work for?'

'The *Daily Worker*, Miss Redcliffe. And we're right behind you. My editor wants me to cover your campaign in detail. Go with you while you canvass the electorate – with a photographer at times – and put your story in banner headlines.'

Isobel thought swiftly. The *Daily Worker* was a very left-wing paper and was clearly supporting her because of her well-known opinions on the Anglo-Soviet Pact and the Russian second front. However, the offer of this free publicity was not one she could afford to turn down. 'That's wonderful news, Miss Throgmorton. I'm delighted.'

'Oh, good!' The reporter gazed at Isobel with an expression that was frankly adoring. 'I've read your book – *A Country of the Heart* – and it's a masterpiece!'

'You're very kind. Glad you enjoyed it.'

'It's a paean to sexual freedom and the liberation of women. We'd like to start with a personality piece – about you and your life. Is now a good time?'

'Now is an excellent time,' Isobel said genially, greatly impressed with this young woman's intelligence. 'Do sit down, Miss Throgmorton. Where would you like to begin?'

෭෮

And that, Isobel reflected afterwards, made two very useful contacts in the Press. Her prior contact had been silent for a couple of days, which had piqued her, so she called him on the telephone.

'You've been neglecting me,' she said.

'No, I've been waiting for you,' William replied.

'Well, here I am. I've just done an interview with a reporter from the *Daily Worker*.'

'I hope you were wearing a boiler suit and brandishing a wrench.'

'They seemed to like me just as I was, darling. Anyway, they're going to scoop you if you don't hurry. Don't you want to interview me for the *Tribune*?'

'In depth,' he replied. 'How about I make you dinner at my place?'

'William, you don't know how to boil an egg.'

'I've developed a culinary dimension that you haven't yet seen. Besides, I can get fillet steaks from an immoral USAF commissary sergeant. Beats anything available in London restaurants.'

'You have won my heart, stranger from across the seas. What time do you want me?'

'The steaks and I will be waiting at eight.'

And this very satisfactory development was capped a few minutes later by a call from *Picture Post*, proposing to send a photographer and a reporter to follow her progress as she went canvassing. They agreed on the very next day, a Wednesday. Isobel was delighted. Bugger Clement Attlee, Mr Perk and the Labour Party!

❦

Wanting to bring William an acceptable gift, Isobel went to Fortnum & Mason. Piccadilly was still jolly, even though Eros – and most shop windows – had been boarded up, and banners exhorting one to 'Dig For Victory' and to 'Keep Calm And Carry On' had replaced the familiar advertisements for Gordon's Gin and Max Factor. Fortnum's itself had suffered some bomb damage during an air raid, but business was being conducted with the usual aplomb, an Aladdin's cave behind a wall of sandbags.

She made directly for her 'little man', an aproned Victorian who understood her requirements better than some of the younger (and more scrupulous) staff. She never needed to tell him that she'd used up all her coupons for the month. He tipped his straw hat courteously and indicated his wall of jars and bottles. 'Anything in particular, Miss Redcliffe?'

'Something a little special, Mr Evans. I'm going to dinner with an old friend tonight.'

He tugged his white moustache. 'What about a small 'amper? You can't do better than arrive with a small 'amper, Miss Redcliffe.'

'What can you do for me, Mr Evans?'

'I can do you a Number Four right away. Military gentlemen are very partial to the Number Four.' It was uncanny how Mr Evans knew without being told the nature of Isobel's old friend. 'Game pie, tinned 'am, potted Stilton, quail in foie gras, rich fruit cake, vintage Bollinger and a nice vintage port. Six pound, five shillings and sixpence.'

'That sounds wonderful, thank you.' As he took her money, Isobel went on, 'Are you a political man, Mr Evans?'

'Oh yes, Miss Redcliff. *"I am an intellectual chap,"'* he sang, beating time with his stub of a pencil, '*"and think of things that would astonish you. I often think it's comical – fal, lal, la! – how Nature always does contrive – fal, lal, la! – that every boy and every gal, that's born into the world alive, is either a little Liberal – or else a little Conservative."'*

Isobel laughed. 'Gilbert and Sullivan?'

'*Iolanthe*, Miss Redcliffe.'

'And which are you? Liberal, Labour or Conservative?'

'Sometimes one, Miss Redcliffe,' he said discreetly, writing the receipt, 'and sometimes another. Depends on instructions from the higher authority.'

'God?'

'The wife. Any reason for asking?'

'I'm going to stand for Parliament,' she said. 'As an Independent.'

'No accounting for tastes,' he said. 'You couldn't pay me to go in that mad 'ouse. But *"in the Parliamentary hive,"'* he sang, '*"Liberal or Conservative – Whig or Tory – I don't know – but into Parliament you shall go!"'*

Isobel took Mr Evans's carolling as an excellent omen and tipped him lavishly, going out of the shop in high good spirits, carrying her heavy 'little 'amper'.

William's rooms at the Adelphi were unexpectedly comfortable. Like Isobel herself, he had a corner where there was a desk on which stood a battered typewriter and several untidy stacks of typewritten sheets, but the rest of the apartment was elegant and orderly. The Adelphi itself, an imposing mid-eighteenth-century terrace on the Thames, had suffered somewhat from the bombing, which prompted Isobel to comment, 'Quite like old times,' as William took her coat. 'Freezing, with a chance of air raids.'

He was amused. 'History repeats itself, they say, first as tragedy, then as farce.'

'Farce? I hope you haven't got a wife who's going to burst in during Act Two and start screaming in French.'

'No wife, French or otherwise.'

'Glad to hear it,' she replied. She delivered the 'little 'amper', which William seemed delighted by. She looked around the high-ceilinged rooms as he explored the contents. 'Nice quarters, my dear.'

'The *Tribune* pays handsomely by British standards. But, as you say, there is the possibility of a visit from Hermann Goering during supper. This is a magnificent hamper, Isobel. We had better try the port after supper. Are you hungry?'

'I haven't eaten all day.' She smiled brilliantly at him. 'I hope you weren't stringing me along about the steaks.'

'I wasn't. All that remains is for you to decide: well done or rare?'

'Rare, I think.'

'Ah. I admire your carnivorous streak. How about a martini to start?'

Isobel settled into the chair he indicated and crossed her legs. 'Better and better. When did you get so domesticated?'

'It just grew on me,' he said, measuring alcohol carefully into the shaker.

'Liar. Some woman has taught you all this.'

He smiled slightly and shook the aluminium cylinder. 'Only one, do you think?'

'Don't make me jealous. You won't like the consequences.'

'You can't be jealous, Isobel.' He poured out the martinis. 'You were the one who ended it.'

'Perhaps I made a mistake.'

He met her eyes as he handed her the glass. 'Did you? Well, here's to past mistakes.'

She toasted him silently. The cocktail was perfect, icy cold and pure. 'Did I hurt you very much?' she asked quietly.

'I can't remember,' he said with a slight shrug.

'Don't be false.'

He drank. 'All right. Yes. You hurt me very much.'

'I know I did. I'm sorry.'

'At least you got a book out of it,' he said with light irony.

'You can write. You could have got a book out of it, too.'

'I didn't care to share any of it with anyone else.'

'I told you. I'm a bitch. You should never have got involved with me.'

'Oh, I wouldn't have missed a moment of it,' he said, sitting opposite her, 'the good or the bad.'

'That's the nicest thing anybody's said to me in a long while,' she replied, smiling.

'Tell me about Oliver Courtfield,' he said. 'The true version this time.'

Fortified by the first martini, and then the second, she told him the true version, this time not disguising how badly she had behaved or how stupid she had been. After she'd run out of words, he sat thinking for a while, as though still listening to her in his mind.

'And Chiara's happy with this doctor?' he asked at last.

'Blissful. They're Darby and Joan.'

'And you? Pining?'

'Not any longer. A lucky escape, I should say.'

'I should say so, too.' He rose. 'I think we'd better see about those steaks.'

She had a third martini while he fried the steaks, which were as thick and juicy as he'd promised. He'd laid the tiny table with silver cutlery and a candle. He opened a bottle of burgundy and served the steaks with creamy mashed potato and parsnip. She looked at the plate. 'There *has* been a woman involved. Culinary dimension be damned. Tell me the truth. I told you mine.'

'There have been two. I wasn't happy with either of them.'

'Why not?'

He shrugged. 'Wartime affairs. You know how they are.'

'Not really. Oliver was the only one in three years. After you, I didn't want anyone else. And Oliver wasn't exactly a tender romance. Afterwards, I got a stinking letter from Felicity, accusing me of deliberately taking happiness away from my sisters. Perhaps she's right. She thinks I took you away from her.'

'That's not what happened. I never wanted anyone but you.'

'Do you think about Spain?'

'Of course. Don't you?'

'I do my best to bury my past. But it has a habit of digging itself out again.'

Willoughby put on the voice of an Indian swami. 'Past, present, future, all same-same.'

The steak – the first she'd had in a long time – and the wine made her sleepy. After they'd eaten, they retired to the sofa with the port from Fortnum's and listened to the gramophone. She laid her head on his shoulder, as though time had not passed since Barcelona. He stroked her hair lightly. 'This is lovely,' she murmured. 'Wouldn't it be nice to believe?'

She surfaced again an hour later to find that she was cradled in his arms, with her hair tumbled around her face. She sat up awkwardly. 'Oh, William. I'm so sorry.'

'Don't be.'

She went to the bathroom and straightened her hair in the mirror. Her face looked oddly young, soft-mouthed and soft-eyed. 'I'd better be going,' she said when she rejoined him. 'It's late.'

He watched her getting ready. 'You could spend the night.'

'I don't think that would be wise,' she replied. 'Besides, I'm canvassing in Stepney tomorrow. I'm starting early.' He helped her on with her coat. 'You could come, if you like.'

Willoughby nodded. 'Maybe I will.'

He called her a taxi and saw her into it. She kissed him on the lips. 'That was a beautiful evening, William. Thank you.'

As her cab trundled off into the darkness, she was remembering the feeling of Willoughby's arms around her, the familiar thrill of his body close to hers. And she was wondering whether she should have stayed and what would have happened if she had stayed. Rekindling her affair with Willoughby would be opening a Pandora's box, right at a time when she needed to be concentrated and undistracted. But, then, when had she ever been sensible?

∽

With paper strictly rationed, she'd had only the tiniest handbills printed, little bigger than bus tickets. They read:

VOTE
ISOBEL REDCLIFFE (Independent)
for Stepney East
END WANT, UNEMPLOYMENT & IGNORANCE
Health Care & Education for All

Armed with a few hundred of these, her copy of the Beveridge Report and a pair of stout walking shoes, she set off for Stepney.

She'd arranged to meet the ladies and gentlemen of the Press at St Anne's Church Hall, which was one of the venues she'd been given for public meetings. They were waiting for her there when she arrived – Julia Throgmorton from the *Daily Worker*, together with a teenaged photographer named Charlie, and a somewhat more sleek-looking group of three from *Picture Post*, comprising a young reporter named Frances Spriggs, whose blonde hair hung in a mop over her pretty brown eyes; a photographer; and a driver. William Willoughby was not there.

After a few words to the reporters, Isobel gathered that nobody here had ever covered an election before and that they were all looking to her to see how it was done. There was nothing for it but to muster her courage and march out of the church hall and into battle. The row of houses, built of rough, grimy, yellow brick, was a daunting prospect. She tramped up to the first door and knocked, her audience gathered expectantly on the pavement behind her, notebooks and cameras at the ready.

After a pause, the door opened, revealing a tired-looking woman in a housecoat, holding a baby in the crook of one arm. Isobel took a breath and began her introductions.

∽

By midday, a number of things were starting to become clear to Isobel. One was that she had bitten off much more than she could comfortably chew. Even in a tiny constituency like Stepney East, with fewer than four thousand registered voters, canvassing more than a percentage of the electorate in a couple of weeks was going to be impossible. She would need to make a big impact at her public meetings, since she could personally call on no more than a few hundred households in that time.

Another was that the bombing in this part of London had been savage beyond belief. They would turn a corner to find whole streets gone, nothing left but mounds of rubble. Their progress everywhere was blocked by craters filled with scummy water or the ominous signs warning of unexploded bombs. What had been neighbourhoods were now wastelands where scavengers, including ragged children, hunted for scrap metal and whatever else they could find. Contrary to the government image of cheery, undefeated Cockneys, people here were like wraiths, faces pinched and sharpened, weary bodies wrapped in motley garments against the icy December wind. The skeletons of gas depots, factories and wrecked cranes loomed against the wintry sky. Everywhere was the smell of broken sewers and burned houses.

A third point that became clear to Isobel was that here, in England's green and pleasant land, was deprivation and wretchedness that she had not imagined existed. Even before Goering's bombers had ploughed up their dwellings with high explosives, these people had lived in dire poverty. The cramped houses were crowded with tenants: old people, their lined faces blank with shock; children who had somehow not been evacuated, nor went to school, but worked at heavy tasks in the back alleys and yards, scrubbing laundry on icy washboards; and mothers of all ages, babies in their arms, each wearing the same hungry face. Only the men were missing.

A very few questions revealed the depth of the poverty. They got water at the tap that the fire brigade had installed at the end of the street. Yes, they were all hungry, but the ration went nowhere. Yes, it was safer for the children in the countryside, but, after all they'd been through, splitting the family would be the last, unbearable, heartbreaking blow. Besides, whom could they trust with their children, the only riches of the poor?

'I mightn't see her for ten years,' a mother told Isobel, her hand on her daughter's tangled head. 'She wouldn't even know me again.'

'I wouldn't wish 'em on anyone else,' another mother said with a wry grin, 'they're that naughty. It's all I can do to keep from throttling 'em meself.'

'I've got six,' said a gaunt mother in her twenties, 'and they'd all be split up. They couldn't bear that.'

And so the children had stayed in the East End, where the Blitz was not the only danger: Isobel saw children teetering on chairs to stir boiling soup, children clambering through broken glass and charred wood, children roaming alone in the shattered streets and wading in the bomb craters.

No, they didn't go to school; the school had been bombed, and anyway, extra hands were needed at home.

Yes, there were rats; yes, the children had lice and worse.

Yes, they had seen death in all the forms that modern warfare could design: those burned to cinders; those dismembered; those who seemed alive and unharmed, but whose lungs had been burst within them by the blast, leaving them gently smiling.

Yes, the rents were high, but the East End was where the factories and workshops were, where their labour and lives were. They had to live here. No, the landlords never did any repairs; they only cared about getting the rent on time, and if they didn't, the family was out on the street, no second chances.

Yes, it was hard, very hard.

They listened, frowning, to Isobel's campaign promises, most of them clearly anxious that her arrival spelled yet more trouble and bad luck, more to be taken away, the children gaping at the cameras or peeping from behind their mothers' skirts. They nodded as she brandished the Beveridge Report and promised them that after the war was won, there would be free doctors for them and free teachers for their children. Whether they believed her or not – and they almost certainly didn't – they were too polite to jeer. But Isobel felt more and more wretched until, when they broke off for lunch at a nearby public house, she finally burst into tears and could hardly speak coherently as the two reporters quizzed her.

'Oh, Miss Redcliffe, don't cry,' Julia Throgmorton said anxiously. 'You're doing absolutely wonderfully!'

Isobel just shook her head.

Once they'd downed their beers and eaten their sandwiches, the photographers departed, leaving the three women to continue on their own. Isobel was starting to work out how to do this canvassing lark. The trick was to ask no more than two questions and not to listen to the answers, because you would only start crying. Then you made your speech, got them to promise you their vote, left them a leaflet and moved on to the next house.

She met little hostility, even in households where they told her straight out they were Labour voters and would be casting their ballot for Dobbs. But she was overcome with shame, and after a long and exhausting afternoon, during which she had visited only three streets, she needed to see Willoughby. She telephoned him from Langham Mansions, and within an hour he arrived to find her tearful on her bed, with a raging headache.

'Sorry about today,' he said, 'I had to cover a Press conference at the War Office.'

'It's the children,' she said, as he kicked off his shoes and stretched out beside her. 'They're what really get me. Just like in Barcelona. The same expressions – the way they look at you – I don't know how to describe it.'

'I've seen it,' he said quietly. 'I understand.'

'They're so resigned. So quiet and calm. They accept it all – as though they've done anything to deserve it.' She turned her head on the pillow to face Willoughby, her dark eyes glistening. 'I realised something today. This was just a stunt for me. I started this out of vanity, the way I start everything. Talking about poverty and disadvantage, saying I was a Socialist. But for them, it's real. I made myself a promise, William. If I get into Parliament, I really will help them. I'll do everything I possibly can for them.'

He said nothing but leaned over her and gently kissed her aching forehead.

'You know me better than anybody in the world.' She put her arms around his neck and looked into his eyes. 'Am I rotten to the core?'

'No. You're just honest about your faults. Very few people are. Most are hypocrites who want to pretend they're perfect, even to themselves.'

She sighed. 'You always make me feel better. I don't know if you're good for me or bad for me.'

He brushed her lips with his. 'I try to be good for you.'

'I know you do. You're the only man who's really cared about me. Maybe that's why I ran away from you. I'm not used to it. All the others just used me. But you—'

'Don't you want to be cared for?'

'I don't want to surrender what I am. I want to be in charge all the time. To be cared for – that means I'm not in charge anymore.'

Willoughby studied her with calm, grey-blue eyes. 'It doesn't mean you have to surrender. It just means you can rest now and then. And let me do things for you.'

'What kind of things?' Isobel asked.

For answer, he unfastened the buttons of her blouse and kissed the silken skin over her collarbones. She caressed his crisp hair, closing her eyes. His lovemaking was achingly familiar; a part of her that had lain paralysed now was awakening again. She felt her body respond, each part of her coming to life under his touch and kiss, until his mouth arrived between her thighs, and the greater pleasure began, full and rich, taking away all weariness, all hurt. She didn't want to fight him any longer. She wanted to keep him always close to her, possess him, have dominion over him, never let him go again. How simple it seemed, now. How foolish any other solution!

Would she still feel the same tomorrow? Or would she curse her folly as she'd done so many times before? Right now, she couldn't think how she had done without him for so many years. She had been mad to drive him away. What else was there in life worth clinging to, if not this?

Afterwards, as she lay in his arms, slaked, she whispered, 'If you still love me, tell me now.'

'I love you. You know that.'

She curled up around his strong body. 'Stay with me until tomorrow. I need you.'

'Don't worry,' he promised, 'I'll stay.'

ᑫ

Over the next days, her life fell into a pattern, exhausting and all absorbing. She began canvassing in Stepney East as early as she could each day. The winter days were short, dark and mostly dirty, and she began each morning well before the sun rose murkily over the shattered skyline. Each day, she gathered a bigger retinue, who followed her from house to house through the streets. This group consisted of gangs of children who seemed to regard her as a somewhat solemn entertainment – the odd journalist who showed up to take a look at the lone political lunatic – and a few local people. These last were mainly younger women, who – perhaps persuaded by her Utopian promises based on the Beveridge Report – had decided to spread her gospel. They were by far the most useful group. She gave them leaflets, and they spread through the streets with them, talking to neighbours and often quarrelling with them on doorsteps. 'I'm sick of their bleedin' promises,' she heard one young supporter shout. 'Isobel's the real thing!'

Isobel was so touched by this – though she felt far from the real thing – that she asked the young woman her name. She was called Flossie Fields. She was twenty-two, with a husband in a Singapore prisoner-of-war camp. She hadn't yet found war work, so she was at a loose end, with a lot of nervous energy. When Isobel offered her six pounds a week to act as her assistant, she jumped at the chance. Isobel was grateful for this support.

Now she was able to develop her campaign more professionally. With William Willoughby's help, she had some posters printed, and these were put up by her ragged little army here and there, led by young Flossie. At around the same time, posters for her rival, Frank Dobbs, also started to go up. He was canvassing a few blocks away, she heard. As election contests went, it was a very low-key affair so far. It appeared that the Labour Party were very certain of victory and confident that their candidate would sweep the board. They were not taking I. Redcliffe (Independent) very seriously as a threat. They were probably right, but Isobel was determined to continue the fight to the bitter end.

She was touched by the support that Willoughby gave her. He not only helped with the printing of posters and leaflets, but she would emerge from a house sometimes to find that he had arrived and was waiting in the street with a Thermos of hot coffee and something to eat. Each night she would come home to him and fall into his arms. He was a wonderful, generous lover who could expertly ease her through bliss into a deep sleep. She had little time to devote to him. She promised him – and herself – that when the campaign was over, she would concentrate on him and think about their future together. For now, she was just grateful that he was there.

Christmas was coming. After years of world war, the celebrations were muted. Bing Crosby dreamed languorously of a white Christmas like the ones before, when days were merry and bright; but those days were long gone. There were no Christmas lights strung across Regent Street, as in the gay thirties, no glittering displays to make the children gasp; but decorations went up of a sort, more opulent in the West End, vestigial in the East End. The shops dressed their windows with tinsel, and bunting was hung over the sandbagged entrances to air raid shelters. Many of the decorations had a martial or patriotic air: red, white and blue flags were everywhere, and Isobel saw a Christmas tree decked out with nooses, ready to hang the top Nazis as 'decorations'.

In East End households, hoarded silver paper from cigarette packets and sweets had to do. Pictures of the King, or Winston Churchill, were hung with little Union Jacks. Keeping out the cold was a more pressing concern. Isobel often found herself visiting at the same time as the Salvation Army, who brought food and fuel and whose brass bands played carols in the streets. Frank Dobbs hired a little car with a loudspeaker mounted on the roof and drove around Stepney East for a few hours each afternoon, urging voters to support him in metallic tones that rivalled the Sally Bash. When he ran out of words (he was not a very eloquent young man), he, too, sang 'White Christmas' in a wobbly tenor. Isobel was green with envy at this modern means of mass dissemination, but doing the same would look like copying, as well as cost more than she could afford. Everyone, it seemed, was peddling salvation.

❧

The *Daily Worker* ran two articles on her, both written by Miss Throgmorton, whose adoration for Isobel shone through clearly in every word. And *Picture Post* devoted a whole page to her, describing her as 'a young woman who is thinking of our children's future'. There was a handsome photo of Isobel looking tenderly at two solemn little East End girls and another of her making a speech on someone's doorstep. While the piece didn't actually urge voters to cast their ballots for her, it was excellent publicity.

Least useful of all, but very gratifying nonetheless, a proper article about her, written by William, appeared in the *Herald Tribune*. This touched her very much. There was a small file photo of her and an account of her experiences in Spain to give background to the election story.

'Do you really think I'm "an important contemporary voice", William?' she asked him.

He smiled. 'You are to me.'

'And "an emblem of the political intelligentsia of our time"?'

'Definitely.'

'Sounds like I ought to be in a museum.'

'Yes, a chamber of horrors.'

'You're a beast.' She settled in his lap and put her arms around his neck, looking into his eyes. 'Thank you, darling. You're so kind to me.'

He caressed the curve of her breasts. 'I get my return on investment.'

'Poor boy, not a very substantial one. You hardly see me, and when we make love, everything's for me. There's almost nothing for you. I promise you, when this ridiculous farce is over, I will lavish attention on you. The way I did in Barcelona. Remember?'

He kissed her tenderly. 'Yes,' he said, 'I remember.'

The day of her first public address, which was to take place at the church hall in Underwood Road, was approaching. Needing something noteworthy to wear for it, Isobel went to Geraldo Lopez in the Fulham Road. Lopez, a Spaniard, had trained with Balenciaga in the 1920s in Madrid. Like Balenciaga, he had fled the civil war for Paris and had started his own atelier in the Faubourg Saint-Honoré, with a very distinguished clientele. Unlike Balenciaga, he'd fled again to London a few weeks before the Germans marched in, losing his distinguished clientele but probably saving his life, not being the sort of person the Nazis took to. He had set up shop on a rather shabby little corner, with a dark little window in which could be seen dim mannequins draped in mysterious, half-finished vestments. Within, however, Geraldo's skill with the scissors was evident in a number of beautiful outfits that were being sewn by three elderly seamstresses.

Isobel was received graciously as one of a diminishing number of clients who still required haute couture in these days of austerity.

'What am I supposed to do with these regulations?' Geraldo asked rhetorically, pouring Isobel a tiny cup of very strong black coffee, which was what he drank all day long. 'I must use no more than so much fabric, must charge no more than so many pounds for the work, so many shillings for the cloth, so many pennies for the thread. It's not easy. And then they expect something elegant that looks as though it was made by someone who knows his business. Not all bodies can be gracefully covered by a postage stamp, you understand? Past the age of eighteen . . . and all my ladies are past the age of eighteen.'

Isobel was sympathetic. 'You have the soul of an artist, Geraldo.' Her eye was roving along the rail as she said these words, hoping to find what she wanted.

'That is exactly what Balenciaga used to say to me,' Geraldo exclaimed. ' "*Tu eres demasiado sensible, Geraldo.*" That is what he always said to me. I don't know how he can stand the Nazis. When I think of my beloved Paris, under the boots of those swine—'

'Absolutely ghastly,' Isobel agreed. She had seen something exciting. Swallowing the bitter, scalding mouthful, she darted at the rail and pulled out a dark crimson dress and jacket. 'This is exactly what I'm after!'

Geraldo shook his head. 'Impossible, *cariño*. That is for the Duchess of Argyll.'

'She is only a little smaller than I. It just needs to be let out here – and here!'

'That is not the difficulty. The difficulty is that the Duchess will cut my throat.'

'When did she order it?'

'In November. For Christmas.'

'You can run her up something else.' Isobel pressed the red outfit against herself, studying the effect in the mirror. She would look magnificent in this. 'This is just what I want.'

'So sad. *No puede ser.*'

'How much is she paying you for it?'

'That I cannot reveal,' Geraldo said. But his eye was bright.

'I'll pay you double,' she said briskly.

'To have my throat cut?'

'Name your price.'

'Twenty guineas,' Geraldo said promptly.

'Including the remaining work?'

Geraldo fluttered his hand. 'If you wish to break a butterfly upon a wheel.'

Half an hour later, Isobel emerged into the bustle of the Fulham Road, twenty guineas the poorer but certain of having the outfit she needed for her speeches.

She was very nervous about her public appearances. She had made many public speeches in her life, but somehow this was going to be different – not on her own ground, and with the possibility of a hostile audience. Not that she'd had any trouble so far. East Enders could be very vocal, but she'd never had any abuse from anyone; the worst she'd had to suffer had been a brisk statement that the household was Labour and was not interested in any other party. She prepared her speech carefully, practising on William. But none of her carefully rehearsed phrases sounded convincing to her own ears.

The evening before the address, she received an unexpected visitor at Langham Mansions: Cécile de Robillard, looking very chic in a black dress and a mink wrap, with spectacular pearls at her white throat.

'What do you have to drink?' she said as Isobel let her in. It was her usual greeting.

'Vodka or whisky.'

'Vodka will do. You know how I like it.'

Isobel poured her a large, neat vodka. She hadn't seen Cécile de Robillard since Chiara's wedding. Her relationship with Cécile had never been a particularly warm one. They were probably too much alike to have become friends, but at least they had understood one another well. 'Cheers.'

'*Santé.*' Cécile drank in her usual way, emptying the glass with a grimace. She held out the glass for a refill. '*Mon fils est mort.*'

'What?' Isobel said stupidly.

'Oliver,' Cécile replied with an impatient gesture of the glass. 'Oliver is dead.'

Isobel sat down heavily with the vodka bottle still in her hand. 'Oh, my God.'

Cécile took the bottle from her and poured herself a second drink. 'Perhaps you will tell Chiara.'

Isobel felt numb. 'How? Where?'

'He was captured by the Germans. They shot him as a spy.' She drained the second glass. 'MI5 will not make a public announcement. It is only for next of kin. Tell your sister after the birth. I don't want to upset her now.'

'She'd prefer to be told right away,' Isobel said heavily. She looked at Cécile. There was no sign of grief on her face or in her demeanour except perhaps for the way she gulped the vodka, and even that was the way she always drank, as though taking medicine. 'I'm very sorry, Cécile.'

'For what?' Cécile asked brusquely. 'You didn't fire the bullets.'

'I mean that I'm sorry for your loss.'

'I lost him forty years ago,' Cécile replied. 'We have lived separate lives, and now we die separate deaths. *C'est tout dire.* What more do you want me to say?'

Isobel drank her own vodka, trying to shake off the feeling of unreality that had cloaked her. 'He had a premonition. That's why he was so consumed by the thought of Chiara's child.'

'Perhaps. But you were his last. So I tell you first, as honorary widow.' There was an ironic gleam in Cécile's emerald eyes for a moment. Isobel could only marvel at her toughness – or perhaps her skill at masking her real emotions.

'Did they give you any details about how it happened?'

'Not many. He landed on the German coast. Some mission of importance. He had been to Germany several times before. But this time, something went wrong. He was arrested by the Gestapo. You know what the Nazis are.'

'Yes,' Isobel said in a quiet voice, 'I know what the Nazis are.'

'He told them nothing. That's why they shot him. If he had talked, they would have spared his life. My son did not lack courage.'

'Nor do you,' Isobel said.

'I? I am simply truthful.' She studied Isobel, who was still sitting, stunned, in an armchair. 'Give your sister my best wishes. I preferred her to you.'

'Thank you for that,' Isobel said bitterly.

'You were too much like him. Heartless and ambitious. Like him, you do not know how to break, how to yield.'

'Oh, I broke, all right. Oliver was the cruellest man I've ever known. He destroyed our family.'

Cécile dismissed that with a gesture. 'Then why complain? Your marriage would have been very unhappy.'

'I suppose you mean that as a consolation.'

'In my experience, all marriages are unhappy. If the woman has a brain, that is. Dispense with the woman's brain, and *voilà* – a happy marriage may be made.'

'It's up to us to make our marriages happy or unhappy, Cécile.'

'Have you experienced a happy marriage?'

'Not so far. But I live in hope.'

'A second marriage is the triumph of hope over experience.'

'I don't think you can have been a very good wife – or a very good mother,' Isobel said, angry with this marble-fronted woman, with her terrible pronouncements.

Cécile gave a sudden harsh, dry sob, and buried her face in her hands. Isobel jumped up remorsefully and tried to put her arms around the older woman, but Cécile pushed her away. She cried violently for a while as Isobel helplessly watched. Then she hurried to the bathroom. When she returned, her face was mask-like, her make-up repaired, though her eyes were swollen and red. 'I must go. Angus is waiting in the car. We're going to the Albert Hall. Something modern. British. Not my taste. I like the Germans, but they are out of fashion, *n'est-ce pas?*'

'I suppose they are.'

'The Germans shot my son, so I should hate them.' She pulled her wrap around her shoulders. 'But I don't. I find it difficult to hate anybody. The only thing I find more difficult is to love anybody. That is something of a mystery, is it not?'

After Cécile had left, Isobel was also able at last to cry. She was surprised at her own grief. She and Oliver had parted on such bitter terms. She thought of their relationship now as a catastrophic mistake. Perhaps it was only the shock that was making her weep like this. He was gone, finally and irrevocably. When her fit of crying had eased, she sat thinking about Oliver. His death was the final awful page in an awful story. It would be hypocritical to pretend that Cécile was wrong and that they would have had a happy marriage. Each of them had come to the relationship with selfish desires.

She picked up the telephone and called William to tell him the news.

'I'm very sorry,' he said. 'You must be in a state of shock.'

'*She* shocks me. She's so cold, William. I looked at her and wondered if that would be me in a few years. It frightens me. I don't want to end up like Cécile.'

'You won't.'

'She told me I was ruthless and ambitious.'

'You know that you are both. But you also have a heart.'

'Have I? Sometimes I think I'm like the Tin Woodman in *The Wizard of Oz*, always looking for one.'

'I can tell from your voice that you've been crying your eyes out,' William said gently, 'so you must have one, mustn't you? Try to sleep, my darling. You have a big day tomorrow.'

'I'll work on my speech. Thank you, William.'

'*De nada.*'

After she'd put the phone down there were some more tears. She was still trying to find an adequate response to Oliver's death, some glimmer of self-knowledge that would help her make sense of it.

She and Oliver had been similar in some ways. Cécile had been right about that. But that was the worst of both of them, that merciless ambition. Should she reproach herself for having it? Both Roberto Albarán, her ex-husband, and Oliver Courtfield had been achievers of that sort. If a man had it, people said he was an achiever. In a woman, it was ugly. That wasn't fair. But women were supposed to be better than men, good mothers and good wives, or else they were like Cécile de Roubillard, monsters.

What she needed, Isobel decided, was a better man in her life. And now she had one. William Willoughby had stuck with her through thick and thin. Did she realise just how lucky she was? She had been a fool to lose him. From now on, she would grapple him to her heart with hoops of steel. She reached for the telephone and called him again.

'Did I wake you?' she asked.

'No. I'm working on a story. Are you okay?'

'Yes. I just wanted to tell you something.'

'What?'

'I love you.'

He was silent for a long time. At last he said, 'You've never said those words to me before.'

'I know. I'm saying them now. Do you want me to say them again?'

'No. Once was enough. But I wish you were here.'

'So do I. Maybe it's just as well I'm not. My face is blotchy and my eyes look like oysters, complete with Tabasco.'

'Very appetising. I love you, too, Isobel. I always will.'

After she'd said goodnight to William, she realised that she had joined that group of people who had Lost Someone in the War. Oliver was the first. She prayed he would be the last, too.

She decided not to tell Chiara the news on the phone, but to go down to Oxford and see her in person. In the meantime, there was her speech to prepare.

༺ၜ༻

William drove her to Stepney in his car the next morning. She was silent on the way, feeling weary. She'd slept little, partly because of Oliver, partly because she was worrying about the speech today. William was sympathetic but wise enough to avoid too many questions.

There was a much larger crowd at St Anne's than she had anticipated. The hall was already packed, and there were throngs at the door and even at the windows. The word had clearly been spread. She went in the back way, surprised to find herself trembling with nerves. From the dressing room, she peered through a little window into the hall. The audience was already restive, with shouts and catcalls echoing around the brick walls.

'This could be a rough ride,' William said quietly. 'If it gets too boisterous, come off the stage, okay? I'll be right here.'

'It'll be fine,' she said, trying to smile bravely. She leafed through her notes, her hands unsteady. 'I don't know if I should say all this – or just talk off the cuff.'

'Say what you want to say quickly,' William advised. 'Get it said in the first two sentences.'

Miss Throgmorton appeared. 'Just to wish you luck, Miss Redcliffe! If you hear someone shouting, "Hear, hear," it will be me.'

'And me,' added Flossie Fields. Her hoarse voice had become the leitmotif of Isobel's campaign. She was a tall, raw-boned young woman, unafraid of expressing her opinions. Isobel was glad to have her combative presence in the hall.

The churchwarden came into the dressing room, looking anxious. 'Miss Redcliffe? I think we should begin as soon as possible. The hall cannot take any more people – and I fear they're growing impatient.'

Indeed, slow clapping had begun. Squeezing William's hand one last time, she took a deep breath and walked up onto the stage.

She was greeted with a roar from the audience. At first she couldn't make out whether the reception was hostile or friendly. Everybody seemed to be shouting at once. Some people were standing up and waving their arms. At the back of the hall, she saw two large and stolid policemen, which gave her some reassurance. She lifted her hand. Somewhat to her surprise, silence fell over the hall. She had her typed speech in one hand, but decided to begin extempore.

'Electors of Stepney East,' she began, 'I stand before you today to ask you for your votes. Now, I realise that most of you do not know me—'

'We know you well enough,' a male voice shouted from the front row.

243

Taken aback, Isobel tried to identify the heckler but couldn't. 'Very well, then, if you know me, then you know that I am an ardent supporter of the Beveridge Report. What is the Beveridge Report, you might ask? I will tell you. It is nothing less than a blueprint for a new Britain, a Britain in which the welfare of every man, woman and child will be protected by—'

'Don't you lecture us about welfare!' This time the interruption had come from the middle of the hall. A stout, red-faced man had risen from his chair and was bawling at the top of his lungs. 'You're no bloody Socialist! You're a bloody Fascist, that's what you are!'

'I am not!'

By way of answer, the stout man hurled something at Isobel. Whatever it was, it fell short, but the gesture was met with an uproar. The two policemen moved purposefully forward towards the stout man. He was surprisingly nimble, however, and darted away from them, still shouting. There was a brief and clumsy chase, a few screams as women were jostled, and the policemen managed to capture him with a tussle. Each holding an arm, they marched him out of the hall. His shouts of 'Bloody Fascist' could be heard for some time after he had been dragged out. His departure was greeted with laughter and scattered applause.

Isobel's heart was thumping. 'That man is a liar,' she said in a clear voice. 'I am not a Fascist.' She recalled William's advice to say what she wanted to say briefly and early. 'I want to talk to you today about my vision for a new Britain. I want to nationalise all hospitals. Medical reform, which is as far as the Tories will go, is not enough! I have been in your homes and seen your children sick, your children undernourished, your children abandoned by their government.'

'She's right,' a woman's voice shouted excitedly. 'They've squeezed the life out of us for years!'

'Thank you,' Isobel said. 'When we come to reconstruct—'

A well-dressed woman in middle age rose from the front row. 'Is it not true,' she demanded, 'that you are a personal friend of both Hitler and Mussolini?'

'No. I was—'

'Liar!' several voices shouted.

'What's this, then?' a man shouted. He was brandishing a photograph clipped from a newspaper. 'Look at that! It's her, innit? Shaking hands with Hitler! Both grinning like monkeys!'

The audience was convulsed. The photograph was passed around from hand to hand, causing turbulence as it travelled. There were more shouts of 'Fascist' and 'Liar.'

'Let me explain,' Isobel called out. 'It's no secret that I once supported the Fascist movement.' A silence fell as all the faces turned to her. 'I was seduced by their promises. A lot of people were at the time. Maybe even some of the people who are in this hall today.'

Someone shouted, 'Never!'

'Well, I was. And I've got the guts to admit it. I was in Germany in 1938, and I saw what Fascism really was, with my own eyes. I saw innocent people beaten and murdered in the streets. I changed my mind. I went to Spain to fight for the Republic against Hitler's thugs—'

'I don't care what you changed, Missus.' This came from an old lady, who spoke slowly but with piercing clarity from her seat. A pair of crutches was propped on her knees. 'You supported the men who killed my two sons, and I don't want to hear nothing more from you.'

Isobel was appalled. 'I'm terribly sorry about your sons—'

'I'll tell you what,' the old woman interrupted in the same slow, clear way, 'you got a bloody cheek to come here today and stand up in front of us in your fancy clothes and say your fancy words and tell us how you changed your mind. It was people like you that got us into this war.' She pointed a skinny finger at Isobel. 'You're covered in blood, you are.'

Pandemonium broke loose. Isobel (who was wearing the crimson dress made by Geraldo) tried to shout a refutation, but her voice was being drowned out. Where were the police? They had disappeared with the stout man and were nowhere to be seen. A lot of people had risen to their feet now and were waving their fists. A chant of 'Blackshirt, Blackshirt, Blackshirt' rose up. She caught a glimpse of little Miss Throgmorton standing on her chair, trying to make herself heard above the hubbub.

At great expense, she'd had bunting made to decorate the stage, reading 'Vote Isobel Redcliffe' in large letters. Some rough-looking men were now tearing it down and throwing the red, white and blue stuff everywhere.

She glanced swiftly over her shoulder. William was beckoning her urgently to come off the podium. The situation was slipping out of control, but she was determined not to be shouted down.

'Let me speak,' she called out, raising her arms. 'Listen to me!' Surprisingly, the hubbub died down a little. 'The point of a democracy is that we can all change our minds,' she went on, her voice cracking slightly. 'We realise we've made the wrong choice, and we change our minds. I did. I was wrong – horribly wrong – but I'm on the right track now. I'm asking for your votes because I believe—'

'Oi,' a hoarse voice shouted. 'You, Miss What's-Your-Name! This is the only vote you're going to get in Stepney.'

She saw a burly man fling something at her, and flinched backwards. It sailed through the air, and, though she tried to fend it off, it hit her chest with a squelch. A terrible stench assailed her. The object was a long-dead cat, which had burst open all over her red suit. There was a roar of laughter and a chorus of hideous catcalls. Isobel was too stunned to react. Dimly, she was aware that someone was screaming insults at the cat-thrower. She recognised Flossie Fields's raucous voice. Some of her other supporters had joined in.

A fight had broken out in the aisles, and there was still no sign of the constables. She tried to wipe the disgusting stuff off her clothes. Something else struck her, something hard and heavy that hurt her shoulder. It was a shrivelled turnip. Other missiles were following, rotten fruit and frostbitten vegetables. She was struck twice more and tried to protect her face.

Willoughby jumped onto the stage and, using his big body as a shield between Isobel and the crowd, hustled her off the podium. The fighting had spread through the hall. She wondered in a dazed way who on earth would be foolish enough to fight on her behalf. Two young men appeared from nowhere and attacked Willoughby with a flurry of kicks and punches. Isobel screamed, clawing at their faces with her nails. They disappeared again, leaving Willoughby grunting in pain. He was not distracted, however, from his task of getting her out of the church hall and into the car, which he'd parked outside the back door.

A jeering group of men and women saw them off, shouting 'Fascist!' and 'Bloody Nazi!' after them. She sat rigidly in her seat as Willoughby drove briskly down the road. She was determined not to give way to tears.

'Did they hurt you?' she asked.

He was rubbing his ribs. 'Couple of bruises. You?'

'I'm all right. That was organised.'

'Maybe,' he replied.

'That bastard Perk put them up to this. They didn't let me say a word.'

'I wouldn't call it a total defeat.'

'Wouldn't you?' Isobel retorted bitterly. 'I'm covered in dead cat, in case you hadn't noticed.'

'I had noticed,' he said, with the ghost of a smile. 'But you had a fair bit of support in there. If you hadn't, they would have massacred us.'

She thought back to the chaotic scenes they'd just been through. 'Are you being serious?'

'Perfectly serious. The young mothers were all for you. And there was Miss Throgmorton, of course, and Flossie – she's worth ten. I would say it was about half-pro and half-anti. The antis brought vegetables, which gave them the element of surprise, but they won't have it so easy next time.'

'Oh, William,' she snorted, 'do you really imagine there's going to be a next time?'

'Of course. If you don't chicken out.'

'It's not chickening out to know when you're beaten.'

'You're not beaten yet. You just got a massive publicity boost. The whole borough will be talking about you. When you get back on the streets, every single person in Stepney will know your name. And a lot of people who might not have wanted to listen to you, but don't like to see women being hit with dead cats and rotten turnips, might be prepared to hear you out now.'

She thought in silence for the next mile. 'You're right,' she said finally. 'Thank you, William.'

'My pleasure. Let's not go home just yet,' he said. 'Let's pay your Mr Perk a little visit.'

'That's an excellent idea,' she said grimly. 'I'm going to give him a piece of my mind.'

∾

Upon opening his front door, Mr Perk recoiled, as much from the smell of dead cat as from the expression on Isobel's face.

'Miss Redcliffe!'

'I've just come from my first public meeting, Mr Perk,' she said sharply. 'Your gang of thugs were there in full force. I've come to tell you that you should be ashamed of yourself.'

'Now, hold on. I don't have any gang of thugs.'

'You're a liar.'

'No, Miss Redcliffe, I am not a liar. I warned you this would happen!'

'And you made bloody sure it did, didn't you?'

'That was not my doing!'

'Oh yeah?' William said. 'Who gave them that photo of Isobel with Hitler?'

'Every newspaper has those pictures on file,' Mr Perk said sullenly, but he looked guilty.

'Do we have to discuss this on the doorstep?' William demanded.

Mr Perk stepped back. 'You'd better come in,' he said reluctantly.

She and Willoughby entered the little front parlour. Mr Perk hastily spread a newspaper on a couch for Isobel to sit on.

'Are you going to tell me that wasn't organised?' Isobel demanded. She was in a cold rage.

'Of course it was organised. But not by me.'

'By whom, then?'

Mr Perk gave Isobel and Willoughby a dry look. 'You don't know Stepney very well, do you? Picked the place because there was a by-election, didn't you? Some bigwig in the Party thought it would be a good idea, so you jumped in.'

A woman put her head in through the interior door. 'What's that dreadful smell, Harry?'

'It's Miss Redcliffe. She's been campaigning in Stepney East.'

'Oh, poor lady!' Mrs Perk bustled in sympathetically. 'Let me try to clean that for you, Miss Redcliffe,' she said, and took Isobel's jacket away with her.

'Ever hear of the Battle of Cable Street?' Mr Perk asked. 'No? Where were you in October 1936?'

'We were both in Spain,' Willoughby said, 'trying to get away from Franco.'

'Ah.' Mr Perk began the process of lighting his pipe. 'Well, we had some fun and games here, too. Sir Oswald Mosley and three thousand of his Blackshirts decided to march through the East End. Now, maybe you don't know this, but a lot of people in Stepney are Jewish. I'm a Jew myself, as it happens, though I had bacon for my breakfast. And if they're not Jewish, they're Irish. The police ought to have banned the march, but they liked the Blackshirts better than they liked us. They thought they'd force their way through with truncheons and horses. We fought them with the same things they threw at you today, Miss Redcliffe. And chair legs and half-bricks, too. There was a lot of broken heads and a lot of arrests, but we turned Mosley and his Nazis back. Nobody's forgotten the Battle of Cable Street.' He puffed reflectively. 'Now, here you are. I told you your past was going to catch up with you, didn't I?'

'But what am I to do?' Isobel demanded. 'This is not fair!'

'You have to help her get her point across,' Willoughby said.

'Why? I'm not her election agent. I'm Frank Dobbs's election agent. I can't advise you, Miss Redcliffe.'

'I just want a chance to speak. I'm not a Blackshirt. I'm a Socialist now!'

'You can't catch Socialism,' Mr Perk said ironically. 'It ain't a disease. You're born with it in your bones and blood.'

'I don't believe that,' Isobel retorted. 'Socialism is a question of conscience, not birth. You can be a duke and a Socialist, if you know right from wrong.'

Mrs Perk stuck her head round the door again. 'She's right there, Harry,' she said pointedly.

'I'm buggered if I'm going to help you to run your campaign,' Mr Perk said rudely. 'I've got young Dobbs to get elected.'

'You don't want to see Miss Redcliffe hurt in your constituency, though,' William said quietly, 'do you, Mr Perk? That's no better than Mosleyism. It won't make your candidate look any better. It isn't a pretty story. There's always a backlash with these things.'

'What are you asking for?' Mr Perk asked with narrowed eyes.

'Firstly, you could put the word out on the street that Miss Redcliffe isn't a Blackshirt and doesn't deserve to have dead cats thrown in her face.'

'You're joking, aren't you?'

'Secondly, you must know a few useful types. Local boxing club, maybe. The sort who'll keep order at Miss Redcliffe's meetings.'

'You're asking me to provide a guard of honour for my candidate's rival!'

'You were born and bred in Stepney, weren't you?'

'What of it?'

'This is your territory. Nothing happens here that you don't know about. Be hospitable, Mr Perk. It's no skin off your nose to look out for a lady, even if she is a rival. She's got support. The young women like her. You could think of it as having two irons in the fire – Frank Dobbs *and* Isobel Redcliffe. They're both Socialists, aren't they? Isobel tried to stand for Labour, and your Committee wouldn't have her. If she gets elected, she might join your party. Whichever one gets in, you can't lose.'

Mrs Perk had reappeared in the doorway with Isobel's jacket. She gave her husband a meaningful look. 'No skin off your nose, like he says, Harry. Here's your jacket, Miss Redcliffe. I got the worst of it off, but it'll need dry cleaning.'

'Thank you, Mrs Perk.'

'No need. I like to see a woman in politics.'

Mr Perk was studying Willoughby. 'You fought with the International Brigades, did you, son?'

'Three years.'

'Whereabouts?'

'Cordoba, Jarama, Belchite, the Ebro . . . Pretty much everywhere.'

'Wounded?'

'A couple of times.'

'He nearly died fighting Fascists,' Isobel said sharply. 'I know; I nursed him. And those thugs of yours kicked and punched him while he was trying to protect me. That's not a pretty story, either – and I'll make sure it gets told, if necessary.'

Mr Perk grunted briefly. 'All right, Miss Redcliffe, don't threaten me. I'll see what I can do.'

⁓

William drove her to Oxford to see Chiara the next day, which was a Sunday. The weather was unpredictable, spells of sunshine dazzling off the wet roads in between dark squalls of rain as the clouds scudded overhead. Chiara and Simon had set up house in a little cottage near the hospital where Simon was working. The place was on the edge of a green that was used as a cricket pitch in the summer; it was called Wisteria Cottage and had an arch of wisteria round the gate, though the violet blossoms were on their last legs in this mid-December, a few tattered rags clinging on for dear life.

Isobel had been dreading giving Chiara the news and was glad to find that Simon was home. Chiara, now carrying an impressive tummy, greeted them with joy.

'Oh, darling, how wonderful to see you! Why didn't you tell us you were coming? And this must be William. No, don't shake hands, dearest William. Please kiss me properly.'

There was a coal fire burning in the grate. Wisteria Cottage was warm and spotlessly neat. The Altringhams had made a cosy little nest for themselves and the child who was coming. Chiara's excitement suddenly died down. She took both of Isobel's hands in her own and looked into her face anxiously. 'You've brought bad news, haven't you?'

'Yes, I'm afraid so.'

Chiara's hands gripped hers tightly. 'Felicity?' Chiara whispered.

'No. It's Oliver.'

'Oh, thank God.' She released Isobel's hands and wiped her eyes, which had suddenly spilled tears. 'I'm sorry – I shouldn't have said that. That was wicked. But I'm so glad it wasn't Felicity. Is he dead?'

'Yes, he's dead.'

Chiara buried her face in her hands. Simon Altringham put his arm around his wife's shoulders. 'This could have waited a few weeks,' he said severely to Isobel.

'I'm sorry,' Isobel said. 'I thought she'd prefer to be told.'

'She was right to tell me now,' Chiara said through her tears. 'Don't be angry with her, Simon. I'd much rather know.' She clasped her stomach. 'It won't hurt the baby. When did you find out, Isobel?'

'The day before yesterday. Cécile told me. He was captured by the Germans and shot. There isn't going to be a public announcement of any kind.'

'Poor Cécile,' Chiara said. 'How is she?'

'Like marble. Almost unmoved – at least on the surface. God knows what goes on inside. She sent you her best wishes.'

Chiara nodded and went out of the room without saying anything else. Simon, swallowing his displeasure, set about making a pot of tea. Isobel heard him talking quietly to William in the little kitchen. She felt she'd done the right thing in telling Chiara, but it was a very difficult moment. When Chiara returned, she was red-eyed and wearing a touch of lipstick. 'There,' she said cheerfully. 'Sorry for the waterworks. I'm all right now.'

'You're blooming,' Isobel said. It was true; Chiara was absolutely glowing with her pregnancy. Her cheeks, plumper now, were pink with health. Her skin was soft, her hair thick and lustrous, her breasts fuller. Isobel remembered those changes so well, when she'd been pregnant with her first child, Paul, who died at a year old.

'You'll stay for lunch, of course,' Chiara said. 'Simon doesn't have to be at the hospital until tonight. It's only Spam hash, I'm afraid.'

'Well, we've brought some offerings.' Isobel unpacked the bag she'd brought, which contained a large amount of American steak, supplied by William, and various delicacies illicitly obtained under various counters by Isobel.

'Oh look, real lemon curd from Fortnum's. Remember when you brought me those macaroons? And I threw them out of the window?'

'I'm not likely to forget.'

'Me either. I wept over those macaroons.'

'I think you had other things to weep over,' Isobel said gently. 'You look so well now, darling.'

'I am well,' Chiara replied. 'I absolutely love being pregnant. Funny, because for the first four months I hated it. But things changed. And you look happy, too. He's so handsome,' she whispered, nodding in the direction of the kitchen, where William and Simon were talking. 'Like a film star. I had no idea. Why ever did you let him go?'

'I've been a fool,' Isobel said. 'I'll probably always be a fool.'

The rain had eased off, and the two men announced they were going for a walk, a discreet way of letting the sisters have a private talk. When they'd donned coats and departed, Isobel and Chiara settled down by the fireside together. 'Thank you for coming down to tell me in person,' Chiara said. 'It would have been awful to hear it on the phone.'

'Are you really all right?'

'Yes. I'll probably cry for a day or two. When Simon's at work, of course. I don't want him getting the wrong idea. He's the only man I care about. And what about you? It must have been a shock.'

'Yes, in more than one way. I never felt as deeply about Oliver as you did. But when Cécile told me he was dead, it started a train of thought. About myself and where I was going. It helped me get my ideas straight about William, too. I've realised that he's the best thing that's happened to me, and I'm not going to let him go again.'

'Good. Don't let him go. Don't let happiness go. Hold it tight. You know, I used to live in dread of this every time Oliver went away. I never knew where he was. I never knew if I would ever see him again. Now that it's happened, it's somehow unreal. Like another life. Funny how years of your life can pass by, and it's as though you were just marking time. Am I heartless not to be more distraught? He treated us both so badly. I forgive him, and I'm sorry he's dead. But I can't feel the way I did before about him.'

'No. I know exactly what you mean, darling. I think the same thing.'

'I'm glad.' Chiara laid her hand on the mound of her belly. 'I don't think of the baby as Oliver's. I never did, really. He's mine and Simon's.'

'Yes. He certainly is, now.'

'Do you think they tortured him?' When Isobel didn't answer, Chiara went on, almost to herself, 'I suppose they did. They must have done. That was the world he lived in – getting information by whatever means. You can't be soft and do that.'

'Cécile said they shot him because he wouldn't talk.'

'Poor Oliver. He didn't talk to us very much either, did he?'

'No. He didn't.'

'Oh! Baby's awake!' Chiara lifted her blouse and put Isobel's hand on the warm bulge of her belly. Isobel felt the baby stirring, pushing hard against the walls of Chiara's womb.

'That's a foot, I think,' Isobel said, smiling with delight.

'Yes. He's very obligingly got himself in just the right position. Simon says it should be a very straightforward birth.' She guided Isobel's hand lower. 'There. Can you feel his head?'

'Yes! He's enormous.'

'He's certainly got a good appetite. I'm starving all the time.' As if to prove it, she opened the bottle of lemon curd and began eating it out of the jar with a teaspoon while Isobel pressed her hands to Chiara's belly, thrilled by the baby's stirrings. She was remembering her own first pregnancy vividly. Sensing this, Chiara stopped devouring lemon curd and peered earnestly into her sister's face. 'Does it upset you?'

'No, my dear, not at all. I'm so happy.'

'So am I. I hated hating you. Thank God that's over.'

'Amen. Have you had any more bleeding?'

'An episode a few weeks ago. Simon put me straight onto the ward, and it stopped. I'm fine.'

'Please take care, my dear.'

'I will, I promise. And so you're going to be an MP,' Chiara said, resuming her attack on the lemon curd.

'I doubt it.' She told Chiara about the Battle of St Anne's.

'My God, that's awful,' Chiara exclaimed at the conclusion. 'What if they throw bricks next time?'

'Then I'll retire. I draw the line at bricks.'

'I'm not even sure what a Socialist is,' Chiara said. 'I'm an absolute idiot where politics is concerned.'

'I wasn't much better,' Isobel said. 'I always pretended to be very political, but, you know, in those days I wasn't, not really. I only got interested in the Blackshirts because I liked the uniforms, and I thought Oswald Mosley was very dishy.'

'Really?'

'Well, and then it was fun to be shocking and have everybody wide-eyed with horror. And then along came Roberto and swept me off my feet, and the next thing I knew, I was married to a Spanish Fascist and being introduced to Hitler and Mussolini. I could spout all the rhetoric, but I never understood what any of it meant until I saw them kill an old man on the streets in Berlin. So I joined the other side. But, you know, it's only in the last few weeks that I've really seen how wretched the poor are in Britain. Seeing how those people have to live – and under the bombing, too – made me so angry that I cried tears of rage. I'd really like to do something. But I don't think I'll get the chance.'

'I've always admired you deeply, Isobel.'

'You're sweet to say so, darling, but I'm not an admirable person.' She waved at the cottage, Chiara's tummy, the cosy domesticity. 'None of this came true for me. It was all taken away because I didn't deserve it.'

'Poor Izzy. My poor girl.'

'Don't be sorry for me,' Isobel said with a smile. 'It's been fun. In parts, anyway.'

'I just want to be happy and safe and peaceful for the rest of my life and have two more children.' Chiara screwed the lid back on the lemon curd. 'There, I've eaten half the jar and made myself sick!'

William and Simon returned from their stroll, both damp and tousled from a squall but radiating that indefinable male camaraderie that indicated that they liked one another. William and Chiara, too, had fallen quickly into affectionate familiarity. Isobel was pleased; if the past year had taught her anything, it was that she was not an island. She had done awful things, had wounded a beloved sister and forgotten another, had treated family ties as bonds to be scorned and broken in the desire for personal ambition. From now on, she wanted to hold things together, and a friendship between William and Chiara and Simon would be a very satisfactory development.

❦

In fact, it turned out to be a happy day, despite the seriousness of the errand. The proposed Spam hash, a dish that everybody was growing dreadfully tired of, was replaced with a steak and kidney pie prepared by William Willoughby's own hands. He had also brought along something new to try, a fizzy brown drink called 'Coke', which William claimed Americans drank with their meals, much to the general surprise.

'As a medical man, I pronounce this the most unwholesome concoction ever brewed,' Simon said. 'It will be a huge success.'

They talked about Felicity in Cairo, whose doings were a marvel to them all, and about the war, which was now at the darkest point that any of them could remember since 1939. The prospect of a world subjugated by Hitler was terrible and real. Yet there were signs of a dawn beyond the blackness. Rommel had suffered a major setback in North Africa, and William described what he had witnessed there: the hitherto invincible mechanised might of Germany broken for the first time. In Russia, too, the German war machine had slowed to a crawl, its wheels clogged with Russian blood and mired in the hardening winter.

While they were discussing the war in this way, the ornaments on the Altringhams' mantelpiece started to tremble and rattle. A deep rumble was making itself felt in the air. They all went out of the cottage and looked up. An astounding sight met their eyes: through the ragged gaps in the cloud, a flight of bombers was rolling overhead. Their silver fuselages caught the cold December sunlight above the English rain. The thunder of their engines became deafening. Chiara clasped her womb protectively with both hands, and Isobel put her arms around her. They were not like any British planes Isobel had seen. They were glorious and terrible, craft from some advanced civilisation beyond Earth's knowledge.

'B-29 Superfortresses,' William said. 'They'll be over Germany in a few hours.'

'Well, if that doesn't give us hope, I don't know what will,' Simon said cheerfully.

They watched as the cavalcade roared over their heads, reverberating to the horizon, raking white furrows in the sky. When they had passed, the four of them went back inside the cottage. Despite all the horrors of the past years, Isobel felt a pang of pity for the women and children, ordinary humans like themselves, who would be at the receiving end of that devastating force.

Simon talked about the progress that was being made in obstetrics, which he believed was in part because patients were growing more assertive. 'There are more women working out of the home than ever before. They feel they've got the right to say what they want.'

'I'm jolly well going to tell *you* what I want,' Chiara promised. 'If I ask for scopolamine, I don't want any arguments!'

'You see what I mean,' Simon said dryly.

Isobel came to the happy realisation that she and Chiara were closer than they had ever been. What they had been through had strengthened their love and mutual respect, not weakened it.

As she and William drove back home to London through increasingly heavy rain, Isobel nestled against William's shoulder. 'Do you think we could ever be like that?' she asked. 'Bottling rhubarb jam and calling each other names out of Beatrix Potter?'

'We had our own version of domestic bliss, as I remember.'

'It was rather fiercer, as *I* remember.'

'We could learn to treat each other a little more kindly.'

'We could get married,' she said. She was astonished to hear the words come out of her mouth. William seemed sceptical, too.

'You've had too much parsnip wine,' he replied.

'I have not. I poured it into the aspidistra. It was ghastly.'

'I agree. If we do get married, no parsnip wine.'

And they left it at that.

∽

Isobel resumed canvassing the next day. As William had predicted, there was a lot more interest in her now. Everybody had heard about the meeting. Some commiserated with her, some laughed; but generally, the attitude was sympathetic. They were, at least, prepared to listen.

She was immensely cheered by a telegram that arrived from Egypt. It was from Felicity, and it said simply, 'GOOD LUCK OLD GIRL STOP KNOCK EM DEAD LOVE FELICITY STOP.' It was a sign that Felicity, following Chiara's lead, had decided to forgive her, and she kept it with her as a good luck charm from then on.

Julia Throgmorton, who had been slightly injured in the scuffle, wrote another passionate article in support of Isobel in the *Daily Worker*, and two other papers ran brief stories about her. By comparison, Frank Dobbs was getting less publicity, but he was not putting a foot wrong, either, and it was clear that Isobel had an uphill struggle on her hands. She could hear the dull, flat, metallic voice of his megaphone constantly in the streets, and many households told her straight out that they would vote for him, no matter what.

The date of her next public meeting was drawing closer, and she was very anxious about it. While Mr Perk had said he would see what he could do, he had given no promises that he would help. To face another hostile mob like that, perhaps armed with more than

260

dead cats this time, was a daunting prospect. But since that moment of weakness after St Anne's, when she'd nearly given up, she was determined to see this through.

An idea had occurred to her. During 1941, before Pearl Harbor, she'd toured the United States, giving lectures to raise money for the British war effort. 'I have met Adolf Hitler, and I have looked into his eyes,' her lectures began. They had been very dramatic affairs. American audiences had been riveted. She had raised thousands of dollars that way. Perhaps something similar might work in the East End, rather than a dry recital of the benefits of a national insurance scheme. She discussed the idea with William, who was supportive.

The meeting was to be held in the Caledonian Hall, a barn-like building ominously situated between a burned-out warehouse and the skeleton of a gasometer. Behind it, the mudflats of the Thames stretched, malodorous and black. The sky was so thick with barrage balloons here that it was claustrophobic.

A much larger crowd than before had gathered. There were at least six hundred people already, and the hall was full. She and William were greeted when they arrived by a group of four burly men in their sixties or seventies, radiating menace for all their grey hairs. With their broken noses and scarred eyebrows, they struck alarm into Isobel.

'Harry Perk asked us to keep an eye on you,' their leader said gruffly. 'We checked everybody for fruit an' such as they came in, but I can't say there won't be a rotten cabbage or two that we missed. We'll be in the front row. We won't do nothing unless things get out of 'and – or you tip us the wink. Okay?'

'Thank you,' she said faintly.

The audience, like last time, was already restive, with catcalls and shouts punctuating the general rumble of conversation.

'Are you nervous?' William asked her.

'Terrified,' Isobel said.

There was no point in waiting too long. The sense of tension was rising by the minute. With a squeeze of William's hand, Isobel walked quickly across the stage to the lectern.

Upon seeing her – she was wearing the same red suit as last time – the audience erupted in a roar. There were hisses and boos as well as a few appreciative wolf whistles and a couple of cheers. Isobel waited for the tumult to die down, studying the crowd. People were bundled up against the freezing cold in coats, scarves and hats. There was no heating in the hall, and whether they had come to throw turnips or applaud her, they had come out on a very cold night. Clouds of condensation rose up in the dim light. She could see Miss Throgmorton and some other reporters sitting in the middle of the hall, with cameras and notebooks at the ready, and a figure near the back who looked suspiciously like Harry Perk. She also caught sight of some of her young women, occupying a block near the front, wearing pink rosettes with her name on them, made by Flossie Fields (Flossie had chosen pink as Isobel's campaign colour). And in the front seats, her four minders sat in a stolid row, arms folded, faces like granite.

When there was something approaching quiet, she asked in a conversational tone, 'Anybody brought a dead cat?'

There was a flurry of laughter and a few more catcalls.

She put her hand in her pocket and closed her fingers around Felicity's good luck telegram. She raised her voice. 'I've met Hitler.' The noise died away to an absolute silence. 'I shook his hand,' she went on. 'I looked into his eyes. They're grey. He smiles a lot, and he makes lots of little jokes. You find yourself thinking, "What a nice man, with his funny moustache and the hair hanging in his eye." When he talks to you, he's very polite.' There was not a sound in the hall. 'He's charming, in fact. He wants you to like him. Just like any man with something to sell.' She looked around the sea of faces. 'Oh yes – he's a salesman, just like those fellows who come knocking on your door with a suitcase full of rubbish in one hand and their hat in the other. Smiling little men, and by the time they leave, they've got your last shilling in their pocket, and you've got something you didn't want in the first place.'

She moved away from the lectern. She didn't need her notes – she could do this speech by heart – and with an actress's instinct, she wanted to be seen as a lone red figure on the stage.

'Well, he's sold us this war, hasn't he?' she went on. Every eye was following her. 'We didn't want it, but we've got it all the same. He's left us to pay for it, too. The rich pay with golden guineas; the poor pay with blood. That's the way it's always been. Hasn't it?'

She'd thrown that question at the audience, and several voices shouted in answer, 'Yes!'

'I didn't come here to talk about Hitler – or the war – because I know we're going to smash Hitler and win the war. You know it too – don't you?'

Again, she'd thrown the question at her listeners, and again there were shouts of 'Yes! Yes!' She saw Julia Throgmorton scribbling furiously. Flossie was nodding vigorously. A flashbulb went off, catching her with her hand outstretched.

'So you don't need to hear it from me. What *I* want to talk about is the kind of Britain we're going to have *after* we've won the war. Are we going to go back to business as usual?' She looked around. 'Are they going to rebuild the tenements, so you can go back into them – cold, damp slums, swarming with rats – and work your lives away in them, so you can pay the landlord his rent?'

There were shouts of 'No!'

'Are you going to go back to seeing your children hungry and ragged? See them working before they've learned how to play? See them taken out of school before they've learned how to read, so they can follow you into the factories?'

The audience were spellbound. 'No!' they shouted.

'See them sick – and not have money to pay the doctor? See them cold – and not have coal to warm them? See them despair – and not have hope to offer them?'

'No! Never!'

She lifted her face. 'Or are we going to build a better Britain? A Britain where every family has a decent, clean home; a Britain where every child can finish school and make the most of what life has to offer; a Britain where the sick are treated, whether they be rich or poor, where the old are cared for and where every man and woman has a decent job?'

This time there was a roar of 'Yes!' Isobel caught William's eye at the edge of the stage. They exchanged fleeting smiles. She had the audience in the palm of her hand now.

'You and I can build that Britain. We've got the blueprint already, thanks to the Beveridge Report. We know it can work because the figures have all been added up. But it may not be easy to get this through Parliament. There are a lot of people who don't want to see a new Britain. Smug people, comfortable people. People like Mr Have, who's afraid someone's going to put their fingers in his pocket and give his money to Mr Have-Not. But I tell you, here and now, that unless there is a redistribution of wealth after this war ends, we're going to go back to the same slums, the same misery, the same injustice – and the same wars!'

This brought the house down. Isobel had to wait until the cheering died away before she could continue.

'We also have to contend with the Conservative Party, that great, dead weight on our country's progress. The Tories will tell you that a welfare state runs contrary to our national character. That's because they believe our national character is a mean, selfish, miserly character. The Tories will tell you that if you give a poor family a decent home, they'll turn it into a slum.' She put her fists on her hips. 'What a bloody cheek!' To laughter, she went on, her voice rising, '*We* didn't build the slums! The *rich* built the slums! Shoddy little hovels they could thrust the working man into and suck the lifeblood out of him and send in the bully boys to throw him out onto the street if he got sick or injured and couldn't pay their extortionate rents!'

Again, she had to pause while the audience stamped their feet and applauded.

'We have to make sure the Tories get the message, ladies and gentlemen of Stepney East. The message is that their day is done. The next government is going to be a Socialist government – and if you elect me, you'll be taking the first step to kicking them out!'

She spoke for another hour and a half, interrupted regularly by applause. When she sensed the crowd's attention flagging, she spoke about her time in Germany and what she had seen on the streets of Berlin, and then about the last days of Barcelona. Afterwards, she took questions for another twenty minutes. By the time the crowd began to drift away, not a single dead cat, rotten turnip or insult had been thrown at her. But Felicity's telegram was damp and crumpled from her tightly clutching fingers.

She consented to be interviewed by Miss Throgmorton, who was bright-eyed with excitement, and posed for a few photographs. There was a throng of admirers around her. At the back of them, she caught sight of Mr Perk. He tipped his hat to her, a small gesture, but one that pleased her greatly nonetheless.

'Where the hell did you learn to speak like that?' William asked her when they were finally alone in the car together.

'Listening to Oswald Mosley,' she said without hesitation. 'He's the best speaker I ever heard – and that includes Hitler.'

'Okay. Just don't mention Mosley and Hitler as your mentors.'

'Was I good?' she asked.

'No. You were colossal.' He grinned. 'You're going to be Prime Minister yet.'

❦

On her return to Langham Mansions the next night, after a very cold and wet day in Stepney, Isobel found a card waiting for her at the porter's desk. One Herbert Brabham, Conservative Member of Parliament for Folkestone, had invited her to join him for a drink at the House of Commons at five fifteen the next day.

This raised her eyebrows greatly. 'Do you think I should go?' she asked William.

'Of course.'

'What do you think he wants?'

'To put you in a sack with some scrap iron, I should think,' William replied, 'and drop you in the Thames.'

Despite this dire prediction, Isobel couldn't help but feel her heart beat faster when she arrived at Westminster the next evening. Sandbagged and shuttered as the great Palace was, it was a magnificent sight in the last gleams of dusk. The thought that she might one day walk in here as an MP was thrilling. Parliament was still in session, and the building was crowded. She was led by an usher through the noisy throngs to a little teak-panelled bar upstairs and ensconced in a dark corner to await the pleasure of Herbert Brabham, who had yet to arrive.

Important-looking persons, mostly male and elderly, were rattling their newspapers and consulting silver tankards all around her. With wistful fingers, Isobel stroked the faded green plush of the banquette she sat on; sniffed the musty aroma of beer, whisky and cigars; and absorbed the atmosphere of ancient political power – or so she imagined – that hung in the air along with the stale tobacco.

'My dear Miss Redcliffe, do forgive me. Unpardonable.' Brabham, a spare young man with a cheerful manner, had arrived. He offered her his left hand to shake – his right arm was an empty sleeve, pinned to his jacket. 'Sorry about the flipper – left the other one in France. I know I'm awfully late, had to slip out of the Chamber while the Whip was distracted. What would you like?'

'A vodka and tonic, please,' Isobel said.

'Excellent. Think I'll join you.' He got the drinks from the bar, juggling efficiently with his remaining hand. Watching him move, Isobel realised he had also lost a leg on the same side. But he appeared fit and had nervous energy in abundance. His sharp profile reminded her of some hungry bird digging for worms on a lawn. 'I expect you're wondering why I've asked you here,' he said as he settled down next to her on the banquette.

'Yes.'

'I've been asked to sound you out.' He clinked his glass against hers. 'Good health.'

'Cheers. Who has asked you to sound me out?'

He leaned close to her confidentially. 'There's a group of us on the backbench, forty or fifty at present, who think alike. You could say we're on the progressive wing of the Conservative Party. We call ourselves the Tory Reform Committee. We're very enthusiastic about the Beveridge Report. We're planning to put pressure on the government to enact the recommendations as soon as possible.'

'I see.'

'The Prime Minister's inclined to put it off. But we believe that if Beveridge isn't implemented, we have no chance of winning the next election, after the war.'

'I agree,' Isobel said, somewhat maliciously. 'You're going to be out like a shot.'

Brabham cocked a bright eye at her. 'You're standing as an Independent in the East End. We hear you're creating quite a stir.'

'Well, I've had a dead cat thrown at me.'

'You'll get worse,' he assured her. He lit a cigarette deftly, one-handed, and exhaled smoke through his beaky nose. 'They wouldn't throw anything at you if they didn't think you had a chance of winning. I read a transcript of your speech in the *Daily Worker*.'

She smiled. 'Not your usual reading, I would think.'

'You'd be surprised at what we politicians read. Anyway, it was an excellent speech. You've got the touch.'

'Thank you.'

'If you do get in – as an Independent – we'd like you to join us.'

She was surprised. 'Join the Tories?'

'Join the left wing of the party,' he said. 'You could do a great deal of good.'

'Mr Brabham, I think you've got the wrong idea about me.'

'Have I?'

'If Stepney East elects me, and I were to join the Conservatives, I'd be betraying my constituents utterly. I'd be joining their class enemies.'

'Stepney East is at least a third Conservative.'

'But it's two-thirds Labour.'

'Then why aren't you standing for the Labour Party?'

'I tried. They turned me down in favour of Frank Dobbs.'

'I see. May I ask why?'

Isobel smiled. 'Let's just say I'm a disgrace to any civilised group of people and better off on my own. I'm very flattered by the invitation, Mr Brabham, but the answer's no.'

'Well, Miss Redcliffe, the invitation stands open. It sounds as though you don't owe the Labour Party anything. The Conservative Party needs reformers, and I'd say you'd be an asset. We're a very determined group. We'll vote against the government, if necessary, to get the legislation implemented. We don't see why the Beveridge recommendations should become part of Tory policy.'

'There hasn't been a scream of excitement from your party so far,' Isobel pointed out sarcastically.

'That's why we need people like you – to ginger things up a bit. Do give it some thought. I think we can promise you a very bright future.' He checked his watch. 'I'd better get back for the division. Good of you to come along – and please call me if you want to discuss anything.'

He hobbled off swiftly. Isobel finished her drink and with great reluctance tore herself away from the House.

Discussing the episode in bed with William later, Isobel said, 'They know they're not going to win the next election. After this war's over, nobody will want to go back to the old system – otherwise, all this death and suffering's been for nothing. Brabham thinks the Beveridge Report is their salvation.'

'Were you tempted?' William asked, kissing her breasts.

'Not in the slightest. You know me.' She drew him down to her. 'I like to be on the winning side.'

♋

The call from Brabham had, if nothing else, confirmed that she was making an impact. But campaigning was made difficult by heavy snow from now on. The blankets of white buried some of the ugliness that the bombing and poverty had inflicted on the East End, but the streets soon turned to slush and black ice, making it hard to get around. Isobel pressed on, but nobody wanted to stand on an icy doorstep to listen to speeches, and many would not even open their front doors to her. Even faithful Flossie was chastened, her teeth chattering and her nose blue with the cold.

The vote was due to take place on the Saturday after next, which meant that only ten days of canvassing remained. It was very frustrating.

Unexpectedly, she received a call from Cécile de Robillard.

'Oliver's will is to be opened on Wednesday morning at ten thirty. His lawyer has suggested that you and your sister should attend.'

'He can't possibly have left me anything,' Isobel replied. 'There's no point in our coming. And it's hardly convenient. Chiara's heavily pregnant, and I'm very busy with the by-election.'

'Nevertheless, you might spare an hour of your valuable time,' Cécile said ironically, 'if only as a gesture to one whose bed you shared.'

'Oh, really, Cécile!'

'And it would be a courtesy to me.'

Isobel sighed. 'All right. Do you want me to tell Chiara?'

'I'll take care of that. *A bientôt.*'

It was an unnecessary interruption, but it was at least an opportunity to see Chiara and Simon again. Isobel called Chiara, who had already spoken to Cécile and seemed happy to come up to London. They arranged to have lunch at *Le Café Anglais* in Soho after the reading.

A solicitor's clerk received them at Broderick & Broderick, the lawyer's chambers in Sackville Street, on Wednesday morning. There were just five of them – Chiara and Simon, Isobel and William, and Cécile herself. Cécile, as always, was inscrutable and immaculately turned out, but Chiara seemed to have found the journey to London fatiguing and couldn't find a comfortable position on the hard waiting-room chairs, sighing breathlessly and wincing. Remembering Chiara's fragile womb, Isobel kept an anxious eye on her. The clerk gathered identity documents from each of them and took them to the lawyer.

'This is positively Victorian,' Chiara whispered to Isobel. 'Gathering to read the will – I mean, really!'

'Oliver *was* a Victorian,' Isobel replied. 'He was born while the old Queen was still on the throne.'

After a brief wait, they were ushered into a meeting room, where the senior Mr Broderick was waiting for them. He was an elderly, hairless, pink man who received them courteously and arranged them around a mahogany table, with himself at the head. He had a manila envelope with him.

'This is Oliver Courtfield's last will,' he said when they were all seated. He laid his hand on the envelope. 'I am the executor. I drew this up myself, according to Mr Courtfield's wishes, in his presence, the day before he left these islands for the last time in July of this year. His death has been confirmed to me by the War Office, although it will not be published in any of the casualty lists or, indeed, be announced anywhere outside these chambers. I might add, though I do not wish to tax your patience, that I was Mr Courtfield's friend for many years, and I know that he would wish to be remembered as a man who served his country well. As there will be no other ceremony, perhaps we can remember him now.'

They sat in silence, with heads bowed, each thinking his or her separate thoughts about Oliver. Despite herself, Isobel felt tears steal into her eyes and wondered if they were in Chiara's, too.

After a minute or two, Mr Broderick looked up. 'Thank you all. We can proceed, if you're ready.' He cut the seal on the envelope with a penknife and drew out a document that was only a few pages in length. 'The will is quite straightforward, though much of it is couched in legal terms which may be tedious for the layperson. Oliver wrote a preamble in his own hand, which he intended would explain his intentions to his heirs. I'm going to read it now.'

He put on his spectacles and extracted a sheet of writing paper from the will.

271

'*"I made this will in case I should not return,"*' Mr Broderick read, '*"and it is my intention that my estate be divided as follows: I leave my house and domain at Courtfield Park, together with all its contents, to Chiara Redcliffe, who lost her own home to the German bombs. It is hers to dispose of as she wishes, but I hope that she and her family will choose to live there and make it their home."*'

Chiara gasped in astonishment, her pink cheeks suddenly pale. She grasped her husband's hand tightly. Isobel looked swiftly at Cécile, who seemed unmoved.

'*"To my friend and the son of my friend, Simon Altringham, I leave the sum of ten thousand pounds, to be taken from my estate."*'

Now it was Simon's turn to look startled. His eyes met Chiara's.

'*"To my companion, Isobel Redcliffe, I leave the sum of ten thousand pounds, and I ask her to remember me with kindness."*'

Isobel squeezed William's hand. She'd had no expectation of anything from Oliver, and she felt touched. It was a handsome sum of money, with which she could do much.

'*"To my mother, Cécile de Robillard, I leave the remainder of my estate, including all residual funds, and my villa in the South of France."*'

Mr Broderick laid the letter before them. 'I hope that's all clear,' he said calmly. 'You may like to look at the letter yourselves. With your leave, I'll read the will itself now.'

❧

'Did you know about this?' Isobel demanded of Cécile when they were seated in *Le Café Anglais* together.

'He consulted me that last morning,' Cécile replied. She was, as ever, coolly detached. 'At first it was his intention to leave Courtfield Park to the child. I told him I thought that might cause problems. He agreed. The result was what you have just seen this morning.'

'But didn't you want it?' Chiara asked. 'Courtfield Park, I mean?'

'I told you once, Chiara: to me it was never a place of happiness. It was always a prison. You, on the other hand, will have contentment there. He has left me a considerable sum of money – and when the Germans are driven out of France, I will have a beautiful home there. I agreed with him that the will was a good one.'

'Well, I feel very uncomfortable accepting such a large sum,' Simon said. 'I expected nothing of the sort. I don't feel I deserve it.'

'You will be a rich man in your own right, Simon, but not for a few years. Maintaining Courtfield Park is not a cheap business. You could consider the money as a means of bridging the gap. It is interesting, is it not, that Chiara could not afford to keep Courtfield Park without your money – and that you could not have it without her.' Cécile was studying the menu, apparently more interested in it than in the conversation. 'What a wretched menu, *mon Dieu*. Why have we come here?'

'It's only five shillings,' Chiara said apologetically.

'*Et alors?* None of you are poor people.'

'Well, we were until an hour ago,' Simon said. 'We didn't know we could afford the Ritz when we woke up this morning.'

'I'm the only one here who didn't know Oliver,' William said, 'but I think we should drink to him.'

'Yes, but only with champagne,' Cécile replied. 'He would like that.'

They ordered a bottle of champagne, which cost far more than the meal they ate, and talked of Oliver with kindness for the rest of the meal, which would perhaps have pleased him.

☙

Cécile departed early, giving them a chance to discuss Oliver's will among the four of them.

'I'm taken aback,' Chiara said. 'I don't understand why Oliver did this.'

'I think it's clear,' William said. 'He wanted to make you and Simon his heirs because he saw you as his only family.'

Chiara looked at Simon rather anxiously. 'But we're settled so happily in Oxford. Courtfield Park is twenty miles out into the country. Would we have to live there?'

'It's yours,' Simon replied. 'You can do what you want with it. I have very happy memories of the place – I've known it since I was a boy, and it was where I met you. We do have a very strong bond to the place. And one day it will belong to our child.'

'But it's so big! How would we fill all those rooms?'

'You could turn it into a private clinic,' William said. They all looked at him in surprise. 'You have lots of progressive ideas, Simon. You're ahead of current medical thinking. In a few years, you could have your own maternity hospital there. Run things the way you want.'

'That's not a bad idea,' Simon said thoughtfully.

'It's a wonderful idea,' Chiara gasped. 'William, you're so clever!'

Isobel put her hand on William's arm and smiled at him. 'You *are* rather clever, you know, darling.'

'You two should make it permanent,' Chiara said firmly. 'How long have you known each other? Years. Through thick and thin. It's silly not to.'

'William might think the opposite,' Isobel said wryly. 'Perhaps it would be silly to tie himself to such a troublesome person as I. Redcliffe, Independent.'

'Perhaps it would. But I've always been drawn to hopeless causes,' William said.

'I don't deserve you,' Isobel said. 'I know I don't. I don't deserve any of this.'

But she had never felt happier.

'I think we should order another bottle of champagne,' Simon said.

୧୬

A wonderfully cheering piece of news was announced the next day – the battered remnants of Rommel's Afrika Korps were withdrawing from North Africa. The battle for Egypt was over. A great danger had passed. Some church bells rang in celebration across London. Coincidentally, William noticed an announcement in the papers to the effect that oil paintings of the battle of El Alamein by the war artist Orlando Hescott had arrived in London and would be on display in the National Gallery that week.

'That's Felicity's beau,' he told Isobel. 'We have to go to the exhibition.'

'Oh yes! I'd love to see his paintings,' she replied. 'But when? There's no time!' She was now back canvassing in Stepney, despite the snow that was building up. The last few days of the campaign were proving arduous for Isobel. She was tired after weeks of campaigning; by now, slogging through the battered streets in the snow, repeating her message again and again, was gruelling work. But a chance – or perhaps not so chance – encounter with Mr Perk gave her flagging energies an added boost.

She came out of a dead-end street to find him sauntering through the snow.

'Mr Perk! Fancy meeting you here.'

'I was just passing by.'

'Rather a chilly day for a stroll,' she remarked. There was a minor blizzard blowing.

'How's the canvassing going?' he asked casually.

'Very cold,' she said meaningfully, not wishing to stand talking to Mr Perk in the snowstorm.

'You made a damn good speech at the Caledonian the other day.'

'Thank you.'

'Got one more to come, haven't you?'

'Yes.'

'Back at St Anne's Church Hall?'

'Yes,' she said with a gleam in her eye. The final speech of her campaign was to be at the scene of her rout – and she had a debt to repay there. 'It's going to be a good one.'

'I imagine it will, Miss Redcliffe,' Mr Perk said, stamping his feet to keep them warm. 'I imagine it will, indeed. We've 'ad a bit of a straw poll. You and my candidate are very close. Neck and neck, you might say.'

Isobel looked sharply at the election agent. 'Really?'

'Frank Dobbs is a very good sort of young man, but he's not going to set the Thames on fire, if you get my drift. He's not what you might call a rousing public speaker.'

'If you recall,' Isobel replied acidly, 'I pointed that out to you at the beginning.'

'Perhaps you did,' Mr Perk said, 'perhaps you did. I do what the Committee tells me to do, Miss Redcliffe. I'm an agent, nothing more.'

'Well, I'd better be getting on, if you don't mind.'

'Hold on half a moment.'

Isobel's teeth were starting to chatter. 'What is it?'

'I hear you had an enquiry from the Tory Reform blokes.'

'You do have long ears.'

'That's my job, having long ears. Might I ask what you said to them?'

'I said thank you, but no, thank you.'

Mr Perk nodded, as though he'd expected this answer. 'Still, nice to be fancied, ain't it?'

'I'm standing as an Independent, Mr Perk. If they vote me in, they'll vote me in as an Independent. I wouldn't betray my constituents by joining the Conservative Party. And, just in case you're about to ask, I wouldn't join Labour, either.'

'But you'd be closer to Labour than you would to the Tories.'

'If you say so.'

'We can talk, at least.'

'Of course we can talk.'

'I'm glad to hear that.'

'Anxious I'm going to win, after all?'

'Anything's possible, Miss Redcliffe.' He squinted at her through the whirling snow, his eyes more like brown river pebbles than ever. 'Nasty weather, mind. You'd be better off indoors, toasting your toes by the fire.'

'I have no intention whatsoever of staying indoors and toasting my toes by the fire,' Isobel retorted, though indeed that was a very attractive prospect right now. 'What, and lose the election? No fear. I'm going to keep going to the end.' She handed him one of her pamphlets. 'Have one of these.'

He nodded, putting it in his pocket. 'Mind how you go. See you at the polls.'

He tipped his hat to her and disappeared into the snow.

ॐ

There were now three days to go to polling day. The news that she was neck and neck with Frank Dobbs was thrilling. With a rousing speech at St Anne's, and another few streets visited, she could perhaps pull off the impossible.

'I'm beginning to really believe I can do it,' she told William as they settled into bed together at midnight.

'Didn't you believe before?'

'I don't think I did.' She had brought a bottle of whisky to bed – it helped her relax – and now she took a swig, then passed it to him. 'This is the first one of my stunts that I've really taken to heart. What are you laughing at, you brute?'

'You've been in Berlin with the Nazis and in Barcelona with the Anarchists. Didn't you take any of that seriously?'

'I can't remember now. It was so long ago. *"This life's a dream, an empty show."*'

'What's that?'

'It's a poem that hung in our nursery when we were children. We used to read it together, the three of us. *"This life's a dream, an empty show, But the bright world to which I go, Hath joys substantial and sincere; When shall I wake and find me there?"*'

He passed the whisky back to her. 'All right.'

'All right what?'

'All right, I'll marry you.'

'Now that I've got ten thousand, *now* you want to marry me.'

'Ten thousand be damned. That's not enough.'

'What are you doing it for, then?'

'The sex,' he said, pulling her close.

After they had made love, Isobel lay with her head on his chest, feeling dreamy and happy. 'Are we really going to get married?' she asked. 'Everything is so uncertain, my love.'

'I've lost you twice before,' William said, stroking her hair. 'I never want to lose you again. I love you, Isobel. You're my life. Whatever happens, I want to be able to come home to you. Always and forever.'

'Oliver's money means I've got a dowry,' she said. 'I lost everything in Spain. Roberto got the lot. Now that they've won the war, he sends me nothing.'

'Perhaps it was Oliver's way of apologising to you.'

'You don't mind?'

'Of course not. It's your money.'

'Yours, too, if we marry.'

'No. I don't want it, even if we marry. It's yours, to keep you safe.'

She nestled against him and drifted swiftly into sleep.

◯◯

She was due to deliver her third and final speech at six in the evening. The day was a busy one. She spent all morning knocking on doors in Stepney, with flurries of snow forcing her to take shelter in any protected corner she could find, making everything difficult. She had word from the *News of the World* that a reporter and a photographer would be coming to St Anne's Church Hall to cover the speech and would make a feature of it, to be published on the day of the vote. This would be a magnificent boost! The paper was lurid, but popular in Stepney, and potential voters would find her on their breakfast tables on the nineteenth of the month. Nothing could be better. Faithful Miss Throgmorton of the *Daily Worker* would also be there, of course, and there were rumours that other Fleet Street papers would be present, too.

She was as jumpy as a cat on hot bricks that afternoon, pacing around William with her speech in her hand, trying out phrases on him.

'Keep it natural,' he urged her, 'just like you did at the Caledonian Hall. Be warm. Friendly.'

'What if they throw things again?'

'They won't.'

'Or if that old lady is there, the one who lost her two sons? That would stop me dead, William!'

'You could tell her you also know what it is to lose a son,' William pointed out gently. 'Be sympathetic, but say that it wasn't your fault. There isn't a single person in Britain who hasn't lost someone. It doesn't help to blame each other. We all have to pull together.'

'Brilliant.' Isobel scribbled notes on her already rumpled sheets. 'I want you in the front row, William, not on the side. I want to see you at all times.'

'I'll be right in front of you, darling,' he promised.

'This is the most important speech of my life. If I lose sight of you, I'll panic.'

'You're not going to panic, and you're not going to lose sight of me.' He glanced at his watch. 'We'd better get going. We should be there early.'

She took a deep, shaky breath. 'All right. I'll get my coat.' The telephone was ringing. 'Can you get that, beloved?' She ran to her dressing table and applied lipstick. If only she could get rid of these blue shadows under her eyes! She was starting to look positively haggard. Politics certainly took it out of one. Another few years of this life and she would be white-haired and lined.

William appeared in the doorway. 'It's Simon,' he said, his face grave. 'Chiara's collapsed. Simon's taken her into the hospital. She's calling for you.'

Isobel rose from her chair in horror. 'Has she lost the baby?'

'He's still on the line. Speak to him.'

Isobel ran to the telephone. 'Simon? How is she?'

'Not good,' Simon replied, his voice tense. 'She had a convulsion. It's acute toxaemia. She's weak and in a lot of pain. She may have to have a Caesarean, but it's five weeks early – and she's very delicate right now. She wants you to be with her, Isobel. Please come.'

'I'll call back shortly.' She replaced the receiver and turned to William. 'But my speech!' she said wretchedly. 'What am I to do?'

William stared at her. 'It's your decision, Isobel.'

'The *News of the World* is going to be there! And all the other papers!' She looked at her watch. 'Oh, God. It's too late to cancel now. What if I make the speech and we go down afterwards?'

'You won't finish until around midnight. There won't be any trains. And driving to Oxford at night, with blacked-out headlights, would be crazy. It's much too dangerous. It would be better to go in the morning.'

'That would be too late. She needs me.' Isobel's shoulders sagged as she realised she had no choice. 'I have to go to her.'

William nodded and took her in his arms. 'I'll drive you. Let's go.'

౷

Racing down to Oxford in the last light of the day, Isobel was silent. How many times in her life had this happened to her? Was it her destiny to have everything she wanted snatched away from her at the last moment? She was on the brink of a dazzling success, of transforming her life from that of a dilettante into someone who mattered, someone who did some good in the world. And once again, fate had laughed at her.

It just wasn't fair. How much of her life had been wasted! How much effort, all gone for nothing! She fought back the tears as she thought of St Anne's Church Hall and what might have been.

Reading her thoughts, William said, 'You've done so much, darling. Maybe enough to win.'

'Maybe,' she said tersely. She stared out of the window at the darkening landscape. Wartime roads were terribly dangerous. With the headlamps of all cars shuttered for the blackout, and no streetlamps anywhere, traffic groped blindly along once the sun had set. It was only where cat's eyes had been set into the roads that one could tell where one was going. The endless convoys of trucks and other military vehicles produced added perils.

'It might still be okay. We'll get back as soon as we can.'

'Of course,' she replied. 'Thank you for trying to comfort me, beloved.' But she felt as though a heavy weight had been tied around her heart and was pulling her down.

They arrived at the hospital just at the time she would have been beginning her speech. However, any sense of bitterness evaporated as she entered Chiara's darkened room and saw her sister lying on the bed, so white and sick-looking and with such an expression of misery on her face that Isobel cried out as she ran to her side.

'Oh, darling! What's wrong?'

'Izzy,' Chiara whispered, groping for her hands. 'So glad you came.' She peered into Isobel's face. 'Can't see very well. Awful headache. I'm no good at this pregnancy lark. Might have known I wouldn't be.'

'Of course you're good at it,' Isobel said. She stroked Chiara's forehead. Her sister's face, she saw, was swollen and sweaty. Her hands, too, were puffy. 'Where's Simon?'

'Somewhere close by. He doesn't go far. So kind of you to come down, darling. I'm sure it must have been dreadfully inconvenient.'

'It wasn't at all inconvenient,' Isobel said. 'Tell me what happened.'

'Oh . . . Can't really remember. Just feeling awful. Fainted. Next thing, Simon put me in here. Is that William?'

'Yes,' William said, taking her other hand, 'I'm here.'

'It's wonderful to see you, dearest William. I'm so grateful.'

Simon came into the room, and Isobel turned to him. 'Simon! We've just arrived.'

Simon led her and William away from Chiara's bed. 'Very glad to see you,' he said in a low voice. 'It's acute toxaemia of pregnancy.

Eclampsia. It's a killer. I was watching out for it, but it came on so suddenly I was caught by surprise. I've given her a magnesium injection, but she's not responding well. I always knew she would probably have to have a Caesarean, and I told her that, but it's almost six weeks early – and she's so weak.'

'Isobel?' Chiara's voice came anxiously from the bed. 'Where did you go?'

Isobel hurried back to her. 'I'm here, darling,' she said, smoothing the damp blonde mop away from her sister's brow. 'I'm here.'

'I thought I'd dreamed you.'

'No, you didn't. I'm right here.'

'I was thinking of Waltham. Do you remember, Izzy?'

'Waltham? No, I don't think I do.'

'You must! Where we used to go for holidays, years ago . . . at the seaside.'

'That was Weston-super-Mare, darling, not Waltham.'

'Oh. Silly me.' She tried to say the right name, but seemed to be struggling with the words. 'Weltham . . . Wilson . . .'

'Don't worry about it now.' She kissed Chiara. 'We'll go there when the baby's born. In the summer. Though I think the bathing huts are long gone now. And it's been badly bombed, of course, like everywhere else.'

'Bombed?' Chiara frowned. Her face was beaded with sweat. 'Waltham?'

'Weston. It was in the papers—'

Chiara interrupted her. 'But how terrible! Why?'

'Don't think about it.'

'They didn't tell me – I don't know why – when we used to—'

Isobel tried to soothe her. She knew that Chiara must have heard of the bombing at Weston, where there was now a large RAF station, but she seemed to be confused. As Chiara babbled on, Isobel realised that her words no longer made any sense. She was talking incoherently, mixing up fragments of sentences and meaningless words. 'Simon!' she called.

Simon took her pulse, looking worriedly at his watch. 'I'm going to give her another magnesium shot,' he said. 'Take her blood pressure, please,' he added to the nurse who had come in.

Isobel gripped William's hand, feeling helpless. As Simon and the nurses bustled around, Chiara's bed began to rattle. At first she thought it was an air raid or a low flight of American bombers, but then she realised that Chiara herself was shaking the bed. She was no longer talking. Her head was thrown back, and her arms and legs were quivering spasmodically.

'Doctor Altringham, she's having a seizure,' the nurse said urgently.

'Keep her on the bed.'

Her heart racing, Isobel went to help. Chiara's spasms were growing stronger. The bedclothes had been pulled back. Her puffy hands and feet were twitching. The dome of her belly was being shaken violently to and fro. Not knowing what else to do, Isobel put her hands on the mound and tried to hold it still to protect the precious contents. Under her palms, Chiara's skin was hot and slippery with sweat.

William had gone to Chiara's head and was supporting her, trying to stop her from biting her tongue – she was chewing violently, and there was already a streak of blood on her lips.

'Good man,' Simon said, preparing the syringe. He gave the injection deftly. The seizure continued for a few more dreadful minutes and then began to weaken. Chiara's arms flopped down. Her eyes were still rolled back, only the whites showing, but her body was relaxing. 'Thank you, everybody,' Simon said. 'Can we clear the room now, please, while the patient is stabilised.'

Standing in the corridor, Isobel felt her own skin clammy with sweat. She was trembling. 'She's going to die,' she said to William.

'No, she's not.'

'She is. It's Oliver. He's going to take her with him.'

'Don't think like that,' William said, putting his arms around her.

'He's killed her,' she said, refusing to be comforted. 'He wants her with him, and he's determined to have her – her and his child.'

Simon and two other doctors were discussing Chiara in low, serious tones. One of them was urging Simon to continue to treat the eclampsia and wait for the natural onset of labour.

'But that could be weeks away,' Simon said. 'I'd have to keep her sedated all that time with morphine and chloral hydrate. Keep her on oxygen to keep her breathing going. Give her digitalis to keep her heart going. The effect on the foetus could be disastrous.'

'You can't let her keep having the convulsions. They'll disrupt all her major functions, Simon. She could die – with her baby.'

'There's another complication – the placental abruption she had at the end of the first trimester. There's probably a weakness there. I had anticipated a Caesarean section in the thirty-ninth week, all being well, but—' He broke off, seeming to realise that Isobel and William could hear this rather grim conversation. Excusing himself from his colleagues, he came over to them. 'I'm so glad you're here,' he said. 'I know it was a bad time for you. You can go in again now. They've made her comfortable. She might sleep intermittently, but she's very restless. I'm going to have to take a decision soon. I'll keep you informed, I promise.'

Chiara was now lying still, her eyes closed. She didn't stir when Isobel sat at her bedside and took her hand. Isobel looked at the pale, swollen face and felt a lump rise in her throat. She had been Chiara's playmate, her mother, her rival, her enemy, her friend. She hadn't been very good at any of those roles. They had spent so many years apart, too, years that should have been close. The prospect of losing her now was terrible. She would give her own life cheerfully to save Chiara's. But nothing was as easy as that.

Simon was so young, so inexperienced. The other two doctors with him in the corridor now were no older, also obviously recent graduates. Did they know how to treat Chiara? Had some oversight, some negligence of Simon's, contributed to Chiara's collapse? She had to keep such thoughts at bay and trust him to know what he was doing.

But that nagging, superstitious dread remained at the edge of her mind. Oliver had been so desperate to have Chiara and the child. Was he pulling them to him now, wherever he was in the darkness? She shuddered with horror, and it was as though the shudder was transmitted through her into Chiara, because Chiara gasped, stirred and half-opened her eyes. 'Izzy,' she whispered through dry lips, 'you came.'

'Yes, dearest, I'm here.'

'The baby . . .?'

'The baby's fine. Simon's just outside.'

'I feel so very strange. Am I very sick?'

Isobel didn't know what to answer. 'You need to rest. They're taking good care of you.'

'Don't go away again, please.'

She squeezed Chiara's hand gently. 'I won't, I promise.'

'I've missed you so much. All those years.'

'I know.'

'"*This life's a dream, an empty show . . .*"'

'No, it isn't,' Isobel said, leaning forward to kiss her forehead. 'It's real and it's ours, and we're going to live it and make the best of it.'

Chiara slipped into a restless doze, but to Isobel's eyes, she was looking worse. William sat quietly in the corner, writing an article in longhand in his pad. A nurse came in every twenty minutes. Simon was still discussing a course of treatment. The hospital was quiet, now. Isobel tried not to think about Stepney, but her thoughts kept returning to the subject. She was still wearing her crimson suit. She had called as many people as she could to tell them that the meeting was off and had asked Flossie Fields to spread the word, but she hadn't been able to reach everyone. People would be arriving at the hall only to be turned away. Reporters would be putting their pencils back behind their ears and trudging back through the snow, cursing her. She had missed the most important night of her campaign. It was a catastrophe. But perhaps she could do something yet. If Chiara rallied, she might be able to get back to London this evening for one last impromptu speech; find a hall, get the word out, try to get the voters to attend. The voting began tomorrow morning at 8:00 a.m. It was a forlorn hope, but it was all she had.

She was drifting into a doze when Chiara suddenly cried out.

'Izzy! Oh, God, Izzy!'

Isobel jumped to her feet. Chiara was writhing on the bed, her head thrown back. 'What's the matter?' Isobel asked.

'Hurts! So much!'

Isobel saw that Chiara was clutching her abdomen. She pulled back the bedclothes and, to her horror, saw the deep red stain on Chiara's nightgown. 'Chiara!'

William was already heading out of the door. 'I'll get Simon.'

Her heart pounding, Isobel tried to comfort Chiara, but the blood was flowing steadily. 'You're going to be all right, darling,' she kept repeating, knowing how idiotic the words were. Chiara was deathly pale now and starting to lose consciousness.

Simon came in and pushed her aside unceremoniously. He took Chiara's pulse briefly. 'She's having another abruption,' he said.

'This is the third bleed. I can't put it off any longer. She'll have to have an immediate Caesarean.'

'Will you operate yourself?' William asked as Simon put up a drip.

'I'll assist. One of the other surgeons will do the operation.'

'Will the baby be all right?' Isobel asked. Simon didn't answer.

The room filled with nurses. Isobel watched helplessly as Chiara, now limp and all but unconscious, was transferred onto a trolley and wheeled out. She watched the group of white-clad medical staff disappear down the corridor with her sister, and felt a crushing wave of desolation overwhelm her. William put his arm around her.

'She's going to be fine,' he said. 'She'll get the best possible care.'

'I keep telling myself that,' Isobel said. 'It doesn't seem to help.'

It was around 4:30 a.m. by now, and the day's bustle was already beginning, with the rattle of steel and china, nurses' voices calling down the corridors with cheerful disregard for sleeping patients. There was nothing to be done but wait. Isobel and William walked slowly to the day room, where an orderly was mopping the linoleum floor. They sat side by side on the bench. Isobel put her head in her hands. 'How long do you think they'll be?' she asked.

'A couple of hours, I imagine—'

A new male voice cut into their conversation. 'There you are, Willoughby. We've been looking for you everywhere.'

Isobel raised her head. A man of about William's height and age, wearing an Army greatcoat still wet with snow, had arrived. William got up. 'Hescott! Where did you spring from?' They slapped each other's backs like old friends. 'Isobel, this is Orlando Hescott, the artist. You remember me telling you about him?'

'Very vividly,' Isobel said, taking in Orlando.

Orlando grasped Isobel's hand in his own very cold one. 'Very pleased to meet you. Your sister's around here somewhere, looking for you frantically.'

'She's just gone into theatre,' Isobel said in some confusion.

Orlando shook his head. 'No, I mean your other sister.'

As he spoke, Felicity rushed into the waiting room and threw herself into Isobel's arms. 'Oh, Izzy! What's happened to Chiara?'

Isobel burst into tears, partly of shock. 'Felicity!' she managed to get out. 'What are you doing here?'

Felicity peered into her face anxiously. 'Is she having the baby already?'

'She's having a Caesarean.'

'But I thought the baby wasn't due for weeks.'

'It's five weeks premature.'

'Then why—?'

'She's awfully sick, Fee. And she's haemorrhaging.'

'Oh no!' They sat down, holding on to each other. 'Is she going to be all right?' Felicity asked. Her face was pale and taut.

'They're operating now. Oh, Felicity, she looks so awful. So much blood!'

'Darling, I don't know a thing about obstetrics. Please tell me what's happening in plain words.'

'I hardly know myself. There are two problems. One is that the baby is apparently poisoning her for some reason, and she might die from that. The other is that her placenta is tearing away from the womb and making her bleed. Both things mean she has to have the baby out.'

'Is this husband of hers any good?' Felicity demanded.

'I think he is.' She tried to explain Chiara's medical dilemma as she herself understood it. She didn't know whether she was doing a very good job or whether Felicity, who was wide-eyed with horror, understood any of it. 'In any case, thank God you're here. How on earth did you get to England?'

'We got a lift in a Liberator bomber, with some American airmen. We nearly froze, didn't we, Orlando? Now I know why they all wear sheepskins up there. We landed at Gibraltar and warmed up a bit, but the rest of the way there was ice everywhere.'

Felicity recounted all this as though it were a bus journey across London. 'You might have told me you were coming!' Isobel exclaimed.

'It was going to be a great surprise – seeing you and Chiara for Christmas, you know. And Orlando's got an exhibition. We thought it was such a lark. I had no idea Chiara was in this ghastly state.'

'What about the Embassy?'

'I don't work for them anymore,' Felicity replied dismissively. 'I think they were glad to get rid of me. They said I was a bad influence on the other girls. And Zippy made Farouk get rid of me, too. After Rommel was beaten, she decided to stay on, you see, so I was supernumerary.'

'What on earth are you talking about?'

'Oh, I'll explain later. Anyway, I applied to the WAAC and got myself appointed as Orlando's assistant. Haven't I, darling boy? I can keep an eye on him that way. *"Entreat me not to leave thee, or to return from following after thee: for whither thou goest, I will go; and where thou lodgest, I will lodge: thy people shall be my people, and thy God my God: Where thou diest, will I die, and there will I be buried: the Lord do so to me, and more also, if aught but death part thee and me."* So help me God, amen.'

'God, you've changed,' Isobel said. Like Orlando, Felicity was wearing a greatcoat. Her fair hair was wet and tangled around her face. She was the same Felicity in appearance, but altered in manner. She had lost the diffident, rather bookish manner of the convent years and had acquired a very worldly confidence.

'Have I? I suppose I've joined the grown-ups club.' She held her hand out to Orlando. 'This is Isobel, my dear. Isn't she just as beautiful as I told you? Only, you're not allowed to fall in love with her. There's been a bit too much of that sort of thing.'

'Nobody is going to love me except William,' Isobel said.

Felicity turned to Willoughby. 'Hello, William. Are you going to make an honest woman of her?' she demanded. They were the first words she had addressed to him.

He studied her, evidently struck, as Isobel was, with the change in her. Then he kissed her on the cheek. 'Hello, Felicity. Yes, and she's going to make an honest man of me.'

Felicity hugged him, dispelling any stiffness between them. 'You're in for a simply terrible time, but then we all are unless we learn to be good to each other.'

'You're both frozen,' William said. 'Your face is like ice, Felicity.' He produced a flask from his pocket. 'I brought some medicinal brandy.'

The four of them sat in a corner of the waiting room, swigging surreptitiously from William's flask of brandy, discussing Chiara. 'What about your election?' Felicity asked Isobel.

'The vote's tomorrow,' Isobel said. She checked her watch. 'Today, I mean.'

'Shouldn't you be hurrying around, roping in the voters?' Felicity demanded.

'I'm not leaving until I see that Chiara's all right,' Isobel replied.

Gently, William explained how Isobel had abandoned her campaign to come down to Oxford. Felicity's eyes filled with tears. 'That's the noblest thing I ever heard, Izzy.'

Isobel laughed briefly. 'Not really. Most of what I've done is pretty ignoble. I'm always letting somebody down. This time it's my supporters.'

William put his hand on hers. 'You know what Forster said. Better let down the country than a friend. Two cheers for democracy, and all that.'

'Oh, I quite agree,' Orlando said. '"One must be fond of people and trust them if one is not to make a mess of life."'

'But Isobel's jeopardised her chances of getting into Parliament,' Felicity exclaimed. 'It's all very well quoting Forster. Don't you see what a sacrifice she's making?'

'Of course I do,' William said.

'It's not a sacrifice,' Isobel replied. 'It's a choice.'

'Well, it's a noble choice!'

The day had by now dawned, with flurries of snow and a lowering sky only a shade or two lighter than night. They were all starving. Orlando and William went off to forage. Isobel, who was by now starting to feel tired, leaned her head on Felicity's shoulder. 'You're different, Fee.'

'So are you.'

'Orlando's a very handsome man.'

'So is William. I don't begrudge you him anymore. I was angry with you for years. Raging inside. Especially after that book. Now it's all gone.'

'I'm so sorry about everything, darling.'

'Don't be. It wasn't until Orlando that I realised William never loved me. I kept telling myself you'd taken him away from me. But that wasn't what happened. I was terribly naïve, you know. Probably still am. I mean – I know that Orlando's probably not my *beau ideal*. But he's mine for the time being, and I'm having so much fun. I've had more experiences this year than in the rest of my life put together. That's been the good part of this war. It broke open the coffins we were living in. Or, at least, I was.'

'I think I was in a coffin, too.'

Felicity stroked Isobel's dark hair. 'What if Chiara dies? How will we survive that?'

'I keep thinking about that. I think Oliver's drawing her to him, refusing to let go of her.'

Felicity shuddered. 'Don't. He wasn't that sort of man. He was very kind to me.'

'You only saw the best of him. At the end, he was ruthless. He terrified me.'

'Anyway, she's not going to die,' Felicity said firmly. 'God's punished us all enough.'

A nurse hurried in. 'Miss Redcliffe? Please come quickly.'

∽

Isobel and Felicity followed the nurse at a run down the busy corridor. Through a double-swing door they reached a ward, where Simon was standing, with his back to them.

'Simon?' Isobel said in dread.

He turned. He was holding a little baby in his arms. The small fists were clenched and the eyes were tight shut. The baby was fast asleep. Felicity grasped Isobel's hand.

'Is that him?' Isobel whispered.

'Her,' Simon said quietly. 'It's a girl.'

'And Chiara?'

'You can see her in a little while. She's in the recovery room. She lost a lot of blood.'

'Oh, my God,' Felicity said, peering at the infant. 'We're aunts.'

Simon held the baby out to Isobel. 'She's going into our brand-new American incubator shortly. Hold her.'

Isobel reverently took the little bundle from Simon. The baby was surprisingly heavy. She looked down into the child's face, so perfect, and at the little hands with their pink creases and their tiny fingernails. A sweet ache rose from her heart up into her throat and then spilled from her eyes in two warm rivulets down her cheeks. 'She's so beautiful. Is she healthy?'

'Very. I don't think she's quite as premature as we imagined. Chiara may have been confused about the dates.' Simon was listening to the little chest with a stethoscope, his face tender. 'There's no respiratory distress, and her heart is fine. But we'll keep her in the incubator for the next week, with oxygen, just to be sure.'

Isobel couldn't speak. She was flooded with emotions – memories of her own first baby, who had died at only a year old, shattering her life, feelings of joy and gratitude that this little life had been spared. 'Take her,' she whispered to Felicity.

Felicity took the child. She wasn't used to babies, and she was awkward at first, but Isobel saw the same reaction moisten her eyes. 'I've never seen anything more beautiful,' she murmured, staring at the baby's face as though hypnotised. 'Clever old Chiara.'

'What will you call her?' Isobel asked Simon.

'We hadn't decided on a name yet,' Simon confessed. 'It sounds strange, but it all happened so suddenly. And Chiara always thought it was a boy.'

A midwife took the baby from Felicity and placed her in the incubator, a cosy little box with clear sides and its own heating system. She unwrapped her carefully and connected the oxygen tube. The small, rose-coloured body, wearing only a diaper, lay at peace, arms outflung trustingly, little mouth slightly open. 'She's had her first feed,' the midwife said. 'She'll have another when she wakes up.'

'She looks like Snow White in her glass case, doesn't she?' Felicity said.

Simon smiled. 'Let's go and see Chiara.' They tore themselves away from the baby.

Chiara was in a darkened room, a blood transfusion going into her arm and an oxygen mask over her nose and mouth. Her eyes fluttered open as her visitors came in.

'Look who's here,' Isobel said, leading Felicity forward. Chiara's eyes focused vaguely. She held her hand out to Felicity, who took it and kissed it.

'Just seen your baby, Chiara,' Felicity said. 'Nice work. I told you I'd be here for it, didn't I?' Chiara's eyes closed again, and she seemed to drift back into unconsciousness. The visit was over. Simon led them out.

Isobel had been frightened by Chiara's weakness. 'Is she going to be all right?' she asked Simon.

'It took a long time to stop the bleeding,' Simon replied. 'She lost a lot of blood.' He hesitated. 'I'm not sure that she'll be able to have any more children. We considered a hysterectomy but decided to take a chance. She's so young. In any case, she needs to recover from this before we can be certain. At least the eclampsia will improve now.'

'You'll have to do your bit, Fee,' Isobel said wryly. 'Three of us and only one child to show.'

'I doubt if I can do any better,' Felicity replied. 'It looks hard. I think I'll skip it.'

❧

Isobel had hoped to get back to London that day, to at least put in an appearance at the polling station, but Chiara was calling for her each time she surfaced. In the absence of a mother, and as the only sister with some experience, she didn't feel she could leave Chiara. And, by now, she had resigned herself to losing the election. Though William tried to comfort her, she was certain of failure.

They finally had time to catch up with each other's news. There was so much to tell Felicity – beginning with the death of Oliver and the distribution of his estate. As William had said, Orlando Hescott was very polished – good-looking, smooth and amusing, and quite possibly a ladykiller; but he and Felicity were obviously on affectionate terms, and there was no point in worrying about Felicity's future now. Felicity had her own life well in hand.

Felicity, in turn, told Isobel about the last months in Cairo, how she had been hauled over the coals by the Ambassador because her association with King Farouk was deemed inappropriate, how she had been assigned to Orlando Hescott as an assistant by the WAAC, and how she now accompanied him in his work, even into battle zones.

'But you'll be in danger, Fee,' Isobel protested.

'I'd rather that than be useless,' Felicity retorted. 'I had far too many years of *that*.'

Simon Altringham put Wisteria Cottage at their disposal. With the four visitors taking up every available inch of space, the little house was crammed. Though the first night was an anxious one, by the next day Chiara had begun to rally and was taken off the oxygen. Although she was not yet out of danger, she was able to breastfeed the baby. The three sisters sat together in the darkened room – Chiara's eyes were still sensitive – while she gave suck.

'I still can't believe you're here, Felicity,' Chiara said. 'I was convinced you were one of my dreams yesterday. Isn't it wonderful to be all together at last? It's been so many years!'

'We won't let that happen again,' Felicity vowed, 'will we, Izzy?'

'No. And we're not going to fight anymore, either.'

'*That* might be a little trickier.'

'What are you going to call her?' Felicity asked, stroking the baby's downy hair.

'Simon likes "Maud," but it's so old-fashioned now,' Chiara said. 'I had a dream we called her "Elizabeth".'

'Oh, I like that,' Felicity said.

'So do I,' said Isobel.

'All right, I'll tell Simon the aunts have decided,' Chiara said, looking down with a smile at the baby at her breast. 'I don't think he'll want to argue.'

When Elizabeth fell asleep, they sat quietly, talking over old times. Isobel tried not to remember that, now, in Stepney East, the votes were being counted. But when she emerged from Chiara's room, William was waiting for her.

'I called the returning officer,' he said. 'The counting's going to be finished by this evening. We have to be there for the announcement.'

'Of course,' she said brightly. But driving up in the car, she felt heavy and sad, thinking of all those she had let down; not just the voters – Miss Throgmorton, Flossie and the rest. They had all worked hard for her, and they would be bitterly disappointed at the result.

◠◡

The whirling snow beat against the small crowd that had gathered on the steps of Limehouse Town Hall, where the count was taking place. It was already growing dark, and of course there were no street lights. A few cars rolled past, their dim headlamps barely illuminating the slush underfoot. In the bitter cold, Isobel huddled against Willoughby. Frank Dobbs was there, together with Mr Perk and a group of supporters holding a banner. There was some chanting from a collection of women that seemed to consist mainly of his family members, but she recognised nobody else. A solitary photographer was on hand, trying to keep his cigarette alight in the blizzard. There was no sign of Flossie, Miss Throgmorton or any of her other supporters. They had abandoned the sinking ship, and she knew she deserved it.

A large policeman, stationed at the door, implacably rejected all applications to be let in.

'We're freezing to death out here,' someone entreated. 'Let us in, Officer!'

'The votes are still bein' counted,' the constable replied firmly. 'Nobody goes inside till the results are official.'

There were groans of dismay. People stamped their feet, beat their hands together and hugged themselves to stay warm. An enterprising boy arrived, wheeling a brazier of hot chestnuts. He was chased off by the constable for 'showing a light', but not before he'd got rid of his entire stock to eager and half-frozen customers. William got them a newspaper cone of chestnuts, and they juggled them in their gloved fingers, burning their mouths on the kernels, which offered some comfort.

'How do you feel?' William asked her.

'Resigned,' Isobel said.

He smiled ruefully. 'Is that all?'

'Yes.' It was true. She had no expectation of having won – indeed, the whole campaign and all the effort she had expended during the last few weeks now seemed somehow unreal to her. So many things had happened in that short time that had given her a new perspective: the death of Oliver, the reading of his will; almost losing Chiara, the arrival of baby Elizabeth; and the growing realisation that, after seven years, William Willoughby was the man who knew her best and loved her best, and was going to be her husband – all this had made a difference, a great difference, to her outlook. She felt there were many things she hadn't understood before that were becoming clear to her now.

At length, the door of the Town Hall opened, and three men came out, led by the Mayor, wearing his chain of office. There was a burst of applause and an upsurge of excitement. His teeth audibly chattering, the Mayor introduced the returning officer, who stepped up to the microphone. In a tinny voice, he began to read the results. There was a sudden ragged burst of cheering from the Dobbs contingent, who then broke into 'For He's a Jolly Good Fellow'. Isobel couldn't understand why. Perhaps someone had made some sign to the Dobbs supporters.

'Quiet please,' the returning officer said, raising his voice querulously. 'Let me complete the reading of the figures.' He waited in vain for silence, then struggled on against the singing. Isobel could just about make out his words. 'Francis Wilfred Dobbs: three thousand, nine hundred and ninety-three votes. Isobel Barbara Redcliffe: one thousand, one hundred and five votes.'

She had lost by almost two thousand votes. The cheering grew louder. Isobel stood, cold and silent, huddled into William's arm as Frank Dobbs's supporters lifted him onto their shoulders and chaired him up the stairs to the microphone.

'And I duly declare,' the returning officer concluded doggedly against the hullaballoo, 'that the aforementioned person, Francis Wilfred Dobbs, has been duly elected to serve as Member of Parliament for Stepney East.'

William hugged her tight, but said nothing. Frank Dobbs, just visible in the darkness, unfolded a piece of paper and began to speak.

'Mr Mayor, may I first of all express to you – may I take the opportunity to say – in all my dealings with the electoral officers—' As he stumbled on, trying to read his speech in the dark, Isobel was wondering whether she was going to cry. It turned out she was. The tension left her in a brief shudder of sobs.

'Thank God *that's* over,' she said through her tears. A figure materialised beside Isobel and William. It was Mr Perk.

'Well, Miss Redcliffe,' he said dryly, 'you appear to have snatched defeat from the jaws of victory.'

She nodded, blotting her eyes with William's handkerchief. 'That's my speciality, Mr Perk.'

'I thought you had it in the bag, I really did. Whatever possessed you to drop everything at the last moment? That was a bad move.'

'My sister was having a baby. I needed to be with her.'

He peered at her through the large flakes of snow that were coming down. 'That sort of thing doesn't do. Really, it doesn't. You ought to have stayed for the finish, no matter what.'

Isobel thought of the things she'd been through in the past few days: the anguished hours beside Chiara's bed, the dramatic arrival of Felicity from Cairo, the miracle of that tiny baby, the sight of the colour returning to Chiara's cheeks. 'No,' she said, 'I oughtn't. I did the right thing.'

She and William turned and walked away down the dark, snowy street. Mr Perk stared after her, shaking his head.

ᘒ

Chiara strengthened daily. There were hopes that she would be able to come out of hospital for Christmas, even if only for a few hours. They agreed to spend it at Wisteria Cottage and started making preparations.

Orlando Hescott invited them up to London to the National Gallery to see his exhibition, an offer that they took up eagerly. London was grey, huddled under a lowering sky, with the atmosphere of a city weary of war and trying vainly to cheer itself up with flags and bunting. Trafalgar Square was full of young people in uniform, looking for amusement, which was mostly to be found in picking up members of the opposite sex. The National Gallery and the embassies crouched disapprovingly under sandbags. The four people in their little party mingled with the viewers who had turned out to look at Orlando's work. Depicting a victory – the first real victory of the war so far – it was a popular exhibition. The Gallery had been almost completely emptied during the Blitz, with all the great treasures crated and transported to Wales, and the empty, echoing halls made a strangely appropriate setting for the display of war art that now hung on the walls once graced by Rembrandt, Da Vinci and Titian.

It was immediately evident that Orlando was a fine artist. The paintings were also much bigger than Isobel had anticipated, panoramic battle scenes in ochres and iron-reds that were yards wide, in some cases. They showed tanks ploughing through the dust and smoke, the silhouetted figures of men running beside them, vulnerable and exposed. Some of the most touching works portrayed exhausted soldiers resting between battles, sprawled in tents or asleep in the shade of fighting vehicles.

They obviously depicted scenes familiar to Orlando and William, who discussed each work, remembering the grim scenes they had witnessed. Isobel and Felicity left the men to talk, and walked round the exhibition arm in arm. 'He's very good,' Isobel said.

'Yes, isn't he? When you see the world through his eyes, you learn a lot. That's what war artists are for. Photographs can't interpret a subject the way paintings can.' They stopped in front of a large canvas showing smoking wreckage spread across a rocky desert. 'You made a wonderful sacrifice for Chiara, darling. I've never admired you so much.'

'Not like my usual lamentable form, was it?'

'It was like the best of you.' She slipped her arm around Isobel's waist. 'You could have won that seat. It must have hurt so much – losing. Does it still hurt?'

'A little,' Isobel admitted. 'I went home afterwards and howled like a baby on William's chest. But compared to the idea of losing Chiara – or you – or any of us – it was no more than a flesh wound. I'm getting over it.'

'Will you have another go?'

'I don't know. I think I'll do something sensible for a while. Dig for victory, or something like that.'

Felicity snorted. 'I don't see you digging for victory, Izzy. Not your style.'

Isobel smiled. 'Well, I might go back to the States with William. Do some more fundraising. I was rather good at that.'

'Of course you were. That sounds much more like it.' A distinguished-looking middle-aged man had joined William and Orlando and was discussing the paintings with them. 'That's Sir Kenneth Clark,' Felicity said, 'the director of the National Gallery. He arranged this exhibition. He's very keen on Orlando.'

'That's wonderful.'

'Sir Kenneth is the person who got me appointed as Orlando's secretary. He used his influence with the War Artists Advisory Commission. Orlando's very ambitious. He's determined to get everything he can out of the war, make a name for himself and come out of it famous. With a knighthood, he says, and his work in all the big galleries. Getting top prices for everything he paints.' She glanced at Isobel. 'Do you think that's the right attitude?'

'I don't know. Is it your attitude?'

'I don't see why it shouldn't be. We all sacrifice so much for this war. Why shouldn't we make the best of it? Why shouldn't we get something back?'

Isobel gazed at the painting before her, tracing the sweeping, confident brushstrokes with her eye. 'I've been thinking about Oliver a lot lately. He was one of the last Victorians. He was old-fashioned in the worst way – and in the best way. He took what he wanted. He was selfish and he could be very cruel. But he didn't hesitate when there was a sacrifice to be made for his country. And he didn't ask for anything in return. He stood up to the Nazis to the end, and that can't have been easy.'

'And he was a bastard to you and Chiara.'

'All men can be bastards to women.'

'If we let them.'

'Anyway, as he left me a small fortune, I'm inclined to forgive him.' Isobel sighed. 'I keep trying to believe that there's honour in this war. Honour and nobility and principle and all the rest. I think of what I saw in Germany and Spain, and I imagine what the world would be like if those people took over. But I know we aren't so very different ourselves. We're bombing their women and children, just as they're bombing ours. We can also be savages. I mean, the only way we're going to win is if we kill more of them than they do of us.' She indicated the painting of military wreckage in front of them. 'There's always going to be this, isn't there? It's what men do.'

'So what's the point of it all?' Felicity demanded.

'If there's one thing Stepney taught me, it's that we can't go on in the same way. We shouldn't have hungry, sick, ignorant children cooped up in slums. Not in Britain. That has to change.'

'So you're really a red-hot Red, now?' Felicity smiled.

'I don't know what I am. But it's the only thing that makes sense to me. People living better lives. Otherwise, all this carnage means nothing. It's just blood in the sand. Like this painting.'

'Isobel's awfully deep these days,' she heard Felicity tell the men as they walked down the steps into a world of snow and sleet. 'You chaps could learn something.'

‿

To everyone's joy, Chiara was declared well enough to come home for Christmas. Since the birth of little Elizabeth, the eclampsia had faded away, and apart from the residual pain of the operation, she was doing well.

'And you still have all your bits and pieces in place,' as Felicity pointed out. 'It won't fall to me to perpetuate the Redcliffe line. Thank God for that.'

Elizabeth, having weighed little more than four and a half pounds at birth, was now over five pounds, and thriving. Felicity was cautiously interested in the phenomenon, but it was Isobel who derived the greatest joy from holding her, feeding her and staring into her sleepy little face. It was as though there had always been a hole in her heart, ever since her own first child had died, so many years earlier, which was now filled. Elizabeth was a serene baby whose eyes (when open) were large and deep blue, and she had been born with golden curls. She was angelic, in Isobel's opinion, and being with her brought a deep comfort to her soul.

By general agreement, the Christmas meal was to be in William's hands. He was the only one of the six of them who could cook. Chiara, as an invalid, was excused all duties. Felicity and Orlando, as the representatives of the Arts, were in charge of the tree and the decorations. It was Isobel's duty to help Chiara with Elizabeth. Simon, who could be called out at any and all hours, was excused Christmas duties but told to make sure he was present for the festive dinner at all costs.

By dint of scouring the surrounding Oxfordshire farms, William secured a goose, half a ham, two dozen links of pork sausage, a tub of lard, a sack of King Edward potatoes, plenty of vegetables and, most miraculously of all, the materials to produce a Christmas pudding.

'He's an old hand,' Isobel pointed out dryly when the others expressed amazement at this rare haul. They had first met during the Spanish Civil War, when William had plundered her vegetable garden on a foraging raid. William merely smiled, and set to work in the tiny kitchen.

Felicity and Orlando had found a Christmas tree, which they set up in the parlour, decorating it with cut-out paper angels and stars, painted in watercolours by Orlando, and with things they found on countryside walks – holly berries, pink rose hips and red haws, conkers, immortelles and acorns. They strung ribbons of ivy leaves around the mantelpiece and hung mistletoe from the lintels.

It didn't fail to be a white Christmas. The snow began on Christmas Eve, drifting down from a softly glowing sky and covering the slush and mud with white. The waits and the Church Army could be heard in the lanes. Baby Elizabeth slept almost through the night and was taken to her first church service on Christmas morning, where she was also baptised Elizabeth Mary Caroline (the second and third names being those of her two grandmothers). Her godparents were Isobel, William, Felicity and Orlando.

They'd agreed that presents were to be minimal that year, since they had all received such an abundance of blessings already; but, nevertheless, there were a number of bottles presented and received – whisky for the men, perfume for the women.

From the kitchen came the fragrances of a splendid Christmas lunch such as none of them had smelled since the start of the war. The more frivolous of them made a snowman in the garden and stole a carrot from the kitchen to provide him with a nose. The others watched from the windows, taking a quiet delight in being together.

The long-awaited meal materialised in the afternoon at the point of maximum hunger. They crowded around the little table and ate, knocking elbows. The goose was golden indeed, perfectly cooked and accompanied by crisp roast potatoes. Isobel had secured some bottles of Bollinger from Fortnum's, which went perfectly with the meal.

It was suitably dark by the time the pudding made an entrance. It arrived in the hands of its creator, William Willoughby, enveloped in blue flames and emitting exotic scents of spices and fruits.

Little Elizabeth Mary Caroline lay fast asleep in her crib, having contributed, without effort, the most magical ingredient of the feast, the presence of the Christmas baby. Chaos stalked the world outside, but in this warm circle, love and laughter and light ruled.

The last corner of the last stomach was filled, and the table was eventually cleared. While the men stretched out beside the glowing fire with whisky to drink and nuts to crack, the three sisters put on their coats.

'Where are you three going?' William asked Isobel.

'Outside, for a walk.'

'Can't we come?'

'No. You boys can stay here and congratulate each other on your good fortune.'

'Or commiserate on your tribulations,' Felicity put in.

The three women went outside to breathe the cool night air. The world was blanketed in snow, so that, in spite of the dark sky, everything was bathed in a pearly glow.

Chiara could not walk very fast or very far, so Isobel and Felicity each took an arm. They passed through the gate, under the last mauve wisps of wisteria, and onto the common. Some others were also walking off Christmas dinners, and a few dogs scampered through the knee-high snow. Otherwise, peace and silence were all around.

Chiara looked up at the night sky. 'Together for Christmas! I never thought it would happen again.'

'I've hated Christmas for years,' Felicity said. 'It was worst in the priory. I just cried for days. I missed you two so terribly.'

'We missed you more. This has been the best Christmas ever,' Chiara replied. 'Like being children again.'

'I don't know about that. Maybe we've started to grow up at last,' Isobel said.

'Maybe the worst is over. Maybe there'll be peace next year.'

'There's a long way to go,' Isobel warned. As if to underscore her words, the distant throbbing of bomber engines reverberated across the clouded sky. Even on Christmas, the war continued. Somewhere in the night, people just like themselves, caught up in a war not of their making, would be huddling in terror.

'I wonder when we'll all be together again?' Chiara said, her voice catching. 'Maybe not for years and years.'

'I can't lose you two again,' Isobel said.

'We can't lose you,' Chiara said.

'Monster that you are,' Felicity added.

Chiara sighed. 'We've all made such dreadful mistakes.'

'Dreadful,' Isobel repeated with a shudder. 'When I look back, I can hardly believe we're all here.'

'But it's going to be all right now,' Felicity said, 'isn't it?'

'We'll always be together from now on,' Isobel said, drawing her sisters close together in her arms. 'Maybe not in ways we can imagine. But there will always be the three of us.'

And she kissed them each.

ACKNOWLEDGEMENTS

My grateful thanks go to my editors at Lake Union, Sammia Hamer and Emilie Marneur; to Jenny Parrott and Jill Pellarin, who licked the manuscript into shape; to Sana Chebaro of Amazon Author Relations; and to my agents, Annette Crossland and Bill Goodall. It's a privilege to work with you all.